The Draftsman's Daughter

SIMON YATES

PAGE PUBLISHING
Conneaut Lake, PA

First originally published by Page Publishing 2024

This is a work of fiction. The author stayed true to historical facts as much as possible, and some historical characters from the time are used to enhance the story. Otherwise, the names, characters, businesses, places, events, and incidents in this book are either the product of the author's imagination or used in a fictitious manner. Any resemblance to actual persons, living or dead, or actual events is purely coincidental.

ISBN 979-8-88793-884-4 (pbk)
ISBN 979-8-88793-892-9 (digital)

Printed in the United States of America

Dedication

For my beloved wife, Shannon, and our amazing kids, Lily, Ben, and Chloe, who supported me throughout.

Acknowledgement

I have many people to thank for their encouragement and support throughout this project. Most importantly, thanks to my wife Shannon for putting up with my many hours alone writing, her enthusiastic support as she read through my drafts, and her excellent cover design. Many people read full drafts and sections and provided excellent feedback including my parents-in-law, John and Trish, my nephew Rick, niece Sarah, Shari Frost, and my good friend and work colleague, Chris Ross. I also want to thank the crew at The Landing in Marblehead — especially Billy and Kim — who kept my spirits up in the early days. Also, particular thanks are due to Katie, who was kind enough to let me use her name, Katherine Daring, for one of the characters in the book.

Prologue

Soviet Sector, East Berlin, 1978

On a normal day, he passed through the checkpoint into West Berlin with ease. His papers were up-to-date, his identities clean—a testament to the work of his masters.

But today was anything but normal.

Today, he was being hunted by the Stasi. They didn't know they were hunting him specifically, but with the blood of a Soviet diplomat still wet and sticky on the steps of his Treptow District apartment, he knew they were coming. More than likely, they had already assembled at the Stasi's Lichtenberg headquarters.

The dead Soviet was, in fact, a KGB officer with a long history in espionage, coaxing vulnerable western businessmen to betray their country for sex, money, revenge, or idealism—the bread and butter of intelligence work in Cold War Berlin. He was well-known to both MI6 and the CIA.

Stasi Oberstleutenant Meyer, responsible for the eleven districts of Berlin, and his KGB counterpart, Major Ivanov, were certain it was the work of a western agent and moved quickly to shut down his limited options to escape.

He could cross at one of the border checkpoints, so the Stasi tripled the Grenztruppen "Grepo" border guards at every one. He could take the Interzonal Railway to West Berlin or all the way back to the safety of West German soil in Osnabrück. Stasi officers would check papers on every platform, search every train car, and question passengers at every ticket office. He could hide in East Berlin hoping to avoid arrest, but they wouldn't give up searching for him until he was found. Word would spread quickly, forcing the scared citizens of East Berlin to scrutinize their neighbors for any reportable transgression. There was little doubt that, by the time this was over, blood would stain the floors of the basement interrogation rooms of Hohenschönhausen prison.

With the forces of the KGB and Stasi amassed against him, the Draftsman chose to make his escape by crossing the most heavily trafficked checkpoint in the city, Friedrichstraße. He'd passed through Friedrichstraße at least once a month for the last six months. He knew the procedures, the guard changeover schedule, and how to blend into the crowd, knowing that he might one day need to get out of East Berlin in a hurry. Wednesdays at 8:00 p.m. were the best when the Grepos switched shifts and the midweek traffic was light.

He carried no foreign currency, no photographs, no receipts from the bars in Prenzlauer Berg where foreigners and locals mingled—nothing that would give the Grepos manning the border crossing more reason to question him.

It was madness, but he developed his escape plan for a situation just like this. Well, not exactly like this. There was never a plan to shoot a Soviet spy in an unauthorized operation with no extraction team to get him to safety. He was on his own.

Here, at least, some of the Grepos might recognize him as a regular. They wouldn't let on, of course. The procedure never changed. They stopped and questioned everyone and searched every vehicle. Their superiors watched their every move from the towers, ready to punish even the slightest lapse. Informers from within their own ranks lurked in the dark corners, smoking foul-smelling Belomorkanal cigarettes and watching for any mistake to report for their own advantage.

The Draftsman gave himself a less than a fifty-fifty chance of getting through unscathed. He felt the anxiety build. He'd escaped before and would do so again, but the sweat soaked through the back of his shirt, and as usual, he urgently needed to go to the bathroom. He closed his eyes and took ten deep and slow breaths to push his discomfort down.

His money was wrapped in tight plastic rolls floating inside the petrol tank of the car, a 75-horsepower piece of shit Moskvitch 412 with the acceleration of a farm tractor. His prized Makarov pistol was hidden in the engine compartment, inside the collector box where the filter was supposed to be.

He parked about five hundred meters down from the checkpoint, on one of the side streets. As usual, the streetlights were out. Some apartments were lit by candles, but most were dark. A steady rainfall had eased off in the last twenty minutes, but rainwater leaked in through the worn-out door seals and a rear window that didn't close all the way. A damp mildewy coldness filled the interior of the car, and he shivered. Outside, the fog and drizzle had a softening effect on the harsh edges of the concrete, colorless buildings that lined the street.

Waiting made him edgy, but the timing was important. Sitting in the car too long would no doubt arouse suspicion. Some nosy hausfrau could pull back her curtain and call the authorities about a strange man sitting in a car on a dark side street.

In the drizzly silence, he checked his watch again: 7.52 p.m. Almost time to move. He took a deep breath and turned the engine over. It sounded like a choke followed by a dry cough. The engine knocked loudly, the painful sound bouncing off the building walls. A few seconds later, the headlights flickered on. One immediately failed with a pathetic buzzing sound. He clambered out of the car, cursing under his breath, and hit the dead light with a clenched fist. It blinked back on. Would it stay on? There was nothing he could do about it now. He had to go.

He gripped the steering wheel, perhaps a little too tight, knuckles blazing white. His doubts crept back and crawled up his spine. If this went wrong, it was into the Stasi van to Hohenschönhausen. He'd be disavowed, tortured, killed, incinerated, and then forgotten. His wife and children would never know what happened to him, and his ashes would be added to the pile of countless others who went before him and washed away in the city drains.

He turned left onto Friedrichstraße, the lights of the checkpoint glowing in the distance. A giant spotlight swung around as he approached, swamping the road ahead in a dazzling light. He felt the rifles trained on the rattling Moscovitch from the bleak, square, whitewashed watchtower. Rifles came off the Grepo's shoulders, radios raised to their mouths. He stopped at the gate. There were no other cars or bikes trying to cross. A grim-faced border guard ordered him out of his car for a pat down and scrutinized his papers while two others searched his vehicle.

Eyes watched from the shadows, the amber tips of their cigarettes the only indication they were even there. Searchlights roamed the Wall from north to south and back while terrible music or emphatic speeches blared out over loudspeakers from both sides of the border. Three sharp gunshots popped, and someone cried out in the distance.

The Grepo took his papers into a nearby shed, and he felt the barrel of a gun dig into his spine.

"Nicht bewegen. Hände in die Luft."

With dread, he realized his luck had finally run out.

Part 1

We dance around in a ring and suppose,
but the Secret sits in the middle and knows

—Robert Frost

Chapter 1

Vero Beach, Florida, 2009

H e didn't look dead from the back. Just an old man dozing peacefully in his armchair. As she stepped through the front door, Ana could see his wispy white hair waving gently in the warm breeze coming through an open window.

"Hello? Dad? You sleeping?"

The silky tones of Shirley Bassey whispered quietly in the background. *Scattered pictures of the smiles we left behind, smiles we gave to one another, for the way we were.*

When she put her hand on his shoulder from behind, his head fell forward awkwardly. She saw bloody, charred hair around a tiny red hole at the base of his skull, and the front of his golf shirt was stained with dried blood and brain matter.

The autopsy report would be unequivocal. The victim, Brandon Pike, eighty, was tortured and then executed. The coroner noted that deep, round burns from a cigar pockmarked his arms and the soles of his feet, burns so severe they penetrated almost to the bone. His hands were bound with double zip-tie handcuffs. His missing teeth were not found at the scene, suggesting that the killer may have taken them. He was punched in the face at least ten times, breaking his jaw in three places. The cause of death was a single 9mm gunshot that entered the cranium at the occipital bone at the base of the skull and exited through the frontal bone.

Later, long after she ran from the house screaming, the young police officer, as green as they come, interviewed Ana on the front steps.

3

"I need to ask you some questions, ma'am. Just some background, then the detectives will need to talk to you."

He gestured toward a cluster of people standing in a circle at the end of the driveway. They were talking, pointing, and occasionally looking in her direction.

His questions were basic.

"When did you arrive at the victim's home?"

"About 9:00 a.m. I'd been away on a business trip."

"Where?"

"Dayton. I was working on a story. I'm a reporter for a local TV station. I was there for almost a week."

"I see. How were things with your father?"

"He was dying of cancer, so not great actually."

In truth, they had parted on sour terms. His watery eyes, buried deep inside the dirty gray cloth of what was left of his face, had pleaded with her to stay.

"Please don't go, Anabel. Your mum's going to visit Sean and that Bible-thumping wife of his. I'll be here alone. What if something happens?"

"It's my job, Dad. It's just a few days."

It was a big opportunity, an exclusive interview with a girl who had escaped from a psycho who chained her up in a basement for years and forced her to bear his children. A career game changer with follow-up TV interviews in Chicago and maybe even CNN, an escape from her lonely life in Dayton.

His head had dropped, and he mumbled under his breath. She wasn't sure if he was genuinely scared or just being difficult. Mum delayed her trip to see Sean a day or two, but in the end, she left too.

"And does anyone else live in the house?"

"My mother, Adeline."

"And where is she?"

"Visiting my brother in Fort Myers."

His constant use of the "and" at the beginning of every question was annoying.

"And have you spoken to her recently?"

"No. I was busy. With work and everything."

"And how would you describe your relationship with your father?"

"Complicated."

"Complicated?"

"Yes, complicated. I didn't spend much time with him until he got sick and my mother needed help caring for him."

The police report noted that no weapons were found at the scene, but a bullet, recovered from the ceiling, had been sent to the FBI ballistics lab. The scene had been scrubbed with hospital-grade disinfectants on the floors, doors, and windows.

They buried him two weeks later following a small service at St. Augustine's Church. The altar was decked out in bouquets of Anouska rose lilies, an oriental varietal her father loved because it reminded him of lotus flower.

Ana stepped up bravely, gripping each side of the lectern for stability, to heap praise on a man she hardly knew for the first thirty-five years of her life. Growing up, he was rarely home. Baby Ana rejected him, thrashing mercilessly when he picked her up. Toddler Ana pretended not to recognize him when he came home and sulked alone in her room. Teenage Ana made sure that she was out with friends when he returned. He missed her senior high school prom, her touchdown against Darien in the powder-puff football game, and made her graduation by the skin of his teeth. She left to study journalism at Ohio State and never looked back.

But it was what happened before the funeral that had left her shaken. An hour earlier, as she sat on the end of her shitty hotel bed with gin and tonic in hand watching the local TV coverage, her mobile rang.

"Ms. Pike, Ms. Anabel Pike? I'm so sorry to bother you. My name is James Mattinson. I'm a solicitor in the UK. It's about your father. Do you have a few minutes?"

"It's not a great time actually. I'm about to bury him. What's this all about?"

"I represent your father, and I have in my possession a legitimately signed will. He had one in the United States and another one here in the UK signed before he emigrated."

"I'm sorry? Two wills?"

"He left instructions to call you on the day of his funeral. The estate amounts to eighty-one million pounds, to about $129 million."

Chapter 2

Ana was sitting in the back of the town car, gliding down the A1A toward her hotel, when detectives called to ask if she could spare a few minutes.

They were waiting for her on sofas in the lobby. They looked the part—slightly scruffy, convenience-store coffee cups, flipping spiral notebook pages, and looking more than a little conspicuous.

What do they know?

Mattinson, the English solicitor, told her that her father's mysterious UK will was not in the jurisdiction of the local police investigating the murder. She wasn't a lawyer, but it was hard to imagine that the will and his murder were unconnected.

If they ask, I'll tell them.

The two detectives stood up as she walked over.

"Apologies for the inconvenience, ma'am. We know this isn't the best time, but we need to ask you some additional questions."

"It's fine. Can we make this quick? I have to get ready for dinner with my family."

The initial theory was that it was a home invasion and robbery gone wrong, but upon a closer inspection of the evidence, it didn't seem like the most likely scenario.

Really? He was tortured and executed. Then the killer took the time to sanitize the scene before leaving. And you suspect something more sinister than a home invasion? What on earth are the taxpayers getting for their money?

What came out of her mouth, thankfully, was "I'm not sure what you mean. Do you think he was targeted for some reason?"

"It looks like a professional hit. He had something they wanted."

This is where they ask me if he had any enemies, anyone who might have a grudge.

They surprised her.

"What was the nature of your father's work? There are...irregularities...in his professional life that...companies we can't find any record of, for example."

The detective, the more rumpled of the two, didn't look up from his notebook, but Ana felt his partner's eyes boring into her from the other armchair.

"We really don't know much to be honest. He traveled a lot. He'd be gone for weeks at a time without contact. He sold textile machinery."

"And do you know where he went?"

"Eastern Europe, Russia, and China, places like that. We joked that he was some kind of spy. He was full of interesting stories, if you put a couple of Scotches in him. Mum said it was all rubbish and that he was just a storyteller."

"And what about work colleagues? Did you know any of them?"

"A few. Our move to America was sudden. One day I'm studying for my O-levels, and the next we are on a plane. We never saw or heard from most of the people he worked with again, except for a couple of the Americans. Bob and Bruce. I don't recall their last names right now. I'm a little rattled by all this, you know."

I need to speak to them first. They could be dead for all I know. Bob Schier and Bruce Lasher.

Bob was quiet for a New Yorker, kind and interesting to talk to, but serious. He'd been her father's boss for many years. She had a vivid memory of being six or seven years old when he brought a delegation of Chinese visitors, four men and a woman, to their home for dinner. They wore traditional Mao suits, dark blue or light gray with Mandarin collars. The men smoked sweet-smelling Chungwa cigarettes. She had loved the name so much that it became synonymous with any sweet-smelling incense smoke. She even told her college roommate to "light up some Chungwa" to hide the smell of the weed they smoked in the dorm. The woman, Madam Yee, took a particular shine to Ana and would laugh and kiss both cheeks whenever she heard the little girl with the English accent speak.

Bruce Lasher, on the other hand, was a flamboyant Texan in the tackiest sense of the word. He gave them his monstrous Cadillac El Dorado until they could get a car of their own. One of the many indignities of her early years in America was learning to drive in the high school parking lot in that thing as her new friends looked on.

"And have you seen, spoken to, or heard from these two men recently?"

"Not in years. They're probably dead by now."

"Anything else you think we should know?"

"Not that I can think of. I'm sorry. It's been a difficult day."

They're going to find out about the will eventually, and I'll have to be the one to tell them.

Later that evening, the immediate family gathered at her father's favorite restaurant, Buca di Beppo. He once said it reminded him of a place he used to go in Positano. None of them had even been to Positano. The waiter arrived, on queue, with a couple of bottles of his favorite wine, Allegrini Amarone Della Valpolicella Classico. Apparently, he discovered it on a trip to the Veneto region. Again, none of them had been to Veneto either.

It was a running joke in the family that he traveled the world, leaving everyone else stuck at home in the dreary north of England eating fish fingers and beans-on-toast. As usual, mother jumped to father's defense with a cheeky smirk.

"Now, now, enough of that! It wasn't all fun and games for your father over there. His hard work paid for all this," she said with a flamboyant wave of her arm.

In chorus, Ana, Sean, and Stephen responded in the usual way, "There's now't wrong wi' gala luncheons, lad! I've had more gala luncheons than you've had hot dinners."

It was the laugh they all needed at that moment.

After dinner, Ana herded her mother and brothers into the bar. "I got a call from a lawyer in England today. Dad has another will. Apparently, he stashed a lot of money in banks around Europe."

The mystery of her father's life had been a family joke, but the call from Mattinson had changed everything. Her father was tortured and killed weeks before a natural death, leaving millions in offshore bank accounts that no one knew about. Whoever killed him was looking for something, and more than likely, it was the money.

"How much?"

"About $129 million."

She said it with a matter-of-factness that surprised even her. She'd come to grips with news that validated what she and her brothers had suspected for years—that her father was probably involved in something sketchy. She pushed on. "Dad named me the executor, and so now I'm supposed to go to each bank and claim the funds. I have to leave tomor—"

Sean interrupted, "I'm sorry but...*129 million* dollars?"

"That's what the lawyer told me. It's an esti—"

"How can we not have known about it? It has to be some kind of scam, right?" His head pivoted from sister to mother to brother and back to sister.

"It could be, yes. I'm going to find out for sure. It's definitely Dad's signature. I have to figure out if the accounts are real and try to access them."

Ana pulled a faxed copy of the will from her purse and handed it to Sean. Stephen, always the oldest brother, snapped "Let me see that!" and ripped the pages from Sean's hand. His nose is out of joint that once again has father chose the youngest of the children over him.

It was a pretty straightforward document—aside from some arcane legalese about an executrix and the Trustee Act of 1925—that included the locations and numbers of the accounts.

"This is strange. It says that some of the beneficiaries might have moral issues with the source. If they cannot accept and transfer the funds to banks of their choosing, the money will go to an organization called Disclose International. Any idea what Disclose International is?"

A quick search of the Web had turned up nothing—no website, no contact info provided, no news clippings naming them, nothing.

"There's an address in Pimlico, London, and the name of a law firm that represents them."

Sean piped up, "Maybe some kind of charitable foundation? Although I can't think of a single charitable cause he cared about."

"We have twenty-one days left to actually process the transfers and execute the will."

More than likely, their father was a criminal—a thief, a mobster, a con man, or something worse. If the source of the money or its transfer was suspicious, especially in this age of money-laundering schemes to fund terrorist groups, the authorities would freeze the assets while they investigate.

Ana's mother sat ashen and silent. She wasn't a crier. She was a resilient and stubborn force of stoic British strength. Stephen sent her the same Christmas card every year, a family standing around an overdone turkey with the message, "Merry Christmas to a tough old bird." But this news has shaken her to the core.

"Who was he? This was supposed to be our sixtieth wedding anniversary year, and now I don't even know who he was. He lied to me for sixty years!"

Someone had to console her and, not surprisingly, the job fell to her daughter, the one who had been there for her through all his cancer treatments.

"It'll be okay, Mum. Let's not jump to conclusions, eh? Like Sean said, this could all be a big scam."

Something in her eyes revealed the depth of the betrayal, like her mother had suspected something for years but refused to believe.

"He left me alone, a working mother, to raise you three during the day and then work nights at that bloody hospital. I trusted him while he was off gallivanting. I always worried he had girls in every port. And now, all this money?"

"Come on, Mum. Let's get you upstairs with a cup of tea. We'll find out the truth, okay?"

She coaxed her mother into the elevator and took her up to her room on the third floor. They sat on the end of the bed for a while, then Ana helped her mother into bed and stayed with her until she cried herself to sleep. The tea never arrived.

Downstairs, Stephen and Sean were still talking and drinking heavily when Ana returned.

"I always thought that Dad was involved in something."

"We all did, Sean. I just expected something a little more humdrum. Not something that would earn him millions of hidden dollars."

When Stephen was young, his father gave him coins from everywhere he went. "I spent hours separating the bloody Polish zlotys from the rubles and yuan. I'd sell them back to him at the current exchange rate when he was going back."

"We did the same thing with stamps. He'd buy stamps in whatever country he was in. When he went back, I gave him the stamps, and he would send a postcard from that country."

Ana settled back into her seat and took a healthy slug of her vodka tonic. He was so much closer to the boys than her. He hadn't done anything like that with her, and it hurt. She felt forgotten.

Stephen said, "We need to tell the police about the money, don't we? If we wait, it will look like we are hiding something."

"Too late. The detectives interviewed me after the funeral, and I didn't tell them about it. They did ask me about his work history, suggesting fake companies."

Ana was just about to get up and head to her room when Sean chimed in. When he helped his parents pack up the house for the move to Florida, he found something strange in the attic, a binder. It had labeled photographs of people with foreign names and job titles like "Minister of Light Fabrics." But they didn't look like ministers of light fabrics at all. One was a burly-looking guy carrying a couple of metal suitcases through what looked like an airport.

And yes, he still had the binder.

Chapter 3

Tipsy and completely exhausted, Ana returned to her room to plot her first move. Bruce Lasher and Bob Schier were the only people she knew that could possibly shed some light. But if they were involved in some kind of criminal enterprise, they weren't likely to tell her anything useful.

Sean's binder was the key. Why had her father collected these photos? He was an avid photographer and always had a camera hanging around his neck. Recently, he had told her that when he was young, he wanted to be a photojournalist, a war correspondent.

Maybe he was building some kind of trail for the authorities to follow? She felt better thinking that perhaps he had an altruistic motive.

Why did he collect all this only to abandon it to an attic, never to be seen again? Insurance? Information he could use if he were ever caught and prosecuted or to protect him from retribution from the people he was working with?

The weariness took over, and she fell into a restless sleep. The next morning, nursing a considerable wine headache, she called 411 for Bruce's number. A woman picked up the phone.

"Lasher residence. How may I help you?"

She introduced herself and asked if Mr. Lasher would be willing to meet with her to talk about her father. "I barely knew him, and now that he's gone, I just want to know more about him."

"Of course. I'm sorry for your loss. One minute, please?"

The woman put the phone down with a clatter and returned a few minutes later.

"Ms. Pike? Yes, of course, Mr. Lasher would be delighted to see you. When should we expect you?"

"I'm driving my brother back to Fort Myers this morning and staying overnight with his family. I could make it to Boca Raton by midmorning tomorrow?"

The woman put her hand over the receiver to muffle her voice.

"That would be fine. The address is 5 Eucalyptus South in Boca Raton. It's a gated community, and there's a guardhouse at the entrance. I'll let them know to expect you."

She called 411 again and was connected to the home of Bob Schier in Greenwich, Connecticut. Another housekeeper answered. What's the deal with all these housekeepers answering phones? It was like she was dialing back in time.

Ana made arrangements to meet Bob, booked a flight from West Palm Beach to LaGuardia and then a red-eye from JFK through Frankfurt to Larnaca airport in Cyprus, the first bank on Mattinson's list.

An hour later, she and Sean set off for Fort Myers in her rented Mustang convertible, leaving his wife, Sarah, and the kids with their car to head home later. They drove with the top down. You didn't rent a convertible to keep the top up.

For the first twenty miles or so, State Road 70, they sat in silence, soaking in the sun and fresh air. Sean tapped his fingers to the Black Eyed Peas' "I Got a Feeling." He didn't seem to know the words even though the song was all over the radio.

Sean used to be fun, but his marriage to Sarah turned him into a homebody. When the kids came along, he grew very serious and became deeply involved in the Sarah's church. Sarah and her family, evangelical protestants, insisted he convert to secure his relationship with her. Eventually, he genuinely embraced the faith.

How will they feel about the money? If any of them felt some moral opposition, it would probably be Sarah and her family.

Sean's conversion had created a rift with his Catholic father that never really healed. He had told Sean recently that his main flaw was that he was easily influenced by others and lacked a strong character of his own. In response, Sean had called his dad an "absentee father who never gave a fuck about anyone but himself." Sadly, those turned out to be his final words with his father.

"One hundred twenty-nine million dollars," he said to finally break the silence.

"It's a lot of money. Has to be illegal, don't you think?"

He nodded slowly but didn't say anything else.

"I'm going to see Bruce Lasher and Bob Schier. You remember them? I think this binder of yours will help me get started. I want to show them some of it and see if it rings any bells."

"What if all this puts you in danger? The killer wanted something. What if it was this money? Or to keep him quiet about something? Like the people in this binder?"

The same fears had kept Ana up most of the night. The money and the murder had to be connected. The binder was a new twist. No doubt the entire family was in danger.

The easy, safe answer was to let Disclose International take the money and be done with it, but that didn't mean that the danger went with it. The best chance for safety was exposing whatever this whole thing was to the light of day and letting the authorities catch the killer.

"Don't get me wrong," Sean was saying, "this money will solve a lot of problems. Stephen's job is on the rocks, and we're going to need to find a nursing home for Mum soon. Sarah and I are fine right now, but with everything going on with banks and the economy?"

Ana, single and happy about it, made a decent living as field reporter for the local ABC affiliate but desperately wanted to get out of Dayton. She had no one there, a couple of friends from work and a college roommate an hour's drive away in Cincinnati. Money wasn't her issue. Ambition was.

They arrived at Sean's home by late morning. Ana put coffee on while Sean scoured his office for the binder. From the kitchen, she could hear him grunting as he heaved piles of paper, books, and folders around his office. He returned a few minutes carrying a thick three-ring photo album and set it on the dining room table.

The outside cover was plain black with a small cellophane pocket on the front to slip a small name card in. Each page featured an 8×10 black-and-white photograph. They looked more like surveillance photos than the artistic work of a photographer. Some were taken from a distance and a few included two or three people leaving a building or getting out of a car. Others were taken from close range and featured a single individual doing something—walking through an airport, sitting on a bench reading, or waiting for a cab. There were at least fifty pages of photographs. Underneath each one was a carefully typed label with names, occupations, and what sounded like company names or government departments.

One was of an Asian woman in an elegant wool suit and hat labeled "Yee Xiu Ying, Director, Shandong Sunshine Textile Co. Ltd." A small handwritten addendum to the label reads "means elegant and brave in Mandarin." She looked familiar. Was that the same woman from the Chinese delegation that came over for dinner?

Another page had a burly, bald-headed man in sunglasses carrying two metal briefcases through what looked like an airport terminal. His label read "Andrey Kuznetzov, Minister of Light Fabrics." In a back pocket, there were extra pictures that obviously never made into the main section. They were loose and unlabeled and of varying sizes. One was of a group of people standing looking at a large machine at a conference. A sign read "Saco-Lowell/Lawrence Textile Group" and another, hanging overhead, reads "Polksa Innotextile Xpo '52." Standing to the left of the shot, in a dark suit and Buddy Holly glasses, his arms folded and not looking at the machine or the camera, was her father. He was in his early twenties, trim at the waist but with broad shoulders. A second photograph at the same location was paper-clipped behind it. It showed an austere man, dressed in a white military suit with gold epaulets and buttons looking at the machine. He had silver hair brushed back from his forehead and a bushy gray mustache. There was no mistaking him—it was Stalin!

"Oh my god! We have a photo of Dad with Stalin! What the fuck? I can't even believe what I'm looking at."

This could be one of the last photographs of Joseph Stalin. He died of a cerebral hemorrhage in 1953 and was rarely seen in his final years, and yet here he was standing within twenty-five feet of her father at a Polish conference in 1952.

They scanned the rest of the binder and thumbed through the loose pictures in the back. It was clear that their father moved in unusual circles and must have had a reason to create this binder.

"What do you make of all this, Ana? Seems very sketchy to me."

"We need to put this somewhere safe. The people who killed him were probably looking for it. Do you think Dad knew you had it?"

"No idea. We never discussed it. I never told him I found it, but there were a bunch of boxes in the attic that I left. When I went back to finish the move out, they were gone. Maybe he forgot about the binder and just rid of the rest?"

She didn't say it out loud, but that seemed highly unlikely.

The last page in the binder was side-by-side photos of two men labeled "Maksym, London 1968" and "Oleksandr, New York 1968." They seemed important. They looked like brothers.

Chapter 4

Boca Raton, Florida

Bruce Lasher's waterfront mansion was perched on the end of a small peninsula in one of Boca's most exclusive gated communities on the inland waterway, The Anchorage.

When Ana pulled up the next morning, the gate was down and the gatehouse empty. A large man in an ill-fitting uniform suddenly popped out from behind a bush, startling her. His pants were baggy, but his jacket was so tight the buttons looked ready to shoot off at the first wrong move.

"Sorry, ma'am. Had to take a leak. Please don't say anything to anyone."

"Of course, not. If you gotta go, you gotta go. I'm here to see Mr. Bruce Lasher. He's expecting me."

He lumbered back into the gatehouse, a large sweat stain spreading across the back of his jacket. He picked up a phone and, after exchanging a few words with someone, hung up. The barrier struggled and wobbled on the upswing and before settling shakily at the top of its climb.

She drove about a mile before arriving at Eucalyptus South, took a right, and pulled up in front a large, whitewashed home surrounded by willow trees in full bloom.

The housekeeper answered the door before Ana could even ring the bell. She was dressed in actual housekeeper regalia—a gray cord dress with a white collar, a white tea apron around her waist, and her hair tied up in a tight bun on the back of her head.

"Ms. Pike? Pleased to meet you! I'm Maria. Please come in. Mr. Lasher is down on the dock. I'll show you the way."

Maria led her through the house to a large sliding window that opened onto a deck overlooking the inland waterway.

Bruce, well into his eighties, was fussing over a gorgeous triple-engine sport fishing boat at the end of his dock, resetting fishing rods with giant reels.

"Well, Ana Pike, I haven't seen you since you were a tot. Can't say I wasn't surprised to suddenly get a call from you. I'm gonna guess that you have some bad news for me about your dad?"

He grinned up at her from inside the boat, like the bad news was actually good news. She was a little taken aback. *What the fuck is wrong with this man?*

"Yes, he was murdered. Someone broke into his home, tortured him, burned his hands and feet, beat the shit out of him, then shot him in the back of the head."

Shock value.

"My god, I had no idea!"

"You don't watch the news down here? It's everywhere. I think my mum invited you to the funeral too. Perhaps you don't open your mail either?"

Bruce gave her a hard stare. In his youth, she could have imagined him being intimidating, but now he looked soft. His face sagged, and he said, "I don't watch much TV, okay? Watch your attitude or I'll have Marta escort you out of here."

"Maria. Her name is Maria."

What an asshole!

If she was going to get anything out him, confrontation probably wasn't the way. She apologized for her rudeness and spent the next ten minutes blowing smoke up his backside about his beautiful home, his amazing boat, and inventing compliments her father made about him "let's go inside. I need a refresher."

"I'd like to talk to you about my dad's past. The two of you worked together for quite a long time. He and I weren't close until recently when he got the cancer. He traveled a lot, and so I want to know him better. I thought maybe you could help."

"He was quite a guy, a real Freddie Benson, you know?"

Bruce was casting himself as Lawrence Jamieson in *Dirty Rotten Scoundrels*, the sophisticated playboy con man living on the French Riviera while her father was Freddy Benson, the rough-around-the-edges protégé learning the trade. He totally missed the point, of course. Benson and Jamieson were rivals, competing in a winner-takes-all competition—not mentor and apprentice.

"So when did you and my dad start working together?"

"I met him in the early fifties. He was as a draftsman at British company we acquired. We picked them up for pennies on the dollar."

"Why?"

"Subsidies as part of the postwar rebuilding undercut their margins. Moscow went for cheap, low-quality product from East Germany and Hungary. The Brits were caught in a squeeze play. He and I cut deals all over Poland, Romania, Czechoslovakia, the Soviet Union, and Soviet Ukraine. Eventually, I left the company, and we didn't see each other much after that."

"Why did you leave?"

"I lived in Italy, had plenty of money, and got sick of the shitty quality of life in the Soviet countries."

Ana reached into her backpack. "I'd like to show you some pictures that my brother found. I'm wondering if there's anyone you recognize."

His demeanor changed noticeably. He shifted awkwardly in his chair and focused his attention on the gin and tonic as if to steady himself.

"It was a long time ago," he says, "memory's not what it used to be. But he always had that damned camera with him. Made everyone very nervous."

"Why?"

"Why? The Commies kept tabs on everyone, and people really didn't want some guy taking their picture."

A tall, black woman swept into the room, waving a glass of champagne, wearing a flowing silk robe that had her gliding on air. She was stunning and didn't look at day over fifty.

Ana immediately recognized her from one on the photos. It was taken in the 1970s in midtown Manhattan. She was elegant and had a kind of intellectual sense of style, a brown leather jacket belted at the waist, white trousers and high-heeled shoes. She carried a big white purse on her shoulder and white ushanka fur hat.

"Hi, I'm Regina, Bruce's wife."

Her voice was silky smooth and cool, her personality friendly and engaging as she extended her free hand. Ana introduced herself, apologized for the intrusion, and explained that her father used to work with Bruce. She expected Regina's face to light up with the pleasant memories, but that wasn't the reaction she got at all. In spite of her hard look, Bruce didn't look up from the binder.

They knew something. Whatever they were up to together was dangerous. "People didn't really want some guy taking their picture." There was more to it than that, Ana could feel it.

Regina sat down next to her husband, the binder opened on the coffee table in front of them. They flipped through it. Every once in a while, they looked at each other, and Ana watched their body language.

Discomfort. Guilt. Exposure.

Ana flicked on the tape recorder in her pocket without telling them. "I'm guessing that you know some of these people?"

"Yes, there are a few. This guy is Artem Ponomarenko. He was a big shot in the Soviet Ukrainian government. He had a lot of sway over our deals in Kiev. He became the first secretary of the Soviet Ukraine government and a very powerful man."

Regina chimed in, "He died years ago."

"Yes, they found him in the bed of his niece, who was studying in Kiev."

Regina shot him a sharp look of retribution. He shook her off. "It's fine, love. They're dead or close to it by now. She's just trying to understand who her dad was."

The second, Miloje Petrovic, was trying to rebuild the Yugoslav textile industry and an ally of Tito in the early days. The last photograph that Bruce identified was Marius Popescu, a Romanian.

"Marius was a partner of ours, blew the whistle on some stuff the Soviets were doing."

He flipped to the last page, the one with the photo labeled "Maksym and Oleksandr, London, 1968." He took in a deep breath and looked with resignation at Regina.

"That's the Palatnik brothers."

Apparently, they started the company in the late 1940s. Oleksandr fled Odessa before the Nazis invaded while Maksym stayed behind. Their parents were killed during the invasion, and Maksym ended up in one of the camps. Oleksandr started a sweatshop in the Garment District of Manhattan called Lawrence Textile and purchased Saco-Lowell, a company on the brink of closure. They brought Bruce in to be the managing director. Maksym became their Ukrainian partner as the US government blocked companies from doing business there. They did business in Ukraine through Saco-Lowell.

"So you and my dad were the link between this guy in New York and his brother in Ukraine. How did it work?"

"Listen, dear," he began in that condescending way, "it was a mess over there. There was no infrastructure, a broken financial system, and a lot of corruption. Saco-Lowell gave us the financial channel to do business there. Oleksandr hired me create the link to do the job, and after my interview, I never met him again. Now, if you'll excuse me, I have some important business to attend to."

Maria appeared next to her, gesturing for Ana to stand and follow her toward the door. Bruce sipped his gin and tonic, but there was the slightest of tremors in his hand. Regina, sitting next to him with her hands resting on her lap, gazed toward the window overlooking the dock. Her face said, "Enjoy the view while you have it. It's all going away."

Ana had hit a nerve.

Chapter 5

S urprisingly, it was an uneventful flight from West Palm Beach to New York, followed by a peaceful ride up I-95 from LaGuardia. Ana crossed the New York state line at Port Chester into Greenwich, Connecticut. Through the open window, she could smell the familiar Arnold's Bakery factory that instantly took her back to her high school days. It was her first time back since she graduated from St. Mary's Academy twenty years earlier.

Greenwich was one of the wealthiest towns in America, the domain of old money and Manhattan's wealthiest financiers and corporate moguls. When the state legislature introduced a personal income tax offset by a reduction in corporate taxes, hedge funds, investment banks, and real estate developers from the city set up shop in Stamford and Greenwich. The population got younger, wealthier, and more social. Yacht and golf clubs, once the stuffy domain of the aging, became havens for future America's Cup winners, tennis pros, and PGA Tour hopefuls.

How on earth did the Pikes end up here? It was a ridiculous gear shift for a middle-class school girl from Blackburn. It hadn't made much sense to her until the call from Mattinson.

She wound her way through the quaint town and took a quick drive past St. Marys before heading down the back country roads of Lake Avenue. Well-manicured colonial homes gave way to mansions with BMWs and Land Rovers parked out front and ultimately to long driveways with everything hidden from view by tall trees.

Five miles in, Bob's driveway appeared on the left. It was easy to miss, just a small wooden sign with the number 760 mostly hidden by ferns. The driveway was a dirt road that wound through a small forest so overgrown that both sides of her car brushed against the encroaching shrubs and tree branches.

She emerged in front of a single-story gray home of wood and stone. Thirty years ago, it was probably a nightmare of modern design that gave his neighbors fits. There was an old Volvo 240 in mint condition parked in front of a three-car garage off to the left.

The front door opened, and a woman with a big, toothy smile beckoned Ana toward her. This must be the housekeeper, Lila, who had taken her call. What was about wealthy white widowers of a certain age and housekeepers? Honestly, it was like something from a bygone era.

"You must be Ana, Bran's girl, right? We were so excited to get your call but so sad to hear that your father had passed. I'm so sorry for your loss."

Ana thanked her and stepped into the house. The entrance opened into a huge living room with twenty-foot floor-to-ceiling windows on the far side. The living room was a seventies style step-down into a recessed living area with couches and a fireplace in the center with glass tables, orchids, and ornaments from years spent traveling the world—Buddhas in prayer poses and sleek, dark figurines carrying baskets. On the wall were masks, shields, large format photographs, and decorative quilts and tapestries. It was a bit much but at least no elephant tusks or weapons.

Bob was in his late eighties and lost his wife, Gloria, a decade earlier to an aggressive cancer.

"It's just me and him these days, so he gets a bit lonely," Lila was saying.

Bob was sitting in a chair on the back deck, a blanket over his legs and a glass of Scotch in his hand. Lila slid one of the huge windows open with ease, and Bob turned quickly to greet his guest.

"Oh my lord! As I live and breathe, Anabel Pike. I haven't seen you since you were in high school. I'm so sorry about your dad. Your father passing is one thing, but the way it happened? It's just so horrible. I can't imagine what you and your family are going through. Please, sit."

She thanked him, and they reminisced for a while—recollections of her antics during childhood meetings, stories of interfamily barbecues gone awry, and shared memories like graduations. Lila stepped through the glass door with coffee and baked goods.

"Mr. Schier," Ana began.

"Please, call me Bob. We're old family friends."

She decided on the way up not to tell Bob about her unnerving meeting with Bruce and Regina. It would introduce a bias, color the information she needed to gain from him. She went straight for it.

"Okay, Bob…you and my dad worked together for a long time, right? Well, the police are asking a lot of questions about who would do something like that to an old man, you know? Was it a home invasion gone wrong or something else? Maybe they wanted something from him?"

"Yes, I see. And if you don't mind my asking, which way are they leaning?"

"That he was targeted. The fact that they tortured him before killing him then cleaned up the scene suggests a hit."

It hung in the air like a bad smell with no obvious source. Ana waited for him to speak, but Bob just nodded slowly and took her hands in his. A sympathetic gesture from an old family friend struggling to find the right thing to say in the uncomfortable moment. He either knew nothing or he was an amazing actor who knew how to play the game. Her gut told her it was the latter, and she decided to play her first card.

"So apparently, while my dad worked for you, he earned a lot of money that he kept in banks accounts around Europe without telling any of us. It appears to have just sat there, and then he left it all in a will that he signed before we moved to America. Do you know anything about that?"

Bob stiffened. His body language transitioned from caring family friend to helpful-but-slightly-bemused coworker.

"Well, you know, they all had bank accounts in the countries they worked in. It was difficult to get around without local currency and some places required it for entry visas. Safer too. You know, these places were corrupt and dangerous most of the time. Criminals robbed western businessman for foreign currency so they could trade them on the black market. Besides, they had a lot of palms to grease, cash bribes to factory managers and government officials. It was seedy but just the way things worked."

"What kind of money are we talking about? In a bank, at any one time."

"Hard to say, maybe $25,000? I wasn't part of the company in those days, but we did the same thing in Asia."

It was a predictable move—not around when it happened, just guessing about the amounts, don't hold me to it. Ana let the pause turn into an awkward silence.

A staring contest. Who blinked first?

Bob blinked first, leaning back in his chair and opening up his torso and arms like a man about to explain the world to a woman. Ana was at her best in these moments. Let him pontificate while she prepared her weapon for the kill shot.

"You know, none of us were making much money. I wouldn't be surprised to hear that some people padded their cash requests and stashed a little extra away for a rainy day. I was about to say it's not a crime, but it probably is!"

Card number two, the binder. Ana reached into her purse for a manila envelope, opened the clasp, and pulled out a batch of photographs. Bob's discomfort increased. He must have pressed a button somewhere because Lila appeared at the sliding door.

"Yes, Mr. Schier?"

"Another, please Lila," he said, pointing to his glass. "Can we get you anything, my dear?"

Ana declined, ready for the kill shot.

"Sean found these in the attic when my parents were moving to Florida. I was hoping you could help me understand who some of these people are. This is a just a few of them."

Bob put on his reading glasses and began to thumb through the photos, shaking his head occasionally at some of the earlier black-and-whites—Artem Ponomarenko, no; Jakub Nowak, no; Marius Popescu, no; and Miloje Petrovic, also no.

"I joined the company in the midsixties, and these people all seem to be from before my time. In the fifties and early sixties, they were all over Eastern Europe, Poland, Czechoslovakia, Hungary, and Romania then later more in the Soviet Union and East Germany. But when the Soviets invaded Czechoslovakia in 1968, it was the beginning of the end. I came in, and we started to shift more of our business out of the region and towards Asia and that was where I focused."

He tapped on the page for Yee Xiu Ying, Director, Shandong Sunshine Textile Co. Ltd. "This is Madam Yee. You met her. Do you remember? You were just a little girl, but your dad and I hosted a delegation from China, four men and a woman? They all came to your house for dinner? You remember?"

"Yes, I was thinking about them at the funeral. The smell of their Chungwa cigarettes and Mao suit stuck with me. So this is her?"

"Yes, she loved you, the little English girl with the funny accent! They were a funny group. Never left China before and ended up being sent to Blackburn!"

The photos of the Palatnik brothers were at the bottom of the pile. Bob froze when he got to them.

"Do you know these guys?" she asked. He paused. Whatever color had been in his face before was gone.

"I do. They're the Palatnik brothers. This one," he said, tapping the photo, "is Maksym. What a piece of work he was. Bruce Lasher, your dad, and Maksym worked together for many years. I met him once or twice in the early days. He had a rough time with the Nazis. After the war, when the Soviets reclaimed Odessa, he somehow managed to take control of the port. He was very powerful and a shady character for sure."

"Would he come after my dad now?"

"He's probably been dead for years. But why would he?"

"Well, someone did. And they wanted something specific."

"Like what?"

"These pictures, maybe? Maybe someone doesn't want them out there? They're not exactly family snapshots, are they? He was involved in something."

"Perhaps. I wouldn't know. I'm sorry."

He clearly knew more than he was telling, but this was as much as she was going to get out of him. He completely shut down.

Why? What does he know? Whatever it was, Bob was in on it too. Just like Bruce.

They made small talk for a few minutes. Update on his grandchildren. Plans for the holidays. Promises to stay in touch.

As she drove away, Ana couldn't help but feel like Bruce, Bob, her father, and this character Maksym were in cahoots. And whoever was running the scheme today wanted these photos out of circulation. And would kill a dying man to make sure.

But who? And if the binder is the motive for the killing, they didn't get it. What if they won't stop until they get it?

*****

Later, as an enormous full moon bathed Bob's property in a milky blue light, a black Suburban eased slowly up the driveway with its headlights off. The engine was almost silent, but the heavy tires cracked small branches and twigs and crunched over the pea stone. It passed the garage and parked in a dark corner under a cluster of maples. The engine cut and sat silent. No one inside moved.

An owl hooted from high up in one of the trees, and a startled animal—perhaps a possum or a raccoon—scampered through the underbrush to hide. Leaves shuffled in the upper branches of the trees. Tiny feet and noses ferreted around in the dirt for food.

The doors of the Suburban eased open with an almost inaudible click. Three figures in black jumpsuits and balaclavas stepped out with the delicacy of ballerinas performing a perfectly executed adagio. They slid silently across the gravel, pressing their bodies against the side of the house. Hand signals and eye movements were all they needed.

They didn't want to be there, but now that the Draftsman was dead, they had no choice. Every trick in the book had failed to get him to talk. There was a lot of money unaccounted for, and their employer wanted it back. But there was more to it than that.

There were secrets that he wanted to remain buried in the past. The Draftsman knew where the skeletons were, and he kept records.

The skeletons must stay buried because the Malina ran New York now. As one after the other, the Italians went to jail, the Malina of Brighton Beach had filled the void.

They reached the front door and rang the doorbell. It seemed like an overly polite gesture given their reasons for being there, but it was part of the plan.

A housekeeper opened the door and immediately took a bullet between the eyebrows. The small caliber round rattled around inside her skull for a second before she fell. No gaping exit wounds or mess on the polished marble floor. She just dropped heavily to the ground, her eyes wide in shock.

The old man was sitting on a couch in the living room. They saw him immediately and saw the panic on his face when he heard her fall. A drink slipped from his hand, the glass shattering on the tile.

They stepped inside, swinging weapons left and right, up and down. A trail of red laser dots on the walls, doors, and ceiling.

"Wait, I'm on your side! There's no need for this! I was going to tell you everything. There was no need to kill Lila."

"You're going to tell us anyway, Mr. Schier," said one. He turned to look over his shoulder and laughed. "You got a light?"

Behind him, someone lit a large cigar, and Bob's eyes widened.

Two hours later, Bob was dead, killed in the same manner as Brandon Pike, the Draftsman—bound, burned, then shot in the back of the head. The leader of the hit squad dialed a number on his mobile to deliver his report.

"Yes, boss. We took care of him. The boys are cleaning up now. Sang like a bird. Told us that the Draftsman left a lot of photographs. His daughter showed an envelope full of photographs, asking questions about who the people are."

He pulled his ear away from the phone as his employer yelled, "*Naydi etu suku bystro!*" (Find that bitch quick!)

Chapter 6

T he trip to Nicosia had been a horror show—a drive to god-awful Newark for an overnight to Zurich on Swissair then onto Larnaca Airport after a four-hour delay. After Cyprus, her next stop was Luxembourg, Switzerland, on Thursday and Manchester on Friday to meet the solicitor, Mattinson.

In the taxi, she had booked the next leg of her journey. There were no direct flights between Larnaca and Luxembourg Findel Airport. Every routing either had a change of airline or a long layover. She settled on a Lufthansa flight through Munich with a ninety-minute layover and a change to Luxair. It would be tight but felt like the best option.

Going to Cyprus first was Mattinson's idea. He said it would help her "get her feet wet dealing with continental private banking types." It was a small account, and he said it was better to look like an amateur there than at one of the Swiss banks with a long history dealing with a secretive clientele and hiding money from the police and the taxman.

She arrived at HellenicBank of Cyprus exactly on time at ten and stepped into a lobby that smelled of wild roses and lavender. The whole island smelled of roses and lavender, as a matter of fact. A severe woman with a tight hair bun sat at a desk off to the right but paid no attention to her. Most of her face was hidden behind a colorful array of orchids. Ana felt like one of the plants, just part of the scenery.

Suddenly, an impeccably dressed man with immaculate manners appeared by her side. He introduced himself as Mr. Kypianos, the manager of HellenicBank, and she disliked him right away. He was quite young, maybe midforties and perhaps fancied himself a bit of a player. He openly looked Ana up and down, judging her worthiness to be in his presence, like the arrogant owner of a super yacht docked in Limassol Marina vetting who could step aboard.

She had been expecting it and spent an hour or two shopping in the boutiques on Ledra Street to be ready. She wore an alluring Delfina white cotton summer dress that fell well above the knee, had a slightly puffed sleeve, and an empire waist. It was almost see-through when the sunlight caught it in just the right way. She added the perfect local handmade black leather sandals with straps that ran between her toes and wrapped around her ankles and a Zeus and Dione black leather shoulder purse.

Kypianos had seen it all before and was not so easily manipulated. Attractive young women came into the bank daily to check up on the accounts of their aging husbands. This American woman—attractive, with long legs and good taste in clothing—was no different.

"I would like access to my father's accounts with your institution. I have the necessary credentials, Mr. Kypianos, provided to me by the attorney for his estate."

His brow furrowed, and his glasses slid down his long ski jump of a nose as he looked down on her. His body language oozed suspicion and nervousness.

"Certainly, Ms. Pike. My associate," he said, gesturing toward the tight bun behind the orchids, "will help with the verification procedures and—"

Don't let the man drone on about bank policies. Stay in control.

"Yes, Mr. Kypianos, I am well aware of the procedures and what needs to be done. Let's just move this along, I don't have a lot time."

Tight-bun-orchid lady rose from her desk and hurried to Kypianos's side. Her skirt was so tight and her heels so high that she sounded like a terrier in tap shoes on the marble floor.

"Please excuse me." Kypianos, with a slight bow, turned on his heels and disappeared through a door.

She spoke perfect English, tinted with a slight Greek accent. "Can I offer you one of our famous Cypriot coffees? Sekto, metrio, glyko, or frappe?"

"Yes, please." Ana picked a frappe, a word that was at least recognizable. It turned out to be right choice for her—cold instant coffee with ice and whipped milk cream. She waited patiently, sipping her coffee, for the next step.

Tight-orchid-bun lady returned to her desk and began tapping on her computer keyboard. The lobby was silent once again. A phone buzzed on the desk and signaled to Ana that they were ready for her.

She was ushered her into a private room with a computer with an antiquated green screen. She entered the account information, and the screen flipped to the account activity. There were just three deposits.

HellenicBank of Cyprus
75 Stassinos Street, Nicosia, Cyprus
Account: 98-45743-1432-05790

Deposit $450,000 EUR—Mar 4, 1952
Cash Converted from Ukrainian Hryvna
Deposit: $750,000 EUR—Jun 10, 1953
Cash Converted from Romanian Leu
Deposit: $1,250,000 EUR—Sep 12, 1963
Cash Converted from Polish Zloty

Current account value:
10,627,000 EUR/13,380,000 USD

The money had been sitting in cash, earning interest but not invested in anything for almost half a century. No one had ever inquired about the account after the deposits, and there was no information about the source.

But she has learned two important things—her credentials were good enough to gain access to the accounts and her father's accounts made people nervous. There was no "Oh, you're Mr. Pike's daughter! It's so wonderful to meet you. He was a lovely man!" Instead, Kypianos had visibly blanched when she mentioned her father's name and insisted on having yet another colleague verify her credentials and observe her access to the account records. Both were important lessons for her next stop in Luxembourg.

She left instructions with Kypianos to transfer all the funds to a new account in the Channel Islands immediately. Mattinson had told her to put all the money in one place, under UK jurisdiction, where she had easy access and he could oversee it.

Chapter 7

Boca Raton, Florida

It was the housekeeper's day off. She was lucky, but the guard at the entrance to The Anchorage was not so fortunate. When the black SUV pulled up to the gate, he took a bullet to the right side of his head before he even had a chance to turn to see who was trying to enter.

They positioned his body to make it look like he was sleeping on the job and left the gate up. They drove down Eucalyptus South until they arrived at number 5, Bruce Lasher's home.

Regina opened the door with a flourish and an enormous smile. Clearly, she was expecting someone else. Her eyes widened, and she turned to run into the house just as the bullet entered the back of her neck. Her body dropped like a stone, but she didn't die right away. She lay paralyzed, desperately trying to signal Bruce.

"You fool! That's not the fucking housekeeper. It's his wife. We needed her alive."

It was a big mistake. She knew a lot. She knew the Draftsman very well, but whatever she had to tell was lost in an instant. Sometimes, things just didn't go according to plan on a kill mission. This kind of operation required people to think on their feet, recognize a change in the situation, and adjust accordingly. They knew that there would be a price to pay for her death, and it would be paid with one of their lives. When the price would be paid was less clear.

They moved silently through the house. One carried the Draftsman's Makarov pistol, the one used to kill Bob Schier the day before. They learned little from the old man except that the Draftsman's daughter had visited and that she was asking questions about people in a binder. He knew nothing about the money. He had died in the same way as the Draftsman.

They found Lasher hiding in the bathroom, lying in the tub behind the shower curtain. The front of his well-worn Nantucket Red shorts was wet with urine, and he was desperately trying to dial a number on his phone. The man reached into the tub and took it—not aggressively but gently and with pity.

"You can change your clothes. We expect to speak with a professional, not a man who soils himself in the bathtub. You must pull yourself together, Mr. Lasher. Yes, we know who you are. This is not a robbery. We are here for information, and you would do well to cooperate with us. We regret the death of your wife. She was quite lovely. We would have liked to talk to her too."

Bruce clambered out of the bathtub and scampered toward his closet. Apparently, he and Regina each had their own. He emerged in fresh clothes and cologne, his hair coiffed the way he liked it.

They bound his hands and feet with the double zip-tie cuffs before placing him in his favorite armchair and removing his socks and shoes. They gagged and duct taped his mouth to prevent his screams from resonating through the neighborhood. The old man struggled to control his bowels again.

The leader, the one holding the Makarov, lit his cigar and buried the burning tip deep into the soles of Bruce's left foot. Bruce's eyes bulged in agony. With a puff to revitalize the heated embers, the leader did the same on his right foot. For a while, he asked no questions at all, just fired up the tip of the cigar then drove the burning tip into his feet and arms. Another man dragged Regina's lifeless body into the room and dropped her near his feet.

"Mr. Lasher, this is just the beginning of your pain unless, of course, you cooperate and answer our questions. You may be able to live out your final years in peace and go fishing in that beautiful boat at the end of your dock, if you play your cards right. Is that something you would be interested in doing?"

Bruce nodded vehemently. The gag and the tape were removed, taking most of his mustache with it.

"You were visited by the Draftsman's daughter? What did she talk to you about?"

"Yes, she showed up here yesterday. She wanted to talk about her father's past, how we got into business in Eastern Europe, and his murder. I'm guessing you were responsible for that?"

"I'm asking the questions here. What else?"

"Not much else that I recall. She didn't stay long."

The leader shook his head slowly, took a big puff on his cigar as another man covered Bruce's mouth from behind. He let the cigar linger on the sole of Bruce's foot until the flesh sizzled and smoked.

"This is not what I would call playing your cards right, Mr. Lasher. I'm starting to think that perhaps you aren't that interested in living after all."

He looked up at his team and said, "Settle in for the long haul, gentlemen. I fear we may be here for a while."

Panting, Bruce stuttered, "I'm sorry. I'm sorry. She had a binder with pictures of people in it, and she was asking me if I knew any of them. I identified a couple for her, just trying to get her out of my hair."

"Whose pictures were in this binder?"

"The Palatnik brothers, Ponomarenko, Popescu, pretty much everyone who was there at the beginning, and then some people from the later years in China that I didn't know."

"Who did you identify?"

"Like I said, the Palatniks, Ponomarenko, and a couple of others. I can't remember now."

"Did she mention the money?"

"No, she didn't say anything about any money, I swear to you!"

He took another huge drag on the cigar, blew the smoke in Bruce's face, and planted the burning end right in the middle of his forehead.

"The bullet that I put in the back of your head, Mr. Lasher, will come out right there. So I ask you again, did she mention the money?"

Bruce shook his head vigorously. "She didn't like or trust me. Our conversation was not friendly. She asked if we were con men or spies, and when I told her were con men, she got mad and left. Maybe she was hoping to find out something good about her father."

"Anything else we need to know, Mr. Lasher?"

"Nothing, I swear it!"

The bullet entered just above the first cervical vertebrae and exited through the cigar burn, as predicted. The killers disinfected the scene, left Bruce in his chair and the body of his wife lying at his feet.

Chapter 8

Washington, DC, 2009

T he Director's office was buzzing when Special Agent Sam Isherwood was escorted into the wood-paneled room. It was only the second time he had been called to a meeting here during his FBI career. The first had been after 9/11 as a member of the Joint Terrorism Task Force. He had briefed the director and others on their common-call analysis, a sophisticated program to aggregate and analyze phone and text records of passengers on all four planes to identify the hijackers and trace their communications back months and years.

Everyone in the office moved toward the secure anteroom through a heavy steel door, dropping their cell phones in a wooden box with an engraved gold label that said simply "Phones, please."

The group all stood behind their assigned chairs. There was one more open down at the end that Isherwood assumed was his, a fact confirmed by the table tent with his name, "SA Isherwood, Criminal Investigations Division."

He recognized a few of the faces around the table—the assistant director of International Operations, director of the Counterterrorism Division, and a former colleague climbing the ranks of the Office of Partner Engagement, Katherine Daring. She was sharp. Her job was to liaise with the web of military and civilian intelligence agencies on behalf of the FBI.

It was an impressive group all around, the kind who had their photographs mounted in conference rooms for their awards and commendations.

The director brought the meeting to order.

"Please, everyone, be seated. There'll be no standing on cere-mony today, ladies and gentlemen. We have a situation on our hands, as you know. I'd like to introduce Special Agent Isherwood to you all. I haven't told him yet, but he'll be leading this investigation and briefing us daily on his progress. I'm sorry about the lack of warning, Special Agent. All will become clear, and I have complete confidence in you to grab the ball and run with it."

A young agent, maybe thirty years old, strode confidently to the front of the room and placed himself in front of a huge screen.

"I'm Agent Josh Parker from the Miami field office investigat-ing the murder of Brandon Pike of Vero Beach, Florida. We received a call from the field office in New Haven about the murder of one Robert Schier in Greenwich, Connecticut, with the same MO."

The screen behind him snapped on with a video link to the Firearms/Toolmarks unit lab at Quantico. A very serious-looking man in spectacles turned toward the camera.

"This is Assistant Executive Laboratory Director Bernstein. He's running the analysis on the bullets that killed our two victims. Director Bernstein? The floor is yours."

"Thank you, Agent Porter. I can confirm that the bullets that killed the two victims, Brandon Pike and Robert Schier, came from the same weapon, a 9mm Makarov, a standard Soviet military-issued side arm from the 1950s until 1991. This weapon is rarely seen out-side Russia and former Soviet satellite states."

He went on to report that there was no record in the FBI data-base of this weapon being used in a crime or registered in the United States.

"In this case, the weapon was the MP-71 variation of the Makarov. It has a threaded barrel for a suppressor and was generally reserved for Soviet special operations and state security. We weren't surprised when we were unable to match it with any other in the FBI database."

No guns or casings were found at either crime scene, but bullets were retrieved from the walls, and a third was removed from the body of Schier's housekeeper. She was shot with a Heckler & Koch Mark 23, a powerful and precise weapon used by US Special Operations in the early 1990s. This weapon also failed to match any crime in the database. However, it was registered to the armory at Fort Bragg and assigned to the Third Special Forces Group (Airborne) and reported missing from the inventory in August of 2007 after a refit of the armory was completed.

Agent Parker thanked the lab director, who turned back to his microscope as the screen went blank and the FBI insignia appeared on the blue background.

"This was not a run-of-the-mill double homicide. The male victims, Pike and Schier, worked together for many years at a company called Saco-Lowell, which had business ties to the Soviet Union and the People's Republic of China. Both were tortured and then executed with the same MO, zip-tied hands and feet, cigar burns, blunt force beatings to the soles of the feet, and a single gunshot to the back of the head." He paused, scanned the table, and said, "And now we have a third."

"Who's the third and what's the connection?"

"Bruce Lasher of Boca Raton. He also worked with Pike and Schier. He was found dead in his home this morning with the body of his wife, Regina Brooks, at his feet. A security guard at his gated community was found shot in his booth also."

"Same weapon?"

"Waiting for the confirmation, Director, but everything else about the killing lines up with the other two."

One was a problem, two was a pattern, but three was a serial.

Katherine Daring leaned forward and said, "Are we concerned about national security concerns? You mentioned Russia and China specifically."

"It can't be ruled out, but our current thinking is that it's more likely to be the Russian mob."

The director had one elbow planted hard on the table, rubbing her chin and staring hard at the young agent. She felt bad for the kid. Great work putting the pieces together, but this one was about to be taken out of his hands and handed over to the more experienced Isherwood.

"Thank you, Special Agent Parker. I'll be writing a personal commendation into your record for your work on this, but this case is going to require an experienced investigative lead from here. You are excused."

The young man deflated for a moment but quickly pulled himself together, straightened his tie, and nodded his thanks. A personal commendation from the director of the FBI would boost his career in ways he couldn't understand today. Simply presenting a case in front of a group like this would change his trajectory. But he was still pissed.

After the door closed, the director stood up. She was a woman of incredible intellect who rose through the ranks and earned her appointment by a Republican president despite her progressive credentials.

"What do think, Katherine? Is this a national security concern?"

"Three men in their eighties with ties to the former Soviet Union and China murdered in close succession with a standard KGB firearm that isn't registered? It could be the Russian mob in the US tying up loose ends but—"

"But?"

"But it sounds like the killers were looking for something. And who knows how far back that could go?"

She turned and said, "Special Agent Isherwood, this is your case now. What do we do next?"

"We need to know if that weapon has a history outside of the US. That means working with INTERPOL to see if it shows up in IBIN or iARMS. It's a hit squad, and we need to figure out who is next on the kill list. And quick."

Chapter 9

Lyon, France

P ascal Benoit woke up early, as he always did, expecting his workday to be just like every other—long hours quarantined in the basement of INTERPOL headquarters, doing the thankless work of digging through the Eastern European organized crime cold-case files.

What he didn't know was that by the end of the day, he would be leading an international investigation into the murder of six Americans, three with connections to the Ukrainian mafia going back a half century—blackmail, murder, political assassinations, and corruption. There wasn't a crime on the books that these people and their associates couldn't be connected to.

Lyon's noisy tourists had kept him up all night, eating and drinking late into the night in the Irish pubs and Bouchon Lyonnais restaurants on the street below his window. He had tossed and turned in his overheated bed, waking up sweaty every hour to check his clock, hoping it was time to get up and have his first cigarette of the day.

He lived alone in a small but functional apartment in the historic Fifth Arrondissement of Vieux Lyon near the Cathedrale Sainte Jean-Baptiste. Two years ago, almost to the day, his wife of twenty years, Claudia, had passed away of breast cancer. He sold their farmhouse near Charbonnieres-les-Bains—the memories and reminders just too painful—and bought this apartment to be closer to work, hoping it would help him overcome the loss and move on.

It hadn't helped at all. He had no one but convinced himself everything was fine as long as he has his work. Those who knew

Pascal, however, watched him slowly spiral into loneliness and depression. He had rebuffed all their efforts to help him find someone.

At five thirty, he had dragged himself out of bed, showered, shaved, and dressed for the day. He rarely deviated from his morning routine unless the weather was particularly bad, but September in Lyon is beautiful. He grabbed his Gauloises Vertes, kissed the picture of Claudia that hung by the door, and stepped into the street. It was a three-kilometer walk from his apartment on Rue Mourguet to INTERPOL HQ on the Quai Charles de Gaulle.

As usual, he stopped for his first cigarette on the Pont de la Feuillee, a bridge connecting the Saint-Paul district of old Lyon to Les Charteux. Lyon's elderly citizens walked their tiny dogs along the banks of the Soane, and the taxi drivers leaned on their cars arguing about football and politics. His next stop was the Cafe de Bruno, across from the Croix-Paquet Metro station. He ordered a café creme, a copy of Le Progrès, and enjoyed his second cigarette at one of the stand-up tables outside.

He has his last cigarette of the morning on the Pont de Lattre de Tassigny. The long bridge was heavy with people heading to the consulates and the expensive car dealerships that dotted the Cite Internationale sixth arrondissement. At the end, he turned left onto Avenue Grand Bretagne and then onto Quai Charles De Gaulle.

The HQ was an ugly building, a white square block surrounded by concrete blockades, an eyesore that had the Rhone River on one side and the beautiful Parc de la Tete D'Or on the other. The place was a hive of activity before Pascal even passed through the security gate. In the hours before sunrise, word came down from the highest levels that investigators should prioritize a request sent in by INTERPOL's National Central Bureau (NCB) office in Washington, DC, in cooperation with the FBI.

Everyone got the message. INTERPOL and the FBI had endured a frosty relationship in recent years. The US applied unwelcome pressure to the agency in the hunt for Al Qaeda killers, financiers, and enablers as part of its War on Terror. A lingering distrust that INTERPOL was more inclined to support autocrats and oligarchs with deep pockets than its democratic members didn't help matters.

The election of a new administration in Washington brought with it a warming trend between the two law-enforcement agencies. The secretariat encouraged a "collegial rebuilding of mutual trust."

Overnight, INTERPOL had added the ballistic and forensic details on two weapons—a Makarov MP-71 and a Heckler & Koch Mark 23—to its Illicit Arms Records and Tracing Management System (iARMS) and the INTERPOL Ballistic Information Network (IBIN) databases. IBIN matched the Makarov to one owned by an Andrey Kuznetzov.

The alert flashed across his screen as soon as he logged on. Kuznetzov was well-known to Pascal and his colleagues working on Project Caspian in the Eastern European Organized Crime Unit. He was a villain with a list of crimes longer than the average arm. The fact that his name came up as a person of interest in the murders of six Americans on US soil sent shock waves through the few people that knew who he was.

According to the FBI, three of the murder victims worked together for years, much of it in Eastern Europe. The similarities between their murders were undeniable—cigar burns on the feet, hands, and forearms, blunt force trauma wounds, and a single 9mm gunshot to the back of the head with the Makarov. All three crime scenes had been scrubbed with hospital-grade disinfectants.

The first victim, Brandon Pike—a dual British and naturalized US citizen, living in Vero Beach, Florida—was tortured and then executed. Two days later, the body of Robert Schier, a US citizen, was found murdered at his home in Greenwich, Connecticut, in a similar fashion. His housekeeper, Lila Hernandez, was shot in the head with the Mark 23. At the most recent scene, the FBI found three bodies— Bruce Lasher tortured and then killed with the Makarov, along with his wife, Regina, and a security guard, Jorge Alvarez, both of whom were killed with the Mark 23.

This wasn't Kuznetzov. Kuznetzov's roots ran deep in the Ukrainian mafia, going all the way back to the 1950s when the Malina first organized and smuggled drugs and weapons through Odessa. He was on every INTERPOL watchlist but hadn't crossed an international border in almost five years, at least not using his real identity. He was also probably eighty by now and surely would not to be the one to fly halfway around the world to torture and execute a bunch of old Americans and their housekeepers. But still the gun was a match, and that was disturbing. It hadn't been used in years, and now, out of the blue, it was used in three separate crimes in the United States.

Pascal picked up his phone and dialed.

"Bonjour, Francois…yes, I'm looking at the report now…ballistics seems like a perfect match, but I just can't believe that Kuznetzov did this himself… I know… We'd have picked up his signal somewhere unless he traveled on an entirely new identity which is possible, I suppose. Could you take an extra hard look at the ballistics and confirm the match? Let me know as soon as possible. There are lots of eyes upstairs on this one."

He spent the next two hours searching though the online files and the old case files down in the basement for any possible reason why Kuznetzov's gun would suddenly show up in America. Makarov pistols were rarely seen outside Russia. How did it get into the US? Why even bother trying to get it through when you could buy much better handguns at gun stores all over Florida?

The gun's ballistics were first captured and entered into the database in 1953 when it was used in the killing of a Bulgarian mobster, whose body was found floating in the harbor in Burgas. Next, a bullet from the gun was retrieved from the body of one Grigor Balan, a Romanian business executive, found at the bottom of a strip mine in 1956. The last time was in 1978 when it was used to kill a Soviet attaché in East Berlin. In between, it had shown up in three killings in and around various Black Sea ports.

Pascal started digging through Kuznetzov's files down in Records and Collections, looking for any connection to either victim. Around lunchtime, just as he was about to rip out his remaining hair and smoke a cigarette in a "Ne Pas Fumer" section of the building, he found something—a cold case from the 1960s that referenced one of the victims, Pike, and Kuznetzov. It wasn't much. Nothing in the file suggested that two met or even knew each other, but that didn't matter at all. There was a connection.

Kuznetzov was associated with well-known Ukrainian criminal, Maksym Palatnik. Palatnik was the de facto head of the Malina. He dropped off the radar in the late 1980s. Pike worked for Saco-Lowell, which was acquired by an American company owned by Oleksandr Palatnik, Maksym's brother, and Kuznetzov worked for one of Maksym's other companies. The goal of that investigation was to establish an illegal financial relationship between the two companies, but the whole thing petered out when the agent in charge retired. It went cold and wasn't pursued any further.

By early afternoon, he realized that he'd skipped lunch—a crime almost unheard of in France. The cafés and restaurants were still full, and no one was in a hurry to get back to work. Pascal grabbed falafel from the window at L'As de Falafel, a stand-in-line spot near the bridge, and pondered his next steps.

When he got back to his desk a half hour later, he found a report from the National Central Bureau in Cyprus there. A man named Christos Kypianos had called the European Union & International Police Cooperation Directorate of the Cypriot police to report an inquiry by someone named Ana Pike regarding an old account. She had the right account number, was listed as a person approved to access the account, and presented a copy of a will from the primary account holder along with her passport.

Pascal picked up the phone, and the switchboard put him through to the NCB office in Cyprus on a secure line.

"Yes, hello? This is Pascal Benoit in Lyon... We received your message about the bank inquiry into an old account by an Ana Pike... Yes, thank you, that would be appreciated. I'll hold."

What a coincidence, a person with the same last name of one of the American victims, was asking for access to an account using a will. Pascal did not believe in coincidences.

"This is Detective Ahmet Ersoy, Cyprus Police. How may I help you, Agent Benoit?"

"Detective, what can you tell me about the woman who inquired at the Hellenic Bank of Cyprus today? It may be connected to a case I'm investigating."

"We sent the report over, Agent. That's all we have on it."

"Is Ms. Pike still in Cyprus? I need to interview her."

"I was told that she was leaving Cyprus today for Luxembourg. She told Mr. Kypianos that she had appointments at a number of banks in the region over the next few days. That's what prompted him to report the inquiry. He said that it seemed strange."

"Did she leave a way to contact her? Or the name of the bank in Luxembourg?"

"She did not, but I suspect, from experience, that it is likely to be Banque Euro Internationale à Luxembourg."

"Do we know how much money is in the Cypriot account?"

"I don't know. You need to talk to Ms. Pike about that. Our assumption is that INTERPOL can supply the right legal documentation to trace the movement of funds through the financial system?"

"Of course, thank you for your time, Detective Ersoy. If anything comes to light that you think might help, please call."

"How can I help if I don't know what you are working on?"

Detective Ersoy smells an opportunity. What can I offer him to get more cooperation?

"The FBI contacted us about the murder of six Americans. We traced the weapon used back to the Ukrainian mafia, a cold case from years ago. One of the victims was named Pike, and now someone with the same last name is visiting a number of banks around Europe."

"I will reinterview Mr. Kypianos to see what else I can ascertain. I'll call you tomorrow."

It was almost five thirty when Francois called to confirm the ballistics match. At six, Ersoy called back.

"The woman's name is Ana Pike, American. She told Kypianos that she had access to the account as the executor of a will. She left instructions to transfer the funds. She left a mobile phone number with Mr. Kypianos."

It was time to take the case upstairs to his boss, Dieter Fischer, Director of INTERPOL Project Caspian. He stepped into the lift and swiped his card for access to the director's floor. The doors opened and directly in front of him was the desk of Director Fischer's assistant, a well-polished Swiss man with a long nose and beady eyes.

He never smiled but said, "*Bonsoir, Monsieur Benoit. Le directeur vous verra maintenant.*"

The director's office door opened, and his head appeared around the jamb. He seemed agitated or maybe just urgent.

"Come in, Pascal. Please, have a seat. What have you discovered thus far? As you know, we want to help our friends at the FBI if we can."

"Yes, sir. I've found an indirect link between Brandon Pike, one of the American victims, and Andrey Kuznetzov, the owner of the Makarov used in the killings. They both worked for companies with connections to the Malina."

The director's eyes widened at the mention of the Kuznetzov name. He walked over to the window overlooking the park. He scratched the back of his shaking head.

"Kuznetzov. That's a name I haven't heard in years. I thought he must be dead by now. I can't believe he would fly to America to kill these people."

"Agreed. The gun has made its way to the US and is now in the hands of someone else. It was used only on the three men, presumably the primary targets. My theory is that the Malina went after these three for a reason. And there's something else. A relative of Mr. Pike, an Ana Pike, is currently visiting banks in Europe, with account credentials as the executor of a will. Can't be a coincidence."

"Okay, I'll take it up to the general secretariat to get you the people and resources you need. You're in charge of the investigation now."

Chapter 10

Grand Duchy de Luxembourg

A na was in the taxi, idly looking out of the window, heading to Banque Euro Internationale à Luxembourg. Her talkative driver was pointing out the Luxembourg American Cemetery and Memorial, where General Patton was buried, when her phone rang.

It's a +33 number. France? I don't know anyone in France.

"*Allo*, Ms. Pike?"

"Yes, who is this, please?"

The voice introduced himself as Pascal Benoit, a Principal Agent at INTERPOL in Lyon, France, and explained that there are a couple of issues he would like to discuss with her.

Shit. The visit to Cyprus triggered something. Stay calm.

"I'm in a taxi right now about five minutes away from my destination."

"I'll be brief. I need your help. Yesterday, we received a request from the FBI about the murder of a man named Brandon Pike. Are you related to this person?"

"He was my father."

"I'm sorry for your loss. Two of his former colleagues, Robert Schier and Bruce Lasher, have also been murdered. Do you know…?"

Stunned.

"It appears, Mademoiselle, that the killers are after something specific. I would not scare you unnecessarily, but we believe they are connected with the Ukrainian mafia and a hit squad known as the Chauffeurs."

The name apparently derived from the "Chauffeurs de la Drôme"—a gang of home invaders in France in the early twentieth century. They tortured their victims into revealing the location of their valuables by burning the bottom of their feet with a branding iron. They held respectable jobs during the day but tortured and robbed by night. They were eventually caught, convicted, and guillotined in public in 1909.

"They used the same gun, which is registered to a man in Ukraine. Does the name Andrey Kuznetzov mean anything to you?"

It did not.

"He is a member of the Ukrainian mafia, the Malina. Did your father have any business relationships with the Malina that you know of?"

Not that she knew of.

"Also, the manager at the HellenicBank of Cyprus called the Cypriot police about a flagged account. Mr. Kypianos informed the police that you are the executor of a will that provides access to this account and left transfer instructions."

"Is there something wrong with that? My father left this will, and I'm the executor."

"Well, it's certainly possible that something is wrong, madame. Your father was murdered. The FBI investigation did not alert us to your travel plans or mention this will. Perhaps you failed to tell them before you left the country? Also, you are transferring the funds to another account. Suspicious, no? We can, of course, freeze the assets, but that will not help us find his killer."

So they know. What to say? What to say? Think quickly.

"I'm sorry, Agent Benoit. I don't know what the FBI know and don't know. I must speak to the solicitor who represented my father. Could I call you later today?"

"Please do not make me wait too long. I am asking for help and can be helpful to you in return, but my patience is not unlimited. I hope your visit to the Banque Euro Internationale à Luxembourg is fruitful. Please say hello to Herr Muller. He and I know each other from university."

And he hung up.

How does INTERPOL know where I am? Are they tracking me? Maybe I'm being followed.

She looked left and right, evaluating the people around her like she could even spot a professional tail. The taxi driver eyeing her in the rearview mirror? The old man with dog sitting on the bench reading a newspaper? The young couple holding hands and chatting as they walked?

She called Mattinson and told him everything Agent Benoit had said.

"Work with the agent but don't give up authority over the accounts. Concealing information from the him will lead to trouble. Just execute the instructions the will."

She pulled herself together, brushed imaginary flakes off her shoulders, gave the driver twenty euros plus a healthy tip to buy his silence, and stepped out of the taxi.

The Banque Euro Internationale à Luxembourg building was an ugly mix of tope block concrete and glass dropped like a turd in the leafy Hollerich, a district dotted with embassies and bound by the curvaceous Pétrusse River. The air was fresh with a slight chill, the wind gently rustling the leaves of the oak trees that surrounded the bank.

As she passed through the enormous automatic sliding glass doors, Herr Gerhard Muller himself welcomed her, just as Agent Benoit had predicted. A polite and polished man with wire spectacles and a pencil-thin mustache, he was cold and businesslike.

"Ms. Pike, welcome. Please accept my deepest condolences on your loss. How can we help you today?"

Ana, conscious of the possible collusion between Muller and Agent Benoit, decided to follow Mattinson's advice to the letter.

"Thank you, Herr Muller. I am the executor of my father's will. I have account access credentials, and I think you'll find everything is in order. I will leave with transfer instructions for the funds."

"Of course, Ms. Pike. As you can imagine, there are procedures and verifications..."

"Frankly, Herr Muller, I don't have time. Please take these documents and verify them."

He explained that her father's account was flagged and that any new activity on it could trigger an inquiry from the authorities, leading to a possible freeze on the assets.

"I am in contact with the authorities, Herr Muller, so if we could just move this along..."

Muller waved over an eager-to-please young man anxiously hovering next to a tall shrub in the corner and instructed him to verify the documents immediately.

Within minutes, Ana was seated in a private office with a computer looking at the list of transactions from 1955 to 1971, all deposits, held by the bank in cash to the tune of 24,250,000 EUR or about thirty-five million dollars. Almost a fifth of his earnings were deposited in this bank. The payments got bigger over time—not a surprise given the suspicions of her brothers, the cryptic wording in the will, and Stephen's binder.

The next morning, she went through the same dance at the second bank in Luxembourg before heading back to the airport for her midday flight to Zurich. Just three more to go, then a flight to Manchester to meet with Mattinson to discuss next steps.

Ana's bank visits in Zurich went very much like the others—erudite and elitist bank managers looking down their noses at her until she produced her credentials, at which point they became twitchy, called in colleagues for support, and reluctantly gave her account access after offering a coffee while making her wait. Transfer instructions for almost fifty-five million euros—about eighty million dollars—were in various stages of execution.

She needed to call Agent Benoit before he started making things "official." She had a direct flight from Zurich to Manchester to meet with Mattinson. Could she continue to put off the INTERPOL agent until she had a chance to talk to the solicitor?

Probably not.

Chapter 11

A gent Benoit was sitting in his office waiting for his phone to ring and reading the latest report from the FBI. Despite marshaling every law-enforcement resource at their disposal, they still had no concrete idea who was next on the Chauffeur's list. Every single person that knew or worked with any of the victims was being contacted. Anabel Pike was definitely on the list.

Outside his window, tourist families ambled through Parc de la Tete D'Or, eating ice cream arm in arm, their steps kicking up a fine white dust that rolled around their feet in billowing clouds. As lovely as it was outside, Pascal knew he would be working late in the INTERPOL HQ records basement for most of the evening. He had nowhere to go or anyone to see, so what did it matter?

Ana Pike had broken their informal agreement to call him back later in the day after speaking to her solicitor. But his main concern at the moment was her safety and that of her family. Possibly large sums of money were involved, and the killers were following the trail to either retrieve it or tie up all the loose ends before it was too late.

Either way, if Pike Sr., Schier, Lasher—or any of the victims for that matter—had mentioned her name or given up any intelligence on what she was up to, then she was next in line for a visit from the Chauffeurs and Kuznetzov's Makarov.

If they can't figure out where she is, her mother and brothers will be very easy to find.

It turned out that, as expected, that Kuznetzov was not the killer. Agents from the INTERPOL NCB in Odessa showed up at his dacha outside of Sevastopol in Crimea. They found him wheelchair-bound

53

and unable to speak. They learned, from the attractive young woman with long legs and a short skirt that tended to him, that it was the result of a stroke. He had a pile of euro bills on the table next to him. Each time he reached up her skirt to grab her backside, she giggled and took one the of the bills. They tried to interview him but got nowhere. The woman was equally unhelpful, claiming that she was just sent there by her agency and barely spoke to the old man.

Someone else had his gun.

Pascal was shaken out of his thoughts by the ringing of his desk phone. It was an American number.

"Good afternoon, Mademoiselle Pike. I was beginning to think you had forgotten about me."

His tone was, by design, terse and cold. He'd waited too long, and he wanted her to know that she was testing his patience. She was playing games, talking to solicitors, failing to live up to their agreement, and he was not about to allow it to continue. He wanted to scare her.

"Yes, I'm sorry," she was saying, but he interrupted.

"We have much to discuss including some new developments. This is not a game, and you do not decide when and how to cooperate. Do we understand each other?"

Not waiting for a response, he rolled right into it.

"What was the relationship between your father, Robert Schier, and Bruce Lasher, and I'm particularly curious about their work here in Europe?"

He was skeptical of her claim that she didn't know much beyond the fact that they worked for the same company when she was young, that her father spent a lot of time traveling for work, and that he never really talked about what he did. She said he was a salesman in the textile business and that she had known Bob since she was a child and he was a regular visitor to their home. Bruce had given her father a monstrous Cadillac El Dorado when they moved to America, but she couldn't recall meeting him prior to her visit a few days ago.

"And what is your theory about what they were doing to generate the sums of money we appear to be talking about as you hop from private bank to private bank in Europe's most notorious tax havens?"

"We have our conspiracy theories, of course. Spy, con man, or something. He never discussed work. Agent Benoit, we do have something in our possession that I think will help with your investigation, but I need to be able to execute the obligations of the will. Perhaps we can help each other out here?"

"It is not the time to be making deals. These killers are looking for you or other members of your family."

"Hear what I am offering before you say no. We have a binder that contains photographs of people, with labeled names, timestamps, and locations. They are not people that any of us have ever seen or heard of before, and most of them had Russian or Chinese sounding names."

This binder could be the key to unravelling an entire international criminal network. She's not going to hand it over.

"Yes, Ms. Pike, that does sound like a document that could help with my investigation. Would it be possible for you to share it with me? I presume you aren't carrying this binder with you?"

"No, I'm not. What I have are names that I recall. When I get home, I will make some copies for you and the FBI. In return, I would ask you allow me time to transfer all the funds to a single account in Channel Islands and not freeze the assets before I can do so. If your investigation finds that the funds are criminal in origin, you can freeze them. Is something you could do?"

"Give me the names and I will consult with our leadership."

"Maksym Palatnik, Artem Ponomarenko, Miloje Petrovic, and Marius Popescu."

Pascal could hardly believe his ears. Hearing someone outside of the Eastern European Organized Crime Unit mention the names of Maksym Palatnik and Artem Ponomarenko in the same sentence was astonishing. Separately, Palatnik and Ponomarenko were well-known—Palatnik was a Ukrainian mobster and Kuznetzov's employer. Ponomarenko was the first secretary of the Communist Party in Soviet Ukraine and, later, a key advisor and ally of Alexei Kosygin, Soviet foreign minister and lead arms treaty negotiator under Brezhnev.

There was a legend within the organized crime unit that Palatnik and Ponomarenko had once joined forces in a plot to remove a government official loyal to Moscow and pursue Ukrainian independence from the Soviet Union. There was no investigatory evidence to support the theory, and, of course, independence didn't happen until the Soviet Union collapsed almost forty years later.

In 1954, however, several years after Ponomarenko's ascension to first secretary, Moscow transferred control of Crimea back to Soviet Ukraine. It was cast as a symbolic gesture to commemorate the three hundredth anniversary of the Treaty of Pereyaslav, the agreement that united the Cossacks with the Duchy of Moscovy and bound Ukraine to Russia forever. "Eternally Together!" posters had popped up all over the region.

The unit's historians had some good unanswered questions. Why would Moscow put a known Ukrainian independence advocate in charge of the entire country? And why, the following year, turn over control of Crimea and the Soviet Naval base at Sevastopol to the Ukrainians? How could Ponomarenko—contrary to Moscow's strategy in every other Warsaw Pact country—possibly demonstrate enough loyalty to Moscow to warrant such a move? It seemed inconceivable that Moscow would sacrifice so much to commemorate a three-hundred-year-old treaty that had no practical connection to the modern day.

If Palatnik were also involved, then Ponomarenko's crowning would have given the mobster a lot more power over ports in the entire Black Sea region. Yalta, Kerch, and the smaller ports along the western shores of the Sea of Azov were all appealing bases for smugglers, crooks, and killers. Perhaps Palatnik could even strong-arm his way into the solidly Russian port city of Rostov, in far northeast corner of the Sea of Azov, a city of considerable historical significance to Moscow. Rostov-on-Don was where the Soviets forced the first significant withdrawal by Hitler, leading to the Battle of Stalingrad just a few months later.

Pascal was not one of the conspiracy theorists—and even the believers gave up caring about it long ago. The fact that a Ukrainian politician and a mobster were connected was hardly surprising in a country with the reputation for corruption like Ukraine.

But now someone who knew nothing about Palatnik or Ponomarenko used their names together, referencing a binder that included pictures of both. It was hard not to imagine that there was at least some kernel of truth buried inside the legend.

Pascal rose from his desk and marched out of the door and headed down to Records and Collections. It would not be easy to piece together the separate investigations into Palatnik and Ponomarenko, but knowing that the murdered Englishman, Brandon Pike, knew of both of them and had their pictures might trigger something.

He took the elevator down to the main lobby and walked across the leafy atrium to a special elevator that gave access to the basement levels. He exited at B3: Records and Collections.

"Bonsoir, Monsieur Benoit. Shouldn't you heading home at this hour?"

"Ah, *bah non*! Research to do on a new case. I'm going to be here all night. Is that okay?"

"*Oui*, no problem at all. Perhaps I can help you find whatever you are looking for before I leave?"

"I'm looking for a connection between two Ukrainians and an Englishman. Can I search the database for anything that includes them all?"

"We can try. What are the names, *s'il vous plaît*?"

"Maksym Palatnik, Artem Ponomarenko, and Brandon Pike."

He tapped a seemingly endless number of keys. Pascal stood helplessly on the other side of the desk.

"There is no single investigation that includes all three, Agent Benoit, but there are records that include at least two in some form or another. There are more that include these individuals separately."

That was enough to indicate that the three were connected at least. "I'll start with those. And there are two other names I need to get, Miloje Petrovic and Marius Popescu."

More endless tapping and then "*Oui*, Monsieur, we have records on investigations that included those individuals. And, interestingly, three of those investigations also cite either Maksym Palatnik or

Brandon Pike. They were all left open and are now considered cold. You are going deep into history, Agent Benoit."

"*Putain de merde*! I need them all."

The records that included both Ponomarenko and Palatnik were thin, poorly sourced, and cases that withered away with no definitive conclusion. One report, however, caught Pascal's attention. It was an uncorroborated account provided by an "unnamed source within Palatnik's security organization." Only someone very close to the action would have this kind of intelligence unless it was a fabrication, of course, and that possibility had to be considered. If true, Kuznetzov seemed the most likely source.

Apparently, the first secretary of the Communist Party in 1953 was a man named Leonid Minkov, a post given to him when his predecessor left to work for Khrushchev in the Kremlin. Minkov was something of a playboy.

Moscow probably had their eye on him, and a year into the job, he got caught taking drugs and sleeping with a suspect American woman who worked at a strip club he frequented. The KGB went to his apartment one morning when he didn't show up for work and discovered him unconscious. A search uncovered a camera containing top-secret photographs of the new KGB organization and the leaders of its departments. They took him to Lukyanivska prison in Kiev for interrogation.

He was apparently held in the same cell once occupied by "Ironbelly" Felix Dobrinsky—a legendary leader of the KGB who was imprisoned there by the Tsar's Okrana secret police before the 1917 revolution. Fascinating but irrelevant!

After a few days in the interrogation room, it appeared that Minkov was set up, caught in a honey trap. They presumed that he shared the documents with the American woman. The KGB knew that Minkov would never have had access to the information on the camera. Clearly, the woman was CIA, and Minkov was forever compromised. He was recalled to Moscow, and Ponomarenko was elevated to first secretary. Pike's name came up in that file as one of Minkov's "several guests" at the club.

Something didn't add up about the source. How would someone working for Palatnik have so much detail on the trap, the KGB arrest, and what happened inside Lukyanivska? Perhaps Kuznetzov was playing for both teams? It seemed unlikely given his long relationship with Palatnik, but it was possible. Loyalty and betrayal were fluid in those days. At the same time, however, nothing in the report implicated Palatnik directly in any crime or even suggested he was involved in the honey trap, but he was also identified as a guest that evening in the strip club.

A second report on Palatnik focused on security and docking fees added to shipments arriving and departing from the ports of Odessa and Kerch. While these "fees" were commonplace, one company—Plastoteknika Simferopol, a joint venture with a British textile company, Saco-Lowell—was exempted from almost sixty million rubles in fees over a span of five years upon Ponomarenko's signature. Suspicious? Definitely. Why would Palatnik and the party willingly sacrifice the equivalent of twenty million euros in today's money for nothing?

Palatnik disappeared in the late 1980s. During the Autumn of Nations, the revolutions that led to the ultimate collapse of the Soviet Union, the KGB kidnapped and killed known conspirators, of which Palatnik was undoubtedly one, with abandon. There was no definitive position on what happened to him, but he never surfaced again, and a man named Jakub Nowak assumed leadership of the Malina in Odessa in his place.

A blurry picture was forming in Pascal's mind. These individuals were all part of the same network, a network that Palatnik built first in the port then expanded into Ukraine's political infrastructure and then even further into the other Soviet satellites. Palatnik wasn't a small-time criminal twisting arms and beating people up in the Port of Odessa. He was a lot more.

Pascal needed to get his hands on that binder. There were no known photographs of Maksym Palatnik anywhere in the Eastern European Organized Crime Unit records, but there was more to this. That binder could unlock the entire network.

Chapter 12

Manchester, England, 2009

Ana's arrival in Manchester brought back a million early childhood memories. It was her first trip home since moving to the US.

In the taxi, she passed stores she hadn't thought about in years—Marks & Spencer, Boots, ASDA, and the Co-op, which the northerners pronounced "quawp" for some reason. She saw road signs for towns she vaguely remembered, like Wythenshawe and Altrincham and one for Reddish, where her Nana had lived. Nana had lived in the same terraced house since getting married in the 1920s.

During the war, they put an antiaircraft gun and searchlights on a patch of land across the street. When the Manchester Blitz began in late 1940, Adeline, Ana's mother, sat on the wall in the front yard watching the searchlights scour the night sky for Luftwaffe bombers. When the air-raid sirens went off, Nana took her down to the basement, and they cowered in the corner as the huge gun tried to blast the planes out of the sky before they could drop their payload on the city of Manchester, a few miles to the north. As a child, Ana had played rounders on that same vacant patch of land with a few of the children on the street.

Mattinson's office in Piccadilly Gardens, Manchester's bustling city center, was decorated with modern furniture, a few healthy plants, and a picture window overlooking Market Street. The desk was small, stylish, and uncluttered for a lawyer.

"I know," he said as they settled into two large armchairs, "it feels more like a psychologist's office than a solicitor's. I don't have many clients, but they have a lot of money, little interest in managing it, and even less desire to meet. My wife's an interior designer and said that if I was going to go into an office and be by myself all the time, it should look any way I wanted."

He pulled out a stack of papers including confirmations that the funds had transferred. It wasn't everything, but the ones she had visited were the most stringent. Other accounts in the Netherlands, the Channel Islands, and Ireland would be easier to deal with and could be handled over the phone as long as he was present and could certify the documents.

"Are you going to distribute the funds to the beneficiaries quickly or wait? We only have a few days to get everything set up. If you are going to let it all go to Disclose International, I'll need to make arrangements."

"Are those our only options? What about setting up some kind of charitable foundation and just giving it all to worthy causes, UNICEF, Save The Whales, OXFAM, or something?"

"Certainly, if you'd like to spend the next ten years in British courts being challenged by the government, the other beneficiaries, Disclose International, or anyone else that feels like they deserve a piece of the pie. Regardless, the assets would be frozen before the paperwork even landed on His Right Honorable's desk. Where are you with the gentleman from INTERPOL?"

"Agent Benoit asked me for the binder. I gave him a few names of people I remembered to look into. I figured it would buy me some time."

"It might work but perhaps not. They are reluctant to intervene without a strong case, and in fact, your father was the victim of the crime, not the perpetrator, so they may not have anything on him to justify a heavy hand."

Ears must have been ringing back in Lyon because, at that moment, Ana's phone buzzed. It was Agent Benoit's number.

She panicked and flashed a look toward Mattinson.

"As the executor of my client's will, I can represent you but only in a fiduciary capacity. I am not a criminal lawyer."

She accepted the call and put him on speaker. "Hello, Agent Benoit. I'm here in Manchester with our lawyer, Mr. Mattinson, and we are on speaker. Is that okay?"

"That's fine. I'll be very brief as I must attend a meeting on the investigation with my superiors to update them, but I wanted to let you know what I found out about the names you gave me. When I report this in the meeting, they are going to insist on seeing the actual binder, and I want to tell them that you will cooperate."

Mattinson nodded to her, and Ana gave her ascent.

"Thank you, Mademoiselle. Now, I should mention that nothing I am about to tell is evidence of anything and does not implicate your father in anything at this point. Maksym Palatnik is the founder of the Ukrainian Malina, the mafia who ran the port of Odessa in the postwar years. If his picture is in your binder, it's the only known picture of him. Artem Ponomarenko was the head of the Communist Party in Ukraine who later served as advisor to the Kremlin on nuclear issues. Miloje Petrovic was a wartime comrade of Palatnik, and they were involved in a blackmail scheme that went horribly wrong and led to the shooting of a government official. And Maruis Popescu was a childhood friend of Palatnik. This is the big one as it involves the US government in a kidnapping plot. The body of the CEO of a Soviet-Romanian joint venture mining uranium ore was later found in the mine, but he'd been tortured, recorded a video confession, and then killed. I think, Mademoiselle Pike, that your binder could be the key to unravelling the Malina's entire criminal network in Eastern Europe, something we've been trying to do for almost a half a century."

Ana stared open-mouthed at Mattinson, unable to speak. He scribbled on a piece of paper, "agree to get him the binder. Tell him it will take a few days."

"Well, thank you for this information, Agent. I'm obviously still taking all this in. I will get you the binder in a few days. What about the FBI?"

"We are working closely with them and sharing all pertinent information. They are focused on the murders committed on US soil, whereas I am interested in the activities of this criminal organization here in Europe. We have different interests with the overlap being the capture of whoever killed your father and his colleagues before they find and kill you too. I cannot overemphasize the depth of my concern for your safety. The Chauffeurs know the clock is ticking, and they will accelerate their hunt. You, your mother, and your brothers are probably top of the list right now. I believe it is imperative that you alert them. I have spoken to the FBI, and they will deploy extra security."

Ana hung up and immediately called Sean in Fort Myers. No answer on his cell phone. She called the house and, again, no answer, just the usual answering machine message: "Hi, you've reached the Pike family," followed by his wife and kids all shouting "Hi" in the background and "Leave a message at the beep and we'll call y'awl back!"

In her gut, Ana knew that she would never hear her brother's voice live again.

Chapter 13

Fort Myers, Florida

Sean's hands and feet were already bound when the house phone sitting on the kitchen counter rang. His wife and children were locked in the basement, forced down the stairs by four heavily armed men in balaclavas. Through the floorboards, he could hear the crying of his youngest daughter and consoling words of his wife as the children's terror swelled.

The only thing that mattered was protecting his family. He knew that he was going to die. They had killed his father, and they were going to kill him too. God would take care of him.

Shadowy figures moved around the house, searching in silence, room to room, drawer to drawer, with surgical precision. Not a word had been uttered since his daughter innocently answered the doorbell. They didn't ransack or destroy. They knew what they were looking for, and it wasn't there.

He was really starting to panic, a fear far beyond anything he had every known in his life. He remembered the terror that set in swimming through the underwater cave in the Virgin Islands. It seemed so incredibly long, and he remembered how quickly he ran out of breath with no idea how far it was to the fresh air. This felt a lot like the panic of suffocation. But a million times worse. His eyes darted left and right, trying to see what they were doing. He chomped on the gag in his mouth, hoping to create enough space to make a sound that someone could hear. But it seemed to just make it tighter, ripping at the corners of his mouth. Sweat poured down his face, into his eyes, and his shirt was soaked. The need to urinate grew—as it always did when he was nervous—but this time, he was so afraid that he might actually shit himself. He'd read somewhere that it was an almost guaranteed outcome when you knew you were about to die that you soiled yourself in the final moments.

With every movement, the bonds grew tighter. A man sat on the arm of the couch, a large pistol with a silencer resting on his lap, watching him. He eyes never moved, and he said nothing. Was he the leader or just a guard of some sort?

Suddenly he spoke, monotone and quiet. His accent was strange, a mix of New York and some blend of Russian and Hebrew. "Do you like my gun?" He stroked the barrel lovingly. "It's such a perfect weapon. I'd never seen one like this until I met your father. It was his, you know. I found it in the house. It's a piece of history. This model, a Malakov MP-71, came out in 1955 when the manufacturer, Izhevsk, added a threaded barrel for a suppressor. Do you know the company? Perhaps not. Today, they are called Kalishnikov. Interesting, no? Anyway, this particular weapon has been used in the killing of some very important people. Your father would know this, of course. He used it on many them. Wait a minute. You didn't know what kind of man your father was? I feel terrible to be the one to break it to you."

The phone in the kitchen rang for what seemed like an eternity before the cheery family voice mail greeting rang out. The man with the gun looked at Sean and appeared to smile under the wool of balaclava. "Such a cute message," he said with a sickly smile and empty vacant eyes then looked back at the machine.

"Sean, it's Ana. Where the fuck are you? I need to talk to you right fucking now. It's critical that you call me back as soon as you get this. And when I say critical, I mean fucking critical, okay?"

The man with the pistol turned back to Sean with a pitying, wistful look in his eyes. "I think, Mr. Pike, that your little sister is trying to save your life. Such a shame for her to be too late. Perhaps she will tell you to put the binder in a safe place. That would be a mistake as we have methods to get the information we need. Just ask your father. Oh, sorry. You can't. We already killed him."

When the search of the house turned up nothing, another man removed Sean's shoes and socks and rolled his sleeves up to his forearms. One of the men lifted his balaclava over his mouth and lit a cigar. When the tip was bright orange, he pushed it into the sole of Sean's left foot then the right, took a few puffs to get it going again, and did the same to the tops of his hands and forearms. The burning lasted about five minutes before anyone asked him anything.

"So where is the binder? Tell me and all this pain stops and your family will be freed. Deny me and I will kill you with your own father's gun before going to your mother's house. I am very short of time, Mr. Pike, and patience."

"I don't have it. My sister took it and put it in a safe deposit box."

"And where is your sister now?"

"Europe."

"Right, Europe. So far away. So safe from harm. And why is she in Europe?"

"Dealing with my father's will."

"A will? How interesting? I expect someone with your father's history has a sizable nest egg saved up. How nice for you all! Perhaps you should call her back. Convince her to tell you where the binder is and how to access it."

"She'll know."

The man gave a nod, and one of his men disappeared down the basement stairs. A child then Sean's wife screamed at the man. He returned with Sean's youngest daughter, a gun pointed at her head. The leader walked up to her, and with a felt tip pen from a kitchen drawer, he drew a small circle in the middle of her forehead.

"If you fuck with me, Mr. Pike, this is where the bullet will exit your daughter's skull, and you will have the pleasure of watching it happen."

They retrieved his phone from the kitchen, redialed the last number, and put it against his ear. When his sister picked up, he tried to sound normal, but the quiver in his voice gave him away.

"Hi, Ana. How's it going? What's going on?"

"Sean, you need to get the fuck out of the house and take the whole family with you. Now! The guys that killed Dad have gone through a couple of his business associates, looking for the binder probably. INTERPOL says that you are probably on their list. You need to get out."

"Oh, come on, Ana! That's crazy. Why would they come after us?"

"Because you know about the binder, jackass! This is all connected to some kind of Ukrainian organized crime thing that Dad was mixed up in, and they don't want the people in the binder on anyone's radar."

"But the binder is ancient, and most of the people in it are probably old or dead at this point. What possible value could it have?"

Ana was silent on the other end. Sean could feel her brain ticking over. He'd obviously changed his tune, and being the suspicious type, she'd picked up on it. He pressed on. "Look, I'll get everyone away from here, but I don't think we should let the binder get in the hands of the police or FBI. If we just give the binder to people coming after us, they'll stop. Right?"

There was a long pause before Ana spoke. "You know I can't do that. We can't hide it. I've already told the FBI and INTERPOL I'd give it to them, when I get back…in a couple of days. Sean, is everything okay?"

He couldn't help himself and burst into tears. Ana heard the gunshot from thousands of miles away.

Part 2

Forever is just ashes and dust,
Years and nothing is erased
Who will sweeten your nights?
Who will listen to your crying?
Who will stay by your side?
Take a coat, it'll be cold.
If the days are hard, remember me sometimes

—Afar Ve'avak, "Ash and Dust"

Chapter 14

London, England, 1963

Emerging from the Pimlico station onto Rampayne Street was usually a miserable experience in January, and today was no exception. The cold, wind-driven rain coming off the Thames soaked through the man's overcoat and turned his old umbrella inside out, breaking two of the spokes. His collar was pulled up to shield most of his face from the weather and from view.

At St. Saviour's Church, he turned left onto St. George's Square, with its whitewashed Georgian homes reeking of old money and class privilege, before taking a quick right on Chichester Street toward the safe house.

Known in his circles as Dolphin Square 807, the safe house—or more accurately safe flat—was on the top floor of an upscale Pimlico complex, home to spies, crooked financiers, and international ne'er-do-wells of every persuasion.

Under the wary eye of a doorman, he took an intolerably slow lift up to the eighth floor. The apartment door was ajar, but no one was waiting to greet him. He hung up his coat on a hook and left the mangled umbrella in the hall to dry.

Dolphin Square 807 smelled of mildew and stale cigarettes. A mist of fine dust and ash hung in the air. The windows were shuttered, and the only light came from an old floor lamp in the corner that leaned awkwardly against the wall and a white-stained-yellow shade with a single bulb dangling from the ceiling in the kitchen.

On the dining table, there was a cup of sticky black coffee, still hot, and a pack of Benson and Hedges cigarettes.

"Thank bloody god!"

The flat was the home of John Dougal until MI6 took it over. Dougal had served as a naval attaché at the British Embassy in Moscow. His sexual proclivities left him lonely and ostracized until a colleague introduced him to the seedy homosexual underworld of Moscow. He was lured to a party where the KGB took compromising pictures of him with some young men. When he was recalled to London to work for Naval Intelligence, the Soviets blackmailed him. It was a classic honey trap. He fed the Soviets secret torpedo, radar, and anti-submarine equipment designs for a decade until he was unmasked as a spy by a Soviet defector.

It was the ideal venue for a debriefing with the deputy director of Counterintelligence in the Soviet Division, the inimitable Giles Bancroft.

Light came through a gap between the floor and the bottom of a bedroom door. He was watching shadows move around the room when suddenly, the door opened, and a shaft of bright light flashed across the table.

Giles, a giraffe dressed in tweed of a man, strode into the kitchen carrying an ungainly bundle of file folders in his arms. "Morning, Draftsman. Thanks for coming in today."

"Nice to see you too, sir. This is a rare treat indeed."

Pushing Giles's buttons with unwelcome familiarity was one of life's few remaining pleasures—along with making fun of his privileged upbringing and aristocratic demeanor. He liked to joke that Giles spent most of his time behind a desk in Whitehall, smoking a pipe and enjoying his two martini lunches.

In reality, Giles had his hands full. The MI6 was a bloody shambles after a string of embarrassing defections in recent years, and the last thing Giles had time for was a liquid lunch.

Why was he here? Why now? It felt like an exit interview, a final interview to tie up the loose ends before they put out him out to pasture once and for all. Balan was dead, and Yellowcake had run its course, a report filed away in some dusty filing cabinet in the basement of MI6 headquarters at Whitehall Court and forgotten.

He passed the time smoking a cigarette and staring at his reflection in the coffee. Deep lines and prematurely graying hair made him look much older than his thirty-five years. It wouldn't be all bad, would it? Take an early retirement with a nice pension, potter around in the garden, spend time with Adeline and the children, and forget the last fifteen years ever happened.

Or maybe they needed something else from him? The Soviet situation was unstable, to put it mildly. Khrushchev's reign was foundering. He'd strong-armed every bugger in the Communist Party leadership to hold onto power, but his mishandling of the Cuban missile crisis finally turned them against him. Leonid Brezhnev waited in the wings to wrestle power from his former mentor and patron. With business connections that stretched from Moscow down to Odessa, no one had more access and experience behind the iron curtain than the Draftsman.

A stern-looking fellow in long gray overcoat and a gray Trilby hat marched in from the bedroom carrying a suitcase. He dropped it on the table, and the skinny metal legs wobbled nervously under the weight. He opened the lid to reveal a reel-to-reel tape recorder.

"Ah! A Sony TC-102, if I'm not mistaken?"

The Draftsman was no aficionado of recording devices by any stretch, but there weren't many good icebreakers to use in a situation like this. The man in the gray Trilby said nothing. In the kitchen, Giles fussed with his papers, licking his thumb with each page flip.

He turned on the recorder. The machine lit up, and he ran the tape back and forth a couple of times.

"Saya sumethin' into tha microphone." He was a Geordie lad, all right, Newcastle through and through. He felt an immediate northern kinship. They were the worker bees, the real people, the opposite of the overeducated, upper-class twattery of Giles and his colleagues.

"Blackburn Rovers totally outclassed Spurs at Ewood Park back in May, thrashing them 3-nil. Jimmy Greaves, England legend and Spurs center forward, was quoted as saying that Spurs were beaten by the better side."

Giles, a lifelong Spurs fan, gave a low growl from the kitchen. The Geordie, who can barely contain a grin, dutifully—and loudly— plays back the recording to make sure everything worked, and they shared a quick conspiratorial smirk.

No doubt he and the Draftsman shared a mutual disdain for the class snobbery of their employers, but his role in this interview was not clear. Surely Giles could manage a tape recorder without a babysitter? It was very unusual to have someone without a clear need-to-know present once an interrogation got underway, but the man seemed comfortable behind his tape recorder, sitting back, arms folded.

The Draftsman wasn't one of their traditional spies. He wasn't identified at Eton, monitored at Cambridge, and recruited over martinis at the Pimlico Badminton Club to join the British diplomatic core as consular attaché. That class of idiots—the likes of Maclean, Burgess, Philby, and the rest of them—sold out their country and the Service to the Soviets. He didn't do microfilm dead drops under park benches or tap-coded messages into a box in the dark of an attic. He's part of the new breed, a businessman. He shared information in exchange for clean passports and Her Majesty's Government turning a blind eye to some questionable business dealings.

In the aftermath of the defections, entire MI6 networks across the Warsaw Pact were rolled up by the KGB, leaving the Service and its reputation in tatters. Some agents were extracted in time, but many disappeared or turned up dead. So they turned to a new breed of spy—businessmen who operated in the region without diplomatic protection. They received information on who was gaining or losing power, how much influence Moscow had, and what opportunities there were for the western countries to upset the Soviet apple cart.

That's how it started out anyway. Even before the Berlin Wall went up in 1961, fences, checkpoints, and minefields popped up along the German, Czech, Hungarian, and Yugoslav borders and made moving between countries harder. MI6 knew that clean papers kept these solo operators out of prison.

Giles settled into his chair across the table, apologized for the delay, which he blamed on the bad weather and the "bloody nuisance" that was his drive from Romford in the suburbs, and started the tape recorder.

"The date is the eighth of January 1964. This is a recording of the scheduled debriefing of code name DRAFTSMAN by the deputy director of Counterintelligence for the Soviet division, code name RUGBY. This recording and transcript is Eyes Only Secret and protected under the provisions of the Officials Secret's Act of 1920, amended 1939. DRAFTSMAN, please confirm that you have signed the Official Secret's Act contract and understand the obligations and penalties included therein." He did so.

Giles shuffled his papers and cleared his throat, perhaps a little too loudly, and said, "I'd like to open the bowling today, DRAFTSMAN…"—always the avid cricketer, Giles peppered most of his conversations with metaphors like this—"by talking about your history with a man named Maksym Palatnik. Tell me about him and how the two of you got going. Naturally, leave nothing out whether it seems important or not."

"Well, I first met Maksym in 1951, but to understand how he built his criminal organization, you have to go all the way back to the war."

Chapter 15

Odessa, Soviet Ukraine, 1941

The Siege of Odessa began in July 1941. For at least a month, the Palatnik family slept, when they could, to the sound mortar fire along the coastal cliffs to the north of the city and the pounding of heavy artillery to the west.

They lived in a small apartment overlooking Pryvokzal'na Square. By day, they ran a stall in the Privoz market selling spices, herbs, almonds, raisins and worked in and around the port's loading docks for extra money. At night, Maksym and his father, Vadim, played traditional Roma folk music in a Klezmer band with a few Romanian friends. A blend of Christian, Hebrew, and Romani gypsy music, it bound the scared communities that lived together in the neighborhood.

Day by day, the fighting drew closer. Eldest son, Oleksandr, had left on a boat to America in June, leaving younger brother, Maksym, to look after his parents.

In October, the Red Army's defensive encirclement finally gave way, and the Nazis marched on the city. The Palatnik family hid in the darkest corner of the kitchen and waited.

The silence was broken by the metal-on-metal screeching and rumbling engines of tanks and gunfire as soldiers of Wehrmacht 11th Army made their way carefully from street to darkened street. Within hours, they heard crunching boots of the main invading force, goose-stepping in formation past their apartment window.

Maksym watched through a small hole in the curtains. He watched his neighbors, taken from their homes, huddled together for protection and warmth in the chill of October on the pavement.

He saw an old man, hit in the face with the butt of a rifle, crumble to the ground like a pile of dry sticks. His wailing wife crouched to help him but got a kick in the stomach from the soldier's steel-toe-capped boots.

"*Verpiss dich, Jude!*"

A group of soldiers rounded the corner and immediately opened fire on the families standing on the pavement. They forced a wounded mother and her child to put their heads together and killed them both with a single shot, the bullet passing first through the brain of the child and then into the mother.

The sound of boots kicking in doors in their apartment building grew closer.

"*Du kommst jetzt hierher, Jude!*"

Mother decided that she should be the one to answer the door. Maybe they'd take pity on a mother. She opened the door a crack, and the heavy boot of a soldier kicked it in, smashing her in the face. Blood spewed from her nose as they grabbed her. At least ten soldiers burst in, grabbed Maksym and his father, and threw them down the stairs. More soldiers waited at the bottom to drag them outside and line them up on the pavement with the others.

The shouting, the crying, the gunshots, and the beatings increased. Some were shot on the spot, their bodies dragged away and thrown in the back of a truck.

Maksym made eye contact with Andru Popescu, father of Marius, one of the Romanian members of their band. He was talking to an SS officer carrying a clipboard. Not in a desperate way but like a colleague. The officer looked up, scanned the assembled families, marked something on his board, and signaled to one of the soldiers with a casual wave of his hand. Maksym knew instantly that they'd been betrayed by their friend.

A soldier grabbed his mother and dragged her into an alley, pulling at her clothes and forcing her into a dark corner. Maksym screamed at them to stop as they beat him with their rifles, kicked, and punched him in the face until he was coughing up blood. His mother fought back against her rapist, kicking and screaming, but tired of her shit, he pulled out his Luger and put a bullet right between her eyes before pulling up his pants.

His father stood under a lamppost with a rope around his neck, begging in broken German for his life. They hoisted him. He twisted and squirmed, pulling at the tightening noose until his neck snapped. The soldier let go of the rope, allowing his body to plummet to the ground in a heap. They shot him just to be sure. Popescu watched from the other side of the street. Maksym took one final blow to the face from a rifle butt, and darkness followed.

He woke up on the floor an open-topped lorry on a road he didn't recognize. It was dark, and the bitter cold of October bore deep into his body. The lorry was packed so tight with people that they stood bolt straight, arms pressed against their sides.

Someone above him shouted, "He's awake!" Two people grabbed him under the armpits and hauled him to his feet.

"If you're awake, you're standing," one said.

The lorry left the main road and bounced down a long dirt path. A wet autumn had turned the dirt into mud and the mud into a swamp. The lorry plunged into a deep hole, throwing everyone in the back to the floor.

Maksym heard someone scream in Romanian for everyone to get off. It was pitch black on the roadside, the mud halfway up their shins. Maksym pushed his way angrily through the group to get to a Romanian soldier who was firing his gun in the air to control the crowd.

The driver pulled a Mauser C96 automatic pistol from under his seat and fired rounds straight into the group. Bodies fell, and the smell of sulfur and blood filled the air. He yelled for everyone still standing to form a single line and start walking toward the village, *"Jetzt eins nach dem anderen! Einzelne Datei!"*

More lorries pulled up behind, disgorging a long, straggly line of confused people. They began a long march through the mud up the hill toward the village of Bogdonovka. The noisiest or the slowest movers were shot, their bodies left on the side of the road for everyone else to step over. Soldiers yelled in a mix of Romanian, German, and broken Russian to keep everyone moving in the right direction.

Curtains shifted uneasily, and lights snapped off as the human train passed through the village. Dogs barked inside, their owners desperately tried to muzzle them in hushed but urgent tones behind the doors.

Beyond the village, the landscape opened up, and the line began a steady climb up the hill toward a barn with a thatched roof at the top. The roadside was littered with forgotten bodies slowly being consumed by the earth. It was a slow climb—a shove for the slow, a bullet for anyone who fell.

The barn turned out to be a row of twenty-or-so barns, hastily built and spreading over the field down the back side of the hill toward a forest in the valley. Each has its own wire fence and a single light mounted over a front door. Armed guards were posted at each one. The unfinished barns further down the hill were dark and unguarded. This prison was expecting more people.

Separations began at the first barn—men separated from women, adults separated from children, young separated from old, strong separated from weak. The groups were directed to different barns on the right and the left of a main path. The process was eerily quiet. The old and the sick kept walking through the main camp toward the barns on the edge of the forest, clearly separated from the rest of the camp. By daybreak, the barns were filled with hundreds, perhaps thousands, of cold, hungry, scared, and separated families. They didn't know it, but they were the first victims of the *Vernichtungskrieg*, the War of Annihilation, in Ukraine.

Maksym was housed in one of the large barns with a hundred others. There were no beds, just dirty blankets on the floor. Each morning, they shook out the rat droppings and rolled them up. They shared one toilet, which had no door, and a pile of newspaper for wiping. It clogged and overflowed daily. No one ever came to fix it, so the inmates did it themselves.

Within weeks, filthy rags hung off their frames like the discarded clothes of a person three times their weight. The skin on their faces looked like cardboard left out in a rainstorm then allowed to dry wherever it lay for weeks—once brown but faded to a moldy blueish-gray. There was no water to wash, so they prayed for rain during their time outside.

At night, they slept in piles. There wasn't enough room for everyone to lie down, so some sat up against the wall or lay with someone else on top of them. The rats scurried between the emaciated bodies, gnawing on the flesh of those too decrepit to fend them off. Mites and bed bugs burrowed into the inmates' skin and laid their eggs. People scratched and bled on the dirt floor. Hideous skin infections ran rampant. And in the dark of night, the sounds of severe fevers, crippling diarrhea, and bouts of vomiting punctuated the silence.

The typhus outbreak that followed was inevitable, and the disease spread through the camp like wildfire. Oberfuhrer Eberhardt, the Nazi advisor to the Romanian camp administrators, arrived to supervise the solution. He stood in his open top car at a safe distance and wore a perfectly pressed, medal-laden uniform that gleamed proudly in the morning sun. He watched through binoculars as hundreds of sick inmates limped down the hill to be packed inside the two large barns on the edge of the forest.

Once the doors were barricaded, soldiers clambered up onto the roofs and doused the thatch in kerosene and set the buildings on fire. Within minutes, both were ablaze. The cries of the people inside echoed across the valley. The smell, carried up the hill by the wind, was indescribable.

The next day, a smoky haze hung over the camp. Looking out of the only window, Maksym could see the soldiers clearing the site, raking up remains and taking away the ashes in wheelbarrows.

The disease continued to spread uncontrolled through the camp. The newly sick slept outside in the cold. The healthy still shared toilets, food, and blankets with them. The guards stayed on the perimeter, and the cooks stopped showing up for work. They found cases of typhus in the nearby village, passed on by guards who ate and drank in the homes of the locals.

It was a week after the mass killing when a guard, unwilling to step into the cabin and covering his face with his hand, ordered everyone outside. They lined up, and Maksym could see the residents of the lower barns already marching single file toward the forest. Gunshots, hundreds of them, rang out in distance. Everyone knew death was coming for them. Their only hope was to see loved ones housed in one of the other barns one more time before they all went to their grave.

Maksym fell in line with the people in front of him and began a slow march toward the burned-out barns, now just a pile of smoldering ashes. Drawing close, the smell was so thick that he could almost taste the copper, iron, and sulfuric remnants of blood and hair in his mouth, and he felt the sticky smoke, black and acrid, grip his face and seep deep into his skin. Even a week after the barn fire, soldiers still hacked apart blackened remains with axes, loading the pieces onto rickety farm carts to be wheeled into the forest for disposal.

They arrived in a huge clearing in the forest with trenches fifty yards long in rows. The first was already filled, soldiers piling dirt over charred and bloody corpses. Next to it, prisoners were digging another half dozen trenches, extending to the far side of the field.

"*Richten sie sich jetzt alle aus!*"

Prisoners climbed out of the trench and lined up along the edge, facing their grave. In quick succession, they were shot in the side of the neck, the bullet sometimes passing into the neck of the next person. A second line formed along the edge of the same trench, standing in the blood of those who had gone before them. They, too, were shot, and their bodies fell into the pit on top of everyone else. A third line formed up along the edge.

Romanian soldiers handed shovels to Maksym and fifty others, indicating that they should start digging. "*Începe să sape! Acum! Acum!*"

One or two refused and shouted back in Ukrainian "*Ya ne budu*" ("I will not!"), throwing their shovels to the ground. They were pushed into the pit with the dead, forced to scramble amid the bloodied bodies. The Romanian soldiers, watching from above, shot each one in the back as they clawed around—not quite enough to kill but just enough to bleed out and die slowly.

After an hour of trench digging, Maksym took his place on the edge with the others. The gunshots started immediately, and one by one, the line of prisoners fell. The man next to him shook violently and vomited when it was his turn. The bullet entered the left side of his neck, a plume of burgundy blood erupted from the right side. The bullet only grazed the back of Maksym's neck, but he fell into the trench, pretending to be dead, hoping the shooter would just keep moving down the line. A new line formed along the edge of the trench, and the bodies fell quickly.

He lay at the bottom of the pit as the dead and dying fell on top of him. Most were still alive but bleeding out quickly, unable to breath or make much sound. He closed his eyes so he didn't have to see their faces. But he felt their blood and other bodily fluids dripping onto his face and soaking into his clothes.

In time, the groans and cries of the dying dwindled. The proximity and frequency of gunshots faded into the distance.

Maksym clawed his way up through the bodies to the edge of the trench. They hadn't even bothered to fill in the graves yet. In the shadow of the trees, he vomited and cleaned himself up as much as possible then sat down to cry. He stumbled into the forest, expecting to die at any moment but determined to get home and make these monsters pay for what they had done.

On the road back to Odessa, Maksym heard countless stories of the atrocities—Bila Tserkva, where hundreds of children were lined up next to a mass grave and shot in the back after witnessing the murder of their parents, the Piryatin massacre during Passover, and the murder, in a matter of days, of about a hundred thousand Jews at Nikolaev and Babi Yar.

His blood boiled. Bogdonovka wasn't the only death camp but part of a systematic slaughter of the three million Ukrainian Jews. Slave labor, extermination, internment, and transit camps for Jews appeared all over Ukraine. For months, the mobile death squads of the Einsatzgruppen Schutzstaffel (SS) swept up families from every town and village after the Wehrmacht passed through. They either slaughtered the population at will, squeezed them into ghettos, or shipped them off to die somewhere else.

By the time he reached the Odessa ghetto in mid-1942, Maksym was determined to fight back. He sought out the resistance group, Slava Ukrayini!— *"Glory to Ukraine!"*—who lived in the 1,600 miles of limestone catacombs and tunnels under the city. They ran operations against the occupying Nazi and Romanian forces and the Ukrainian Insurgent Army (Ukrayins'ka Povstans'ka Armiya), an anti-Soviet Ukrainian independence group collaborating with the Nazis.

He entered the catacombs through an entrance in the Moldanovka section of the city, the old Jewish quarter of Odessa before 1917 and now home to some factories and, ironically, the mostly Romanian people who worked there before the invasion.

The entrance was little more than two rusty doors in the ground that groaned and squealed when he opened them. A ladder led down to the catacomb floor. He followed the rusted rails that once carried the mining carts filled with limestone and coquina through the dimly lit tunnel for about one hundred yards. It was dark, but ahead, there was light. He was met by a large, neckless lump of a man called Artem, who carried a torch and an SS standard issue MP-35 submachine gun.

"Pass phrase?"

"With the wrongs of our nation, for vengeance we burn."

The catacombs would be his home for another two years until liberation by the Soviet Red Army in November 1944 that ended the *Reichskommissariat Ukraine* forever. It was there, in the gloom, that Maksym met many of the people that would chart the course of his postwar life.

Chapter 16

Giles was only mildly interested in Maksym's life story and made it clear that he wanted to get back on track. He was irritable and checked his watch frequently.

"Let's talk about Maksym's cronies, shall we? So he gets back to Odessa somehow, joins this resistance group, survives the war etc., etc. By the time you came along, Maksym was already running the show in the Port of Odessa, I presume?"

"That's right. We got there in 1951. He had an organization around him, security people, and plenty of money."

Maksym, still only in his twenties, was a hard man. He was a 5'5" wiry bundle of hard muscle on a compact frame with a small, cold heart and deep, piercing eyes. His body was scarred—scars on top of tattoos and tattoos on top of scars—and he had a blood-orange burn scar on the right side of his face that claimed a few inches of his hairline. He was a nasty man with a short fuse.

The wounds of his wartime experiences were still evident. Sometimes, he struggled to stand. His ribs never fully healed from the beatings in the camp. He was missing enough teeth that it was difficult to eat, so he chewed everything on the left side of his mouth. And he was almost blind in his left eye from repeated facial beatings to the point where the pupil had drifted away from center.

"And, yes, he was a real bastard. You didn't bugger about with Maksym. Running the docks was a rough game, and he was the roughest of the lot."

He was about to go on and say that he didn't know how they made contact with Maksym when Giles interrupted.

84

"But Bruce knew him before, right?"

Bruce Lasher was the brash American hired to run Saco-Lowell—the British textile machine builder that the Draftsman worked for—after it was acquired by Massachusetts-based Lawrence Textile. Even before the war, the Lancashire mills were closing. Postwar, the government focused on rebuilding what the Allies and the Axis spent five years bombing the bloody hell out of over on the continent. The cheap, poor-quality fabrics coming out of Eastern Europe hit demand for Lancashire textiles hard. Bruce's plan was to sell machine designs instead of fabric to governments of the Warsaw Pact, an illegal practice for American companies at the time.

"Before?"

"He knew Maksym's brother, Oleksandr? Oleksandr owned Lawrence Textile Company. And you knew that Oleksandr sent him to England with the express goal of establishing a business connection with his brother in Soviet Ukraine?"

He'd never given that possibility a second thought before. The two of them had acted like strangers when he and Bruce showed up in Odessa. It was plausible, he supposed, that Bruce knew they were brothers, but why keep it a secret? Hiding it from him would have been a pointless lie with nothing to be gained. And that wasn't Bruce.

"That would be news to me. Can't see the point of hiding it from me."

"Maybe he was afraid that you would think you were being roped into something nefarious, some kind of illegal plot."

He stood up and moved back to the seat in front of the tape recorder. The Draftsman caught his eye and felt a warm thread of sweat trickling down his back. Something felt very off. He leaned forward to grab another B&H, betraying his anxiety, and flicked open his Zippo.

"I found out later that Lawrence Textile was owned by Oleksandr Palatnik in New York and that Maksym ran Tekstylny Lodz-Odessa, our first partner in Poland. Didn't strike me as anything sinister, just smart business."

"Seems like a bit more than smart business to me. It sounds like an illegal backdoor business connection between the two global adversaries through a Ukrainian emigre in New York with deep pockets and his mobster brother running the port of Odessa. A channel to circumvent laws banning the exchange of money between US and Soviet Union?"

The Americans had laws against commercial relationships with the Soviet Union. In March 1948, the Department of Commerce announced an embargo on exports to the Soviet Union and its allies. Congress formalized the economic sanctions in the Export Control Act of 1949 and strengthened them in 1951 with the Battle Act.

Don't walk into the trap. Move him on to something else.

"Above my pay grade, I'm afraid. I didn't get involved in American politics. All I know is that our deals kept getting tangled up in red tape and Maksym's name kept coming up, so we arranged to meet him."

Giles, of course, didn't take the bait and continued, "Still, it was illegal and you knew it."

Why's he pressing on this?

"I'm surprised you are asking me about this, sir. You were involved from the beginning. I'm sure if we doing anything illegal, you would have put a stop to it."

Giles snapped a look at him. "Rewind the tape to strip that statement from the record, please. Tell me about your first meeting."

"Our first meeting was in Lodz, Poland, at a restaurant called *Nóż i Widelec*, the Knife and Fork. The best bigos in all of Poland. I went as Saco-Lowell's representative in Poland, but Bruce did all the talking."

"And what did they talk about?"

"Maksym had influence all over Eastern Europe. He'd create lots of problems, and then, if you cut him in, he'd make them go away. Eventually, he and Bruce shook on some kind of deal and that was that."

"And how did it work from then on?"

"Bruce and Maksym were tight for a couple of years. I used the Frankfurt office as my base of operations to manage the business. Bruce lived on the Italian Riviera and spent most of his time sipping Cinzano Biancos with the Hollywood jet-set types."

Giles returned to his folder, shuffling and page thumbing. The sound was irritating. Every few seconds, he touched his index and middle finger to his tongue and then planted them loudly on the corner of each page as he flipped. A few times, he paused, brushing his threadbare mustache with his thumb and finger and murmuring under his breath.

Giles suddenly looked up from the unruly pile in front of him, pushed his glasses up the bridge of his nose, and said, "Let's move on then, shall we? Tell me more about Maksym's network. So the roots of his criminal organization begin in Odessa with a bunch of resistance fighters who go off into the postwar world and make names for themselves in all kinds of ways. The bonds of resistance brotherhood survive and become the criminal organization we know today. Tell me about Artem Ponomarenko and the Balan affair."

Chapter 17

M aksym's narrow eyes bore into the young Englishman from the other side of the railcar. His shoulders and head rocked rhythmically with the motion on the old tracks of the Ukrainian rail system.

It was an eight-hour train from Odessa to Kiev-Pasazhyrskyi central station. The first five hours of the northeasterly route pressed against the border of the Moldavian SSR—Romanian territory acquired by the Soviets in the Molotov-Ribbentrop nonaggression pact with the Nazis—before banking northeast toward Kiev for the last three hours.

He's avoided Maksym's piercing stare by looking out of the window at the Ukrainian countryside and taking pictures with the new Argus twin lens reflex camera that hung around his neck. It had taken him almost a year to save up for it.

Ukraine still carried the scars of war—abandoned farmhouses peppered with bullet and mortar holes, burned-out tanks overgrown with weeds, and vacant, boarded-up factories covered in graffiti.

He could feel the Ukrainian's eyes on him. It was unnerving.

They were going to meet an old friend of Maksym from the wartime resistance. Artem Ponomarenko was a power broker climbing the ladder of Ukrainian SSR government. The reason for the meeting, however, was a mystery, and Bruce was not particularly forthcoming.

"Maksym and I don't see eye to eye, Bran," he had warned. "I don't think he takes me seriously. We need a new face in there, and that's you. He knows you from Poland, so maybe you can build a rapport with him."

An expensive Hugo Boss suit hung off his wiry frame. Boss was an active member of the Nazi Party as early as 1931, and his company manufactured uniforms for the SS, the Hitler Youth, and the Wehrmacht.

Maksym smoked Prima cigarettes, another relic of the Nazi occupation. The pack design still used the colors, symbols, and German Blackletter font that defined the awful past. His hair was slicked back with copious amounts of Brylcreem, a British product made by Beecham, pressing his already thinning hair tight against his scalp. He reeked of Prince Roman Petrovich Russian Leather brand aftershave preferred by wealthy businessmen who wanted to broadcast their rustic roots. You don't want to look or smell too rich while wandering around the docks at night. And he wore a double cross of Lorraine pendant around his neck, a medieval symbol of royal power in Poland and Hungary.

"I have heard about you," Maksym said suddenly, looking absently out of the window. "Mr. Lasher speaks well of you. I have yet to see what it is that he sees in you." His English was broken but respectable.

"He and I are very different. I'm a working-class lad from a mill town in the north of England. He's a Harvard University elite type."

"So he is style and you are substance? He is the brain and you are the brawn?"

"He's piss and I'm vinegar."

Maksym looked confused.

"It's British slang. Piss means alcohol and being drunk. Vinegar is the hangover cure that sailors used after they'd been out on the piss. He's the party, but I'm there for you in the morning."

"We call him a *bila vorona*, a white crow. He wears the fine clothes and has good manners, but underneath, he is scavenging bird. He's good at deals but in then out, you know? In Ukraine, being here, knowing people is very important. You know people and do things for them, and they do them for you later. You only work with people you trust. Artem is one I trust, but he is...Andrey? How do say *khod'ba po kanatu* in English?"

His head of security replied "Walking a tightrope" in perfect English.

"Yes, yes. Artem is walking the tightrope." He lit another Prima, and the foul-smelling smoke streamed out of his nostrils. "Ukraine is a complicated country."

Control had passed back and forth between foreign invaders for centuries. The Golden Mongol Horde, the Polish-Lithuanian Commonwealth, the Cossacks, and the indigenous Muslim Tatars of the Crimean Khanate had all ruled over the region until the Russian invasion of 1783. The Russians held it for 135 years until the abdication of Tsar Nicolas II and the Bolshevik Revolution of 1917. The country was assembled from many ethnic groups, tribal alliances, and entangled familial relationships. Some were loyal to the Tzar and pro-Russian, some were pro-independence, some anti-Semitic, some anti-Muslim, some just tried to stay close to family in Poland or Hungary as best they could across borders redrawn after the war.

He explained that resentment of the Soviets ran deep, from Stalin's intentional starvation of the Ukrainians during the Holomodor of the 1930s to the shipping of hundreds of thousands of Ukrainians to the gulags of Siberia. Anti-Soviet and independence-minded Ukrainians had watched with envy as Hitler rose to power in Germany. Many saw Nazism as the path to independence and freedom from Soviet oppression. Others saw it as blueprint to get rid of the Jews. Many Ukrainians in the north and east saw themselves as Russian and were closer to the Tsar than the people in the south and west. After the war, Moscow put loyalists in powerful government jobs in Kiev and throughout Soviet Ukraine then used their power to strip the country of its plentiful natural resources—iron ore, coal, nickel—for their own benefit.

"In business here, we navigate the unknown waters of the past. I do my best to rebuild the country, give people jobs, and try to get our own people into companies and government to change things. The Port of Odessa, the best port on the Black Sea, is very important to Moscow, and my influence there gives me power."

And that was where Artem Ponomarenko came in.

"Artem saved my life when I got to the catacombs of Odessa. He took me in, nursed me back to health, and we fought the Nazis together. He's a communist, an apparatchik, not a businessman."

After the liberation of Odessa, Artem soared through the ranks of the Ukrainian Communist Party to become second secretary, behind Stalinist Leonid Minkov, and the highest-ranking official on Council of Ministers. The position gave him power over the rebuilding of Ukraine's textile industry. Everyone needed clothes and curtains.

"Minkov is a problem for all of us, you also, and Artem can help. I want him out and Artem as first secretary."

This is dangerous talk. Why is he telling me all this? Is it a trap? What the bloody hell do I say? Think, Brandon!

"The times are hard, and there is much to be done to rebuild Ukraine." It was the best he could up with.

Maksym chuckled. "You will do well here to speak with care but not fear. Dostoevsky said taking a new step, uttering a new word, is what people fear most. That is Ukraine today. We say *Posluzhlyvyy duren' hirshyy za voroha*, the obliging fool is worse than the enemy. Your boss is the obliging fool."

It was midafternoon when they arrived at Kiev-Pasazhyrskyi central station, a gargantuan facility in the Cossack baroque style with a dash of Tsarist-era constructivism thrown in for good measure. They took the Kiev tramway to Poshtova Ploscha then walked to Kontraktova Ploscha in the merchant district of Podil.

Yegor Restaurant, named after the owner, sat on the attractive side of the Ploscha with the view of St. Catherine's Church. Yegor hurried his regular patrons out into the street, and two of Maksym's security men entered, their hands on the guns in their side holsters.

"The name of this square, like Ukraine, changed to suit whoever ruled, Alexander Square for Tsar Alexander II, then Red Square after revolution in 1917, the Nazis called it something else, but after the war, it went back to its first name, Kontraktova Ploscha, Contracts Square, the place where merchants traded and made deals. It's also the Jewish sector, so it is where I feel most at home in Kiev. And Yegor's borscht is the best I've ever had."

The security men returned and gave the all-clear signal.

Artem Ponomarenko was an enormous man. His frame took up a large corner of the restaurant. At least six feet four and probably twenty-five stone with closely cropped hair, he looked like a former military man squeezed into a suit that probably fit him years ago but was now stressing the seams to breaking point.

Yegor brought over a large pot of borscht, the bright red beetroot soup that flowed like blood in every kitchen in Ukraine, served with chunks of beef and garlic fritters called pampushki. A bottle of colorless liquid sat in the center of table.

Artem was already a little flushed. He'd been there a while. "This is horilka. An old Ukrainian proverb says the first shot of horilka lifts your spirits ever so slightly, the second one sends you flying like a hawk, and each drink after that, you soar as happy and free as a bird. It sounds better when you say it in Ukrainian!"

It tastes like fire.

Another shot and the conversation turned to the business of the day.

"Minkov is causing us problems, Artem," Maksym began, "forcing me through the Party functionaries in Odessa to put more of his people in powerful administrative roles in the port, blocking shipments with paperwork if I don't."

"He's there to protect Moscow's interests."

Those interests included a series of dams along the Dnieper River and the Soviet Union's largest power plant, DinproHES. The Dnieper ran southeast from Kiev to Zaporizhia before turning to southwest and spilling into the Black Sea near Kherson.

During the retreat of 1941, the Red Army had dynamited the Dniepropetrovsk dam, and the flood that followed killed tens of thousands, including their own troops crossing the river to escape the Nazis. The Nazis destroyed it again in 1943. Rebuilt between 1944 and 1949, it had been generating power for little more than a year.

"And he's there to keep Ukrainian party in line, of course. If we push him out, Moscow will just send another one to replace him and perhaps someone worse. Listen, Maksym, perhaps I can help. Do you remember Marius Popescu?"

"His father betrayed my family to the Nazis, but he proved himself a worthy fighter against the Nazis during the occupation. What about him?"

He looked from side to side to make sure Yegor was out of ear-shot. Walls have ears.

Popescu apparently worked for man called Grigor Balan, who ran two companies in Romania—SovRomCuart and SovRomPetrol. Stalin created the SovRoms to punish Romania for siding with the Nazis and to siphon the country's natural resources for the bene-fit of the Soviet Union as war reparations. SovRomPetrol ran the oil refineries in Ploiești, north of Bucharest. SovRomCuart operated the Bihor quartz mine in eastern Romania, near the border with Hungary.

As Artem told it, Minkov saw Balan as an adversary, a rival for the affections of Tavárisch Stálin and also as a competitor to Ukraine's own energy production in Stalino Donetsk. To Balan, Minkov was an obstacle.

"Balan needs a shipping partner across the Black Sea. Today, he ships over land through Hungary, Yugoslavia, Czechoslovakia, and Poland." He rubbed his thumb and forefinger together and raises his eyebrows. "This will be lucrative for you, Maksym, and it is a chance to poke a stick in the eye of the fucking Romanians."

"Minkov will block it."

"Perhaps, but it might be possible to kill two birds with one stone, as your English friend would say. I can arrange a night out in Kiev with Comrade Minkov? An opportunity to get to know him on a more intimate level perhaps? If you agree to work with Comrade Balan."

By midnight, The Byblos Club, a warehouse converted into a secret strip club behind an abandoned factory, was buzzing.

Minkov had three loves in the world: girls, horilka, and power—not necessarily in that order. It was clearly not his first time there. He knew the bouncer at the door, patted a few men on the back, and smacked the bottoms of the waitresses, laughing and waved his money around.

They had spent the last two days setting the trap. Maksym wanted to hire a slinky seductress or saucy Gypsy Rose Lee type, but fake copies were scattered all over Eastern Europe. They needed a different kind of femme fatale for this honey trap. She couldn't be one of the dancers. She needed to be untouchable, intriguing, and maybe a uniquely exotic.

They hired an American girl named Regina, a rare treat in 1951 Kiev, and certain to catch Minkov's eye. She was a beautiful, dark-skinned woman with waves of raven hair tinged with light brown highlights, and a silver clip to hold it all in place. She had full red lips and eyes of light green with thick black lashes, full breasts, slim waist, and long legs.

They set her up as a bartender with all the American sass that your average powerful Soviet politician might find attractive in some-one behind a bar. She had a huge smile and laughed at his jokes.

Minkov chose a table at the front near the dancers. It started with shots of horilka. He invited attractive women, planted at neigh-boring tables, to join him and spent an hour drinking, flirting with the girls, and having the dancers between sets on stage sit on his lap.

Regina only served Minkov. She came out from behind the bar just for him.

When Maksym, Artem, and the Draftsman drifted away with their girls, and by 2:00 a.m., Minkov zeroed in on Regina and invited her to join him at his table. Within the hour, they were the last two in Byblos, and thirty minutes after that, they were in his penthouse in Lypky, the section of the city where the rich and powerful looked down from the balconies of their newly renovated mansions.

"Drink?"

"More horilka? I don't think I can handle any more of that shit! Okay, just one more, then I want you to try something really fun with me. I brought it with me from the States, and I've been saving it for a special occasion. You'll love it!"

Minkov grinned. "What is it?"

"They call it Milltown. It makes sex unbelievable. I tried it once, and I don't think we got out of bed for days. It's all over Hollywood right now. Interested?"

"*Da*! Perhaps I should stop drinking?"

"Doesn't matter! We can take the pill now, have a couple more shots, and it only takes about twenty minutes to kick in. After that..." She gave him a saucy eyebrow dance and an enormous smile.

The pill was actually twenty grams of meprobamate, a sedative developed at Wallace Laboratories in Milltown, New Jersey. Twelve grams could calm a mentally disturbed person, but forty grams would kill a large man. Twenty grams was just enough to knock someone out for a few hours.

They drank, took the pills, and began kissing on a settee. Within minutes, Minkov slumped forward and fell unconscious. His eyes stayed open for some reason, and a small floret of foam formed at each corner of his mouth. She pressed her fingers against his carotid artery. He had a strong pulse and was breathing.

Before leaving, she planted a small Minox-A camera in his jacket pocket. It contained photographs taken by a CIA asset working in the new MGB headquarters in Lubyanka Square. The pictures documented a new planned structure and leadership of a merged Ministry of State Security (MGB) and Ministry of Internal Affairs (MVD) to be called the Komitet Gosudarstvennoy Bezopasnosti (KGB). The Soviets could decide that the camera was a plant to set up Minkov and that he was not passing information to the West through Regina. In that case, or so the plan went, they hoped the Soviets would tie themselves in knots looking for the mole who passed the information.

A few hours later, tipped off that a high-level official had been seen cavorting with an American woman, MGB officials broke down the door and found Minkov passed out in his underwear, a pair of American brand Roussel women's panties and a bra in his bed.

One of the officers, rooting through Minkov's jacket pocket pulled out the camera and said, "Comrade?"

After a week of interrogation in the basement of Lukyanivska Prison, Minkov was recalled to Moscow, never to be heard from again. Artem Ponomarenko was elevated to first secretary of Ukraine Soviet Socialist Republic, and Grigor Balan got his shipping deal. Artem was installed as first secretary of Soviet Ukraine in an elaborate closed-door ceremony at the Palace of the Facets inside the Kremlin and attended by Stalin himself.

And so it began.

Chapter 18

Balan's ships began their grim, predawn trip north from Constanta, clinging to the western coastal edge of the Black Sea for safety. Early winter snow and ice encased Odessa. The city's rich retreated to the comfort of well-heated homes in Kievskyi while the poor crowded round street corner bonfires of rubbish. Thin pillars of smoke shrouded the city in a gray haze.

The ships, acquired by Moscow under Roosevelt's Lend-Lease Agreement, were hastily transferred to a new Soviet state-owned enterprise under Balan's control called the Azov Sea Shipping Company. They flew the blue, yellow, and red tricolor of Romania and bore proud names, like *Rezistenta* (Resilience), *independenţă* (Independence), and *Curaj* (Fortitude). But the crews were Soviet, experienced seamen of the Black Sea Fleet.

Maksym, standing in front of a large picture window in his office overlooking the port, watched the ship's lights blink weakly as they arrived in Odessa under the cover of the night.

The Draftsman stood nearby, on the other side of his large oak desk. "The first ships are here. This is an important day."

Palatnik grunted, lost in thought. He was anxious about something. Distant and distracted for the better part of a week, he was chain-smoking his way through two packs of Primas a day. He turned suddenly, stamping out the cigarette butt in an overflowing ashtray on his desk.

"Artem and I are meeting tonight. There are issues we need to discuss. Dangerous issues. It's better you do not hear us. But I want you close in case."

"Where? *Tsarske Selo?*" (Royal Village.)

"Of course."

"*My z Andriyem pidemo pershymy pereviryty.*" (Andrey and I will go first to check it out.)

Maksym laughed. "Your Ukrainian is getting better every day."

"*Vy zanadto laskavi.*" (You are too kind.)

They arrived early, a little after eight o'clock, to clear the place out and sweep for Soviet bugs. Andrey, normally meticulous and unwavering in his dedication to the task, leaned idly on the bar drinking coffee and chatting up one of the waitresses. She was just his type, long hair, long legs, and a steady heartbeat.

The Draftsman reached under Maksym's usual table and planted a small device of his own. He tapped his hearing aid and knocked on the table to make sure it worked. He took a Minox B subminiature camera from his jacket pocket and snapped a couple of test pictures.

Andrey was oblivious. The waitress blushed uncomfortably at something he said. She looked over her shoulder into the kitchen area to make sure her boss wasn't watching.

"*Ya ne taka divchyna, ser.*" (I'm not that kind of girl, sir.)

At little after nine, Artem and Maksym arrived. They took their usual table, and the waitress brought over water and glasses of horilka.

The Draftsman was not invited to the table and sat at the bar, watching them talk through a dirty, cracked mirror on the wall behind the bar. They spoke Ukrainian, and the Draftsman, still learning the language, picked up only fragments in his earpiece. No matter. Giles and friends would translate the tape later.

With Andrey stationed outside, the waitress relaxed and flirted with him but decided he was boring and not worth the trouble when he didn't respond to her attempts at conversation. In his earpiece, Artem was saying, "Comrade Stalin, our caring father, did not look well. We may lose him soon."

Stalin was no friend to Ukrainians or the Jewish community, but talking openly about his demise was dangerous. Stalin's campaign—labeling Jews as disloyal "individuals devoid of nation or tribe" and imprisoning doctors of Jewish descent—had made life increasingly difficult for Maksym's friends and business associates.

"He is strong and will persevere."

"The followers are already posturing to assume power."

Stalin's death would create chaos in the Kremlin. Malenkov and Beria were already positioning themselves to take over, but Khrushchev was rumored to be the chosen heir. The three would fight it out behind closed doors, out of the earshot of Stalin.

"Khrushchev is not like Comrade Stalin who wants to make everyone pay for war. The *pizda* Romanians should pay for their betrayal, but Khrushchev will free them. I believe he will shut down the SovRoms and return control of the companies to Romania."

"But that will put an end to our business. The first ships just sailed into port."

"No. The Soviet Union is still their biggest market. The ships will continue. But Khrushchev does not believe in building massive armed forces of men, tanks, and ships. They consume too much and offer nothing in return. He believes in missiles, atomic power, and uranium. And where will he get his uranium? Balan's quartz mine in Bihar. They have found uranium there."

In March, Stalin died in his dacha in Kuntsevo of a stroke. Pravda published the story of his illness and final days in surprising detail, presumably to avoid speculation about a plot to seize power by Beria. But it was Malenkov that replaced Stalin as premier, chairman of the Council of Ministers, and head of the party apparatus. Khrushchev would have to wait his turn. Beria was arrested for treason in June, convicted, and executed two days before Christmas.

For Maksym and Artem, it was business as usual. By late spring, what started out as a trickle had turned into a steady stream of Romanian ships. Balan had business interests that went far beyond quartz and petrol. Heavily laden with wood, coal, natural gas, and coal bound for the Soviet Union, they sailed into the Maksym-controlled ports along the Black Sea.

The rubles rolled in, and the circle of people around Maksym grew. He welcomed an endless stream of supplicants currying favor into his spacious office overlooking the Potemkin Steps. His organization became known as the *Malina*, derived from one of Maksym's raspberry export businesses in an attempt to sound more legitimate.

His operational leaders, known as the Pakhan, ran port operations. They controlled the flow of goods in and out, manhandling the dockworkers at the bottom and fluffing the government officials who ran the bureaucracy at the top. Eventually, they ran their own shipping companies.

In addition to their legal operations, they trafficked Afghan heroin from the Caucasus, counterfeit cigarettes, and dozens of other illegal products around Europe. They financed shipments at usurious rates, ran protection rackets, and loan-sharked the local businesses.

Around the port, violence was rampant. Bodies, dumped into the Black Sea from the causeway leading out to the Vorontsov lighthouse, regularly washed up a few miles south on the beaches of Vidrada and Lanzheron. Knife attacks, shootings, and kidnappings were as commonplace as the kebab stands in the Primoz market.

The Malina expanded into the ports of Kurasu in Turkey and Burgas in Bulgaria. Drug and human trafficking were big business, and it didn't take long for the Malina's criminal activities to draw the attention of INTERPOL.

That summer, the Draftsman secured a lucrative deal in Poland to refit factories in Krakow, Lodz, Warsaw, and Poznan destroyed by the Nazis during the Reich's final days in the winter of 1945. From there, he moved south into Czechoslovakia, Hungary, and Bulgaria, using Maksym's money and influence to pave his way.

But it was the Balan business that really lined Maksym's pockets. Malenkov kept the SovRoms going. Half of Romania's exports were on Balan's ships bound for Maksym's ports. With Artem's support, the Malina took control of the rail lines running north toward Moscow from Odessa, Kiev, and Kharkiv.

In the late summer of 1954, the Draftsman was summoned to Odessa. The city buzzed with activity. Tourists from the north ambled along Deribasovskaya leading to the opera house.

As was his custom, Maksym stood with his back to the door watching the traffic in and out of his port. A dense cloud of Prima smoke billowed around his head. Andrey stood to the left of the office door, his right hand tucked inside the lapel of his expensive suit and resting on the Makarov holstered under his left arm.

The Draftsman was surprised to see Bruce slouched in armchair in front of the huge mahogany desk. He had an unusually large glass of Scotch in his hand. Bruce was a gin man. It was the signal. Whatever was about to happen needed to be transmitted back to Broadway House in London. He winked at the Draftsman to confirm.

He and Bruce were rarely in Odessa at the same time anymore. Almost a year to the day, on the patio at Buca di Bacco, a terrifying drive from his house in Praiano, Bruce had said, "Life on the Amalfi suits me better. A new man will be running Eastern European ops for us."

At their final meeting at the office in Manchester in early 1953, he had introduced him to a tall, ungainly fellow named Giles Bancroft. The Draftsman pegged him immediately as a pompous twat.

"Morning, boss. And, Bruce? What a pleasant surprise! Haven't seen you in donkeys."

Bruce waved his glass in greeting. His face was flushed, and he'd gained a little weight.

Maksym finally turned from the window and said, "Let's get down to business. Time is short. You have done a fine job, Mr. Pike, building our business in the northern and eastern soviet states. We now need you to extend further south into Yugoslavia and over to Romania."

"Okay. What do you have in mind?"

"Our friend, Comrade Balan, has a special cargo he needs shipped every month by rail from the Băiţa mine on the Hungarian/Romanian border up to Minsk and Vilnius."

"It will need to transition in Warsaw, but that shouldn't be a problem."

"It's more complicated than shipping a bunch of fabric from one country to another."

"Is it something illegal?"

Maksym took a long, slow drag on his cigarette, his head bobbing from side to side. He was hedging. The Draftsman glanced at Bruce, hoping for a clue, but he just stared into the bottom of his glass.

"I wouldn't call it illegal, but it is very secret. We will need it set up in a few months. You will be handsomely paid, of course, and you will become one of my Pakhan, with all the privileges that go with it."

"And the cargo?"

"Uranium. Moscow wants to beat the Americans into space, and it's going to require a lot of fuel, and that's made from uranium, or so I'm told."

Space? They want to beat the Americans into space? Bollocks.

"So we need to set up transport of this uranium, but the Americans can't know how much of it they have?"

"Exactly."

"Okay, we'll need a cover, something innocent that we run on that route as well. Any ideas?"

"Well, actually yes, we have one idea. Miloje Petovic."

Chapter 19

Odessa, Soviet Ukraine

The difference between the Bristolskaya Hotel and the other hotels that accepted foreigners in Soviet Ukraine was stark. Most were decrepit, some downright dangerous, but the Bristolskaya was classic Louis XIV. Columns and pilasters stretched up to high ceilings with marble everywhere, gold accents, and epic paintings celebrated the military legends of Ukrainian and Soviet history.

The Draftsman, despite being a man of unpretentious northern English tastes, stayed there because that's where wealthy foreigners had to stay. The hotel overlooked Taras Shevchenko Park. A self-portrait of the Ukrainian poet as young man with wavy hair and plaintive eyes hung in the lobby. He was an advocate for independence who managed to avoid getting caught until Tsar Nicolas I, who could read old Ukrainian, read "Dream." The poem made fun of the Tsarina's frumpy appearance and the facial tics she developed during the Decembrist Uprising. Shevchenko was arrested, imprisoned in St. Petersburg, then forced to march almost 1,500 miles from prison to exile in Orsk in the Ural Mountains.

The Draftsman sat hunched over a truly awful gin and tonic in Le Grand Cru, a bar off the main lobby. It was made with *Duzhe Dobre Dzhyn*, a Ukrainian gin that literally translated to "very good gin." It tasted like a combination of juniper berry and battery acid. He was alone, except for a bartender carefully drying martini glasses and his KGB tail sitting at the far end of the bar pretending to read a copy of Pravda. He stuck out like a sore thumb in a well-worn tweed overcoat with an enormous furred collar, a dockworker's woolen hat, and scuffed government-issued shoes.

The KGB paid special attention to foreign businessmen now, a step up from imprisoning and torturing their own people toward harassing and scaring visitors. Everyone was followed. Every hotel room was bugged, and every contact scrutinized.

Where the Draftsman went, his tail went also. They'd never actually spoken to each other, but they bought each other drinks and raised their glasses, nodding in mutual acknowledgment of the awkwardness of their relationship.

Tonight, however, the Draftsman's thoughts were elsewhere. His contact was late, not by much, but it was still troubling. He needed to get a message back to London about Maksym's new uranium venture with Balan. Uranium was not just fuel to blast rockets into space. A few grams of it had wiped out two cities in Japan less than a decade before, and now the Romanians were mining enough to require a train car to move it every month?

The distinctive rose and jasmine scents of Chanel No. 5 arrived before she did, the gentle tap of her heels, a second or two apart, on the marble floor. She passed behind him, perhaps a little too close for two supposed strangers in a mostly empty bar. The closeness of his cotton shirt and the silk of her sleeve sent a shot of static through his body.

She took a seat at the bar between the Draftsman and his KGB tail. He avoided looking over at her, but he could feel the tail become suddenly alert to the situation. She crossed her legs to the left, her knees pointing in his direction. No doubt she was wearing her favorite pale-pink champagne Pierre Balmain dress and the Salvatore Cangemi creme-colored sling-back heels.

She snapped open her purse and took out a Chesterfield. He could see the newspaper ad in his head. The debonair executive comes home to his aproned wife, apple pie in one hand, long cigarette in the other, and says, "Her cigarette and mine! We choose Chesterfield! You've come a long way, baby!"

The bartender sauntered over to her. "A drink, ma'am?" Even his most flirtatious voice was gruff and a little disturbing.

"Sidecar, please. With the best cognac you have."

She pretended to check her hair in the mirror behind the bar but caught the Draftsman's eye for a moment, smiled, then winked.

He bought her second drink, and they moved their stools closer together, flirting shamelessly. The bartender and the tail watched with fascination. She wasn't the kind of *poviya* they were used to seeing in Le Grand Cru. The pickup was slow and intimate, like two future lovers meeting for the first time. She brushed the top of her foot against his calf.

After about half an hour, they got up to leave, and he helped her down from her stool. As they made their way to the elevator, he looked back over his shoulder, just in time to catch the conspiratorial grins of the two men left behind.

And his KGB tail did not get up to follow. It worked.

Upstairs, they undressed quickly, peeling off each other's clothes, whispering between heavy breaths and zippers. They both knew the room was bugged. Hidden cameras were a distinct possibility in this hotel. The listeners manning the bugs needed to hear the sounds they expected to hear as two people enjoy an evening of passion, so they climbed into bed and made love under the covers as they had many times before.

Afterward, they slept for a couple of hours, just enough time for the listeners in the room to lose interest. In the dark, Regina climbed out of bed, put on a robe, and tiptoed over to the hotel room desk. She turned on one of the bedside lamps and handed him a pen and paper.

He wrote, "Message to RUGBY. Need to meet soon. Very urgent. MP business shipping U ore from Romania. Need help to cover."

She read it, nodded slowly, and scribbled, "YANKEE involved?"

He nodded. "Dangerous. MP trust issues. Perhaps a setup. Gave signal. Scotch."

She dressed quickly into the more conventional attire she'd left in the room earlier and packed the dress and heels in her small overnight bag. Her final note read, "Le Grand Cru, 6pm Thursday with instructions."

Another opportunity to take her to bed, he thought.

He watched her look both directions down the hallway. Turning back to him, she pursed her red lips and blew him a last kiss before quietly slipping away and closing the door behind her.

As usual, the guilt crept under his skin. Adeline and the children back home all deserve better. It unsettled his stomach and made his skin feel itchy. Regina's Chanel scent clung to him. In the bathroom, he washed the experience from his body in the shower. The water was lukewarm at best and slightly dirty. It's probably all he deserved.

Chapter 20

Belgrade, Yugoslavia

Perhaps not surprisingly, as the heir to the trouser cartel, Miloje Petrovic was well-dressed, wearing a high-quality brown wool suit with a fuller cut to downplay the size of his broad shoulders and muscular frame.

Before the war, the Yugoslav textile industry was run by four cartels—the stocking cartel, the sized cotton cartel for tailors, the rug cartel, and the largest of the four, the trouser cartel run by Petrovic's father, Anton. Together, the cartels employed almost a quarter of the country's working population.

When rumors of the Nazi invasion began, young Miloje and his mother fled for Odessa, hoping to catch a boat to America. His father stayed behind to fight with the partisans and was killed at the Battle of Poljana. The Nazis crushed the cartels, shut down the factories, and melted down all the machinery for scrap iron.

Miloje and his mother stumbled into in Odessa in June 1941, just two months ahead of the Nazi Wehrmacht, starved and destitute. There was no ship out of Odessa, so Miloje took a job as a dishwasher in one of the city's many restaurants.

When the Red Army's defense of the city collapsed and the Nazi's marched on Odessa, they hid their Jewish heritage and pretended to be Eastern Orthodox Christian, as most Serbs were. Nonetheless, he was beaten, imprisoned, released, and confined to the ghetto but avoided being shipped off to Bogdonovka with the rest. His mother cleaned toilets at the Nazi headquarters.

He joined the resistance and lived in the catacombs. In mid-1942, he met Maksym Palatnik who appeared in the old mining tunnel, broken, alone, and barely recognizable. Miloje fed him, helped him regain his strength, and the two of them fought together until the Nazis were driven out once and for all by the Soviet Red Army in April 1944.

After the liberation, Miloje, battle-hardened but still a teenager, returned to Belgrade to assume his father's position to find someone else living in his family home. A Nazi collaborator had claimed their home during the occupation. After liberation, the Communist regime declared them enemies of the state and threw them in prison. The home had been given to the new head of the rug cartel as a reward for his loyalty, an odd decision as he, too, had secretly collaborated with the Nazis.

Nonetheless, Miloje had smelled opportunity. President Tito had launched a major revitalization project to rebuild the pile of rubble that was Belgrade, a city flattened by the Nazis on their way in and again by the Soviet Red Army chasing them out. He called it Novi Beograd, "New Belgrade."

Tito put a loyalist named Stankovic in charge of rebuilding the cartels while keeping Moscow at bay. Tito's relationship with Moscow was fragile. His partisans didn't get much help fighting the Nazis, so he didn't think that Yugoslavia owed them much in return. But Moscow had a strong grip over the members of the League of Communists of Yugoslavia party.

The other cartel leaders, already under the thumb of Stankovic, ignored Miloje. His youth and lack of standing within the league made it impossible to follow through on his ambition to refit and reopen a large factory and take back control of the cotton and wool markets from Hungary and Bulgaria, countries favored by Moscow. It didn't help matters that he was Jewish.

Miloje and the Draftsman were sitting in a small outdoor café in the old neighborhood of Dedinje on the eastern slopes of Topčidersko Brdo, just south of downtown Belgrade.

"This is a very nice part of town," the Draftsman commented idly as they waited for their coffee to arrive.

"Thank you. My family home is here, but now it belongs to the state. One of the new cartel heads sleeps in my parents' bed and cooks on my grandmother's stove. I will get it back someday and assume my father's position as is my right."

"He was a great man, from what I understand."

"A true Serbian hero of the Great War and leader of a small band of partisans who fought against thirty thousand Nazis and Croatian Ustase traitors in the second."

"And you yourself, Miloje, a hero of the resistance in Odessa with my boss, Maksym. No less brave than your father."

"That is kind of you, but we were just irritants, hiding in the dark to come up from below and be a thorn in the side of the Nazis. My father never hid in the dark. He stood proud in the full light of day to face down the enemy."

This could get tiresome quickly. Let's just get this insufferable filial piety shit out of the way now or the old man's shadow will hang over this relationship forever. Barely listening, he let Miloje talk as the coffee was served. It was thick and black, Turkish style, but in a much larger cup and poured by the waiter from a small jug attached to a long-pouring handle.

"You'll probably want to add some sugar," the waiter said helpfully before putting down a plate of sweets he called "rátluk." It looked like Turkish delight, gel-like cubes in a variety of colors covered in a fine-powdered sugar.

"So, Miloje, Maksym has directed me to do whatever I can to help you. I am one of his Pakhan, responsible for his business in East Germany, Poland, and Czechoslovakia. Hungary and Yugoslavia are markets we plan to develop, so we are interested in helping you for business reasons as well as your long personal relationship with Maksym."

"I need to get rid of this *drkadžijo*, Stankovic. I only asked him to return my own father's factory so I could get the loans for repairs and machines to reopen it. One of the other cartel heads wants the building and will develop it as a joint venture with Soviet government. I wanted to bribe Stankovic into signing over the factory to me. He's a Jew, you know, but keeps it hidden."

"He'd report you to the UDBA, and they'd put you up against a wall in Glavnjača. What we need to do is threaten his power. What's his weakness? What is he afraid to lose?"

"His weakness is his arrogance, that no one can touch him. He is a bureaucrat. His wife is the one with the money and the family name."

"We have a plan, Miloje."

"I can trust you?"

"You can trust Maksym. And I do what Maksym tells me to do. You must stay away from this so you can't be implicated. When it's done, I will contact you."

Maksym arranged a meeting with Stankovic. He resisted at first, but the presence of Ponomarenko convinced him to take the meeting. Artem's reputation for getting things done and his friendly ties to Moscow were a clear message that this was a real business opportunity not to be missed.

They met in the Belgrade suburb of Palilula. The name came from the expression "*pali lulu*" which means "light a pipe." The Ottoman rulers banned smoking for fear of accidentally setting crops on fire. In the late summer and early autumn when all the crops had been harvested, the smoking ban was lifted, and locals announced this by calling out "*pali lulu*" to their neighbors to let them know it was safe to light up.

Stankovic sat with his arms folded over an enormous belly. He had a permanent frown and a face carved from an intractable piece of gray stone. His gruff demeanor softened after a couple of glasses of rakija plum brandy.

"Thank you for meeting us, Comrade Stankovic."

"Ach, it was good to get away from the city for a few days. I have a home here in Palilula. My wife is throwing a party for her Belgrade society friends. Karađorđević or Obrenović descendants, they are all the same. Talking about the purity of their bloodlines and which of their relatives were mistreated, betrayed, or dispossessed of their rightful inheritances and titles. Just being around all that aristocratic shit upsets my stomach."

"Well, I'll get straight to the point if I may? Our businesses are shipping in and out of Black Sea ports and textile manufacturing. Both are critical to the Motherland's goals. Comrade Ponomarenko met with Comrade Malenkov recently to ensure that he was supportive of continued expansion and the need to bring higher-quality clothing to the people."

"We walk a thin wire, as you surely know, between President Tito's desire for a more autonomous Yugoslavia and demonstrating our loyalty to the bigger goals of the Soviet people."

"It is the same for us in Soviet Ukraine. I believe that both are possible, but poor choices of partner or plan will lead the falcon to see and fall on its prey."

"So what is it you want from me?"

"Guaranteed contracts for Yugoslav clothing, rugs, and drapes taken by rail across Romania to the port of Constanta with our partner, Grigor Balan, then put on my ships bound for Odessa. It gives you greater access to Soviet market with access to the Black Sea and guaranteed buys going direct to the great Soviet people."

"And what's in it for you?"

"For me? Greater use of my ships and ports gives me the power to increase pricing for less desirable shippers and offer favorable docking to my best partners. For Comrade Ponomarenko, it is providing a valuable service on behalf of the people of Soviet Ukraine."

The message was clear. Everyone would make money, and the risk that Moscow would not approve of a little skimming off the top or the lining of certain pockets was zero. Moscow would not care as long as it was all below the waterline.

"Demand for Yugoslav textiles is high, and you are not the first to make such an offer. It cannot be exclusive, you understand."

"I understand. We are only talking about orders that ship to Soviet Ukraine through the port of Constanta. As our confidence in each other grows, other contracts can be negotiated."

"I would be exclusive on that route?"

"We will make no other contracts for the textile business between Yugoslavia and Soviet Ukraine. To be reviewed each year, of course."

"Of course."

"We have one additional request, Comrade Stankovic."

He stiffened. "*Ruka ruku mije*? One hand washes the other?"

"We ask that you support Miloje Petrovic in his claim as head of the trouser cartel and allow him to reopen his father's factory. He is an old friend from the resistance days in Odessa. We want to exploit the demand for textiles in Poland and East Germany and maybe take back dominance of the wool market from the Hungarians."

They knew that there was no love lost between Stankovic and the Hungarians. He grew up in Subotica, a city in northern Yugoslavia that was annexed and occupied by Hungary in 1941. Ethnic Serbs, like the Stankovic family, were driven from the city and most of the city's seven thousand Jews sent to Auschwitz. Three years later, Tito's partisan army, Stankovic, and his father among them chased the Axis forces from the city and spent the next year torturing and executing the Hungarian citizens left behind for retribution.

"The other cartel heads don't want Petrovic to assume his father's position. The ones that survived the Nazis don't want to face the son of the Great War hero, a Jew who fought for Serbian people in both wars, while they gave their daughters the Nazis to preserve their position. The others are leftover Stalinists in the pocket of Moscow."

"You can persuade them or replace them. That's why you have the position you do, Comrade. *Vreme je novac.* Time is money. We have plenty of one and very little of the other."

Chapter 21

Giles's normally well-coiffed hair was messy, his long fingers pinned on either side of the field report lying out on his desk. Deep trenches of worry rolled across his forehead.

The Draftsman sat across the room in an old leather armchair, reading the same report. The tension in the room was palpable.

"So Balan needs a secret way to ship uranium ore from the Băița mine to Minsk. Palatnik has proposed working with this chap Miloje Petrovic in Yugoslavia as a cover. Petrovic is another one of these resistance fighter friends, and he's trying to reopen his father's factories in Belgrade, but this government official Stankovic, who is Moscow's man in the country, is blocking him."

"Yes, sir. Yugoslavia is complicated as you know."

Giles's spectacles hung on the end of his nose as he looked over at the Draftsman. "So Petrovic approached Palatnik for financial help and maybe some scheme to get rid of Stankovic. Is that your read of it too?"

"Yes, sir."

"Well, we can't stop them moving this uranium, but we can learn how much and what they are doing with it. The Kremlin is a mess at the moment. Malenkov is on thin ice. He was close to Beria, and they just executed him as a traitor. The analysts think his days are numbered, and Khrushchev will take the reins soon. We need to see what's happening over there and whether this uranium is for space, nuclear weapons, or some other purpose."

The plan they concocted sounded simple enough. Go along with Palatnik and Balan on the uranium shipping. Set up rail contracts for routes between Belgrade, Budapest, Warsaw, and Minsk. Persuade Maksym to make a deal with Stankovic to support young Petrovic and use the young man as cover for the uranium shipping. He was to document everything and send the intelligence back to Broadway House monthly through Regina and establish a trusted relationship with Petrovic. MI6 needed more sources in Yugoslavia and Hungary, both potential trouble spots for Moscow but for different reasons. In Hungary, the people were increasingly unhappy with the Stalinist government of the Hungarian People's Republic. Revolution could well lead to a Soviet invasion.

The operation was classified Codeword Level Top Secret as YELLOWCAKE. The chief of the Secret Intelligence Service, C, would be the only other person with access.

Chapter 22

B ucharest was once known as *Parisul Estului*, the Paris of the East. King Carol II had built the new Royal Palace, the Archul de Triumf, and the Gara de Nord. With the onset of war, the king declared Romania neutral, but Fascist elements in the government urged alliance with Nazi Germany as their traditional patrons France and Britain collapsed.

Bucharest had served as a major transit point for Nazi troops heading to the eastern front, so the Allies bombed the shit out the city until 1943. When the Romanians switched sides near the end, the Luftwaffe bombed the shit out of it again. The city's recovery, lacking a strong and ambitious leader like Tito, was slow.

Marius and the Draftsman took a table on the outside patio of a boisterous café across from the ruins of the Curtea Veche, the palatial home of Vlad III Dracula from the mid-1400s. A waiter arrived carrying two glasses and a bottle of Fetească Regală, a cheap native Romanian white wine that the Communists found particularly suitable to mass production.

"The first shipments have arrived in Warsaw, Marius. Comrade Balan must be pleased", the Draftsman said.

The young man shifted uneasily in his seat.

"I suppose. The extraction of the ore is proceeding well. We move it to the mill, crush, and leach it to separate the uranium and make the yellowcake powder concentrate that ends up on your trains. We will have to see how much more we have in the open-pit mine before we need to start drilling down. This part is easy and cheap, but once we have to start creating underground shafts and sending men down there, the cost will be very high."

The first containers of uranium ore had arrived arrive at Warszawa Główna railway station, and the Draftsman had traveled there to meet the train. It looked like just another cargo train pulling into a station full of passengers. The people, standing on the platform reading the state-run newspaper, *Rzeczpospolita*, were unaware of dozens of fifty-two-gallon drums filled with yellowcake.

Today, the young man was strangely quiet and pensive. He stared into his glass of Fetească Regală, swirling the golden wine but not saying anything. The silence became a little too much.

"Are we getting close to running the pit dry already?"

"No, but we have other problems."

"Such as?"

"It's nothing. Everything is fine."

The Draftsman just wasn't buying it. He was hiding something, but his body language didn't give any clues to the severity of the "other problems." They sat in an uncomfortable silence for a few minutes, punctuated by weak attempts to start conversation.

"Is there something you need to tell me? I can't help but think you are keeping something from me."

"There are bad things going on at the mine. Balan is using political prisoners to do the mining, and they are all dying. We've gone through thousands already. Their hair falls out. Their skin turns red and peels off. They cough and vomit. Then one day, they don't show up for work. The guards go to their cells to check and find them dead. The crematorium runs around the clock, and their families aren't even told. They are not real criminals. Nobody cares."

"Balan is aware of this?"

"Of course. He gets paid for each new prisoner he takes on. He doesn't care if they die. They'll just send him a new one, and he lines his pockets again. The prison is almost empty. Balan's hiring people from the nearby villages now. They have no idea. My cousin starts there next week. He has children, but I cannot tell him."

It struck the Draftsman, somewhat to his own surprise, that perhaps he was complicit in something he wanted no part of. He could set aside the discomfort he felt about allowing the Romanians to ship uranium into the Soviet Union to gather intelligence on the nuclear program, but innocent people dying by the thousand while Balan got rich? It changed the calculus.

When they met back in Frankfurt a week later, Giles was bewildered by the Draftsman's apparent distress over the issue. It happened all over the Soviet Union. Stalin's Siberian gulags, used political prisoners for all manner of awful jobs from working in coal mines to breaking big rocks into gravel. The living conditions were horrific, and, according to the analysts on the MI6 Soviet desk, more than a million people had died in them.

"There's a much bigger game here than a few prisoners dying of radiation poisoning. We need to know what the bloody Commies are up to."

The difference here, although blurry, was that Sovromcuart was supposedly a legitimate quartz mining business, not a government-run penal colony. It didn't seem to matter to Giles and that horrified the Draftsman.

The Soviets kept a tight lid on what happened to the drums of yellowcake after they arrived in Warsaw. A source who worked in the rail yard had revealed that it was driven to Vilnius in SSR Lithuania in the back of a truck. It left Warsaw at midnight and arrived in Vilnius before dawn. After that, who knew.

"When we know what we need to know, I want you to approve an operation to take Balan out. If you can't do that, I'll drop out right now."

"You can't. And you're being silly. But when the time is right, we will take care of Balan. You have my word. Now, how confident are you in the intelligence from this chap in the rail yard?"

"I believe he's telling the truth. No reason to think otherwise. He was well-paid and took no risk. We did a thorough check on him first. No known connections, family or otherwise, that would suggest ulterior motives to lie. Now, we need someone in Lithuania to tell us what happens next."

Chapter 23

Vilnius, Lithuanian SSR

The small hut, in the middle of the forest outside Vilnius, looked like an abandoned shed. The innocuous exterior disguised its true purpose as one of the hundred or more entry and exit points for the Forest Brothers into their underground network of bunkers and tunnels. Inside was a chair, a desk, a couple of candles, and a pile of blankets that its owner, Kostas Janulis, sometimes slept on. A tattered old carpet with a faded image of *Vytis*, the mounted white knight that symbolized the county's long history of independence, covered a trapdoor leading down into the tunnels.

Kostas didn't spend much time there, especially during the winter. He lived with his wife, Rasa, in one of the concrete tenements Stalin built around Vilnius to house the massive inflow of ethnic Russians. As Lithuanians and Jews, they were fortunate to get one, a benefit of Rasa's job at a new chemical processing plant on the outskirts of the city.

The first frost came almost a month early, driving the Forest Brothers underground for the winter. They survived on scraps and ammunition left in the forest by nearby farmers. They wouldn't surface until March to launch ambush attacks on the Red Army patrols that scoured the countryside for targets, mostly Lithuanian-born Poles and Germans, Catholics, and other anti-Soviet sympathizers.

Kostas wasn't a fighter anymore. A month in Lukiškės Prison had cost him both knees, the trigger finger on his right hand, and a big toe. His left ankle had been broken and never completely healed. His job now was to find food, money, and weapons for the Forest Brothers and look after the hut.

The Soviets annexed the Kingdom of Lithuania in 1940, collectivized the farms, and sent tens of thousands to the gulags of Siberia. A year and a half later, they lost it to the Nazis during Operation Barbarossa. Kostas and Rasa fled the Nazi invasion and headed south with the everyone else. His parents were two of the seventy thousand Lithuanian Jews murdered in the Paneriai Massacre of 1941. Two months and eight hundred miles later, they landed in Odessa and joined the Maksym Palatnik's resistance movement, Slava Ukrayini.

When the Red Army "liberated" Lithuania in 1944, the remaining citizens were beaten, murdered, looted, raped, displaced by an influx of thousands of Russian workers, and driven into poverty by collectivization. It was against this backdrop that the Forest Brothers were born, a guerrilla army of Lithuanians opposed to the Soviet occupation. When Kostas returned home in 1946, he immediately joined the Forest Brothers' fight.

With Stalin's death and Khrushchev's promise to unwind the oppressions of his regime, Kostas hoped things would change. Nothing changed, and, in fact, the KGB increased their operations in and around Vilnius, coaxing a web of greedy informers and scared citizens to name names, reveal hideout locations, and denounce Forest Brother members at sham trials. The hesitant were taken from their homes and held in Lukiškės prison until they buckled.

Kostas published and distributed articles about the Forest Brother's victories and their plight, hoping local farmers and independence-minded patriots would feed and arm the partisans. One of these articles made it out of Lithuania to Poland and from there into the hands of a British diplomat in Berlin.

It was sent to London, scrutinized and authenticated by MI6 analysts, and eventually landed on the desk of Giles Bancroft. Not knowing how to operationalize the intelligence, Giles had filed the document away for future reference.

It wasn't until the Draftsman informed him that the first shipments of yellowcake had traveled to a secret facility in Vilnius that he remembered the document and pulled out the file. Making contact with Kostas Janulis seemed like a good, if dangerous, idea.

"We need to make contact and cultivate this partisan, Janulis, in Vilnius through an asset we have in the government there. He'll make contact, establish a relationship, and persuade him that we're sympathetic to his cause. Then, at some point, we'll make an approach. We need to know where that ore is going and what they are using it for."

"Why would he help us?"

"Resources, dear boy. Food, clothing, weapons, ammunition, and money. He's going to need all of them all if these Forest Brothers are going to keep fighting the Russians. That, and he's an old friend of Palatnik from the resistance."

And so the months passed without further communication to the Draftsman on the topic. The shipments rolled on, and Marius' emotions grew increasingly hard to manage. The prison ran out of healthy workers for the mine. Desperate for work, local villagers took their jobs, and the death count climbed. Marius' sister, a nurse at what passed as a hospital, horrified her younger brother with stories of patients crippled by radiation poisoning. When his cousin died right before her eyes, Marius threatened to blow the whole scheme wide open.

The Draftsman played for time and bought his silence with cash, extra doses of Prussian Blue and DPTA to treat the victims, and countless bottles of Fetească Regală at the café across from Curtea Veche.

The silence from London continued until one night as he sat at the bar of the Hotel Przedziecki Palace in Warsaw, a haven for diplomatic banquets in the early postwar years. Its austere furnishings and decor had faded with a decade of Soviet neglect.

The delectable Regina appeared by his side once again. She picked him up and swept him up to a room on a high floor for sex and the exchange of intelligence. Before she slipped out into the night, she gave him a scrap of paper with a name, meet location, and an abort signal.

The cover story was simple enough on the surface. A western businessman operating legally in the Soviet republics meets with a mid-level official responsible for textiles and transportation. The first two meetings were to take place inside a heavily bugged government building so the tapes could be analyzed back in Moscow for any impropriety. The two strike a deal to allow a factory to reopen, stocked with high-quality western technology. They agree to host a conference and trade show in Vilnius to give the local officials a chance to brag and demonstrate their loyalty to Moscow. Unspoken, of course, was that the factory would be filled with Soviet immigrants, not local workers, a policy known as Russification. For the Lithuanians, reeducation camps or relocation to Siberia were the most likely outcome.

It was a slow and laborious courtship. The Draftsman made regular trips from Warsaw to Vilnius to maintain the facade. From Easter through the State Day of Lithuania on July 6, celebrating the crowning of the only King of Lithuania, Mindaugas, he buried himself in the culture of Vilnius and worked his way around a Communist Party bureaucracy that got bigger and more difficult to navigate by the day.

On Assumption Day in August, Regina confirmed what he already felt, that KGB scrutiny was backing off, leaving him with just his regular tail.

He arranged a meeting with the asset on a bench in Kanlai Park, near the Hill of Three Crosses, a monument to commemorate the beheading of friars in the 1300s. They apparently angered the city's citizens by preaching the gospel and disparaging Lithuanian pagan gods, so the monastery was burned. Seven friars were beheaded, and the rest crucified before their bodies were thrown into the Neris River. It was a bizarre thing to commemorate. The Soviets thought so too and had demolished the stone crosses.

Both men had KGB tails. They ambled conspicuously some distance behind but still within earshot. When the Draftsman and the asset sat on the bench, they stood awkwardly under a nearby birch tree. The language of choice for this meeting was Polish, with a smattering of English to keep the KGB on their toes and some innocent Russian epithets that the idiots charged with listening to them would remember.

They spoke in code, a cleverly constructed language that sounded like the business of textiles but was, in fact, something entirely different. When it was done, they stood, smiled, shook hands, and walked off in opposite directions.

In his report back to Giles, the Draftsman made note of a key piece of intelligence. Rasa Janulis worked in the cafeteria at what she believed was as a uranium processing plant and had agreed to help her husband find out where the material went from there. Naturally, Kostas wanted a steady flow of aid for the Forest Brothers in exchange. And the go-between, now an asset on the official MI6 payroll, wanted a payout as well.

At his next rendezvous with Regina in Warsaw, she confirmed that an agreement had been made and that Rasa and Kostas would be providing information back to him through the asset.

As they lay in bed, he said, "That's a lot of hands to pass this kind of intelligence through. Increases the risk of being discovered, don't you think?"

"We do it sometimes. It's called information laundering. Different people have different pieces of the whole, and it gets rearranged as it moves from one to the next person. No one can figure out what the intelligence is until all the pieces are decoded and reassembled back in London."

Who did she think she was talking to? This wasn't information laundering. For the first time, he questioned her truthfulness with him. And not for the first time, it struck him as odd that Regina and the long-absent Bruce were both Americans working for MI6.

Throughout the summer and into the autumn, shipments from the Băiţa mine ran north every two weeks. Each train car carried about twelve tons of yellowcake ready to be processed. A single car on the first trip became two, then four, and six within months. The horrors of Marius' stories of the mine notwithstanding, production at the mine was ramping up quickly.

The intelligence coming back to the Draftsman from the asset was threadbare, truck arrival times and dates in Vilnius, names of some government officials in the city associated with the project, but nothing concrete about what went on at the plant and where the yellowcake went from there. Giles's money and weapons continued to flow to the Forest Brothers, but the Draftsman grew antsy and impatient.

Regina tried to calm him down. "These things take time to develop. Move too quickly and someone gets exposed, and we have to roll the whole thing up before anyone gets killed."

"But the people in the mine are getting killed. We need to go faster."

"All right, calm down. Do you think we can prod the asset a little harder without exposing him?"

"Yes, but we might need a bargaining chip. Cut back on the supplies to Kostas. Winter's coming, and they'll all go into hibernation soon. Once that happens, we won't get anything useful until spring."

"Okay. I'll talk to Giles. Set up a meet with the asset. Squeeze but gently. This is not exactly your area of expertise. Set aside some of the more thuggish aspects of your personality in favor of diplomacy."

The pressure worked. The asset informed Kostas that the Brits needed results or the supplies would start drying up, starting with weapons and ammunition then moving quickly onto food and clothing, just as the winter approached. In late October, the asset set up a dead drop with the promise of "something special" to share. From under one of the stones of the former Three Crosses monument, the Draftsman retrieved a small cigarette case, and under the three scrawny cigarettes was a tiny piece of film wrapped in paper. He rode back on the train to Warsaw, and in his room at the Przedziecki Palace, the Draftsman cut away a tiny portion of the lining of his suitcase and slipped the film in. It fell all the way down.

He checked out and headed for Warsaw-Okecie airport and his flight to East Berlin, took the Interzonal Railway straight through West Berlin, across East Germany to Osnabrück on West German soil. From there, he jumped in a chauffeured car for the two-hundred-mile drive south to Saco-Lowell's Frankfurt office where Giles was waiting.

Chapter 24

Frankfurt, West Germany, 1956

Giles and the Draftsman stared at Rasa's translated note, the first concrete evidence that the uranium being shipped from Romania was being fed straight into the Soviet nuclear program. The note, projected onto a screen, courtesy of Broadway House Translation Services, read:

> *Vilnius to Gorkiy-130(Горький-130),*
> *also Arzamas-16 (Арзамас-16)*
> *Atomgrad Sarov, Nizhny Novgorod Oblast*

> *Transit between Vilnius and Gorkiy-130 overseen by Colonel Vasily Volvo, Ninth Directorate, KGB*

> *Atomgrad facilities security controlled by Lt. Col. Ivan Novikov, Fifteenth Directorate, KGB*

Atomgrads? That was a new one. The Soviets had dozens of closed cities called *pochtovyye yashchiki*, "mailboxes," where travel or residency restrictions were so strict that only a few people knew they even existed. They weren't on maps, but MI6 knew where some of them were. Presumably, Atomgrads were secret nuclear research, uranium processing, or weapons manufacturing sites.

The next block of text read:

> *RDS1 First Lightning "Первая молния/*
> *Pervaya Molniya"*
> *RDS2 Tritium "boosted" uranium device lev-*
> *itated core*
> *RDS3 Levitated plutonium core and ura-*
> *nium-235 shell*
> *RDS4 Boosted fission plutonium levitated core*
> *design*
> *RDS6 Hydrogen uranium 235 and lithium-6*
> *deuteride*
> *RDS 37 multi-staged, radiation implosion,*
> *Sakharov's "Third Idea"*

The Draftsman asked, "What is this?"

"If I'm not mistaken, it's a list of the Soviet's first seven nuclear weapons tests. They show progress in their capabilities. The naming convention is different with the last one, which suggests a significant change. I don't know what 'Sakharov's Third Idea' means or who Sakharov is."

"Bloody hell."

"This needs to go to the Americans."

"C will never approve it. The intelligence is single-sourced and completely unverified. Rasa could have made this up after a night of drinking Stakliškės. We did put pressure on them to produce, after all."

"Only the Americans have the ability to fly over this so-called Atomgrad and get the pictures to prove it exists. We have no other asset in the field that can corroborate or refute Rasa's intelligence."

He picked up the phone on his desk. "Yes, Marjorie. Would you be so kind as to get Wing Commander Horrocks at RAF Lavenheath on the phone, please? Ring me back when you have him on the line. And get me thirty minutes with C as quickly as possible. It's urgent."

Prime Minister Anthony Eden had approved the deployment of Lockheed U-2 planes out of Lakenheath in January to "study the weather and cosmic rays at altitudes up to 55,000 feet." The first CIA detachment of U-2s ("Detachment A") was therefore known publicly as the First Weather Reconnaissance Squadron, Provisional (WRSP-1).

Two days after Giles's call with the wing commander, the giant plane, dubbed "The Albatross" for its enormous wingspan, took off from RAF Lakenheath, with pilot CIA designation "JP"—one of just five certified U-2 pilots—at the helm. He climbed to more than forty-five thousand feet before he reached Kristiansand on the southernmost tip of Norway, banked northeast toward the Baltic Sea, added another ten thousand feet of altitude. He crossed into Finland near Oulu and entered radio silence. They wouldn't hear anything more until he contacted the tower at Incirlik Air Base in Turkey to confirm his safe return to NATO airspace about three and a half hours later.

JP was in Soviet airspace for an hour when he began his turn south toward Sarov over Veliky Ustyug, where the Sukhona and Yug Rivers met. Savov was only a few hundred miles east of Moscow, so this was the most dangerous segment of the trip.

The plane was equipped with three Hycon 732 high-altitude aerial reconnaissance cameras. They could capture objects as small as two feet across from a height of more than twelve miles. JP had spent countless hours at high altitude over the Arizona desert learning how to fly and take pictures with the new camera equipment at the same time. Doing it within five hundred miles of Moscow was an entirely different kettle of fish.

Chime...five-second pause...chime...three-second pause... chime...one-second pause...chime. He went to work.

The camera had more than 1,800 feet of Eastman Kodak's newly developed Mylar-based film, enough for thousands of photographs. His job now was to zoom in on at the secret nuclear research base near Sarov called *Gorkiy-130* without being shot down.

Ninety minutes later, safely in NATO airspace, he sent the signal, "Albatross 1 to tower. Weather is clear. Returning to base."

Chapter 25

Giles gave the go-ahead for the operation to go after Grigor Balan. The Draftsman and Maksym acquired an apartment in Balan's building, a former Austro-Hungarian palace overlooking Ferdinand I Square in Oradea, the capital of Bihor province. It was about twenty miles from the mine and close to the Hungarian border.

"There can be no, and I mean no, MI6 fingerprints on this op. This is not something we do, at least not in the current climate. Even here in Broadway House, no one can know," he had said, wagging his long index in the Draftsman's face.

He was referring, of course, to the continuing rumors circulating about a ring of Soviet moles buried inside MI6. Paranoia had been rampant ever since Kim Philby tipped off two Soviet spies, Guy Burgess and Donald McClean, that the game was up, and the two fled for Moscow. The details were still murky and not openly discussed around the office, but Burgess, a terrible alcoholic by all accounts, was under suspicion of meeting a Soviet KGB officer regularly. Philby had warned Burgess that an interrogation was imminent, and a cloud of suspicion lingered over Philby until he, too, was forced to leave MI6. Avoiding further embarrassment was paramount to Giles, who had his eye on the top job when C—Lord, help us all—finally gave up the throne. A botched assassination attempt on Soviet-controlled soil would scupper his plans, especially if the operation was exposed by another traitor in the Service.

Operational planning began in the basement of Broadway House. It wasn't quite an unused custodial closet but not far removed either. Desks and chairs were piled up against one wall, but the one opposite had a large whiteboard.

"You'll need to rely on resources in the region. This is your op, and we can't afford to send anyone from the service in there with you. That means it's you, Maksym, Popescu, and anyone else local. No Bruce and no Regina either. We cannot risk exposing them. They are significant actors in operations beyond our walls."

The penny dropped. They were CIA.

It wouldn't be easy to get to Balan. He kept a low profile and maintained his own secret police force to keep the lid on the uranium scheme. Moscow filled his pockets, and he had stashed millions in banks around Eastern Europe.

Six weeks later, the operation began when a nice couple moved into the Oradea apartment, roles played by Maksym's security head, Andrey Kuznetnov, and a Hungarian woman who was supposedly his wife. They got to know their neighbors and started going regularly to Cyrano, a nearby restaurant for the beef tarragon stew and cabbage rolls.

When the weather turned cold, the husband was unable to get out due to knee and hip pain from a war wound. They hired a young Englishman, who was studying in Oradea, to run errands and pick up food for them. He had immersed himself in conversational Romanian and Hungarian with a tutor—just enough to make friends and get by, not enough to raise suspicions.

He tried, unsuccessfully at first, to engage the gruff doorman, a retired officer in the Hungarian army, in some friendly banter. Softening him up was critical to the next part of the plan.

For the first several weeks, the doorman insisted on taking the food up to the couple. Eventually, he let the young man go up, noting which floor he got off the elevator and checking his watch to make sure it didn't take too long. After a month, he just opened the door and didn't pay attention after that, happy to avoid conversation with the annoyingly cheerful young man.

"I want you take this." Andrey pulled out his prized weapon, a Makarov MP-71 with a custom threaded barrel for a silencer. "I have family in Romania and Hungary. Balan dying by a bullet from my gun would be an honor. It's clean, and besides, they will think it was KGB. They are the only ones carrying these."

The Draftsman was about to ask him where he got it from, but thought better of it. Andrey's past was opaque at best, and it would not be a surprise to know that he had KGB connections.

The next day, carrying the usual bag of food, the young man entered the apartment building around 7:00 p.m., got off the elevator at the old couple's floor, then headed for the emergency staircase to climb the additional two floors.

Two men were posted outside the apartment door. They turned when the staircase door opened, reaching into their lapels for their guns. Two quick pops from the Makarov and they fell to ground. The Draftsman dragged their bodies into the stairwell.

Back at Balan's door, he put on his balaclava, quickly picked the lock, and entered the apartment, Makarov in hand.

Balan was sitting with his back to the door at an ornate table eating dinner. A neighbor, tempted by an envelope of money to keep an eye on the coming and goings in Balan's apartment, had confirmed that he was alone that night. The cameras and bugs hadn't picked up anything untoward since Balan returned home from work. He pushed the suppressor into the base of his skull, and Balan froze.

In his conversational Romanian, the Draftsman said, *"Vino cu mine, domnule Balan. Foarte pașnic și liniștit sau te voi omorî."* Come with me, Mr. Balan. Very peacefully and quietly or I will kill you.

The Draftsman marched him down seven flights of the back stairs to a waiting car. The Halothane-soaked cloth rendered Balan unconscious in seconds, and when he awoke, his hands and feet were bound. It was dark except for a small lamp in the far corner of a very big room. In the shadows, a man sat on a stool, staring at him, the long barrel of a pistol pointing in his direction.

"You are awake, Comrade Balan," he said in Romanian. "It's time for you to talk about the uranium and the dead prisoners who worked the mines. Are you ready to do that?"

"Who the fuck are you? I have nothing to say. Now, fucking untie me!"

Behind him, Balan heard the whirring of a tape machine and the slow, deep breathing of another person then the burning pinch of a needle in the back of his neck.

"This will help you talk. And if you don't, I have this."

The muzzle was warm against his neck.

Chapter 26

Balan's body was found at the bottom of his own pit mine. A newspaper report in *Adevărul* noted multiple broken bones and head trauma resulting from a high fall, injuries inflicted post-mortem. It was a single 9mm gunshot to the forehead that was the official cause of death.

All the signs pointed toward a KGB interrogation and execution, which was exactly what the Draftsman wanted them to think. The weapon used was a new Soviet military pistol, a Makarov. The autopsy uncovered multiple injection sites, presumably for sedatives, and marks on his wrists indicating his hands were tied behind his back.

The brutal murder of an important Romanian businessman and political power broker was big news in Bucharest. Prime Minister Chivu Stoica traveled to Moscow to formally protest the killing to Khrushchev.

To avoid further embarrassment and save face, the two signed an agreement to replace the jointly-owned Sovromcuart with a new, wholly Romanian state-owned company—run by a Soviet-friendly man, of course—that would continue mining and processing of uranium ore and delivering its entire output to the Soviet Union. The Soviet stake in the company was set at 413 million rubles, which they converted into debt payable by Romania over the following ten years. Stoica agreed to the terms and claimed victory.

But Moscow's new man in charge, a severe alcoholic presumably banished to the Romanian/Hungarian border as punishment for some indiscretions around the Kremlin, had little interest in running it. The flow of uranium from the mine slowed the following year, and by 1959, the mine closed for good. By the end, the death toll from radiation poisoning topped fifteen thousand, a ton of uranium ore to fuel the Soviet nuclear program for each person who died working there.

Giles and the Draftsman met at Hampden Park, Glasgow, in May 1960 for the European Cup Final between Real Madrid and Eintract Frankfurt. The Draftsman had tickets to be among the 130,000 that descended on the stadium. It was a 7–3 thrashing for the outclassed Frankfurt team unfortunately. Legendary Hungarian Ferenc Puskás scored four, and Alfredo "The Blond Arrow" Di Stéfano added the other three.

"Things are changing, Draftsman. The Cold War has entered a new phase, the Space Race. Everyone's still building nuclear weapons, of course, but getting to the moon is going rely on nuclear fuel too."

The Soviets had developed the world's first intercontinental ballistic missile, R-7 Semyorka, and launched at least fifteen test missiles already. In just a few years, the Soviets had advanced space exploration by first blasting low earth satellites into orbit with Sputnik 1 and 2, followed by Luna 1, the first to achieve escape velocity and break free of the earth's gravitational influence. Luna 2 was the first object to land on the moon, and Luna 3 was busy snapping photos of the dark side of moon. The Americans were falling behind.

"This isn't just going to be about tracking what the Soviets are up to anymore. Our friends across the pond want to get a lot more active."

"I'm not sure I understand. What are you asking?"

"We're drawing it up now. Operation Undercut. It's a long-term plan to undermine relations between Moscow and the other members of the Warsaw Pact. Sow the deeds of discontent, you know. The whole Balan affair put a lot of pressure on the relationship between the Soviets and Romania. We can't do much about a nuclear arms race or the space race now, but Undercut is designed to go underneath. Death by a thousand small cuts as they say."

"And this plan, Undercut, involves me how?"

"Well, you're our most connected asset in the region. And you're not an employee of the Foreign Office or the security services. You have a degree of access that would take years to replace. We just don't have that kind of time. It's your patriotic duty."

They sat in silence for a long time. He was about to claim that he was just a businessman and not bound by obligations of patriotism, but he caught himself. He'd killed someone, several people in fact, and Giles knew it. It was foolish to claim businessman status now.

The final whistle blew. The Real Madrid supporters—joined by the locals who had watched Frankfurt humiliate their team Rangers 12–7 on aggregate in the semifinals—roared. Real Madrid's captain, José María Zárraga, raised the trophy. The East Stand, better known at the "Celtic End," began emptying as the fans streamed out to fill Glasgow's Mount Florida and King's Park area pubs. The Draftsman took a long draw on his cigarette, turning away from Giles to blow out the plume.

"Do we really know what we're doing here, Giles? I have to say that, given all the scandals, defections, doubles, triples, and mole hunts, you are asking me to participate in something that I don't think your office can handle. Things are really starting to get ugly with the Soviets. Then there's the downing of that spy plane."

Less than a month earlier, an American U-2 had been shot down near Sverdlovsk, deep in Soviet airspace, with an S-75 Dvina surface-to-air missile. Initially, Eisenhower had acknowledged only the loss as a civilian weather research aircraft operated by NASA. He claimed the pilot suffered oxygen deprivation over Turkey and that autopilot had carried the plane into Soviet airspace. They were left red-faced a few days later when the Soviet government produced the pilot, surveillance equipment, and photographs of Soviet military bases taken during the mission.

"Indeed, so much for the so-called Spirit of Camp David! Khrushchev is a clever bugger. He let the Americans weave their fantastical story knowing all along that the pilot was alive and most of the plane intact. The Summit in Paris next month will go down in flames just like that U-2."

The stadium was close to empty now, except for the first of the cleanup staff making their way through the lower terraces picking up litter. It was nine thirty in the evening, and a cold wind whipped around the empty stadium.

"Up for quick a pint down on Somerville Street?"

Chapter 27

East Berlin, British Zone of Occupation

The bed in the Hotel Charlottenburg Savoy was not up to the task. It sagged in the middle, but, more importantly, the legs creaked and groaned as the Draftsman and Regina made love for the third time in as many hours. Strong bed frames and firm mattresses were rare even in the best hotels in East Berlin.

They'd had a quick dinner and a few drinks at the Fox and Hound, one of a growing number of tacky nostalgic reminders of home in the British sector, before returning to their hotel. They took a roundabout route, stopping and starting, retracing their steps, and standing in front of shop windows looking for tails in the reflections.

Theirs was a carefully crafted relationship. Their KGB file characterized her affair with the Draftsman as a casual attempt "to poke a stick in the eye of her boss and former lover, Bruce Lasher." They portrayed Bruce as an *obmanutyy muzh*, a cuckold aware of the couple's surreptitious trysts who took pleasure in their shared betrayal of him.

Nothing could have been further from the truth, of course. The relationship between Bruce and Regina was an imaginary bond curated and managed by the agency. In fact, Bruce neither knew nor cared about the libidinous affair between the couple. He had plenty of relationships of his own in Italy with far fewer strings than the agency could attach and more passion than a midwestern American woman could supply. But the image of an emasculated Bruce served KGB purposes.

For his part, the Draftsman told himself that Regina was just a way to pass information from east to west and also satisfy carnal needs on long trips away from home. In-between times, however, he wrote guilt-ridden letters home to his wife, Adeline, riddled with flowery but deceitful excuses for his absence and empty promises to make it up to her when he got home. In time, his feelings grew into something more than carnal. He didn't love Regina, but close, and he felt ashamed.

Naturally, MI6 intercepted and reviewed all his letters before sending them on. The psychologist's assessment was that the Draftsman was teetering, that his affection for Regina was more than professional, and that they were taking him too deep.

"He's at a fork in the road, sir. We ask him to do more than the usual businessman-as-asset program. The Balan operation was an inflection point. We lured him into a kidnap, interrogate, and kill operation. He went along with it because he didn't know what else to do. With Undercut, we've dropping him into more perilous situations, and it's all coming home to roost."

No doubt, he was in too deep with Palatnik. They had to decide what to do with him—either put him out to pasture before he got killed, sold out MI6, or take him all the way down the rabbit hole and live with consequences.

The service could ill afford to lose an asset tied so deeply into the fabric of the Soviet underworld. For more than a decade, the service had cajoled the Draftsman into situations that were dangerous both diplomatically and personally. Losing him would be a disaster, but the world sat a nuclear inflection point, and the Draftsman was in the middle of it.

"What do you suggest, Doctor?"

"Bring him in for an in-depth debriefing. Make him think the game is up. Expose and threaten him, subtly, of course, about his past activities. Then give him a choice, are you in or out for the next phase? And see which way he goes. Let him choose the direction."

"Okay. Let's get Regina to bring him then."

Putting Regina back in had bought them time. She calmed and focused him on the task hand. However, he appeared to be falling in love with her, and fearing exposure, she did little to discourage it.

Sitting naked on the edge of the bed, she lit a cigarette and blew a long stream of smoke up to the yellowed ceiling.

He didn't entirely trust her. She was CIA. Bruce was CIA too. There was just something about Americans that he couldn't quite trust. He understood Giles.

"It's getting harder to move around these days," he said. "They're checking papers, asking more questions, and focusing on westerners."

It was an innocent-enough comment, but her time to respond made him think. Her gaze was fixed on the French door window overlooking the Fasanenstraße synagogue across the street.

Eventually, she said, "It's going to get worse. The analysts are saying that the occupation deal is falling apart. Khruschev wants to sign a separate deal with East Germany to kill the Allied Control Council agreements. They've got thousands fleeing East Germany for the west every month. They'll probably close the border altogether."

Walter Ulbricht, First Secretary of the Socialist Unity Party (SED) and head of the German Democratic Republic (GDR) government, had asked the Soviets for help with *Republikflucht* (desertion from the republic) to West Germany. It all seemed so inevitable. Berlin's four-power status assured free travel between the zones of occupation and forbade the presence of German troops in Berlin. Nonetheless, Ulbricht convinced the Soviet Union that force was necessary to stop its population leaving for the West.

The Draftsman said, "I have a contact inside Ulbricht's government. He came to us looking for a deal to make a hundred thousand new uniforms for the Grenztruppen. He told me that the government is stockpiling materials for a barbed-wire fence and a wall. Hard to believe, don't you think?"

"Not at all. I wouldn't be surprised actually. This contact of yours. Should we be cultivating him? Do you think he wants something from us?"

She still had her back to him, the smoke swirling above her head like Medusa's snakes.

"I don't know, Regina. Recruiting spies isn't really my area of expertise, to be honest. But it sounds like you might have it in your background?"

She turned to him, perhaps a little too sharply. "I'm just a courier, Ben, if that's even your real name. If you think this is someone we should be talking to, I'll pass the message on. That's all. And don't pretend you aren't up to your ears in this shit."

She dressed quickly without saying anything else. He'd hit a nerve. Was she offended by his insinuation or concerned that her role in his life was something other than what she portrayed? Or was she threatening him?

"I didn't mean to suggest you are pretending to be something you're not or that I'm innocent either. I'm just feeling like this whole situation is on course to be something I'm not equipped for."

"No one is equipped for the unknown. If you can't trust me, they can put someone else in here and I'll go home. They want you back in London for a chin-wag."

She snapped on her remaining stiletto sling-back and marched out without looking back. She didn't slam the door behind her, but it felt like it.

At midnight on August 12, 1961, less than a week after Regina's abrupt departure, the government of the GDR closed the inner German border to foot-and-vehicle traffic. East German soldiers tore up the streets, making them impassable for most vehicles, and erected barbed wire entanglements around the ninety-seven miles of the three western sectors and the twenty-seven miles that actually divided West and East Berlin.

The Draftsman, caught on the East German side of the border, was told that he would have to wait until all the new security procedures were in place before he could cross back into West Berlin. As an important businessman in both the GDR and the Soviet Union, he was assured that moving across the border would not be a problem but the Grenztruppen border guards were not completely trained on the protocols yet. It was risky to attempt a border crossing with tensions running so high.

Within weeks, the East German army, police force, and volunteer construction workers had completed a makeshift barbed wire and concrete block wall that divided one side of the city from the other. Watchtowers, gun placements, and sniper positions soon followed.

Chapter 28

East Berlin, Soviet Zone of Occupation

I n late August, the Staatsoper Unter den Linden Opera House performed Wagner's *Die Meistersinger von Nürnberg* to raise the spirits of the East German population—at least the portion of the population with the means and connections to get tickets. The theater was packed with military uniforms and government officials.

The Draftsman was still trapped in East Berlin He and his source sat high up in the balcony, just two businessmen working on a deal to open a textile factory in Marzahn-Hellersdorf. At almost four and half hours long, the two breaks between acts were the only time the two could talk. As the house lights went up, most people around them headed for the bar or the toilet. The Draftsman and the source slipped through a side door into a hallway to smoke, propping the door open with a bucket.

"Belomrokanals burn through quickly, so we must be quick. Blow your smoke back into the theater so they know we are right here. I have something very important for you, a photo of the U-2 pilot shot down over Soviet Union."

The pilot had been convicted of espionage and sentenced to ten years in Vladimir Central Prison. Apparently, his cellmate was a Ukrainian political prisoner who fought the Nazis with Maksym Palatnik.

"And how, exactly, do you know this Ukrainian cellmate?"

"He's a cousin. My father is Polish and my mother Ukrainian. Every summer, we went to Lviv, where my mother's side lived. When the Nazis sent them all to the camps, he escaped and went to Odessa and joined the resistance. After liberation, he went back and pub-

138

lished a pro-independence newspaper. The Soviets got tired of his shit-stirring and hauled him off to Vladimir. He got the letter out to me through a prison guard."

"And why are you telling me this?"

"I want to get out before it's too late. My wife and children left for the American sector a couple of months ago. Now, we are separated and don't know when, if ever, we can be together again."

"What makes you think I can do anything to help with that? Even if I could, it would put me at enormous risk."

"I have no one else. You move freely back and forth, so you must have connections that protect you. If I get proof, can you help?"

"I have no idea. I don't get involved in this kind of thing. I'll talk to my boss when I get back to England. I don't know when that will be."

They left together, shaking hands at the front entrance before heading in opposite directions. The Draftsman turned right on Unter den Lindenstraße. It was a warm night, and the late summer roses were blooming in the beds that lined the wide boulevard. Even with the new interzonal travel restrictions and the prospect of severe Soviet rule, life, at least for now, ran as normal.

How long would it last? Probably not too long if the source's plans for the factory to make Stasi and Grenztruppen uniforms was any indication of the future for citizens of East Berlin.

He felt someone behind him, maybe thirty feet back, steps taken at the same pace but a fraction of a second behind his own. Like an echo. He was used to being followed, of course, so he avoided slowing down or trying to look back. The width of the boulevard prevented him for casually glancing at a window on the opposite of the street to see who it was. But something was off. He could feel it. But picking up his pace would only raise alarms. Was he about to be robbed? The steps didn't sound like a robber. They were colder, steady, and more ominous.

To get back to his hotel in the Mitte district, he had to cross two bridges, and in between, there was an enormous park that was mostly deserted at this time of night.

The Marx-Engels-Brücke Bridge that spanned the Spree Canal was just ahead. If an assault was going to happen, this was the spot. It was quiet and poorly lit. His lifeless body could be easily tossed over and float unnoticed for miles through Friedrichswerder until the canal reconnected downstream with the Spree River.

On the left was the wide-open space of Lustgarten and on his right stood the remains of the Berlin Palace, bombed by the Allies during the war and finished off by the East Germans in the early 1950s. He decided to stick to the right and make a run for the ruins of the palace. The burned-out rubble of the Berlin Palace at least offered places to hide.

But in his stomach, he knew he wouldn't make it that far. The steps behind him quickened. And when he was about halfway over the bridge, the man called out. "*Herr! Bitte! Bitte hör auf!*"

As ordered, he stopped and automatically reached into his coat pocket for his papers and turned back to his tail.

"How can I help you, Comrade?"

The man was clearly Stasi, despite his ridiculous attempt to look like an ordinary citizen of Berlin. It was summer, and he wore a thick wool coat, an ushanka fur hat, and cheap sunglasses.

"I'm sorry to bother you," the Stasi officer began, "but I would like to talk to you about your colleague, Herr Dieter Müller."

"Are you an officer of the GDR government? What authority do you have to ask me such questions? We are business partners working for the good of East Germany and the Soviet Union."

The young man, clearly out of his depth, stiffened his spine and did his best to be intimidating. "I want to know what you and Herr Müller discussed at the opera."

"You still haven't answered my question. Are you an officer of the GDR?"

"I am."

"What department?"

"You would do well not to ask such questions, Herr Pike." The young man was gaining confidence. Definitely Stasi.

"We are working together to open a factory in Marzahn-Hellersdorf, at the direction of Herr Ulbricht. To manufacture uniforms for the East German military. You, with all your suspicions and insinuations, may be stepping into dangerous territory. Do you know what you are getting into?"

"Do not threaten me, Herr Pike. I have the authority to arrest you and take you to Hohenschönhausen for questioning."

"I resent this infringement of my rights and will speak to the ambassador about your atrocious behavior."

"The times have changed for you, Herr Pike. They have changed for us all. You are here now. Your ambassador has left East Berlin. You are alone here. Now, about your conversation with Herr Müller? You left the theater to smoke in a hallway. I would like to know what you discussed there."

"I already told…"

The officer pulled out a Walther PP semiautomatic pistol, pressing the barrel hard against the Draftsman's forehead. "I will not have any more avoidance of my questions. Tell me now the details of your subversive exchange or I will arrest you as a foreign spy. You won't see the outside world for months if ever."

The Draftsman's knee rose quickly into the officer's groin. As he fell forward in agony, an uppercut under the chin reversed the momentum, dropping the German flat on his back. The Draftsman ran hard toward the Berlin Palace. He heard the officer get up, shout something in German, and shoot. The shot was wildly off target, the bullet tearing into a tree about ten yards to his left, sending bits of bark flying in every direction. More unintelligible German and a second shot, still off target but closer. He felt the heat of the passing bullet on his right ear and jumped over a low wall, hiding behind what was once a side entrance to the palace.

The running footsteps coming toward him slowed. The Draftsman carefully retrieved his Makarov from the inside pocket of his overcoat. The officer was so close that as he crept around the corner, the cloud of breath on this unusually chilly evening gave the Draftsman a few seconds advance warning. He slowly raised his arm above his head, holding the Makarov by the barrel.

Step…step…step…turn… The butt of the gun came down hard on the crown of the Stasi officer's head. It sounded like the cracking of an eggshell. He stood frozen for a second before his eyes rolled into the back of his head, and he fell back landing on one of the old palace's stones. A large pool of burgundy blood drained from the back of his skull and spread quickly into large pool on the ground.

Panic surged. He had just killed a Stasi officer on East German soil. He had to get back to West Germany immediately.

He carried his travel permit for the Interzonal Railway that could take him all the way to Osnabrück without stopping. It was a ten-minute walk to Berlin Friedrichstraße station past the opera house, then right on Charlottenstraße, left on Mitellstraße, and a quick right on Friedrichstraße. It was a roundabout way, but these streets were dark, and anyone following, or chasing, was easily spotted.

As usual, Grenztruppen guards were posted at every entrance to the station. From across the street, he reached into his pocket for his travel permit and passport. His fingers fell on a small cylindrical container that was not there when he left the hotel. Someone, presumably the source, had slipped something into his pocket at the opera.

What kind of GDR secret was he now carrying? He took a deep breath and marched confidently across the street to the youngest and sleepiest-looking guard he could find. The boy reviewed his papers, eyed him lazily, and waved him through.

Chapter 29

M16 analysts at Broadway House confirmed it. A negative hidden inside the cylinder in his pocket was, in fact, a photograph of missing U-2 pilot, Frank Porter. On a table to Porter's right was a copy of Pravda dated September 12, 1961.

Porter wrote letters to his wife from Vladimir Prison each month, but they didn't sound like him. Grammatical errors and overly positive statements about the conditions and his treatment in prison signaled to her that someone else was telling him what to write. The fact that the letters still arrived in his handwriting at least confirmed he was alive and gave her hope for his safe return one day. But this was the first photographic evidence that he was alive. Giles and the Draftsman hunched over the enlarged and grainy photograph illuminated by a desk lamp in the darkened office.

The heavy drapes were drawn to block out the midday light. It was a cloudy and cold January London day, so the midday light was hardly a problem. Giles had insisted nonetheless. He pressed a large magnifying glass to his stronger right eye and moved slowly and carefully across the image.

There was little doubt that scene was staged. Porter, still in his flight suit, looked healthy, his hair brushed, and clean shaven. The same could not be said, however, for the poor wretch standing to his left, emaciated and in filthy clothes with a long, unkept beard.

The message was clear. This is what a few years in Vladimir Prison will do to your spy, so act quickly if you want him back.

"Looks like they cleaned him up for it," Giles pronounced as he stood up straight, putting down the magnifying glass and pressing both palms into the small of his aching back. "The Americans are in two minds about him. The CIA Counterintelligence chief thinks Porter defected to the Soviet side and used the spy plane and all its technological wizardry as leverage. He says that he gave the Soviets everything and, therefore, has no trade value. President Kennedy disagrees and wants to get him home. Porter's wife is apparently running all over the Washington social scene demanding action."

"Let me guess. They want us to make the trade and leave the US out of it."

"The president has given the go-ahead." He paused for a moment to light his pipe. "They're flying over some KGB colonel from the Hollow Nickel Case as trade bait."

"The what case?"

"Hollow nickel. Coded messages hidden inside an American coin. Anyway, he got thirty years and has steadfastly refused to confess anything. Won't even tell them his real name. You leave for Frankfurt tomorrow."

"You want me to run this operation? I have no idea what—"

Giles interrupted, "It's your source that's working the Soviet side to get this done. We can't put someone else in there now. The whole bloody thing will go up in smoke. Regina will meet you in Berlin and coach you through it."

It had been a year since their last meeting at the Charlottenburg in Berlin. It wouldn't be the same as before. Adeline had put him through hell about it. After a few Scotches, he'd confessed his betrayal. It made him feel better, but not her, of course. He hadn't tried to blame it on the stress of the job or loneliness of business travel but on a weakness of character that he needed to work on. She'd slapped him so hard across the face that his ears rang for days. Then she walked out, leaving him with the boys, to move back in with her parents for a while. Eventually, she returned, but it was different.

Giles returned his attention to the photograph, gesturing toward the door with his free hand. The Draftsman was dismissed. As he was about to walk through the door, Giles said, "And, Draftsman, do try to keep your hands to yourself. This is an operation, not a romantic weekend in Paris."

He replied "Yes, sir" and, under his breath, added, "You twat."

The next day, Giles handed him a manila folder with the required papers, passport, and personal profile to memorize. He would enter East Berlin as a Romanian businessman returning from a two-day permitted trip to the West. On the train to Potsdam, he would brush up on the language as well as he could. Hopefully, he wouldn't need it. It was highly unlikely that any of the Grenztruppen at the border spoke Romanian or recalled that a Romanian left East Berlin. They might check surveillance logs but would come up with nothing.

"Set up the meet with your source, give him back the same pen he gave you. It now contains a negative with instructions for the exchange. Remember to destroy these documents before you leave the GDR and return to West Berlin with your usual credentials. Now, off you go to the Costume Department for your fitting."

The Costume Department dyed his hair jet-black, adding a few flecks of gray and thin streak of white to age him. He traded in his fashionable Wayfarer glasses for an ugly pair of Soviet industrial style jam-jar bottoms. They handed him a suitcase of prepacked clothes that he could change into before going to the Friedrichstraße train station checkpoint. Finally, he was fitted with a bushy fake mustache and told not to shave for a day or two.

Back in Giles's office for his final operational review, he said, "I look like a bloody fool!"

"Don't be silly!" Giles replied, barely able to suppress a grin. "You can't waltz into East Berlin looking like Marlon Brando, can you? You're a beaten-down Romanian businessman living under a Communist regime. You've got to look the part."

They ran through his personal profile one last time. Giles grilled him on the smallest of details, had an associate bombard him with questions in Romanian, and checked all the papers for accuracy.

After an hour, he said, "Right, on your way, my boy. Regina will meet you at your hotel in Berlin to see what you have for her. Information, I mean."

The innuendos were growing tiresome. Giles knew about their relationship, if you could call it that. Sleeping with him was part of her cover, a cover Giles presumably helped create. Giles's confidence in Regina seemed almost unimpeachable.

Two days later, he left his flat in the Sachsenhausen district of Frankfurt headed for the Hauptbahnhof, a twenty-minute walk down Schweizerstraße and across Untermainbrücke—once known as the Adolf Hitler Bridge—that spanned the Main River. He boarded the Interzonal train bound for Potsdam Pirschheide on the outer ring of the Berlin rail system.

The train rattled north through the regions of Hesse and Saxony before bending to the east at Hildesheim and crossing the East German border. In the bathroom, he changed into his disheveled Romanian business disguise. His well-worn overcoat had a thick but sour-smelling wool collar, an inner lining with seams splitting at the armpits, and a strategically placed missing button. He hid his real papers in the hidden compartment of his suitcase with his camera and the Makarov and slid his Romanian documentation in the inside pocket of his coat.

As expected, the first "stop" in the GDR was Magdeburg. The train was held for over an hour while border guards and Stasi officers rummaged through bags, checked papers, and questioned passengers.

"*Was war ihr geschäft in Westdeutschland, Herr...Lazarescu?*" What was your business in West Germany, Herr Lazarescu?

"*Nur ein treffen mit einem britischen textilunternehmen. Wir stellen Ihnen wärmere uniformen für den nächsten winter her.*" Just a meeting with a British textile company. We are making you some warmer uniforms for next winter.

"*Ich verstehe. Ihr Deutsch ist sehr gut.*" I see. Your German is very good.

"*Danke. Meine Mutter stammte aus Salzburg und lernte meinen vater an der Universität Wien kennen.*" Thank you. My mother was from Salzburg and met my father at the University of Vienna.

The officer seemed satisfied with the explanation, looked him up and down, then turned to one of his colleagues.

"*Sieht aus als könnte er eine eigene neue uniform gebrauchen!*" Looks like he could use a new uniform of his own!

Laughing, they moved on to the next compartment, and the Draftsman settled back into his seat. Through the dirty window, he saw an older man dragged from the train and thrown to the ground on the platform. He was surrounded, kicked a few times, then hauled away into the station terminal.

At Potsdam, he took a taxi to his usual, the Hotel Charlottenburg Savoy. Regina was waiting in his room.

"You look well, Ben. It's been a while. We swept the room for bugs, so no need to entertain the listeners."

The next day, an unusually cold day even for Berlin in late January, he dressed and wrapped himself again in the overcoat, carefully placed the mustache and glasses, and pulled on a wool hat to cover his ears.

Regina inspected him and tugged on the woolen collar.

She said, "*Omul de afaceri român perfect!*" The perfect Romanian businessman!

"I didn't know you spoke Romanian!"

"I don't. I've been practicing that phrase for weeks!"

At the station, he joined a line of people crossing into East Berlin. Not surprisingly, it was short and quick. The GDR was more than happy to let people in but willing to shoot them from one of the towers for trying to get out. Reports of snipers killing East Germans trying to run across no-man's land to the west were common now.

This direction, it was all smiles and welcomes. Off to the side, in a shadow near the steps that led down to the tracks, Stasi officers watched casually, smoking their Belomorkanal cigarettes. One had a camera and took a picture of everyone who came through.

When he reached the front of the line, the guard looked at his papers, smiled, and spoke to him in broken Romanian. Shit.

"*Cât timp ai fost în Berlinul de Vest?*" How long were you in West Berlin?

His accent was terrible, but the words and verbs conjugation were correct. Trouble. Thankfully, the Romanian rolled of his tongue much easier than he expected.

"*Doar câteva zile. Afaceri. Mă bucur că vin acasă.*" Just a few days. Business. Glad to be coming home.

The guard shuffled uneasily, grunted, and flipped through his papers. It was more Romanian than he could handle.

He switched to German. "*Danke. Willkommen zurück in der Deutschen Demokratischen Republik.*" Welcome back to the German Democratic Republic.

He waved the Draftsman through and quickly moved on to the next person in line. "*Papiere, bitte.*"

Chapter 30

Lustgarden, East Berlin

I t didn't seem like the best idea to meet the source on a bench in the still bomb-pitted wasteland of the Lustgarten, a once beautiful garden that Hitler had paved over to hold his mass rallies.

"We'll have a surveillance team on you," Regina had assured him. "Sometimes, it's better to be out in the open than in the shadows. Just don't look suspicious. Look like a miserable East German feeding the flying rats until he shows up," she had told him.

It was mostly deserted but had benches under the lime trees around the outside that had been planted to make it look less like a parade ground and more like a bombed-out parade ground surrounded by lime trees. The Draftsman felt very exposed despite wearing a thick black overcoat, hat, glasses, and a fake mustache.

He sipped a cup of glühwein to fend off the cold early winter wind coming off the Spree River. It was weak and tasted vaguely of vinegar. A half-starved dog in search of food approached cautiously from his right. He shooed the wretched creature away.

The distinctive sound of Stasi boots on patrol passed behind him. They stopped briefly, and the officers exchanged some words he couldn't understand while they lit their cigarettes before moving on.

Once again, it struck him that Regina was deeper in the operation than she let on. "I'm just the messenger, Ben," she had said. Who had set up the meet with the source? They clearly had enough contact with him to arrange it. Why did they need him for this? He recalled Giles's words back at Broadway House.

"It's your source working the Soviet side to get this done. We can't put someone else in there now."

And yet, somehow, someone had made this arrangement without him, and Regina seemed to be at the center of it. He felt like a pawn in a game he really didn't know how to play.

His backside was getting numb. The wind whipped, and the ghosts of Hitler's mass rallies hung in the air. Pigeons gathered and pecked around his feet. He plucked a piece of stale bread from his pocket and began breaking it up into small pieces. He checked his watch. Two minutes more then abort and try again tomorrow. He heard steps come up from behind him, not hurried like someone in a panic or slow like someone about to put a bullet in the back of his head. Eyes forward. Feed the birds.

"*Darf ich diesen Platz einnehmen?*" May I take this seat?

"*Natürlich. Es ist eine kalte nacht und die tauben müssen fressen.*" Of course. It's a cold night, and the pigeons need to eat."

"*Hast du etwas mehr brot zum teilen?*" Do you have extra bread to share?

"*Ich mache. Es wäre eine schande für sie, zu unger.*" I do. It would be a shame for them to go hungry.

A negative response was the signal to the source to abort.

"*Tauben fressen alles.*" Pigeons will eat anything.

Any other phrase was also a signal to abort.

The source sat down and accepted a hunk of bread with the pen buried in the middle. He switched to English.

"I presume your colleagues were intrigued with the photograph?"

"They were."

He broke off a small chunk of the bread, crumbled it into small pieces, and tossed them to the hungry pigeons. They swarmed around his feet, strutting and making prolonged cooing sounds.

"I presume you have a plan for me? The walls are closing in."

"We're aware. The East German authorities were unnerved by our meeting at the opera. Have they come round knocking?"

It was a trick question created by Giles. If the source had been questioned and admitted it, then he was probably reliable. If not, it could be a trap.

"They did. They also stopped by my office to ask questions about you."

"What kind of questions?"

"Well, what kind of business arrangement we had, how often had we met, and if I suspected you were a British spy. I gave them two-thirds of the truth and crossed my fingers on the other third."

"And yet here you are."

"Here I am. I think it was a foolish choice of location to be honest, so open and easily monitored. There are millions of fucking pigeons in Berlin and much safer places to feed them. So is there a plan for me?"

"Yes, but you need to get a message to someone about an exchange. That has to happen first. Then I will come back with the necessary papers for you to cross over."

"Who are you offering?"

"A KGB Colonel. He's been in a US prison for a few years. I've been assured that it will be seen as a fair trade."

The source was quiet. He looked around the remains of Lustgarden wistfully.

"You know, my father came to this place to listen to Hitler. He came home, with a rush of blood to the head, to my mother and I, spouting the lies and xenophobia he heard here. He believed it even as the walls crumbled around him. And now, we have Ulbricht, the Stasi, and the Soviets to put up new walls."

The Draftsman had no interest in a regretful trip down memory lane. Even the pigeons looked around nervously. "We should go now. You have everything you need in your pocket. Take it where it needs to go, and we can meet again to confirm the plan."

He stood up, made a show of their parting handshake, and said, perhaps a little too loudly, "It is a pleasure doing business with you for the benefit of the German Democratic Republic. I look forward to consummating our agreement," and disappeared into the darkness beyond the lime trees.

The pigeons circled around the Draftsman's feet, scavenging the remaining crumbs. He kicked one, and in a mass panic, they all flapped their wings and took off.

The prisoner, was already at RAF Lakenheath. He'd arrived in the middle of the night with a bag over his head and hands and feet shackled. He was led down the ramp of the USAF Douglas C-133 Cargomaster by a man in a dark suit, sunglasses, and a Trilby hat and encircled by armed guards and immediately transferred to another plane to West Berlin.

Once there, as rain poured down on the entourage, he was bundled into a military police transfer vehicle and whisked away to Tegel Prison in the French sector. They passed his food and water through a slot in the cell door and allowed him to walk, his eyes and ears covered, in the yard for thirty minutes a day.

A week later, his ankles shackled to a ring on floor of a van and his hands stretched over his head to another ring on the roof, he was taken in the middle of the night to Glienicker Brücke.

The Draftsman watched the prisoner from a bench on the opposite side of the van.

From under the bag, he barked, "Where am I? What are you going to do with me?"

One of the American guards snapped back at him, "*Zamolchi! Skoro uznayesh, kommunyaka!*" Shut up! You'll find out soon enough, commie!

The guard and the Draftsman exchanged a conspiratorial smirk. The young man spoke Russian well. He even managed to deliver the response with a Yiddish-influenced Odessan dialect, like Maksym's. On a scrap of paper, the guard wrote, "My grandparents fled Odessa in the pogrom of 1905. They raised me."

They sat for an eternity on the western end in Wannasee. The bridge spanned the Havel River, the border between West Berlin and the GDR. It had been closed to West Germans in 1952 and then to East Germans when the Wall went up. Of all the checkpoints between East and West Germany, it was the only checkpoint under complete Soviet control—no Grenztruppen or Stasi.

The rain bounced in heavy drops off the roof of the van. At first, it was fast and regular before slowing to a trickle. The opposite end of the bridge was dark and silent. Where the bloody hell were the Soviets?

Through the drizzle and darkness, a quick double flick of headlights. They were already there.

Chapter 31

London, England, 1963

It was late afternoon before Giles's interrogation—excuse me, "debriefing"—of the Draftsman began to wind down. It was dark outside and raining. Huge drops of water pounded against the window. The remnants of two packs of smoked cigarettes hung in the air, prompting Giles to open the window and let the cold air in. All three men were tired and running out of tape.

It was all on the record now. Fifteen years of the Draftsman's secret life—from an innocent businessman to shipper of nuclear materials to kidnapper to killer of Stasi officers to manager of a prisoner exchange. And yet he still didn't really know why it was happening.

If he was honest, it felt good to get it all out, confident that none of it would ever see the light of day. That wasn't quite true, of course. The Official Secrets Act sealed this report for fifty years, but it would circulate within the Service. The Draftsman, given the unlikely odds that he would live long enough, would be well into his eighties and probably senile by then. Would anyone still be interested in all this in 2013? Seemed unlikely.

At around 6:00 p.m., Giles shut down the tape recorder once and for all. The final tapes were put in box that he sealed with tamper-resistant tape. The Geordie closed the suitcase and strode out of the room with both into the same back bedroom he came in from hours earlier.

Giles poured himself a drink and looked up at the Draftsman expectantly. "You interested?"

"Of course. Who makes it?"

"Balvenie, twenty years old. It was my father's favorite, always kept it on hand in a crystal decanter on the sideboard at the Admiralty. He died last year of a heart attack."

"Sorry to hear that."

"Don't be. He was a pompous arsehole who went behind my poor mother's back with one of my nannies. I'm just working my way through his prized Scotch collection."

The Geordie came back into the room and sat down across from them. His presence and role was peculiar. It was highly unusual for the support staff to sit with an interrogator and his target in such a casual manner. He was not who he appeared to be.

Giles poured him a drink also and added three cubes of ice. He was American!

"Thanks very much. Appreciate it."

"What's going on here, Giles? This lad sounded like he was right out of the Tyne and Wear docks when he opened his mouth earlier today."

The Geordie extended a hand. "The name's Bob."

It suddenly dawned on the Draftsman that he wasn't being put out to pasture or that MI6 was expanding their relationship. No, they were closing the book on him and turning him over to a new master, the CIA. He took Bob's hand and slowly shook it. "What is this all about?"

"We're hoping you might be able to help us with an operation we're planning to run."

"You just recorded nine hours of a classified debriefing about MI6 operations. And then you walked out of the room carrying the box of tapes, tapes that implicate me personally. Is that your leverage?"

"Ben," Giles interrupted, "this is a joint MI6/CIA initiative. The work you've done over the last fifteen years is the perfect foundation for it. It will help undermine Soviet control in Eastern Europe and perhaps in time bring the Soviet Union to its knees."

Just below the surface of his skin, his blood boiled, the pressure building like an active volcano in his chest. He had just confessed to a multitude of crimes on tape. Those tapes, no longer under the control of MI6, sat in the hands of a man from the CIA, who was now asking him to participate in a potentially illegal operation to undermine the Soviet government. Giles and MI6 had betrayed him.

But he was also angry at himself for falling into the trap. The Geordie had played for him a fool. He had suspected CIA involvement for years. Regina for one and Bruce for another. Even Maksym had shared his suspicions.

He had been cornered and knew it. He stared into the American's eyes. The tension hung in the air, thick as a Highland fog. Giles shifted uncomfortably in his seat.

"Well played, Bob, well played. The trap has been sprung, and it's my foot in the jaws. You'd better tell me what you want before I bleed out."

"Now, now, don't be…"

"Fuck off, Giles. Don't bloody patronize me."

He turned back to Bob and said, "What are you asking me to do?"

"Well, in a lot of ways, it's what you are already doing, just with a little more direction from us and done in a more strategic way. Until now, your more unlawful activities were sanctioned and funded by Maksym Palatnik for his benefit. Recently, MI6 funded your operations indirectly. We would like to see you perform those same kinds of actions for the benefit of the free world instead."

Bob picked up his Scotch and leaned back in his seat. This wasn't his first time recruiting a reluctant asset. His network in Eastern European and the Soviet Union was extensive, and every single one of them found themselves, at some point, sitting across from him, going through the mental gymnastics of deciding what to do next—comply, resist, delay, or betray?

As the three men sat in silence, he could see the Draftsman's brain working. The trap had been sprung, and his captive had little choice but to go along with it. But he also knew that the seduction of this particular recruit would take time and care. They weren't, after all, just looking for a man willing to kidnap or kill one time in exchange for money or safety from prosecution or persecution. They needed a man who would spend the rest of his life in peril, participating in operations many times over, for reasons that he wouldn't be privy to and for a country that wasn't his own.

It would be the signature recruitment of his career. If successful and fruitful, it would etch his name in the lore of CIA history—the spymaster who recruited and managed the asset that brought down the Soviet Union.

"Was Bruce Lasher one of you lot?"

The Draftsman's questions were predictable. Every recruit, in the moment, reflected back on the past and questioned every task, every relationship. It didn't matter. He was in a vice, and every question answered just tightened it.

"He and I did have some informal meetings in the early days of Saco-Lowell. But like you, he was an independent businessman who just happened to also be a patriot and wanted to serve his country."

"Did he recruit me for you as well?"

"Well, now we are getting into territory that requires mutual trust, Mr. Pike. The answer is not exactly. His job was to create a connection between Oleksandr and his brother, Maksym Palatnik. You, Maksym, and others fed information to him. He passed it back to Oleksandr, who gave it to us. Once you and Maksym were tight, Bruce backed off. We let that partnership blossom knowing that Giles and his colleagues had it all under control. The exchange for Porter was, as you can imagine, a turning point for us. Your suspicions about Regina, Bruce, and the agency have been growing. We think that 1964 is going to be a pivotal year for US-Soviet relations. Depending on who wins the election in November, Johnson or Goldwater, the next few years could swing in wildly different directions. It looks like Khrushchev is in trouble too. We are on the precipice."

The Draftsman was well aware of the turmoil brewing in Moscow. Khruschev's ouster as first secretary of the Central Committee and the elevation of Brezhnev worried everyone. Brezhnev's goal was nuclear parity with the US. A nuclear arms race was the most likely outcome.

"Intelligence estimates say we have almost ten times the nuclear firepower of the Soviets. Brezhnev is going to build up their stockpile. Then there's space. They sent up Gagarin and then the first woman, Tereshkova, before us. The Russians will have a cosmonaut floating around outside a spacecraft inside a year."

"I know all this, Bob. What I don't know is what it has to do with me. I'm not an American, and I'm not on the government pay-roll. Why me?"

And then it dawned him. It wasn't just him they wanted.

"You want me to recruit and run Maksym as a CIA agent."

Chapter 32

They had a reservation at one of Maksym's favorite restaurants in Odessa's Kievskyi neighborhood. It had a rustic Ukrainian theme with a collection of traditional embroideries and colorful shawls, vintage accessories like spinning wheels, and a wood-burning stove decorated with flower paintings called petrykivka.

In a secluded corner, the Draftsman was going through the mental translation exercise of the menu. As usual, Maksym offered no help. He waved to other guests and occasionally got up to pat someone on the back and compliment them on the attractiveness of their female dinner guest in a way that only a mobster would.

The Draftsman had no experience recruiting spies, and Maksym was not what any recruiter would call a vulnerable target. Two months had passed since the debriefing in London, where he eventually pledged himself to the American cause.

He'd spent several days being coached through this particular recruitment by Bob. He had learned, and immediately recognized, the subtle techniques used to recruit a new asset, the seductive push-pull, the application and absorption of pressure, and the climbing of the trust ladder, Bob's own invention.

Maksym returned to the table just in time to hear the Draftsman place a large order of food in near-perfect Ukrainian. He ordered homemade sausages, potato pancakes, black pudding, and, of course, the Beluga, Ossetra, and Sevruga caviars native to the Black Sea. He added a bottle of Ployez Jacquemart Rosé Champagne to pair with the caviar and a bottle of Khortytsa Ukrainian vodka for the meat and potato plates.

"Your Ukrainian gets better every day, my friend, as does your taste in the finest Ukrainian food and vodka. I must be paying you too well to afford our very best caviar!"

"We've known each other a long time, and you've been very generous to me. It's about time that I bought you a good meal."

"Ach, I have an account here. They've probably already put it on my monthly bill. I'll take it off your next payment."

They took a first shot of Khortytsa. It was a fine, if unremarkable, vodka with mildly sweet caramel flavor. A few small plates of food appeared, and within a few minutes, they were three shots into the meal. The caviar arrived in long-stemmed serving glasses, and the waiter popped the Ployez Jacquemart.

"I'm impressed. Pairing the caviar with the Ployez Jacquemart is inspired. Most people go for Dom Pérignon when spending so much on the caviar, but the Ployez is a wonderful choice."

"I called the restaurant earlier today to get their recommendation. I wish I'd thought of it myself."

"As you say in your country, well played. Now tell me, what is it you need from me? I usually call the meetings."

He had expected his boss to take control right away. Maksym believed that everyone did everything for a reason, that there was always an agenda. In his world, it was true. Very few would spend time with Maksym for the hell of it.

Bob had a method. He called it "climbing the trust ladder." It was simple to describe but hard to execute—two ladders side by side, one for the recruiter and one for the target. Start at the bottom, take one measured step up at time, and convince the target to take one step with you.

For the Draftsman and Maksym, it was decided that the first big step on the ladder was creating a feeling of shared risk, a risk with enough truth in it to believable and enough deception to allow him to manipulate the situation and advance them to the next step together.

"You remember that operation a few years ago, the one where your friend, Marius Popescu, came to us to take care of the CEO who was killing his employees mining uranium?"

"Of course, Grigor Balan. *Yakyy svoloch!*" What a bastard!

"Well, Marius was implicated in his death and thrown into Aiud Prison."

"Very bad place Aiud. The prison of all prisons. They have a box called the *rezervă*, the reserve. They lock political prisoners in it for weeks at a time."

"He spent two years there then fled Romania for Paris when he was released and then paid INTERPOL a visit to tell them about it. They opened an investigation that included your name and mine. On a wall in the Paris office, they are building a picture of the network you built and the operations that are associated with them."

"And you know this how? INTERPOL has no power here."

They weren't ready for the second step on the ladder yet, so he ignored the question and focused on Maksym's statement.

"There is talk that they are seeking permission from the Committee for State Security in Kiev to interview us. I am worried for you and for me."

"They will not grant such permission, I am sure of it. The Committee will not support an intrusion by a foreign law-enforcement agency into Ukraine. And Moscow will back them also."

"But we did cross an international border into Romania, and we escaped through Hungary. What if State Security sees this as an opportunity? There is talk, as you know, of change in Moscow. Would the apparatchiks in Kiev not want to have a feather in their cap when it happens? If they get their hands on the evidence that INTERPOL has collected? What might they do?"

Maksym chewed slowly on a large chunk of black pudding and stared into his vodka glass. Be patient with the first step, Bob had told him. Give Maksym a chance to explore the implications in his own head. If you have planted the right seed in the right way, human nature will let the negative implications weigh on him. Then do something to remind him how good he has it today and what he will miss if he doesn't go forward with you.

The Draftsman rattled the Ployez Jacquemart around in the ice bucket. The noise snapped Maksym back from his thoughts. He poured a glass for both of them and "Which of the three caviars are you favorite, boss?"

"With Ployez Jacquemart, it must be the Ossetra."

Together, they had climbed on the second step of the ladder, distract the target from the risk and focus on a shared pleasure. The Draftsman could feel Bob patting him on the back from somewhere in his fancy new office in Langley, Virginia. The next steps on the ladder had to happen in quick succession—validating that the threat or need for action was, in fact, real and then providing a viable next action.

"You asked how I knew about the INTERPOL investigation. It was Bruce Lasher. You probably already knew that he had some shady government connections in the US."

"I suspected as much."

"I didn't, and I haven't spoken to him at all in recent years. He asked to meet me in London, so I flew back from and met him for lunch. He told me that INTERPOL had alerted the FBI to the Balan case and the FBI took it to the CIA. The Americans are really worried about the uranium, said the Soviets are going to start an arms race."

"Pah! Moscow wouldn't know what to do with it. They probably dumped it all in the Volga. And that mine shut down two years ago. There's nothing left except the mass graves."

"Maksym, the trains are still running from Baita. They want you and I to help them stop the Soviet Union and the United States from wiping each other out."

"In exchange for what?"

"Protection. And the chance to poke a large stick in Moscow's eye."

Chapter 33

Kiev, Soviet Ukraine, 1965

For the first time, *Den Peremohy*—commemorating the official surrender of Nazi Germany to the Allied forces on May 8, 1945—was an official labor holiday. It was a beautiful spring day in Kiev with temperatures well above normal.

At lunchtime, veterans of the Great Patriotic War marched down Kiev's main boulevard, *Khreshchatyk*. It ran from *Ploscha Leninskava Komsomola* (Lenin's Komosol Square) to *Bessarabska Ploscha*. The Red Army turned Kreshchatyk to rubble in their scorched earth retreat of 1941, ending a battle for Kiev that claimed more than eight hundred thousand lives. It set the stage for the Babi Year massacre of thirty thousand of the city's Jews over two days. Two years later, the Red Army drove the Nazi Panzer Army forces back to the Polish border leading to another hundred thousand dead and wounded.

Two miles to the north of Bessarabska Ploscha, every table at Yegor's was packed with families and friends celebrating the holiday. The atmosphere was loud and lively. Guests consumed copious amounts of borscht, chicken Kiev, cabbage rolls, and, of course, liters of horilka. Even the yelling of the cooks back in the kitchen wasn't enough to dampen the mood.

Yegor had died of a massive heart attack a few years ago, so his two able-bodied sons now ran the restaurant. They had expanded into a former bakery next door when the owner was arrested for anti-Soviet propaganda under Article 70 of the USSR penal code. The property was annexed by the government of Soviet Ukraine and given to the boys as a reward for something never discussed out loud.

Artem, Maksym, and the Draftsman sat at the very same table they had that first time in 1951. A small, yellowed card with the word *Zarezervovanyy* (*Reserved*) always sat in the center even though Artem spent most of his time in Moscow serving as an advisor on Ukrainian issues to Premier Alexei Kosygin.

It was at this table that they plotted the ascension of Artem to first secretary of Soviet Ukraine at the expense of the unfortunate Leonid Minkov. It was where they concocted the strategy to facilitate Grigor Balan's shipments of uranium to the Soviet Union that helped the US uncover the depth of the Soviet nuclear program. They had planned the Draftsman's assassination of a rival to Maksym from Zhdanov there. After the war, Mariupol had been renamed for Andrei Zhdanov, who was born in the port city and thought to be Stalin's successor until an untimely death from an intentionally misdiagnosed heart attack opened the door for Khrushchev.

And now, at Artem's invitation, they sat there again. They ate. They drank. They laughed. And they waited. Why had he had called them together after so many years? Artem wanted something.

"It's a fucking disaster in the Kremlin now. With Khrushchev out, Brezhnev, Podgorny, Shelepin, and Alexei are all fighting it out."

They both noted the use of Kosygin's first name. Artem was clearly enamored of his new boss. The Politburo had refused to put too much power to one man's hands after years of Khrushchev's strong-arm tactics. In the process, however, they created a power struggle among its four top leaders.

Artem threw back a sizable shot of horilka, probably a double, and continued, "Comrade Kosygin is a good man, but Brezhnev is determined to get rid of him."

"Why?"

"Alexei is a reformer. Wants to focus the economy on production of light consumer goods for the Soviet people and possibly exports. Brezhnev portrays him as a pawn of western decadence and materialism. He supports agriculture and heavy industry. They speak of Alexei as a repeat of Khrushchev."

"But Brezhnev is Ukrainian. Should we not support him? Kosygin is from Leningrad," said Maksym, fully expecting Artem to snap back at him.

Artem's face changed. Was it anger, irritation, or perhaps frustration at having to justify Kosygin over Brezhnev once again?

"Brezhnev is betraying Ukraine for the sake of power," he sneered. "Alexei and Podgorny together see the Soviet Union's role in the wider world while Brezhnev and that KGB fuck Shelepin want to return us to the days of Stalin. Isolation, repression, and poverty for people. We cannot allow it to happen again."

That was something they could all agree on.

"Also, Alexei does not believe that Brezhnev as general secretary should represent the Soviet Union abroad. This function should fall into the hands of the head of government, which is Alexei's position, and not the head of the party."

"What about Gromyko? Is he not the Minister of Foreign Affairs?"

"Pah! He is an official of the government, not the party. He works for Alexei, and, honestly, he's too busy fighting his own battles against the International Department. They're supposed to manage political relations with other Communist countries but are meddling in Gromyko's business."

"So what do you need from me, Artem? Are we here to eat and drink with everyone else or is there another reason we are all here?"

"I want you to meet Alexei in Moscow with two of his Deputy Ministers, a man called Federov, who oversees *Mintekstilprom*, the Ministry of Textiles of the USSR, and another, Ivanov, who oversees *Minlegprom*, the Ministry of Light Industry. I want you give them information from the West and from the Soviet Republics that will help Alexei persuade the Politburo that the reforms he proposed to Khrushchev are still necessary."

Maksym and the Draftsman were silent, pondering the implications and risks of such a request. Artem was a partner, but neither felt they could completely trust him. As the Ukrainian proverb went, there are no old friendships in business. What he was proposing was a meeting to pass information from the west to the Soviet Premier and two of his supporters with the goal of undermining the positions of Shelepin and Brezhnev.

On the surface, it was an outcome that would benefit both Maksym and the Draftsman from a business perspective, but it could just as easily be a KGB trap. A test of Artem's loyalty to the real powers in Moscow by setting up Kosygin? Perhaps an operation to expose their MI6 and CIA connection. Regardless, whatever was said next would be critical to their long-term well-being. It was the Draftsman who finally spoke first. He had cover that Maksym did not.

"Mr. Ponomarenko, I would, of course, need to get approval from the Foreign Office before agreeing to this meeting in Moscow. I don't pretend to have those kinds of relationships, so it will take time. But I think it is safe to say that none of us want to return to the policies of the past. I don't know who Comrades Kosygin, Ivanov, or Federov are, but I have learned to tread very carefully in this country."

Artem nodded, "Of course, you are right. Our sources of accurate information are, well, unpredictable, but Mak—"

Maksym sat silent, his arms folded across his chest. He was trying to look tough, but the Draftsman sensed his fear. This felt like a classic but clumsy KGB entrapment operation.

The Draftsman interrupted, "And, I don't want to speak for Mr. Palatnik, but he cannot be asked to put his business relationships in jeopardy either, especially if it potentially runs contrary to the policies of the leadership in Moscow."

He meant personal safety but couldn't use those words. There was little doubt that the KGB was eavesdropping on this meeting. Suggesting that he was in physical danger risked, indicating some kind of guilt. It could be a simple trap that would lead to an immediate arrest and time in the basement of Lubyanka, or it could just as easily be the start of a more complex operation to bring down Maksym and everyone around him.

It was just better for him not to respond.

"I understand. We have all known each other for a long time, but I recognize the unorthodox nature of my request. Perhaps we can meet again in a few weeks to revisit this. For today, a day to celebrate our great victory over the Nazis, another bottle of horilka!"

The Draftsman cringed at the prospect.

Two weeks later, in the bar of Kiev's Hotel Mockba, Regina was dressed for what appeared to be a Russian winter, a long wool coat, fur hat, and her trademark bright-red lipstick. As usual, the mostly male contingent, like a pack of hungry wolves closing in on their kill, leered. They all had her scent in their nostrils and licked their lips in anticipation as they moved inches closer to their prey. Regina was used it and knew how look after herself, but it unnerved him every time. As he sat down next to her, all eyes zeroed in on him, and he felt the daggers. He ordered a gin and tonic and said, "You are really turning some heads in here tonight."

"It's the hat. Fur on a woman's head attracts Soviet wolves. It makes me feel more familiar to them. Like something they could charm with vodka and machismo without fear."

"You make it sound intentional."

She turned to him and smiled. "Feeling a little threatened? Like you might actually have to fight one of them to be with me?"

"Always."

"I'm more of a praying mantis than a forest deer."

The banter was enjoyable, but the pack closing in was top of mind.

"Stop it. They're harmless. And besides, I'm armed."

She opened her coat a little. Her dress had a slit that ran all the way up and beyond her hip bone. Tucked into a thin garter belt was a Baretta 950.

"It has a tip-up barrel, you know." She winked and smiled at him.

He found her playfulness a little intimidating as only an intro-verted Englishman sleeping with a confident American woman could. She drew attention toward them that he would rather avoid. It was dangerous.

"I need some air and a cigarette," she announced suddenly and hopped down from her barstool and marched toward the lobby. The wolves were startled, looking from one to the other nervously for guidance on the pack's strategy. Chase? Wait? Regroup? None of them knew.

The Draftsman, leaving his gin and tonic behind, pursued. He found her near the taxi stand, asking one of the drivers in perfect Russian for a light.

"*Ne naydetsya prikuri?*"

The rotund little man was flustered. He'd never been approached by a woman like her, at least not like that. He dropped his lighter twice and struggled to get it to spark. When it finally caught, she leaned in to him, her expensive western perfume unlike anything he smelled before.

Regina scooped up the Draftsman's arm. "Let's walk."

They turned down *Mykhaila Hrushevskoho*, a quiet cobbled street with a few streetlamps, most not working. There was an embankment wall of about five feet on their left side that separated the street from Mariinskyi Park. On the right were historic government buildings, lights off at this time of night. It was a smart choice, hard for the KGB to follow them without being spotted.

Nonetheless, they walked arm-in-arm in silence, stopped, retraced their steps, took a left into the park, and passed Stadion Dynamo, where FC Dynamo Kiev played. They surfaced on the banks of Dnieper River and sat on a bench for a few minutes looking at the beaches of Trukhaniv Island on the other side. They played the roles of lovers, teasing and laughing with each other, before getting up and walking toward the Kiev Pechersk Lavra monastery.

"What did Giles have to say?"

She slipped something small and round into his pocket. A small pen, perhaps.

"The details are in there but essentially continue to nurture Ponomarenko. We'll feed him intelligence he can use to influence his friends in the Kremlin. We want to drive a wedge between Kosygin and Brezhnev but also isolate Shelepin and put Podgorny's obedience-and-order platform in Brezhnev's crosshairs."

"And you want me in the middle of all that? It puts everything we've done at risk. It's a trap! I'll be arrested!"

"We don't think so. The analysts are confident that Kosygin is the winner in this. We're just helping accelerate the outcome."

"Bollocks! Kosygin is a good diplomat, but he can't arm wrestle the politburo into anything at all. The analysts are wrong, and it's my balls on the block here. No bloody way I'm doing this. I expected Giles to squash it."

"Look, we'll start with some innocuous stuff, mostly true and verifiable, and see how it takes."

"With me in the bloody crosshairs?"

The silence between them lingered a little longer than he was comfortable with. The nagging fears of distrust danced in his stomach, climbing toward his heart. She had no answer, but he could hear Giles in the distance.

"It's the best chance we have to destabilize the Soviet Union, to pit the factions against each other. Then we drive distrust between Moscow and the republics. And, in time, the Soviet Union will fall. Hopefully before we blow each other to nuclear smithereens."

Chapter 34

The KGB came for them in the middle of the night. The Draftsman awoke to the slow, measured steps of someone trying to hide their presence. His hand gripped the Makarov under his pillow a little too tight, and out in the hallway, the shoes squeaked with every step on the old floorboards. Maksym was in the room next door. His snoring stopped suddenly.

It wasn't a surprise. They'd been expecting it.

Shelepin was digging into the sources of Kosygin's information. A KGB surveillance team followed them everywhere in Moscow, searched their rooms when they were out, planted bugs in the walls and lamps, and listened to every sound.

But recently something had changed. The faces of their tails, once relaxed and nonthreatening, became a little more serious. Their tradecraft was more sophisticated. New agents, and more of them, were added to the surveillance teams, and they were harder to identify. The clumsy room searches, drawers not closed all the way, or an out-of-place lamp on a side table stopped. On the street and at checkpoints, their documents and papers were scrutinized a little more closely.

Innocent men don't change their behavior when the surveillance increases. Maksym and the Draftsman continued their business as usual, hoping to soothe suspicions. Regina returned to West Germany to lay low for a while.

The intelligence provided to Kosygin over the last eighteen months had helped the Soviet Premier persuade Brezhnev that there was an alternative to a centralized economy driven by heavy industry.

As the Soviet economy lumbered on through slow or no growth, Brezhnev allowed reforms to go forward, using almost 350 enterprises in light industry as a test. The Soviet textile industry—and by extension the Draftsman and Maksym—were the main beneficiaries. Kosygin incorporated free-market ideas, like profit making, efficiency in production, incentives for managers and workers, and stripping away state bureaucracy.

Shelepin didn't like it. And now the KGB were here to arrest them. Or maybe worse.

Out in the hallway, one of the KGB men slowly inserted a key in to the lock on Maksym's door. The Draftsman pressed his ear against the door to listen.

A man whispered, "*Eto ne rabotayet?*" It doesn't work?

"*Ne govori.*" Don't talk.

Another whisper, a little more urgent, "*Mozhet po sosedstvu?*" Maybe next door?

"*Zamolchi!*" Shut up!

They inserted the key in the lock to the Draftsman's room. It didn't engage. The KGB agent turned the knob, but the door failed to open. No doubt, Maksym had charmed someone at the front desk to give the KGB the wrong key.

The Draftsman swung his camera bag over his shoulder and moved to the opposite end of the room, opened the French window, and slipped silently onto the balcony, which wrapped around the entire front and side facade of the hotel.

To his right was Lubyanka Square, which was not a place he wanted to go. KGB headquarters. To his left, *Ploshchad Revolyutsii* (Revolution Square), a park with the Bolshoi Theatre at its northern end.

Maksym appeared on the balcony from next door. He was wearing only his underpants. They were disconcertingly small, and the Draftsman felt compelled to look away as he said, "We can't run. They know we are here. If we run and get caught, it will be very bad, like we had something to hide and fled. If we stay and they arrest us, it will be terrible, but we can protest innocence and maybe we can survive."

"They don't have keys to our rooms. The girl at the desk will live for a year on what I paid her. We go back inside and get back into bed."

"What if they put the screws to her?"

"*Nyet.* Trust me. I already did." It hardly seemed the time for cheeky jokes, but Maksym's grin was endearing. "For tonight, keep your gun close, and we will be safe. I have a car coming to get us after they leave. We will disappear."

In Maksym's world, the KGB were incompetent fools, bumbling along, orders in hand, but without the brains or the street skills to think for themselves. He slithered back into his room and closed the French window, leaving the Draftsman on the balcony by himself.

Two floors below, the Moscow traffic was light. Most of the streetlights had been turned off, and the windows in the building across the street were dark.

Fear possessed him for reasons unknown. The thought of being hauled away and interrogated in the basement of Lubyanka was too much. Maybe he could protest innocence and survive whatever hideous torture methods were in vogue these days, but the odds were slim. How many had been taken there and never returned? Too many.

And the truth was that he was now on the payroll of MI6 and the CIA. Maksym was not, at least in any kind of traceable way. He could afford to be brave. Or he could play his Soviet card, unmask the Draftsman as a western agent, and reveal everything he had done in the past decade for western intelligence. The killings. The kidnappings. The recruiting of traitors to the Soviet Union. Maksym knew about it all and could cover his tracks.

Who would fare best under an interrogation by the KGB? Of course, Maksym would. He had a family in Odessa, in-laws in Kiev, friends from the catacombs scattered throughout the government apparatus of every Soviet republic. But the Draftsman was alone. His family didn't even know where he was or what he did. Giles and the rest of them back at Broadway House would disavow him. Adding his arrest to the laundry list of MI6 embarrassments from the recent past would be out of the question. Who knew how many agent networks across Eastern Europe would be rolled up if he were taken in?

And to what lengths would the KGB go to get the information they needed knowing that they had an MI6 agent shackled to an overhead pipe in the basement?

He was burned. He had no choice but to get out of Moscow as quickly as possible and abandon Maksym to the mercy of the KGB. It was the end of their relationship and the end of his involvement in Operation Undercut. And if he couldn't make it to the safe house in Odintsovo and stay there until an extraction came to get him out of the Soviet Union once and for all, it could be the end of his life.

It was a twenty-foot drop to the street below, *Teatral'nyy Proyezd*. He would land right in front of the main window of the bar and just a few feet to the left of the main entrance. Even at this late hour, the bar would be open, and members of the KGB surveillance team would be lingering by the front door looking for them. He was also very likely to injure himself.

He turned to his left and ran along the balcony toward Revolution Square. Most of the curtains into the other rooms on the floor were closed, but one was open, exposing a couple in the preliminary stages of undressing. They paid no attention to the man dashing past their window in the middle of the night. The balcony bent to the left, wrapping around the darker and quieter side of the building. At the end, thank God, he found a retractable ladder that dropped down to the street next to Revolution Square metro station.

He walked, as casually as he could manage to avoid drawing attention to himself, down the stairs of the Metro station. Inside, there were statues paired on either side that led to the platforms in the socialist-realism style. It was apparently good luck to rub certain parts of some the statues, but he didn't know which ones. So he rubbed the boot of the male football player and hoped for the best. He waited for the eastbound number 3 subway train.

At Kuntsevskaya, he got off, hid in the shadows for ten minutes before switching trains and continuing on to Odintsovo and the safe house. Under normal circumstances, he would have backtracked, taken a train to another part of town, but there was no time for perfect tradecraft.

Like many of Moscow's suburbs, Odintsovo's agrarian past was being replaced with high-rise apartments and factories. He could hide there among the hundreds of thousands of residents until someone came to get him. After that, he couldn't return to the Soviet Union for many years, perhaps never knowing what became of Maksym and Artem.

Part 3

A sail is passing, white and frail.
What do you seek in a far country?
What have you left at home, lone sail?
The billows play, the breezes whistle,
And rhythmically creaks the mast.
Alas, you seek no happy future,
Nor do you flee a happy past.

—Mikhail Lermontov, "The Sail"

Chapter 35

Odessa, Soviet Ukraine, 1988

Maksym's home, tucked neatly on a quiet and well-lit street in the leafy Kievskyi district of Odessa, sat on a large plot of land behind a high wall. His neighbors, older, wealthier, and less interested in spying on the people around them than most, minded their own business and kept to themselves. He had security teams posted in cars at either end of the street and a third sat in front of the house. They kept a low profile and didn't scare passersby, so no one complained.

But all were incapacitated now—four temporarily and two permanently. Cameras covering the major points of access to his home didn't pick it up. The guard who normally monitored them from the basement took the night off to celebrate the second night of Hanukkah with his family.

Maksym was home alone and not expecting guests. His wife, children, and grandchildren had left Odessa to visit his dying mother-in-law in Kiev. He promised to join them for the final night of the holiday that fell on the sabbath this year. He lounged on a sofa in front of a large television watching replays of the Soviet rhythmic gymnastics team winning gold and bronze at the Seoul Olympics.

A ZAZ-1102—a high-end car for the average Ukrainian—pulled up to the curb close to the front gate and turned off its engine and lights. No one got out. A large oak tree with branches extending over the street cloaked the face of Andrey Kuznetzov, the man behind the wheel, with a heavy shadow. A tall man walked his car past in a hurry, the collar of his overcoat turned up to cover most of his face. He opened the front gate and marched up the garden path to the front door without looking around and rang the doorbell. Dogs barked in the neighborhood. At first, there was no answer. Waiting made him edgy.

Maksym was unpleasantly surprised to see the Draftsman standing on his front step when he answered the door. He was nervous and urgently looked up and down the street for his security teams. Someone was going to pay for this. He didn't see Andrey sitting in the darkened car lurking in the shadows under the oak tree.

"What the fuck are you doing here?"

"We need to get you out of here. The KGB are getting ready to arrest you."

"Who's we? And how did you get past my men?"

"You should let me in before your nosy neighbors call the authorities. Mr. and Mrs. Serdyuk, the old couple across the street, are paid to watch the comings and goings at your home. I'm sure there are others who pay attention too." He stepped inside without waiting for an invitation.

They'd last seen each other since a prisoner exchange on Gleinicke Bridge in East Berlin a decade earlier, almost to the day. Maksym sat in car at the Soviet end watching through rain-soaked windows. It was definitely him. Older and grayer, but that was Maksym all right.

The Draftsman barely remembered what happened after his arrest at the Friedrichstraße crossing. He endured a week of interrogations, a regular cocktail of psychoactive drugs, sleeplessness, and countless other indignities. He had been within hours of cracking. He knew, however, that he was of no further value if he told them everything. He wouldn't even have known the bullet was coming.

By some miracle, he'd been taken from cell, thrown in a lukewarm shower with a well-used bar of brown birch tar soap that wouldn't produce foam, and given a clean set of clothes clearly taken from a much larger man.

When they shoved him into the van, it was raining. It was always raining. They rattled along the uneven roads for what felt like an hour before stumbling to a halt.

The Grepos in the back with him, one of whom he recognized him from his trips across the checkpoint, hoisted him up by the armpits as the rear door swung open. The rain had turned to sleet, and he slipped on the step down. No one tried to break his fall. Once upright again, they pushed him toward the bright lights on the other side of the bridge.

The steel grating of the bridge was slippery in the cold morning as he stumbled feebly to the other side. A wretched-looking fellow appeared through the drizzle-distorted headlights heading in the opposite direction. He was carrying a small suitcase, face hidden by a scarf and dark glasses. They passed without acknowledging each other.

He reached the other side to find Giles, Bob Schier, and Regina waiting for him.

He had not set foot in Eastern Europe again until the day he showed up on Maksym's front step. It was Maksym who had secured his release in 1978, and now it was time to return the favor.

Escalating unrest throughout Eastern Europe had the analysts at Langley and Broadway House on the edge of their seats. From the Polish Spring with strikes in the Gdansk shipyards and the coal mines of Jastrzębie-Zdrój to Hungary's Prime Minister Miklós Németh letting East Germans travel safely through Hungary en route to freedom in West Germany, Moscow's grip was slipping.

The Berlin Desk in London was convinced that it was only a matter of time before the Wall came down and the entire Warsaw Pact collapsed. The old hands on the Moscow Desk thought it a fanciful dream at best, more like waking up a sleeping bear, smelly, angry, and hungry after a long hibernation. The Soviets would bring down the hammer on the weak governments that allowed the unrest to continue. Before anything good could come of the unrest, the analysts all agreed, a lot of bad had to happen first, and that included a massive arrest and purge of potential troublemakers. Gorbachev and glasnost made headlines in the West, but the general secretary was still committed to preserving the Soviet state and Marxist-Leninist ideals.

Maksym, for his part, was still running the Malina out of Odessa, but his fingerprints were all over popular unrest. Years of investment by MI6 and CIA in Operation Undercut was finally starting to pay off. In reality, it was a failing war in Afghanistan that was distracting Moscow from the growing rebellions.

In late November—a week before the Draftsman showed up on his doorstep unannounced—the Signals team in Istanbul had reported that Maksym's name was coming up a lot, suggesting that the KGB planned to arrest him within days. If he got a talking-to in the basement of Lukyanivska, with the right amount of psychological and physical abuse and the liberal use of drugs, Maksym would crack. And it probably wouldn't take that long. Dozens, if not hundreds, of people connected to the network would be dragged into the interrogation room, sent to prison, or executed. Maybe all three. His arrest was just not an option.

"We have a team in Istanbul. They'll get you to America."

"Are you fucking kidding me? I can't just walk away from my businesses, my friends, and my family like that. I'm not going anywhere. Let them come for me!"

"It's not an option. They'll bring in a Snatch team to take you by force if they have to, but I want to get in front of that. I'm at least talking about a new identity and a healthy bank account. The CIA Snatch team might not have such a cushy plan for you."

Maksym's anger was really just an attempt to disguise his fear. The Draftsman had known him long enough to read the truth in his bluster. If they came for him, he knew he'd be dragged from his home like a dog, locked in a basement with the excrement of those who were in there before him smeared on the walls, and his blood would permanently stain the prison floors. No, Maksym would rather go down in a hail of gunfire.

Maksym turned angrily and was about to yell "Bullshit! I will not…" when Andrey, who appeared out of nowhere, pressed the chloroform cloth into his face. The Draftsman restrained his arms from behind.

It smelled sweet, filling his nasal passages with peace. Maksym enjoyed the feeling for a moment, then everything faded, and he slumped into a pile on the tiled floor.

Andrey, shaking his head at his betrayal, said, "I fucking hate to do this to the boss." They carried his unconscious body and dropped him into the back seat of the ZAZ.

"Take us to Chornomorsk, Andrey."

The route was winding and unfamiliar. Andrey doubled back a few times and stuck to mostly empty, unlit back streets. Sometimes, he drove fast, other times painfully slow. He stopped at green lights and drove through the reds. A couple of times, he drove through an intersection only to reverse or make a sudden left or right turn. He'd stop frequently for no apparent reason, sometimes for a few seconds, sometimes for a minute. He kept a constant eye on the rearview mirror. If he saw the same car twice, he'd do something unexpected. The Draftsman thought it was overkill and likely drew more attention to them than was necessary.

After about an hour—a trip that should have taken less than twenty minutes—they passed through the gates of the Chronomorsk shipyard and headed for the cargo area where containers marked "Palat-Lojistik" were piled three high close to the dock. The claws of an enormous ship-to-shore gantry crane hovered above. The heavy chains rattled as the enormous claws locked onto one of the containers and hoisted it onto a waiting ship.

Andrey pulled up next to one container with an open door. "This one's yours. Let's get the boss in."

They dragged a still-unconscious Maksym out of the car and carried him into the container. There were two military-style cot beds inside, a box with a few bottles of water, and snack bars but nothing else—not much sustenance for a twenty-four-hour trip across the Black Sea to the Port of Karasu on the northern coast of Turkey.

"He's going to wake up at some point and be really pissed off. What are you going to do when that happens?"

"I'm going to keep sedated him. We don't have much food or drink, so the longer I can keep him down, the better. The car in Karasu is all set, right?"

"*Da*. Instructions are in the glove box. Everything you need, directions, money, reservations, and contacts. If it's not on that sheet, don't trust it. The KGB will know he's gone soon. The cleaners are already taking care of the house, and we even have a guy back there who looks like him hanging around to throw off anyone watching."

"Take care of yourself, Andrey. Disappear. Take your money and vanish. Your work is done. I'll explain to him what I did and why. We've been together, me, you, and Maksym for almost thirty-five years. The bond is strong, and I will make sure he understands. I will look after him."

"And I can expect my payments to keep coming?"

He handed Andrey a piece of paper with some numbers and address on it. "This account has plenty of money in it, above and beyond what you already have stashed. If you ever find yourself short or the Soviets fuck you over, dip in. We earned it together, and we are the only ones who can access it."

They hugged for the first and last time. With a final wave, Andrey closed and locked the container door, plunging the two of them into the pitch-dark for at least the next twenty-four hours.

By the light of a small flashlight, the Draftsman kept his boss sleepy, compliant, hydrated, and fed. The floor was dry at least, but in the dark, he could hear the clickety-clack of the rat's tiny toenails as they scratched and scampered around. They squeaked incessantly.

About eight hours in, Maksym came to, conscious but not all there by any means. He was angry—verbally abusive and mildly violent but terribly uncoordinated. He took a swing that the Draftsman easily dodged.

They used "the shit-and-piss corner" as little as possible, but the odor grew worse every hour. More of the excited squeaks started to come from that corner. The seas grew rough, the huge ship pitched fifteen degrees to port then starboard, and they both puked until there was just stomach bile left. The rats scurried to find sustenance in the vomit.

Eventually, the batteries died on the flashlight, and they spent the last eight hours in total darkness. They lay on their cots and listened to the rats' toenails. When they finally docked in Karasu and the container door opened, even the rats couldn't get out fast enough.

Chapter 36

They emerged from the darkness of the container into the darkness of night. It made the transition easier. It was almost 3:00 a.m. in Turkey. The cranes were hard at work hoisting containers.

A car, parked in the shadows of one of the buildings, caught the Draftsman's attention. Two suspicious-looking men were watching them. He shook his head. It was almost too cliché. While other men worked on the dock as usual, these two sat in their car looking suspicious. One was even smoking and had the window cracked to let the smoke out.

They found their Oyak-Renault 12 looking a lot like a long-abandoned vehicle in the back corner of a parking lot near the cargo dock. The little ashtray was overflowing, and the car stunk of stale Maltepe small cigarettes. There was a small pile of coffee cups and a leftover bag of lamb kebabs on the back seat, adding to the already pungent aroma. Clearly, their providers took great care to ensure that their car looked authentic and wouldn't draw attention to itself.

Andrey's note in the glove compartment gave directions to the Galata Bridge Hotel, in the Karakoy section of Istanbul, with a pre-paid reservation number. His handwritten message was clear and simple: "Goodbye, friends. I sign off here. You are in their hands now. Go with God! AK."

As Maksym read the note, the finality of the situation seemed to sweep over him. "He was a good man. Looked after me, us, for years. Forty years. Gone."

"Perhaps he'll retire to that little dacha in Crimea with the pretty housemaid he always wanted! He must have the money. I think he only bought nice suits, sunglasses, and weapons as long as I knew him."

"That was my money. I bought his fancy suits, his arsenal, paid his bribes, and gave him cash for his girls, on top of paying him for his work. He has plenty of money. I hope he retires now. I will miss him."

It was a four-hour drive to Istanbul along the northern coast. A faster route dipped south on the E80 highway, but would be harder if they had to shake a tail, and that was clearly going to be the case today. Somewhere en route, they needed to take care of the two KGB men from the dock.

Getting rid of them early would give them plenty of places to hide the bodies and their car. The closer they got to the suburbs of Istanbul, the riskier a killing became—more people, more police.

The northern route, on the D014, weaved through farmland dotted with whitewashed houses and dense maple and sycamore forest to the town of Sile, a beachy place where the well-off of Istanbul went to lounge, fish, eat, and drink. Losing the tail in the town's incomprehensible one-way system and narrow streets might help avoid some bloodshed. The Draftsman, however, settled on taking them out earlier on the road to Kandira.

As they drove, Maksym ate the leftover kebabs from the back seat and moaned incessantly about the dirty car, how uncomfortable the seat was, the smell of stale cigarettes, how boring the road was in the dark, the rats in the container, the smell of the shit-and-piss corner, the "fucking KGB assholes," the loss of his business, the weakness of the Ukrainian government.

It was endless.

Draftsman wasn't a regular smoker, but he was relieved to find a half pack of Maltepes and a book of matches under the seat. He told himself that it was okay to have a couple because it would suppress his appetite and give him something do to avoid punching Maksym.

Dumping the ashtray out of the window, he took a peek in the wing mirror and then the rearview mirror to see if anyone was behind them. Not so far. But the KGB probably had several teams along the route to track and eventually intercept them. A moment later, the weak lights of a car rounded a corner about five hundred yards back. One headlight flickered. It must be them.

He finally snapped at Maksym's bitter complaining.

"Please, just shut the hell up! I can't even hear myself think, and I need to think right now. We've got a fucking KGB tail to deal with." Bruised, Maksym looked out of the window in silence.

Draftsman decided to follow the signs along the coastal road toward the Acarlar Floodplain Forest. It was the perfect spot to take out the tail—a mix of lagoons and forested swamplands separated from the Black Sea on the northern side by high sand dunes. But what if a second tailing team further up the route realized that the first team were gone? An alert would go out that they had lost contact, and who knew what would happen then. He'd need to change their route and take alternate roads to the D014. Those roads were few and far between before Kandira.

As if reading his mind, the tail dropped back. Draftsman turned off his headlights and slowed down. Would they panic and try to catch up? If they did, he knew they were alone. If they didn't, that meant there was another team ahead of them ready to take over.

On their right-hand side, it was all sand dunes, and on the other side of the road was swamp.

In the end, it all happened so quickly. Suddenly, the Russians came roaring up behind with headlights on dazzle, threatening to ram them. The passenger was loading a gun, rolling down the window, and undoing a seat belt to lean out and shoot.

As they drew close, Draftsman waited until the passenger was leaning out of the window and raising his pistol then slowed and drifted over to the right. The move forced the Russians over to the left toward the middle of the road. Draftsman slammed on the brakes, hurling Maksym—who had refused to wear a seat belt— forward into the dashboard. The Russians reacted by swerving hard left, and the first bullet whistled into the passenger side mirror. The Russian driver fought with the steering wheel but could not prevent the car from skidding off the road and landing with an enormous green splash in the swamp.

The two men scrambled to escape the rapidly sinking vehicle through the windows and clambered up the incline, only to find the Draftsman standing at the top with the Makarov pointing at them. He shot the both in the forehead, and the bodies sank into the water. The car disappeared below the waterline in a flurry of air bubbles.

When he climbed back into the car, Maksym had something new to complain about—his bloody nose and the urgent purple bulge developing above his right eye.

"What the fuck? A little warning the next time you pull a move like that!"

"You know what they say, belt up for safety!"

Draftsman decided to change the route by getting off the D014 in the town of Üçoluk, just ten minutes up the road. The new route took them south as far as Celyandere. From there they made a right turn onto another country road and rejoined D014 about ten miles further down in the nondescript village of Kuklaki. It had added about thirty minutes to their drive but hopefully threw off the second KGB tail team, if there was one.

The rest of the journey was uneventful. Maksym slept, his head bouncing off the window of the dilapidated car. They entered Istanbul, crossing the Bosphorus into Ortaköy down the Çırağan Caldesi and passing the abandoned palace of the thirty-second Sultan of the Ottoman Empire, Abdulaziz. The thought went through his mind that someone should renovate it and turn it into a hotel. The view of Üsküdar, one of Istanbul's oldest residential neighborhoods on the Anatolian side of the Bosphorus, was spectacular.

In the peace of the early morning, as the sun rose and the Draftsman pulled up in front of the Galata Bridge Hotel, the call to prayer rang out from thousands of mosques across the city. He rolled down the window to listen, and for a few, brief minutes, he felt calm and carried away from bad thoughts that circled inside his head constantly. The reverie was broken when Maksym awoke with a start.

"Where the fuck are we?"

They were tired, dirty, angry, and still stinking of oil and rat shit when they arrived at the hotel in Istanbul. The porter eyed them warily as they climbed out of the Oyak-Renault that smelled like a sewer and an ashtray rolled into one.

"I'm sorry, sir, perhaps you are looking for a different hotel? I'd be happy to help you find it. It can be so hard to find your way around Istanbul, especially with the one-way system."

Maksym's response was direct and quite rude. "We're guests here. We have no bags, so park the fucking car."

An agency man—in a well-pressed dark suit, perfectly trimmed hair, aviator sunglasses, zero expression on his face—emerged from inside and directed the pompous porter away from the wretches and their disgusting vehicle. With a quick flick of his wrist, he called over another man—a local with a bushy mustache and the dark, deeply wrinkled face of a hardworking man—who jogged over, climbed into the car, and drove away.

Agency man ushered them down a narrow alley to a side door that accessed the hotel kitchen then up the three flights of a service staircase to a floor secured with more agency clones. It was all very professional and clinical.

Showered and freshly clothed, they met the agency man, who identified himself as "Michael Sternthorpe," and two other name-less individuals. They sat outside at the Aruna Neptun Cafe under the Galata Bridge that linked the commercial side of Istanbul to the traditional Muslim side, site of the imperial palace and principal religious sites. They ate lahmacun and drank scorching hot Turkish coffee but rebuffed the fortune teller who usually read the coffee grounds at the bottom of the cup. After lunch, Sternthorpe handed Maksym a manila envelope that contained a US passport, a plane ticket to New York, and a birth certificate and Social Security card with his new identity.

The next morning, they were driven to Istanbul airport, flown to London for a quick debrief with Giles in a secure room at Heathrow, before boarding the final leg to JFK.

Maksym, with Sternthorpe in the seat next to him, looked out of the window as the plane chased the remaining daylight across the

Atlantic. He hadn't seen or spoken to his brother in a half century. Would he be welcomed? How would it be to see each other for the first time? Deep down, he resented Oleksandr. He didn't have to see his parents murdered in the street or get shipped off to the camp where only a horrible death awaited. He didn't have to fight the Nazis while living in an underground cave filled with rats. He didn't have to fight and scrap and kill for everything he ever had. But that was all so long ago, and this was a new life. He took out the folder and examined his new life. His new name was Mikel Borova. They had told him that it was a generic name that could originate anywhere in Europe, but he thought it suited him. It sounded sophisticated, worldly—until he opened his mouth and dockworker Ukrainian and Russian came pouring out.

Chapter 37

They arrived in New York the next morning, Maksym with a new identity, a clean US passport, and a flush bank account at Manufacturers Hanover. He spent the first week in a Manhattan hotel room, enduring daily debriefings—a euphemism for interrogation—from a rumpled, bespectacled, and balding man from the agency. His glasses slid down his nose every time he looked down to jot down a note, and the constant need to push them back up became a major irritation to Maksym.

They moved Maksym and his wife, who arrived a few days later after a harrowing journey from Kiev to Warsaw then Oslo, into a small apartment in Brighton Beach, a neighborhood the locals called "Little Odessa." On the day he moved in, they found a bottle of Italian red wine on the kitchen table, an Allegrini Amarone Della Valpolicella with a small note card in the brown paper bag which read: "Welcome to America! ~BP."

He became a regular at a little restaurant on the corner called Tatyana's. She served excellent pierogi, borscht, and Smetannikov cake for dessert, and kept a bottle or two of horilka in the back for him and a few of his friends and business associates. For a while, he kept a low profile, just another semiretired Ukrainian émigré, like many around him. Of course, just keeping a low profile wasn't the same as doing nothing. Maksym had plans.

He and Oleksandr became friendly but not close. His brother ran his business in Manhattan's Garment District and lived in Greenpoint with the Poles who worked in his factory. He had nothing against the Polish Jews, of course, but it would have been nice to have Oleks living with his own people in Little Odessa. The reality was that Oleks hadn't had a connection with Odessa in half a century. Why would he feel obliged?

His nephew, Anatol, on the other hand, worked on Wall Street and lived in Brighton Beach. The young man was a mover, leveraging his Ukrainian roots to persuade local business owners to invest their savings with him. He approached Maksym about doing the same for him. Anatol was charged with managing and investing Maksym's money, and as his uncle began rebuilding his business in America, Anatol became a close confidant.

Anatol Palatnik loved his father dearly, but they were nothing alike. There was a lot to admire in the man who fled Ukraine weeks before the Nazis invaded, arrived in New York months later penniless, and spent the next half century building his business in the Garment District. He was kind and good to his workers who ran the spinning and weaving machines. He built his business pennies at a time and worked fifteen hours a day, six days a week. On the Sabbath, he rested and prayed, but in his head, he was already thinking about the next day's work. Anatol grew up watching his father fight against failing markets, pitiful margins, recessions, new competitors, and the pressure of New York mafia protection rackets.

Anatol had no intention of living that way. He had a knack for the numbers and the charm that made people trust him. His clients were mostly the small-time players from his neighborhood in Brighton Beach, Russian and Ukrainian immigrants running small businesses like his father.

Wall Street had been good to Anatol. He was greedy but not Ivan Boesky greedy, and he was a risk-taker but not Michael Milken level of risk-taking. And he played the corporate leverage game too but not Carl Icahn corporate leverage. As a young bond trader, he'd smoked the rolled up hundred-dollar bills just like everyone else in the business. But they were someone else's hundred-dollar bills.

In the mid-1980s, as the icons of the industry fell, Anatol played it safe at Manufacturers Hanover, sold his own and his clients' stock early, and waited for the scandals to blow over. Black Monday in September 1987 was his cue to get back in. He played the markets and tripled his money by mid-1989.

That was his public face. His private face was that of a financial fixer for some of the midlevel mobsters in the city, capos in the five organized crime families, the same ones running the protection rackets that were such a problem for his father. It was risky business. He had helped a few of them launder money from a New York gas tax bootlegging scheme by opening dozens of shell companies in Panama. There, it was legal for wholesale companies to sell gasoline to each other tax-free, import the gas, and then collect tax on the sale. The wholesaler kept seven cents of the nine-cent per gallon tax and gave two cents to the capos operating in their patch. When the authorities came looking for their tax revenues, the shell company in Panama would be gone and simply replaced by a new one. It was a very profitable business—maybe in the hundreds of millions—until nine members of the Colombo crime family were convicted on racketeering, counterfeiting, and extortion tied to the tax evasion scheme. Anatol's cut, stashed in the Banco Nacional de Panama, was in the multimillions. It sat there, untouched, waiting for the day when he needed to flee the US. He called it his "fuck-off money."

It was that first spring in Brighton Beach when the young man—he was actually in his midthirties, but to the sixty-five-year-old Maksym, that was young—came to him with a proposition.

"Uncle, the wholesalers and the Italians have been running the retail gas business in New York for years, importing the stuff from South America through Panama. I set up the corporate entities down there for them. They were ripping off the tax revenues, and that's why they all went down. But the whole of the US only imports about fifty thousand barrels of Russian oil a day right now. I bet we could sell ten times that amount in New York alone. Everyone, the importers and the gas stations, want to get out from under the thumb of the mafia. And, honestly, the mob wants out, too, before more of them get sent to Rikers."

"I may know someone at Gazneft we can talk to, but it's too early. The whole of the Soviet Union is collapsing. There are rallies all over Ukraine. Gorbachev is visiting Kiev to campaign for his first secretary puppet. The whole fucking thing is falling apart. But when it's over, Yeltsin will have the reigns and privatize everything, sell ownership shares to the people for pennies on the dollar. Those chosen people will get very rich very quickly with protection from the state. We must wait for those people to emerge."

And that was the beginning of the rebirth of Maksym Palatnik. Ten years later, the US was importing more than two hundred thousand barrels of Russian oil a year. By the time that the Draftsman was killed, it had tripled again. Most of it passed through the port of Odessa, sailed for Panama, and then landed in the Port of New York.

Chapter 38

Langley, Virginia, 2009

Marcus Sternwell rubbed his forehead hard, his elbows planted firmly on the desk of his fifth-floor office overlooking the Potomac. He preferred to ease into his day by admiring the view over a hot cup of coffee, but that wasn't going to happen. Today was the beginning of the end of his storied career at the agency, and he knew it.

An open manila folder lay on his desk. It contained a memo from his new boss, Michael Atwater, the Executive Director (EXDIR) of Central Intelligence, asking him to respond to a formal request from the FBI and INTERPOL for investigative support. Underneath was a copy of a preliminary case report into a string of execution-style murders up and down the eastern seaboard by a hit squad. The ballistics report suggested connections to the Ukrainian mafia. Three of the victims had been tortured before their execution, and the same gun was used to execute them.

Atwater probably had no idea who the victims were or how they were connected, but Sternwell was very well aware of the cases and the people involved. They were all former CIA employees or assets from the Cold War years. Just seeing their names on an unclassified document was disturbing.

As the Director of National Clandestine Services in the Directorate of Operations, Sternwell had no desire to see anyone connected with agency activities from those days exposed in the press or discussed in congressional oversight committee meetings.

For the moment at least, the call for help was informational only, but it wouldn't stay that way for long. "Support" was an ambiguous term. Coordination and information sharing between the Agency, FBI, Homeland Security, and international law enforcement was rife with ambiguity and a distinct lack of consistent protocol. His best bet was to slow walk it, hiding behind the classification system and "national security" protections, leaving no crumbs for the FBI and INTERPOL to follow. It would hold them off for a while, but eventually, it would all come back to Langley.

When Atwater found out how deep the links went, would he protect the agency and his Director of National Clandestine Services or use Sternwell as a scapegoat to take the fall for the sins of the past?

The timing could not have been any worse. A new Democratic administration had taken back power in January, and eight months later, the promotions, reassignments, and retirements were still rippling through the senior levels of the agency.

Atwater had been a peer until his recent promotion, running the Directorate of Science and Technology. Like so many in the agency these days, he was a techie and had close to zero experience with clandestine and counterintelligence operations in the field. This wasn't quite true, of course, but Sternwell wasn't privy to much of Atwater's past work. For most of the 1990s, he had orchestrated the partnership between US, German, and Swiss intelligence, known as Operation Rubicon. They sold encryption technology to more than one hundred countries through a company called CryptoTech AG in Switzerland. The technology was packed with backdoors and codes easily broken by the intelligence services.

He now reported up to the director and deputy director of Central Intelligence, both of whom were politically appointees. They were on the more activist side, and Atwater was the buffer between the partisan politics at the top and the day-to-day running of the agency below. He was anxious to show his superiors that the agency could do the right thing just as well as they could do the wrong.

"This is a special situation, one that has eyes at the White House level," he had said to Sternwell the day before. "We cannot afford some embarrassing screwup thanks to interagency turf right now. Do what you can, within bounds, of course, to demonstrate a new attitude of cooperation with our sister agencies."

Sadly, he was going to be very disappointed when the two men met later that morning to discuss the case.

The clandestine nature of Operations gave some protection from the posturing of politicians, but he could feel the noose tightening. Congressional investigations already underway were looking into questionable programs and post-9/11 activities that had their home in the Directorate. This could well be the final nail in his career coffin. Perhaps, it was time to have lunch with his friends at the defense and intelligence lobbying firms down on D Street and prepare for a departure from the CIA.

He needed to set all that aside for a while to really understand the details of this troubling case so far. The investigators were trying to establish recent links between five individuals—Maksym Palatnik, Andrey Kuznetzov, Bruce Lasher, Robert Schier, and Brandon Pike. These men had a multitude of sketchy dealings in their combined FBI files going back to the 1950s, but that paled in comparison to their records at CIA.

Lasher and Schier were CIA case officers who recruited and ran field agents in the Eastern European division. Both had retired when the Soviet Union collapsed.

Schier was known inside Langley as "the Venus Spy Trap." He got the name for a counterintelligence operation he ran toward the end of his career against James Pollard. Pollard, a Naval Intelligence Officer, had befriended a former colonel in the Mossad who coaxed him into sharing documents with an ally. Schier uncovered the scheme and planted disinformation to pass back to Mossad for a few years. But Pollard got careless and was caught by a colleague printing classified documents on a copier and taking the copies home. He was arrested, convicted, and sent to FCI Butner, a medium-security prison in North Carolina.

Schier's true claim to fame was his orchestration of Operation Undercut, a complex program of counterintelligence that ran from the 1960s until his retirement in 1990, designed to undermine relations between the Soviet Union and its satellite republics.

The file on his desk confirmed Sternwell's worst fear, that this operation was the critical link between the killings.

Lasher was all-field operations, managing agents and sources around Eastern Europe for almost half a century without being compromised once. He was embedded in Ukraine to establish the link between Oleksandr and Maksym Palatnik. In cahoots with Giles Bancroft at MI6, he recruited an unwitting Pike to serve as a go-between using the textile business for cover. When Bancroft was promoted to deputy director of Counterintelligence in the Soviet Division, Undercut was launched, and Lasher took a back seat. From then on, Schier managed Pike, known as the Draftsman, and led the recruitment of Maksym Palatnik. Everything coming back to Langley went through Lasher via Regina Brooks, another CIA field agent. Regina later married Lasher and was also killed by the hit squad.

Kuznetzov, a longtime CIA source, was an associate of Palatnik and the last known owner of the Makarov MP-71 used to kill Pike, Schier, and Lasher. Not surprisingly, the CIA ledger on Palatnik and Pike was deep and very, very classified—beyond "Top Secret." Many of the files carried a special code-word classification, limiting file access to an even smaller group than Top-Secret clearance.

They were considered legends by the very limited number of people who had ever heard of them. The Cold War years held a lot of secrets. It was better for everyone that most stayed that way.

According to the case report, the FBI had nothing of substance on any of the victims, and the connections between Pike, Palatnik, Schier, and Kuznetzov were speculative at best. The relationships had surfaced in some INTERPOL investigations from the 1950s and '60s. The last INTERPOL file that referenced both Pike and Palatnik was from Poland in 1972, where a crony of Palatnik was caught siphoning money from a Soviet-controlled company. Palatnik and Pike ran some kind of operation and ended up killing someone, but there wasn't enough evidence to pursue it, and the Polish government stonewalled the investigation until it ran out of steam. After 1972, both men had dropped off the radar of INTERPOL.

Sternwell wasn't surprised. Recruiting people who worked in police and government records departments was the bread-and-butter counterintelligence work in the pre-digital era. It was the best way to make files appear and disappear, generate documents and identities, and ensure that agents in motion avoided arrest with investigative trails that dried up.

Sternwell had seduced—or maybe he was seduced by—and began a relationship with Zeynep, a young woman who worked in records department for Turkey's intelligence service, the Millî İstihbarat Teşkilatı (MIT). They met by chance—or maybe it wasn't—at a nightclub in the Kavaklidere neighborhood of Ankara. Sternwell was sitting alone at the bar when he saw the group of girls at the far end, all drinking and dancing. They were under assault from a clutch of mustached dervishes in silk shirts and gold chains. One of the girls caught his eye and nudged her friend to check out the well-dressed guy at the end of the bar. A few minutes later, they approached, some giggly flirtations and cocktails followed, and he left the club with Zeynep a couple of hours later.

Getting a NATO ally to share information was one thing, but asking a low-level officer inside the government machinery to destroy or falsify records was an entirely different matter. He was romantically involved with Zeynep for a year before he asked her to destroy a file that included photographs of a visiting US senator soliciting a prostitute working at the only the government approved *"genel ever"* brothel in Istanbul's Karaköy district. Zeynep soon realized that he was using her and demanded payment to pay her "poor, sick mother's" medical bills. She accumulated a small fortune by her standards before she was found one morning floating in the Bosphorus with her hands severed and a bullet in the back of her head. Someone found out what she doing. Sternwell, riddled with guilt over her death, was recalled to Langley in a hurry and began his climb up the ladder from the safety of home turf.

He looked at his watch: 8.30 a.m. Three hours until the scheduled briefing with Atwater in one of the secure conference rooms up on the sixth floor. He needed to review the report from Pike's final debriefing after his extraction from Eastern Europe where they tied up any outstanding informational loose ends before a planned or forced retirement from the Service. The debriefing and his last official contact with the agency lasted five days.

Sternwell pulled up the report on his computer. It was classified as Top Secret. A cheery dialogue box popped up, "Request Access?"

The file carried an extra code-word classification, a randomly generated cryptonym, to limit access even beyond need-to-know. He tapped in GREEN MERCURY ORCHID on his keyboard.

"Secondary Authentication Required."

He put his finger on the authentication pad next to his keyboard, and the little wheel swirled on his screen, went blank for a moment, and opened the file.

The report, more than thousand pages long, was dated October 17, 1989, and compiled by the Assistant Director, Office of Soviet and Eastern European Operations, Robert Schier (STANWYCH). A search box gave him the option to focus on sections containing key words, so he applied filters to target the sections containing both Pike (DRAFTSMAN) and Palatnik (KONTROL). The list shrank from 135 to 12. Six topics caught his attention—the CIA's extraction of Palatnik and Pike from Ukraine in 1988; Pike's 1978 arrest in East Berlin; the 1975 assassination of Athens CIA Station Chief, Geoffrey March; the Jakub Nowak killing in Warsaw in 1972; the 1970 Babic operation in Yugoslavia; and the Russian invasion of Czechoslovakia in 1968 that referenced Bruce Lasher (YANKEE).

Extraction of KONTROL and DRAFTSMAN, December 1988

By the summer of 1988, Soviet Premier Gorbachev was under pressure from hard-line party factions opposed to Glasnost and angered by his denunciation of Stalin in a speech celebrating the seventieth anniversary of the October Revolution. Soviet newspapers published an open letter blaming a reformer clique of Jews and ethnic minorities in the Kremlin for undermining Stalinist ideology. It became a rallying cry for anti-reformers and a rationalization for KGB-led operations against Jews. The KGB initiated a corruption investigation targeting Volodymyr Shcherbytsk's Ukrainian government.

KONTROL was a target due to his extensive illegal business dealings, his influence within the local, regional and central government, and his Jewish heritage. Deputy director of Central Intelligence, at the recommendation of the Director of Operations for Soviet and Eastern Europe, authorized his extraction. DRAFTSMAN was recalled from Asia with instructions to fly to Odessa, reconnect with KONTROL, leave Ukraine together by boat to rendezvous with an extraction team in Istanbul. KONTROL was given a US passport and new identity and flown to New York via Frankfurt. Several weeks later, the extraction of DRAFTSMAN was also approved.

STANWYCH. Why did he need to be extracted? What prompted it?

DRAFTSMAN. Kuznetzov called me out of the blue, worried that the KGB were moving in and that Maksym wasn't taking the threat seriously. I reported back to Langley that I was afraid he would be arrested and interrogated, exposing us all. The decision was made back here to get him out early and we did.

STANWYCH. And? What happened after that?

DRAFTSMAN. He assumed a new identity, Mikel Borova, and is living in Brighton Beach as far as I know.

By early 1988, the Soviet Union was disintegrating. The KGB was operating on conflicting and reactionary orders from a collapsing and desperate government. KONTROL's extraction made a lot of sense. It was entirely possible that the operation had exposed DRAFTSMAN. There was no scenario where having either of them taken in by the KGB was acceptable. Their arrest and exposure would have been devastating to the agency's reputation, and more than likely, one or both would have died in the basement of Lukyanivska prison.

Palatnik and Pike showed up in the same operation in East Germany in 1978 when DRAFTSMAN was arrested and briefly imprisoned at the Stasi prison, Hohenschönhausen. Sternwell clicked on the link to jump to that section.

Arrest of DRAFTSMAN in East Berlin, 1978

DRAFTSMAN attempted to cross the border from East to West Berlin as was his usual practice. The Grenztruppen border guards were on high alert following the assassination of a Soviet diplomat.

STANWYCH. Tell me about Preobrazhensky.

DRAFTSMAN. I'd made a half dozen trips in and out of East Berlin that year. My cover was that Lawrence Textile had a major deal with a company called FibrNonwovensTech. It was a shell created by one of our assets inside the DDR. We were actually gathering intelligence on turnover in Hoenecker's government. It was unusually high, and we thought it might be about to fall. I had a regular bar in Prenzlauer Berg. I'd sit at one end drinking my Beefeaters and tonic, and my tail would sit at the other end. This happened all the time over there. We never spoke, but I'd send him a drink, he'd return the favor. On my third or fourth visit, he decides to talk to me. It turns out he wasn't just a tail I exchanged drinks with. He was a KGB recruiter, working over the western businessmen who crossed back and forth between East and West. I was one of those businessmen. He walks over, introduces himself as Alexei Preobrazhensky, thanks me for supporting business in East Germany, and asks if I'm interested in making some new connections in the East German and Soviet government. I was quite insulted that he thought I'd fall for that. I reported the contact and was told to follow it. Well, he was either a complete fucking wanker or the people he targeted were wankers. Anyway, we ended up in an alley one night talking. He tried to recruit me and get me to recruit others. When I refused, he threatened to contrive a story about me that would get me arrested. I couldn't afford to take that risk, so I followed him home one night and shot him on his front steps.

STANWYCH. Why there?

DRAFTSMAN. Where I went, he went. I didn't want it to be easy to pin his death to me. I thought that if he was killed on his steps, it could have been any number of people. I left the alley, went back to my hotel, and when his shift was over, I followed him home. I probably shouldn't have killed him, just left East Berlin and never gone back.

STANWYCH. And then?

DRAFTSMAN. I had to get out of East Berlin in a hurry. I had a shit car, a roll of money, and a weapon that I just couldn't leave behind. I tried to cross at Friedrichstrasse, and I could have pulled it off if it wasn't for the headlights on the car failing. They arrested me and took me to a Stasi prison for interrogation. I was there for what felt like a year. They drugged me, beat me, played loud music twenty-four hours a day, starved me, made me shit in a bucket, tied me up. Then suddenly, they cleaned me up, threw me in the back of a van and drove me to the bridge. I walked towards the headlights, and some guy passed me going the other direction. We looked at each other but kept walking, and suddenly, I was running towards something that felt like safety. Maksym got me out.

STANWYCH. Palatnik? How?

DRAFTSMAN. Don't ask me, but he was there on the Soviet side of the bridge. I had to be him. Nobody else gave a damn. Your lot would have left me for dead.

Sternwell was shocked. But was he really? Actually, nothing surprised him about the CIA's past anymore. It was amazing, however, that Pike was part of a prisoner exchange on Glienicke Bridge and that Maksym Palatnik, a Ukrainian mobster, orchestrated his release. DRAFTSMAN's days in Eastern Europe were over, of course, and he was deployed to Asia, but KONTROL kept working in the region and continued to report back to RUGBY.

He was still knee-deep in the Pike debriefing report when Damon Macatee, agency liaison to the FBI, asked for time on his calendar later to discuss the special operational request from the FBI investigating Pike's murder.

"Have Marsha set something up, Damon. I'm still working my way through the files. Maybe after lunch?"

"Yes, sir. Thank you, sir."

For personal reasons, Sam was particularly interested to read the section about the assassination of CIA Station Chief Geoffrey

March in December 1975. He'd dated March's daughter, Elizabeth, for a year at Georgetown. She had a big heart and even managed to convince him to volunteer at a homeless shelter in Brentwood during their sophomore year.

But she was also damaged. As a little girl, living in a strange country, she watched from her bedroom window as her father was executed and her mother beaten, bound, gagged, and tossed behind a hedge. Not surprisingly, her mother was never the same, and Elizabeth's aunt was the one to raise her from then on.

When the agency showed up at the apartment to recruit young Sam Sternwell, she was none too pleased. And when he agreed to join upon graduation, it was more than she could take, and the young couple split up.

But this was the first he had heard of any kind of agency response to her father's murder. March name and address had been published in the *Athens News*, and he was identified as a CIA agent in the book *Who's Who in the CIA?*, published by two Soviet bloc intelligence agencies. His killing eventually led to the Intelligence Identities Protection Act of 1982.

Geoffrey March assassination and reprisal against 17N

The military Junta in Greece, known as the Regime of the Colonels, fell following a coup d'état in Cyprus and fear of imminent war with Turkey. Parliamentary democracy and free elections were restored in late 1974. Director Welch arrived in Athens in July 1975 after serving as CIA Station Chief in Mexico City. On the evening of December 23, as he and his wife walked home from a Christmas party on his street in Kifissia, three men jumped out of a stolen Simca-Fiat, shot him in the head execution style in front of his wife, then beat, bound, and left her crying behind a bush. Years later, in 1985, a man named Pavlos Serifis confessed to the killing and alleged that he did it with his uncle Demetrius, a tall blond woman known only as Anna who drove the gateway, and another man who was one of the leaders of a newly formed far-left terrorist group called 17 November(17N).

STANWYCH. How were you involved in the aftermath of Geoffrey March's assassination.

DRAFTSMAN. Maksym asked MI6 to intervene on behalf of an old friend from the resistance. The fact that 17N had killed March was actually just a coincidence. 17N targeted other Greek officials, including the chief of internal security, who also happened to be the brother-in-law of a shipping magnate who did business with Maksym. He wanted revenge on 17N and gave us a small fortune to care of it for him.

STANWYCH. And how did you get involved? This was long after you left the region.

DRAFTSMAN. I still worked for the London office, and I didn't see a good reason to get it cleared in Washington. It wasn't a CIA-sponsored job, had nothing to do with March, and the agency wouldn't have protected us anyway. Anyway, Alexandros Andino, a leader of 17N, was untouchable and hard to pin down, always moving around, changed his appearance all the time. We decided to take out his nephew, Xiros Tzortzatos, instead. We knew they were close, but Xiros was not 17N, just a well-known restaurant owner in Athens. Maksym's magnate friend wanted it done in a very public way to send a message, so I shot him from long range while he attended a family wedding. Xiros was standing next to Andino's wife, Anna, when I shot him so that she got covered in her husband's nephew's blood in front of the whole family. A bit blood thirsty for my taste, but it was what the client wanted.

STANWYCH. And yet it never made the press. How did that work?

DRAFTSMAN. The client squashed the story. He just wanted Andino to know that it was him. And the internal security people were happy too. The Greeks could put the Sicilians and the Ukrainians to shame when it to revenge killings.

It wasn't the revenge story Sternwell had been hoping for. He'd often thought about tracking Elizabeth down but never had a good excuse. Avenging her father's death would have been just the ticket even if he couldn't share any details. He decided to let it go and flipped to the next section that focused on an operation involving a man named Jakub Nowak.

Jakub Nowak killing in Warsaw in 1972

STANWYCH. How did you come to meet Jakub Nowak? And what was his connection to Maksym Palatnik?

DRAFTSMAN. He was a customer of Lawrence Textile. In 1972, we attended an industry exhibition in Lodz, Poland. We were working the booth, talking to local manufacturers. One of them was a company called Polska Innotextile. Before the war, it was privately owned, but the Nazis took it over and used the factory to make uniforms and prison clothes for the concentration camps. Then the Soviets took it back, turned it over to Poland's communist government. Jakub Nowak was one of their men. Maksym had a friend, Filip, from the resistance, and Jakub was his uncle. Anyway, Jakub and his cronies had been siphoning money from the company for years undetected. Every six months, the cash was shipped out of the country and deposited in various banks in the West. Rumor was that the SB, the Polish secret police, were onto the scam thanks to an informer in Nowak's organization. Nowak was a solid source for MI6 about Poland, and so he needed to be protected. He was also an excellent customer of Maksym's transportation services.

STANWYCH. And so what did the relevant parties decide to do?

DRAFTSMAN. Nowak was taken by the SB one night to a warehouse. He was given some pretty rough treatment. Somehow, YANKEE knew where he was being held, then Maksym told us and sent Andrey [Kuznetzov] and I to get him out. We got there and found Nowak with his arms chained around a pipe in the ceiling. No one else was there. He'd been beaten around the ribs, and his face was bruised, one eye swollen shut. I went to get him down, and Andrey went to search the rest of the building. When he didn't come back, I went looking for him. I found him on his knees with a gun at the back of his head, whimpering about having a family and begging for his life. I took out the guy about to kill him.

STANWYCH. And who was he?

DRAFTSMAN. No idea, presumably SB. The whole thing was strange. I decided not to ask too many questions. There's always a master plan. Kuznetzov loved me after that though. There was always tension between Maksym's security people and the rest of us. I'd known Andrey since 1951, but we never really interacted. Anyway, after this he gave me his beloved Makarov, and we were like brothers from then on.

STANWYCH. That's false. You had the Makarov since the Balan operation. You want to revise that statement?

DRAFTSMAN. Maybe you're right. It was so long ago. I forget.

And there it was. Pike had been killed with his own gun, a prize given to him by Kuznetzov. DRAFTSMAN had been arrested at the East German border in Berlin with the gun used in the assassination of a KGB recruiter back to the West. Somehow, the Makarov ended up in his retirement home in Florida, and thirty years later, it was used to kill him. It had to be Palatnik. He had arranged the Draftsman's release and probably got the Makarov over the bridge with him too. It was the link the FBI was looking for and maybe just enough to keep them from digging too deep into the agency's past.

Whoever it was that killed Pike knew about the gun. And that was the problem for Sternwell. Maksym Palatnik, nee Mikel Borova, knew. Out of the corner of his eye, he could see the little red light on his desk phone flashing incessantly. The ringer was off, but Marsha always called anyway, knowing that he could not ignore a blinking light.

"Hi, Marsha. What's up?"

"Sorry to interrupt, sir. Damon Macatee is trying to get on your calendar today. He said he spoke to you this morning and that you wanted me to find a time after lunch. But you have a meeting with Director Atwater at two. Mr. Macatee mentioned something about UNDERCUT. Should I make your twelve-thirty slot available? It's currently blocked for an operational review, but you could send a delegate to that."

"Okay. Set it up, and I'll meet Damon here in my office."

Chapter 39

Washington, DC

I t was Pascal Benoit's first trip to Washington, DC, a fact that was surprising even to him given his many years at INTERPOL. The killing of Sean Pike and his daughter had US law enforcement's head spinning. They were targeted innocents, and that was a terrifying escalation. The housekeepers and security guard were innocents, too, but not targets. Just in the wrong place at the wrong time.

Agent-in-charge Isherwood had called Directeur Fischer personally to ask for help. Project Caspian had more information on the Ukrainian mafia than anyone else. Fischer gave Pascal permission to make the trip for meetings on the case at the US National Center Bureau and FBI Headquarters.

"You know about these criminals. And not to mention you are in contact with the daughter and her solicitor. Whoever these killers are, they are closing in on the family, looking for this binder and the money."

Despite the urgency of the case, finance denied him the more expensive, direct flight in business class between Paris and Dulles. He suffered through a layover in JFK on his way down to Reagan Washington National. He was fortunate, however, that one of his contacts at the FBI was able to secure an acceptable room rate at the Willard Intercontinental on Pennsylvania Avenue NW. The location was perfect—walking distance to both US NCB and FBI HQ. Some people were drivers, others rode buses and subways or took taxis, but Pascal was a walker. He learned a lot about a place by feeling the ground under his feet and hearing clips of conversations between passersby.

At US NCB, the small team of American INTERPOL agents liaising with the FBI brought him up to speed on the investigation

206

so far. The identities of the killers were still unknown although the FBI behavioral analysts at Quantico had built a profile. It was clear that whoever they were, the cruelty of their attacks was increasing. What started as a single, brutal murder had escalated to the killing of innocent housekeepers and ultimately to the killing of a child in front of her father, leaving her body at his feet and then killing him. The profilers believed it was part of a ritual, like the burning of the feet and that there were likely more terrifying techniques that they just hadn't tapped into yet.

"We've started calling them the Chauffeurs in Lyon…"

Blank stares.

"After the Chauffeurs de la Drôme, a gang of home invaders who tortured victims to reveal the location of their valuables by burning the bottom of their feet with a branding iron. They were guillotined in 1909."

"You still guillotined people in 1909?"

Pascal reveled in the shock of his statement.

"Oh, yes. In fact, the last public execution was 1939, in front of the Prison Saint-Pierre in Versailles. The crowd celebrated the death and dabbed handkerchiefs in the blood of a German who kidnapped and murdered women for profit."

There was a large whiteboard in the meeting room, divided into two—one half for the United States and the other for Europe. In the middle of each were the Palatnik brothers—Oleksandr on the US side and Maksym in Europe. The victims—Brandon Pike, Robert Schier, housekeeper Lila Hernandez, Bruce Lasher, Regina Brooks, security guard Norbert Quirrel, Sean Pike, and his daughter, Nicole—were dotted around the US side of the board. Each picture was marked with a "D" for deceased. Different colored strings traced the path of the hit squad from south to north and back. The living, marked with an L, were on there too, including Ana, her mother Adeline, and brother Stephen.

On the European side, Maksym Palatnik was marked with a "U" for "unknown," Artem Ponomarenko with a "D," and Andrey Kutnetzov with an L. There were a dozen grainy pictures Pascal didn't recognize.

"Who are all these people?" Pascal ventured, gesturing toward the board.

"Xerox copies of the photographs from the binder that Ana Pike turned over to the FBI—the ones they shared with us anyway. They had to be cleared through national security. Some names were redacted."

"There's an actual intelligence angle to this? My understanding was that it was more about organized crime than spies."

"It could be the usual interagency politics, but Maksym Palatnik appears to be more than just a mobster. He was wired into the Soviet government and maintained numerous relationships with the West. It wouldn't be a surprise to find names in there with Cold War connections that the intelligence community wants to keep under wraps." Pascal was not surprised.

They spent the morning breaking down the actual and suspected relationships between the people on the board. Most were speculative at best. Many of the shadowy figures from the binder had no discernible links. Their names were probably fake. By the time they stopped for lunch, they had a clearer picture of the situation, but a major question still loomed: where was Maksym Palatnik now?

He had dropped off the radar as the Soviet Union collapsed, never to be heard from again. A corrupt and cruel mobster with powerful connections in Moscow, it made sense for the KGB to cut off the head of the snake. A number of his associates fled for Israel, and rumors that the Malina operated in and around Tel Aviv were rampant. They concluded that he was probably dead.

But if he wasn't behind all the killing, who was? His brother was the obvious suspect, but had no record, paid his taxes on time, and ran what appeared to be a legitimate business. The FBI had questioned him but got nothing of substance. He had a son who was a hotshot on Wall Street who they still needed to interview.

The Americans had ordered sandwiches, soda, and cookies to be delivered to the office. While they decided against the whole "working lunch thing," they nonetheless spent the time digging into their email while eating unappetizing sandwiches, potato chips, and guzzling Diet Coke.

To Pascal, it was an unbearable experience. As the only smoker in the group, he headed outside with his trusty Gauloises Vertes and stood in front of a sign that read "No smoking within 25 feet of the door." His mind churned and processed everything he had learned. He was convinced that Maksym Palatnik was alive, pulling the strings from somewhere.

In the afternoon, they turned their attention to the money. A decision had been made not to freeze the assets, which amounted to more than a 130 million dollars. Why? Ana was cooperating with the FBI and had consolidated all the money in a single account under the legal management of solicitor, James Mattinson. She had no access to it and couldn't move it. It was easily frozen.

The main reason, however, was the fear of alerting whoever hired the hit squad to how close they were. Apparently, the general secretariat, in line with Pascal's advice and his own ambitions of a happier and more productive relationship with the Americans, had bowed to FBI's wishes.

"What do we know about the source of the money?"

"Not much. We have some circumstantial links between deposits, people in the binder, and Brandon Pike that seem to line up. Pike appears to have been some kind of enforcer for Maksym Palatnik, getting paid for taking out rivals or politicians that got in the boss's way. We've had Ana Pike under surveillance through NCBs in Europe as you know Agent Benoit. The banks she visited received large deposits in a half dozen foreign currencies beginning in 1951 and ending in 1988. After that, the accounts were untouched. The money just sat accumulating interest and benefiting from inflation."

"And we know this how?"

"Sources. We have them in most of the banks. They help us, so we stay off their backs. Of course, they give us as little as they can get away with."

Perhaps the FBI could shed more light on this. They had a meeting scheduled for the next morning with Sam Isherwood and his team. They folded up the tent for the night.

The first day at NCB done, Pascal took a slight diversion on the way back to the Willard onto Tenth Street NW to see Ford's Theatre, where Abraham Lincoln was assassinated, before sitting alone in the Round Robin, the famous bar in the Willard, reviewing his notes from the day.

The circular bar sat in the center of room of polished mahogany and forest green decor. A sign behind the bar read "All Nations Welcome Except Carrie," a reference to the radical prohibitionist of the Temperance Movement, Carrie Nation, who raged against alcohol and attacked serving establishments with a hatchet.

Behind the bar the spectacled bartender in a starched, white shirt and black bow tie carefully dried martini glasses with a small towel. "Long day, sir?"

Pascal nodded, rubbing his forehead into a million deep ripples.

"What can I get for you then, sir? How about our signature, Mint Julep, known as the Henry Clay. It's made with Maker's Mark Kentucky Bourbon."

"I will give it a try. Thank you."

They lapsed into a comfortable silence, the only sound was the muddling of mint, bourbon, sugar, and the tumble of crushed ice into the tall glass.

"I'll leave you in peace, sir, but if you need anything, please don't hesitate to ask."

The Round Robin was starting fill up, a mix of old men in bowties, polished, well-groomed young men in Brioni suits with starch white shirts but no tie and attractive women in silky dresses that clung seductively to their Pilates-toned bodies. Pascal felt rumpled and behind the times in his French blue tweed and unimaginative tie.

"I'm going out for a smoke. Can you hold my seat? I'm told you have a good selection of Scotches here. What do you recommend for someone on a government-travel budget?"

"Macallan Rare Cask Single Malt, but you might have to chip in some of your own money, I'm afraid! I'll make it double at no extra cost for you though."

Outside, a light snow was falling. The temperature had fallen dramatically since he walked back to the hotel. His overcoat was still hanging on the back of his seat at the bar, but at least he still had his scarf on. This would be quick.

Chapter 40

J. Edgar Hoover Building, Washington, DC

At eight thirty the next morning, after a wonderful night's sleep thanks to the Macallan and perhaps the largest bed he had ever slept in, Pascal strolled out of the Willard and made the ten-minute walk down Pennsylvania Avenue NW to the J. Edgar Hoover FBI headquarters.

He was freezing, grateful that he thought to bring his wool over-coat, hat, and gloves. An icy breeze roared up the Potomac, whipping around the buildings of the Federal Triangle area.

FBI Headquarters was perhaps the ugliest building he had seen in Washington, a crumbling Brutalist edifice across the street from the much more austere Robert F. Kennedy Department of Justice Building.

As was his custom, he was fifteen minutes early. Just enough time for a final cigarette and some casual people-watching. It was strange, he thought, that everyone dashed around in suit jackets, ties blowing over their shoulders, seemingly oblivious to the cold, while he sought protection from the wind under a scrawny tree. He blew out a long stream of smoke and tipped his cigarette into the soil around the tree. He caught several passersby giving him a judgmental sideways glance, and he felt distinctly out of place.

Other members of the INTERPOL NCB team were approaching, so he stubbed out his cigarette on the sidewalk. One of them looked down as he did it, letting him know that it was poor form to leave the butt lying there, so he picked it up and stowed it in his pocket. Probably not a great idea.

The team assembled and marched confidently toward the main entrance, exchanging morning pleasantries and complaining about the crowds on the Metro Blue line coming into the Federal Triangle station. After a multitude of security measures, they were escorted to a large windowless conference room on the third floor.

The walls were whiteboards, sparkling white except for one small segment in the corner with very American-sounding names like Jason Derek Brown, Walter "Bucky" Higginbottom, and Joey Springette. The names were inside a box with the message "DO NOT ERASE" at the top. Pascal wondered who they were and why was it so important not to erase their names. Surely, they were important enough to be written down in a place of greater permanence.

Seating was assigned around the conference table—name tent cards, an official FBI notebook, and ballpoint pen sitting on FBI blotter, with an FBI-embossed water glass half filled already with crystal clear still water. On a sideboard at the far end stood a coffee dispenser, a bowl with cream in small plastic containers, and some pastries wrapped in cellophane. The US NCB team seemed comfortable with this commoditized, corporate experience, quietly talking and laughing while perusing the sideboard for the perfect blend of breakfast items.

Pascal felt out of place and uncomfortable. He liked to pick his own seat. This wasn't a wedding for Christ's sake. He wanted an espresso or a café crème, not a bitter and burned American coffee with a dose of half-and-half. Breakfast was a pain au chocolat in parchment paper, not a stale Danish wrapped in plastic with an indistinguishable red or yellow substance in the middle.

This was going to be a long day, and, God, he needed another cigarette. He could feel the packet in the inside pocket of suit jacket brushing against his shirt, reminding him it was there and willing him to take one out and light up. There were conference rooms back in Lyon that still allowed smoking and came complete with ashtrays and embossed books of INTERPOL matches. Not here.

The agenda—printed on official FBI letterhead and placed perfectly next the notebook—showed that a break was planned for 10.30 a.m. and would last exactly fifteen minutes.

He was surprised not to see his name as one of the people leading any of the discussions. The morning session, that precious time before his cigarette break, was labeled in an elegant Palatino font, "Group Discussion of the Case As It Currently Stands" with "Special Agent Paul Bergman, Violent Crimes and Major Offenders Division, FBI" and "Mary Coopersmith, Transnational Crime Division, US NCB INTERPOL" delivering the information.

The late-morning session, presumably leading into a prefab lunch of turkey sandwiches and potato chips at twelve thirty, was titled "Next Steps: Brainstorming Ideas To Catch The Perpetrator(s)." This session was to be led by "Sam Isherwood, Special Agent-in-Charge" and, surprisingly, Mary again. If adhering to parallel seniority, it should have been Pascal.

This had the earmarks of a power play with Isherwood controlling the pivotal discussion about what to do next. The afternoon would be devoted to "Operational Planning and Execution" led by a generic "Combined FBI and US NCB Team." The day was scheduled to end at 5.30 p.m.

Pascal looked up as Sam Isherwood and his team of FBI investigators marched into the room and took their places standing behind their assigned seat. Several carried Starbucks cups, apparently aware of the distasteful coffee options available on the sideboard.

In his most authoritarian voice, Isherwood said, "Good morning, everyone. Thank you for coming in. I presume everyone knows everyone already? We have a busy day ahead of us, so I suggest we dig right in."

This was one of the many things that annoyed Pascal about Americans as colleagues. They were always so directed, so single-minded, and impersonal in their approach. They focused on the outcome from the start as if the whole thing was just a series of predetermined steps to reach a necessary conclusion and that the meeting would end when agreement was achieved and the next steps put into motion. He could almost hear the closing statement of the day, "Thanks for your time today, everyone. This is a great plan. Let's put it into action!"

This wasn't France. He had to set his prejudices aside. These crimes had to be solved before more people were tortured and killed.

He took a deep breath and sat in his assigned seat at the table, counting the minutes to the first break and his chance to grab a cigarette.

He returned the greeting, but Isherwood started speaking before he could finish it with grace.

The morning session passed without incident, both teams open to sharing whatever information they had to date. There were a few times when Isherwood would pipe up that "that information is not currently available to our investigation, but we are working on it."

The fifteen-minute break was barely enough time to get downstairs and back. Lunch was awful, as expected, and Isherwood micromanaged every detail throughout the day. But by the time they all closed their folios for the day and stood up to leave, they had a plan that they could execute, and as much as he resented the FBI's control, their efficiency in decision-making was impressive.

At the end of the day, the FBI and INTERPOL had hatched a plan to catch the perpetrators. The bait was Ana Pike, and Pascal had enough of a relationship to persuade her. Or so they believed. It was going to be a difficult conversation.

The next morning, just before 7:00 a.m., Katherine Daring, the Assistant Executive Director of FBI's Intelligence Branch and the most senior liaison with the intelligence community, pulled up to the entrance of the Potomac Overlook Regional Park trails. She was met one of her frequent running partners for a planned 5K, twice around the Donaldson Run Loop. A stiff, cold breeze whipped off the river, and she was glad to have her winter gear, concerned that perhaps it was overkill for September. Clearly not. She plugged her earphones into the iPod on her upper arm, started her workout mix, and put on her ponytail ear warmer headband and gloves.

Her partner appeared next to her, a fleece running hat, dark glasses, and only his nose and mouth exposed. He quickly applied some Blistex to his lips, and with a flick of his head in the direction of the entrance, they were off. They were both experienced trail runners and set a fierce pace from the start. The first loop took about ten minutes. Halfway through the second loop, they stopped to sit and hydrate on a fallen tree trunk set back about fifteen feet from the trail.

"I need your help with something," Katherine said, "a case we are working on. You guys are already aware of it, a series of targeted hits on people associated with the Ukrainian mafia. You know which one I'm talking about."

"Mm-hmm. We looked at some of the photographs. Some shady people in that group, for sure. I think we gave the FBI investigators all the information we could. What do you need?"

"We need to get a message to someone, someone who might be able to let the right people know. They aren't going to stop until they have what they want, the binder of photographs and the money paid to the first victim. It's in the millions, and we're pretty sure someone wants it back. We need to catch them. The director and his new-found buddy in the general secretariat at INTERPOL have made it a top priority. Can you help?"

"I don't know. I'll run it up the chain. I'm not cleared to that level, so I can't tell you what we have or what we can do one way or another. Either way, we'll need to be read in on any operation. What's your timeline?"

"Three days."

Chapter 41

Maksym Palatnik, now known as Mikel Borova, had the protection he needed. He wasn't worried. If his name came up in the investigation, they'd whisk him away to safety as they had twenty years before when they brought him to America to escape the KGB. Some of his Pakhan and their people would go down, but they all understood the risk. The survivors would join other organizations as long as they followed the code. The thieves' code had never been more important, and everyone knew it. Their future prospects, and even their lives, depended on it.

His handler had called for a meeting, the first in several years. No doubt time was short. He needed that binder whatever the cost, whether it was paid in dollars or lives. And he wanted the money back too. More out of principle than necessity.

And now Maksym was waiting for his contact to arrive at the designated spot, a bench in Asser Levy Park, named after one of the first Jewish settlers in the Dutch colony of New Amsterdam and the first Jew to own a house in North America. Seemed appropriate.

"It's good to see you, Mikel. I trust you are well? It's been a long time. You must know it's an important matter, right?"

The old man—still wiry and lean, the scars on his face less obvious now, one eye drifting to the side in blindness—just looked at his contact who continued on.

"As you know, there are many matters from our shared past that we wish to remain in the past and I—"

216

"What's this all about? I'm a busy man. It's not good to be seen lingering in a deserted park next to children's playground with someone not from the neighborhood."

"The Draftsman, and several of your former colleagues have been murdered. And now his son and granddaughter are also dead. This string of murders is a top priority at the FBI. The name Maksym Palatnik has come up as part of the investigation, but so far Mikel Borova has not. They think you died at the hands of the KGB, but I don't think that will last. If they haven't already, they'll be interviewing your brother soon as a prime suspect. Do not make contact with him. He is already under surveillance. Andrey Kuztnezov's name came up too. A weapon used in all the killings was a Makarov registered in INTERPOL's database under his name. Andrey is doing well, by the way, living in his dacha with a long-legged young nurse who lets him feel her up for money. Somehow, that weapon made its way here, sat unused for thirty years, and was then used to kill the last man known to use it. Fascinating, don't you think? If I were a betting man, I'd say that whoever killed him understood the significance of that weapon and is now using it kill the Draftsman's family and friends to send a message. Anyway, the working theory within the FBI is that the killers are looking for something specific. Our concern back at Langley is that there is some record of his past that might expose some things or some people that we don't want exposed. The only persons that would care as much about that kind of exposure are the people who might themselves be exposed. Are you following me here?"

"Of course. You don't need to be so cryptic. I believe he kept photographs. When I knew him, he was never without a camera. I told him it was not smart. People, including me, would be suspicious, but he always had one with him."

"I see. So there are many people who potentially didn't want their identity or association with him known. That's good. Plenty of fool's errands for the FBI to chase. We only care about ourselves and you and your family. We can handle the Draftsman being exposed, a fossil of the Cold War when those kinds of intrigues were just part of the job. I guess the point is that we want those photographs destroyed or turned over to us as well, and it is our suspicion that someone in your sphere is the one looking for them. We'd like to get a message to whoever that is with some information about where and when they might be found. We also need the killing to stop, of course, so in exchange for the information, we'd like some assurances about the safety of the person we believe has possession of them. Is that something you can help us with?"

An hour later, Maksym and his nephew, Anatol, were alone at Tatyana's. She brought a fresh bottle of horilka to the table, and Maksym ordered her to turn up the music. It was a composition called "For His Kind," a piece written for choir, brass, and percussion with lyrics based on the poems of Oksana Zabuzhko by a young Ukrainian composer. He enjoyed this piece immensely, but its main purpose today was to drown out the conversation with his nephew.

In the van across the street, a lone FBI agent, smoking a cigarette and hunched over a recording device, watched a video screen showing the inside of the dimly lit restaurant. The music coming through his headphones was unbearable, a cacophony of blaring trumpets overlaid with a dramatic reading of Russian prose or poetry. The mics planted in the restaurant captured some but not all the conversation between the two Ukrainian mobsters. The FBI agent didn't understand a word of it, but someone would read the translation. He'd taken photographs of everyone who came out through the front door.

The screen showed the last two men still huddled at a large corner table, both facing the door, looking at something on the table, maybe a map? They seemed nervous, looking up at the front door every few seconds. The older one appeared to be giving instructions to the younger one, who nodded frequently. There was a gun sitting on the table, a pistol with a suppressor attached. They talked for almost ten minutes before the paper or map was folded and put in the older man's overcoat pocket. They had another drink, lit up a cigarette, and ate more of the food. The business portion of the meeting was apparently over, and the FBI man was none the wiser about the content of the conversation than he was before it happened.

Chapter 42

Naples, Florida

Pascal flew down to Fort Myers on an FBI jet and was met by a car to take him to the hotel. Ana, back from her whirlwind trip around Europe, and her mother had driven over from Vero a day earlier and were staying at a nearby Best Western in Bonita Springs. They were there for Sean and his daughter's funeral and to support Sean's widow, Sarah, and the other two children

He called Ana from the car and explained that he needed to meet with her. He had the unenviable task of convincing Ana to be a part of the FBI/INTERPOL plan to catch the killers.

He knocked on her door. She had sent her mother down to the hotel restaurant to get a table for lunch. It would give them time to talk in private.

"Good morning, Ms. Pike. It is good to meet you in person. Please accept my deepest condolences on the loss of your brother and niece. I just can't imagine your pain."

"Thank you, Agent Benoit. Please come in, and call me Ana. My mother is downstairs and expecting me for lunch so—"

"Yes, of course, I'll get to right to the point, and, please, I am Pascal, not Agent Benoit. Anyway, I spent the last week in Washington, DC, at FBI headquarters, reviewing all the evidence and formulating a plan. The killers do not know that you have turned over the binder to the FBI, so they will still be looking for it. We do not know what they know about the location of the money, but perhaps they want that too. The assessment of the profilers is that they will escalate the pace and the cruelty of their actions. We must keep your family safe."

"But what about me?"

"That is why I am here. We need your help."

Ana was in no mood. The death of her brother and niece was too much.

"Not interested, Agent Benoit. I've turned over the binder to the FBI, and they have shared it with you as promised, and my mother and I both have round-the-clock protection. It's not my job to catch these people. It's yours. It's too dangerous."

"I understand, but unfortunately, there's no other way. We can sort through all the photographs and try to make connections, but it will take too long. We need you to draw these people away from the rest of your family."

"No. I won't do it."

"I have seen it before, Ana. Our best plan of attack is to draw them into the trap rather than wait for them to come anyway when we are not ready. I am asking a lot of you, but you will be perfectly safe, and I will be there, I promise."

Her resistance was weakening.

"This will work. I know it. We will catch them. They won't even get near you. I will be there with you the whole time anyway. Will you help us, Ana?"

Chapter 43

Brighton Beach, New York

Tatyana's restaurant cleared out around 6:00 p.m., an hour before the sunset marking the beginning of Rosh Hashanah. Customers headed to temple and then home for the traditional candle lighting, challah bread, apples, and honey. Rosh Hashanah marked the beginning of the Ten Days of Awe when God determined all creatures' fate for the coming year and inscribed the names of those that would live through the following year in the Book of Life.

To Maksym, religious orthodoxy was a weakness to be exploited, another weapon in his arsenal of manipulation. For as long as he could remember, he had played to the traditions. He even put up a yolka tree, similar to a Christmas tree, that was part of the secular New Year's celebration in the Soviet Union. He was a Jew, a Christian, a tribalist, an atheist, a Muslim—whatever he needed to be at the moment.

Today, he was all Jew, and he used this holiday to play God, adding or removing names from his own Book of Life. It was he who decided who was favored and who needed to perform teshuvah to atone for failing him in hopes of seeing their name added to his Book before Yom Kippur when it was closed for the year. Disloyal minions and impudent rivals who couldn't atone were condemned.

Tatyana dimmed the lights a little and flipped the "Open" sign to "Closed."

It was the tenth year in a row that his top leaders, the Pakhan, had gathered at Tatyana's for this purpose. His nephew, Anatol, sat to his right. There was an empty honorary seat to his left for his brother,

Oleksandr. The other six Pakhan filled the other seats around the large table.

Tatyana marched in and out of the kitchen with plates of salo, pierogi, and potato pancakes. In the center of the table, she dropped a large bowl of bloodred borscht, two bottles of horilka with shot glasses, and a bucket of Ukrainian Chernihivske beers.

They spoke in hushed Ukrainian. Even here, the walls had ears. The Russian mafia was deeply entrenched in Brighton Beach. Tatyana fed a lot of local Russian mouths, but few Americanized Russians could understand Ukrainian. Several of his Pakhan were Belorussian or Polish and could speak and understand Ukrainian with ease, sharing the same Slavic language roots.

For an hour or so, the men whispered about their own book of business in loan sharking, bootlegging, protection rackets, prostitution, and arms trafficking. Maksym's only rule was no drugs, and it was always the first topic on the list for the Rosh Hashanah Book of Life meeting.

For years, the Russian mafia, who ran the Black Sea ports of Poti and Batumi in Georgia, trafficked opium, cocaine, and heroin from Azerbaijan and Afghanistan into the hands of the Russian mob in Brighton Beach for distribution throughout America. The war on drugs had taken a toll on many of these organizations. The new administration had abandoned the moniker, but the investigations, raids, and arrests continued unabated. Maksym wanted no part of it and demanded the same from his Pakhan. There was no atonement for the violators.

Ten names were left off the list to go in the book this year for violations of the policy—some with minor violations would be told atone before Yom Kippur. For the others? They made plans to eliminate them.

"The number of drug traffickers in our ranks gets lower each year," Maksym noted. "We must continue to work to eradicate it from our organization. This new president will not change the policies of the last when it comes to drugs. We cannot get caught in the Russian trap."

The discussion moved on to rivals, other outfits encroaching on the Pakhan's business, expanding their geographical reach, or poaching their men with promises of riches. The final topic was law enforcement, clean versus dirty cops, who could be bribed and who was trying to bring them down.

The book, in this case a spiral-bound notebook from Staples, sat on the table, and Maksym scratched his notes in the margins. The Pakhan, like a pack of slobbering hyenas over the corpse of an antelope, wondered how much that book would be worth in the hands of rivals. None dared take the thought to action.

In time, Maksym put down his pen, closed the book and lit a cigarette. He took a long drag, blowing a stream of thick smoke toward the already yellowed ceiling.

"Our efforts to find the binder and retrieve the money from the Draftsman have proven fruitless so far. He was killed and nothing. His associates were killed and nothing. His son and granddaughter were killed and nothing. The FBI and INTERPOL are after us and closing in. We have one last chance."

He looked over at one of his Pakhan and said, "If you want to find your place in the book, this is that opportunity. The teshuvah for failure will be great."

"Of course, boss. I won't let you down."

Another Pakhan voiced what they were all thinking. "Boss, could we be drawing too much attention to ourselves? Surely, that binder is old news from the old world. How valuable can it be today? The FBI are going after the bastard Russians right now, Moglievich, Dvoskin, Ginzburg, Ivankov, and the rest of them. Maybe it might be better to let them spin their wheels on those guys and not put a target on us?"

"They are already looking at us, and besides, that's not part of the code. I hate the fucking Russians, but we won't let them go down. They foolishly traffic in drugs, and we can't stop them, but in the end, we protect them, they protect us. Break the code, and the whole system falls. We manage our own business, protect our rivals, and keep the problems between us between us."

The Russian mafia and Ukrainian Malina lived by *Vorovskoy Zakon*, the thieves' code—very different from the family structure of the Italian mafia. The code forced members to relinquish family and other binding relationships, protect the secrets of others, take responsibility for the actions of another so that they could continue to operate and not lose your ability to make good decisions when consuming alcohol.

He took a deep breath, eyes piercing, making clear exactly what he needed them all to know. "I need that fucking binder, and I want my money back. Am I clear?"

Chapter 44

Dayton, Ohio, 2009

Ana hated her apartment. She'd rented it as a place to drop her bags, do laundry, and get some sleep between journalistic adventures. The two-bedroom, in a nice new building overlooking the Benjamin Shuster Performing Center in downtown Dayton, lacked any of the homeyness that it deserved. There was nothing to suggest that someone loved it or even really wanted to live in it. Long hours at work, it turned out, were not the same as adventures, so she spent more nights than she wanted there but never bothered to decorate.

She opened the front door for the first time in weeks. Bills and junk mail had piled up. Was it really that long since she'd been there that the landlord had to empty her mailbox and come into the apartment to dump it on the floor?

A couple of open, but still full, U-Haul boxes sat in the corner of the living room. Pictures hung on the same hooks the previous tenant had left in the walls. The furniture—old, threadbare, or just wobbly—was a mishmash of dated pieces given to her by her parents, leftover from her college apartment, or picked up on the cheap on eBay. The whole place felt like an abandoned office after a downsizing with mismatched chairs and random odds and ends waiting for a new tenant to breathe life into it.

At least the Wi-Fi and cable TV worked. Something in the kitchen smelled, but she was afraid to open the fridge to find the source. On the counter, she found a half pack of Marlboro Menthols and a lighter. A wine rack that held sixteen bottles had only one in reserve, a $10 Sangiovese. She realized, with a degree of horror and shame, that her drinking and smoking activities were in complete alignment with the rest of the apartment—low brow and without real taste.

She was an emotional mess, devastated by the killings and terrified of what was to come. At times like this, she generally turned on herself, reverting to the bad habits of her past, and usually ending with a late-night call to her sometime boyfriend on the fifth floor.

Her apartment served as a proxy for her life—the equivalent of a college dorm that was clearly not up to the standard of someone at her stage of life. She set to work cleaning up. If they were going to come in and take her, the place was going to look decent. It was a silly thought, but it reminded her of something her mother used to say, "Always put on clean underwear each day in case you have to go to the emergency room."

Her meeting with Pascal had been sparse on the details.

"It has to be this way," he had said. "We don't know when they will come, but they will probably watch you for a while first. Act normal. Go to your job. Go to the grocery store. Visit your favorite bars and restaurants. They won't do anything in public. Come home at the same time and leave each day at the same time. Give them a predictable pattern and force them to act during a narrow window of time where you are always home alone. We will always be there to protect you, I promise you."

There was a sincerity and caring charm to Pascal, like he had lost someone and couldn't bear the thought of losing another. The FBI people, and especially that stiff Isherwood, were all business, so formal and impersonal. But with Pascal, it felt more like a father talking to a daughter about to take her driving test or leaving for her freshman year of college. Despite what he was asking her to do, he made her feel safe.

And yet he wasn't that old, maybe five or ten years older. That was nothing these days. She wanted to kick herself. "Really, Ana? Falling for a French detective in the middle of your father and brother's murder case? What the fuck is wrong with you?"

No one would have called her trusting or welcoming of others. In high school, her mother had told her that her body language "repelled" others, that she appeared "suspicious of everyone," and needed to "lighten up a bit and let some people in." The words were burned into her self-esteem, motivating her in good times to dig deep into a story to reveal an unexpected truth but driving her into solitude, cigarettes, and alcohol when it all became too much.

Over the years, her mother's lunchtime martinis at the Stanwych Club with the ladies of Greenwich had opened the door to even more criticism and judgment when she came home. Her father's long absences made things worse, and the distance between mother and daughter widened every year. When she finally left for college with a chance to chart her own course without her mother's liquor-soaked, passive-aggressiveness to drag her down, she had thrived.

In time, she came to realize that her mother had always been lonely, abandoned by a husband who lived a second, secret life that didn't include her. Her two sons, Sean and Stephen, were peas in a pod. They took care of themselves and didn't give any indication that they needed her at all. When her husband moved the family to America in a hurry, leaving the older two and everything she knew behind, all she had left was a young and fiercely independent daughter with her own high school life to lead. It wasn't until much later, when her father's cancer kicked in, that she began to see her mother differently.

Pascal had said, "Force yourself to go out during the day. You'll see a laundry delivery service van in the car park. I will be in that van. Wherever you go, one of us will follow. I will always be watching and listening, and there will be many others from the FBI tracking you. It won't be long, I promise."

She desperately wanted to believe his promises and assurances. Why was that? Her life was a minefield of broken promises. The only person who never failed her was her father who promised her nothing and delivered on it. Now, she was putting her life in the hands of a Frenchman she didn't know but who made her feel safe and important. It was so cliché. Daddy issues. She wanted to punch herself in the throat.

She lit another cigarette, opened the Sangiovese, and prayed to God that she wasn't about to make another enormous mistake.

For the next two agonizing days, she pretended to live a relatively normal life, taking the 7:00 a.m. bus to the studio, standing in line for lunch with everyone else at Marty's Sandwich Hut at one thirty, having a couple of drinks after work with colleagues, before going out for dinner and getting back to the apartment around ten. The laundry van popped up in different locations around the parking lot but always had line of sight of the steps that led up to the front door of her condo.

On the third morning, Pascal was waiting for her at the bus stop, sitting crossed-legged on the bench with a newspaper on his lap and a Starbucks coffee in his hand. He was trying to look American but probably craving a cigarette, she thought. He didn't seem to know what to do with his hands. As she sat down next to him, he tried not to notice her too quickly. Eventually, he looked up from his paper and gave her a polite nod and a good morning. There were other people standing around, waiting for the bus. When it arrived, he touched her arm, signaling for her to wait and take the next one.

He said, under his breath, "We think it's tonight. Don't ask me how we know that. An FBI agent named Dack, Bradley Dack, will meet you at your office at 4:00 p.m.. He'll give you an earpiece so that we can communicate, okay? It will look just like a hearing aid, and he'll teach you how it works. You can return to your home at any time after work. Pick up food if you want to, but no alcohol tonight. We don't expect anything to happen before 10:00 p.m. They may even wait until everyone in the building is asleep and come in the middle of the night. We think they will try to take you somewhere. Do not put up a fight. Just go with them. Nothing will happen to you. Agent Isherwood and I will be in the van, but our team will be all over, okay?"

A second bus arrived, and without saying another word, Pascal stood up, tucked his newspaper under his arm, and stepped aboard, leaving Ana sitting on the bench. It was happening—whatever "it" was. An FBI guy was going to show up at work and ask her to undress so he could stick wires to her body. Then in the middle of the night, a serial killer would enter her home, torture her, and then put a bullet through her brain. If she was lucky, they would take her. Even for someone as pragmatic and stoic as Ana, it was a lot. The bus pulled away with Pascal sitting in the window in front of her. He never looked at her as it pulled away.

The sun set at eight thirty. Every thirty minutes, Pascal spoke into her ear. "Nothing to report yet. Are you doing okay?"

At first, she'd been sassy in her responses, but as time wore on and her nerves frayed, her answers had been reduced to "so far" or "I can't do this."

Every creak freaked her out. Even with the TV on, she found herself listening to every sound. She really wished she had a dog right now whose ears would perk up at the slightest sound and hop down to investigate the source. He would patrol the perimeter of the condo, and when assured that it was secure, he'd lie down next to her on the couch, one eye and one ear always open.

At eleven thirty, Pascal said, "You should go to bed now. Start turning out the lights. We haven't picked anything up yet. Don't worry. We have a lot of people watching over you. I won't let anything happen to you, I promise."

There it was again. Another promise. These kinds of operations went to shit all the time on TV. Someone makes a mistake, falls asleep while on watch, or waits too long to intervene. She turned out the living-room lights and headed for her bedroom, brushed her teeth, and lay down on the bed to read.

There was no way she was going to sleep and no way she way she was getting into her pajamas. If these fuckers were going to take her somewhere, it would be wearing her jeans and sweatshirt. Her pepper spray was tucked under her leg, just in case. She should have known better. Reading in bed put her to sleep in minutes.

"Wake up, Ana."

The accented voice was calm, like a late-night radio DJ playing slow jazz. At first, she couldn't tell whether the voice was in her dream or in her room. But in the darkness, as her eyes adjusted to the low light, she saw the shadowy figure was standing at the end of her bed.

"Don't be afraid or make any sound. Everything depends on that."

From her bedside, she sensed a shuffling movement as a cloth was pressed over her nose and mouth. The smell was sweet, but the taste was chemical, like a dentist's office. For some bizarre reason, she once again she remembered the words of her mother—"Always make sure you're wearing clean underwear in case you are taken to the hospital"—and she felt comforted because she was, in fact, wearing clean underwear.

Her final thought before the darkness was *Where are you? You promised...*

From a secure room in the basement of CIA headquarters, Sternwell watched the drone footage of the slow-speed pursuit of the kidnappers, their arrival at Wright Brothers Airport, and escape by helicopter with disgust. After twenty-four hours or more at the office, the stubble on his chin was rough, and heavy bags were forming under his eyes. This was an absolute fucking mess. Sternwell knew his neck was on the block. Damon Macatee was the only other person in the room with him. He shook his head and mumbled "Amateur hour" under his breath.

It was too easy. "What the fuck was Isherwood thinking?"

Inside the FBI van, they had watched as Ana's unconscious body was carried out to a car, an Audi with Pennsylvania license plates. The trunk opened, and her unconscious body was loaded in. It was just a three-person team, the two who entered the apartment dressed all in black with balaclavas and sunglasses hiding their faces and a driver for the getaway.

On the audio recording, they heard, "Okay, everyone, on your toes." It was Isherwood's voice. "Signals, do we have tracking on the vehicle? Are we getting a signal?"

"Yessir. Her earpiece is still active. It doesn't look as though they found it."

"Let's see where they go. Team Alpha, do you have eyes?"

"Yessir. The vehicle is headed east on West Second Street, about to make a left to head south on North Perry...correction...the vehicle is continuing on West Second, heading towards I-75...heart rate and blood pressure stable...still unconscious we believe...vehicle turning onto I-75, heading south...speed steady at 57 mph."

The Audi, never breaking the speed limit, continued south on I-75 for about fifteen minutes.

"Exiting at Exit 41, Austin Boulevard heading East. I think they're going to the Dayton-Wright Brothers Regional Airport, sir… Turning right on 741 South, North Springboro Pike…they've passed the main airport entrance…turning left now on West Tech Road into the helicopter area. Should we intercept, Agent Isherwood?"

"Not yet. I want to know which copter they are going to so we can trace it."

Sternwell looked at Macatee, elbow planted on the desk and his hand over his mouth and said, "That's the moment this operation failed."

On the video, the Audi sped up suddenly, hitting 75 mph as it approached the security gate, which lifted just in time and instantly dropped behind them, leaving Team Alpha stuck on the outside. What followed over the radio was the clatter of voices barking at the security guard, the urgent requests for instructions, the sound of a dashboard taking a beating, and the scramble of people trying to get out of the car. Someone shouted at the gate operator who shouted back in Spanish, trying to sound confused. Then silence.

They watched the Audi disappear around the side of a hangar, and two minutes later, a helicopter rose above the roof and disappeared into the night sky.

Sternwell could not believe it. Why had they waited so long? Why hadn't they taken the kidnappers out before they made it to the highway? Why the fuck hadn't Isherwood just stuck to the plan? When operations went sideways, it was usually because someone involved deviated from the operational plan, throwing everyone else into confusion and indecision.

"The director must be losing his shit."

By all accounts, the FBI director was incandescent. Not only did this botched operation expose the department to a very public humiliation when it came out in the press, but it also threw a massive wrench into his plan to build a good working relationship with INTERPOL and would also cause problems with the Department of Justice.

"Indeed. Inspector Clouseau from INTERPOL is apparently quite close to the victim and was the one to convince her to be the bait in the trap. So far, the lid is still on this thing, but that won't last."

"Setting aside for a moment what we know, what does the FBI really know about the kidnappers, the escape chopper, and where it went?"

"At this point, not much," Macatee said. "They were really caught with their pants around the ankles."

"What about our exposure?"

"At the highest levels, they probably know that Agent Daring came to us for help. They have the names of the Palatnik brothers, but so far, we don't think they've connected Maksym to his new identity. They tried to interview Oleksandr Palatnik, but we swept him away on a 'surprise vacation' to an undisclosed island a week ago with no contact with the outside world. They have the video and audio captured inside Ana Pike's apartment, the audio from her wire and the license plate of the rented Audi. They've interviewed the security guard at the airport who told them it was not uncommon for their private clients to request unusual security measures, cheating husbands whisking mistresses off to Paris or trying to ditch private investigators. The helicopter had its N number blacked out, filed no flight plan, made no call to the tower, and dropped off Airport Surveillance Radar about twenty minutes into the flight. We assume it landed somewhere nearby, and that's about it."

It was a lot of assumptions, and that made Sternwell extremely nervous. It was only a matter of time before everyone put the pieces together.

"We need to get KONTROL out of the country and out of reach of the FBI and INTERPOL ASAP."

Chapter 45

Tatyana's was officially closed for the afternoon. Maksym sat alone at his regular table, a copy of the *New York Post* open in front of him. The headline read "NY Synagogue Bomb Defendants Claim Entrapment!" With his glasses perched precariously on the end of his nose, he read the story aloud to Tatyana, who was standing in the kitchen doorway.

"You remember those four ex-cons plotting to bomb New York City synagogues and shoot down planes with missiles? They claimed in federal court that they were lured into the conspiracy with $25,000 in cash and an open credit line at their favorite fried chicken store!"

He was chuckling derisively and enjoying his racial epithet as Sam Sternwell walked in. Tatyana was startled to see a well-dressed and well-built black man standing in the doorway and barked, "We're closed! Read the sign!"

Maksym looked up from the paper and frowned. Tatyana might have been mildly horrified to be enjoying a racial joke with a black man standing in the door of her restaurant, but Maksym was completely unfazed. He looked up, pushed his glasses up the steep arch of his nose, and carefully closed and folded the newspaper without taking his eyes off the man in the shadow of the door.

"Do I know you? I don't think so, but you look familiar for some reason. From a long time ago."

"Istanbul. I met you and the Draftsman at the hotel. My name is Michael Sternthorpe. We had lunch at the restaurant under Galata Bridge. Ringing any bells for you?"

The lights of recognition went on. "*Bozhe mir!* Tatyana, leave us, please."

She disappeared into the kitchen at the back, and they heard her leave through the rear door of the building. "I knew I recognized you from somewhere. You met me at my worst, drugged up and smelling like the inside of a rat-infested container. You appear to have done well for yourself, Mr. Sternthorpe. I'm guessing that that's not your real name. So where is my usual guy?"

"The situation is far above his pay grade and clearance level now, so you got me. He spoke to you about the murder of the Draftsman and others and the FBI sting to catch the perpetrators. Unfortunately, they fucked it up and let them escape with the target, so now the FBI are closing in on you, and we can't let that happen."

Maksym feigned innocence then indignation then anger. "Careful what you imply, *pindo*! I had nothing to do with that, and I don't take kindly to threats."

Sternwell knew very well what he meant by "*pindo*," a derogatory Ukrainian slur used to describe Americans they didn't like, particularly black Americans like him. He was tempted to snap back at the pockmarked, greasy-haired, wizened old asshole with the cheap cologne and rancid cigarettes but caught himself. It was more important to convince him to leave the country without a fight. A standoff with the FBI followed by either a hail of gunfire or an arrest was exactly what he wanted to avoid a message delivered by the director of the CIA in no uncertain terms before he boarded the agency jet that morning.

"Spare me the bravado, *zalupa*." Calling the old man a dickhead in Russian still felt pretty good. "I'm here to get you out of here. I have a jet waiting at Republic Airport in Farmingdale. The FBI are about thirty minutes behind me right now. They've had your brother under surveillance and took him in an hour ago. They've got pictures of the two you from years ago, and an informer in your organization who's confirmed that Mikel Borova, supposed boss of the Ukrainian Malina in New York, is, in fact, Maksym Palatnik and the man who put out the contract on Brandon Pike. How long do you think it will take them to pin the others on you, Schier, his housekeeper, Lasher and his wife, the security guard at Lasher's gated community, Sean Pike, and his daughter? Then add in the kidnapping of Ana Pike that hopefully won't become another murder, and you've got some angry FBI agents coming after you. You want to be here for that?"

Sternwell's cold delivery of the lie was flawless. The idiots in the FBI were still chasing their tails, but Palatnik didn't need to know that. He stood with his hands stuffed into his overcoat pockets, his right hand resting on a Baretta M9, just in case.

Palatnik stared at him for a long time without saying anything, probably one of his tried-and-true intimidation tactics. It wasn't particularly effective against a seasoned operator like Sternwell, especially delivered by a man in his eighties, alone in a dingy shithole of a Russian restaurant in dilapidated Coney Island.

A door creaked open at the back of the building. Odds-on, it wasn't Tatyana coming back to stir the borscht.

"Call them off. This isn't a situation you can win by thinking you can take me out. I wouldn't come here alone, and whoever that was that opened the back door has about five seconds to live unless you call him off."

Maksym, stubborn mule that he was, did nothing. There was a pop and a puff of hot air and the sound of a heavy body falling to the ground. The silence and the stare down lingered. Sternwell didn't even turn around to see what happened.

"I hope you didn't just lose someone close to you, Maksym."

The sound of a body being dragged across a wood floor echoed around the empty restaurant. The back door must have opened as a coldness crept round the corners and circled around them. Light footsteps moved around in the back, moved into the kitchen then stopped.

A sudden look of sullen defeat fell over the old man's face. He drew in his breath, sniffed, and stood up. He put on the woolen overcoat that hung on the back of the chair and slid his pale, veiny hands into a pair of leather gloves he pulled out of his pockets. With the newspaper tucked safely under his arm, he said quietly, and with the weakness of an old man resigned to his fate, "After you, Mr. Sternthorpe."

They moved toward the back door where a well-armed man in a black suit, dark sunglasses, and the black hat of a limo driver was waiting. He put out a hand to block them momentarily while he slowly opened the door, looked quickly in both directions, and then signaled that it was safe to leave the building. A car was waiting with the rear door open, and Sternwell and his charge stepped in. The door closed behind them, and the man in the black suit climbed into the passenger seat next to the driver.

"Let's go" was all he said. He didn't turn around, but they could see his eyes—or rather his glasses—watching them through a mirror attached to the sunshade in front of him.

They passed under the railway bridge and drove up Coney Island Avenue. Maksym stared idly out of the darkened window, knowing it would be the last time he saw his adopted home. Someone would take over, but at least it wouldn't be Anatol. His nephew made him rich on Russian gas, of course, but the stink of Wall Street never left him, and Maksym was convinced the kid was plotting to replace him. Anatol had jumped at his mission to track down the binder and the money, his chance to cement his position as the top Pakhan and step into the shoes of his aging uncle to run the Malina for years to come. In reality, he stepped into Maksym's trap, one that would land him in solitary in a maximum-security prison in the middle of nowhere.

Maksym's wife was long dead. His girlfriend, a former prostitute that he was putting through college now that she was clean, would find another man. Maybe she'd go back to her old life and die from the heroin overdose that seemed inevitable when he plucked her off the street corner.

It was over. He removed his gloves, grabbed a wet nap from the package in the seat pocket in front of him, and rubbed his palms together, washing his hands clean of this place and wondering where he would land next and what his new name would be.

They made a right turn onto to Belt Parkway and picked up the pace. It was a forty-minute ride to Republic Airport.

"So, Mr. Sternthorpe, where are we going after we get to the airport?"

"Up in the air and far away," was the only answer he got. "It would be great if you could give us a clue where Ana Pike is. It will make everything that happens from here on out a whole lot easier for you."

"Do you have a pen and paper, Mr. Sternthorpe?"

They drove the rest of the way in silence, the eyes of the man in the black suit always watching.

Chapter 46

She tried to open her eyes and keep them open, but they didn't comply. Her lids felt sticky, lashes clinging to each other like school glue—not quite strong enough to keep them closed but just enough to make opening and closing difficult. She could see shadows and blurry shapes, vaguely human, standing in a row. Their voices sounded like Charlie Brown's trombone-voiced teacher, Ms. Othmar. And then, in a moment, she was gone, and the shapes faded away with her.

The next time she opened her eyes, it was mostly dark except for a light in one corner of her peripheral vision. She tried to turn, but her neck didn't respond. There was a lot of noise. It might have been music but not something she liked. Her mind, as muddled as it was, realized that she was in trouble, that the FBI and Pascal had failed her, and now the fish had the bait. She thought about the slow, painful death of her father and the horror of her brother seeing his daughter executed right in front of him.

What did they have in store for her? She felt something move off to her left, like someone was standing there, a shadow, arms folded with no face.

Her mind was foggy. She tried to move her arms and legs, but they didn't respond either, like they weren't connected to her anymore. It was as if her brain sent the instruction to move, but whoever was sitting at the control panel turned to the captain and said, "I'm sorry, Captain, I'm not getting any response," and the captain barked back, "Goddammit, man! Keep trying!" Something in her head reminded her that this internal dialogue was ridiculous. Then the darkness returned.

When she came around the third time, her situation was clear. She was, in fact, restrained, her hands and feet bound. The gag in her mouth was very tight and tasted like a car mechanic's oily rag. She was clamped into some kind of dentist's chair. A chin strap held her head in place, and her feet were bare. She wiggled her toes, relieved to reestablish contact with her body parts.

The vast room was dirty, standing water on the concrete floor underneath overhead pipes that dripped. There were vents stretched across the low ceiling, so she was probably in a basement. Something small scampered across the floor. She thought she was alone until, behind her, the foot a chair screeched as someone moved. A plume of cigar smoke drifted over her left shoulder and snaked its way up to her nose. She struggled against her restraints, but they just tightened, digging into her skin and cutting off the circulation to her hands and feet.

The voice was quiet, almost soft-spoken but with a clear New York accent. "You should resist the urge to move, Ms. Pike. They will just keep getting tighter."

She needed to see who it was.

The feet of the chair squeaked again, but he stayed out of view. The acrid smoke drifted over her shoulder once again. He coughed, more of a throat-clearing really, and spat noisily. The disgusting sound echoed around the basement. He mumbled something into a radio in another language. It sounded like Russian. She could hear every sound he made—every sniff, the smacking of his lips that reminded her of a dog licking its balls, the draw on his cigar, and then the release of smoke.

A door creaked open, and heavy footsteps came up behind her. There was a flicking sound of a fingernail on plastic and a sharp pain as a needle entered her neck. It burned fiery hot for a moment. The heat softened to warmth as the chemical coursed through her veins.

"Thank you, Doctor."

There was a long pause before the voice behind her spoke again. "Sodium pentothal. It suppresses higher cortical functions temporarily. You need not be alarmed, Ms. Pike. It just makes the interrogated individual a little bit more compliant and likely to tell the truth. And the truth is all we seek here."

Another wisp of cigar smoke snaked around her neck and up toward her face.

"They say lying is a complex mental activity that relies on these higher cortical capabilities, so it's just easier and more natural to tell the truth. Fascinating, no? Perhaps not. I'm not sure I believe it anyway. We have more reliable methods. I'm sure you know what I'm talking about. I'm sorry, are you trying to say something? I will remove the gag, but you should know that we are miles from anywhere and underground. No one will hear you."

Her vision blurred, and a persistent ring developed in her ears. In the left, it sounded like church bells in the distance. In the right ear, it was just a steady tone. The combination was disorienting. She felt herself begin to cry, but inside her head, she bellowed, *Don't you fucking do that, Ana! Don't give this fucker the satisfaction!*

Nonetheless, she felt the tears stream down her face. Someone tugged at the back of her neck, and the cloth tearing at the corners of her mouth released, finally allowing her to cough and splutter. She wanted to scream every insult she could think of at this man, but nothing came out.

The door opened again. A metal cart rattled across the uneven concrete floor before stopping somewhere behind her. Really? If she was watching a movie and someone brought in a cart of torture instruments, she would have rolled her eyes at such a trite intimidation technique. They couldn't come up with anything better than that?

"Thank you, Doctor. That will be all," she heard her inquisitor say. The metal door behind her clanged shut, and she knew they were alone. Nothing happened for a while. She found herself counting the drips of water from the pipes. They marked the passage of time. Seconds felt like minutes. Minutes felt like hours.

Eventually, he spoke. Slowly, carefully, enunciating every word to make sure she understood. It wasn't menace exactly, but like menace with a dash of aloof arrogance.

"You know, Ms. Pike, this doesn't need to be ugly. You know what we are looking for. We can avoid any unnecessary unpleasantness. What do you think?"

Ana wanted to scream "Fuck off!" at the top of her lungs, but she felt the pressure of a warm gun barrel at the base of her skull. Somewhere behind, someone was sharpening a knife.

"I was very surprised, actually, that your father and everyone we visited after him were so unwilling to tell the truth. But you, Ms. Pike, have been most difficult to track down, hopscotching all over Europe like a high school graduate on a gap year. And right after the terrible murder of your father, no less. You must have had some important business to attend to. I would like to know what that business was, so let's start there, shall we?"

Isherwood, Pascal, and the rest of the FBI team raced north along I-75 toward Sandusky, toward a little used warehouse north of town on Lake Erie. Agent Daring had called in the location based on a tip from Damon Macatee. It was just an address, but a quick search of the records revealed that Oleksandr Palatnik owned the property. Unused for the last decade and boarded up, it was less than fifteen minutes flying time by helicopter from Wright Brothers Airport, which explained why it dropped off the radar so quickly.

Why would Oleksandr own an abandoned factory in Dayton, Ohio?

The team argued about whether Ana was there or not, but there was nothing else to go on. And so they went. The bigger question was whether or not they could get there in time.

Isherwood barked orders into his phone as they drove, setting up the tactical team that would storm the facility with the control center management team in Manhattan.

"Keep them quiet and out of sight until we are on scene, do you understand? No lights and sirens. Our ETA is eleven minutes. And get a negotiator out there in case it becomes a hostage situation. The very best one we have."

Pascal sat next to him in the back of the black armored Escalade. They weren't really on speaking terms, so he stared out of the window as they wove through northern Ohio. They'd used him and his relationship with Ana to bait the trap. Her blood was on his hands.

Isherwood turned to him. "Assault Team Alpha and Beta are in place, a perimeter of a hundred and fifty meters around the building. We should be on scene soon."

"*Bon.* I hope we are in time, *Agente.*" Pascal was a cold-case investigator and had never been part of a tactical assault and rescue operation. He'd been vocal in his criticism when they let Ana slip away so easily. Everyone knew that it was a total disaster, and if they found Ana dead, Isherwood's career—and probably his pension—were gone, a thirty-year career flushed away.

Pascal knew something else was going on. It was like the kidnappers knew the plan and then someone gave the FBI her location. It smelled fishy, but Isherwood was operating like it was normal procedure. Perhaps it was normal in this complicated country with its web of law enforcement, Homeland Security, and intelligence fiefdoms. Pascal was much more comfortable with the arcane command-and-control structures of Eastern Europe. At least you knew where you stood and who was going to come after you. From the front seat, someone piped up, "ETA eight minutes, sir."

When the invisible man behind her started asking questions, Ana's only concern was survival. He could smack her around a little, maybe even burn her with his cigars. She'd recover from that in a couple of weeks, perhaps spend a day or two in hospital. But once he started playing around with the tools on his cart, all bets were off. Death was the most appealing possibility. Every person who met this man before her had suffered for a long time then died with a gunshot to the back of the head.

What led to the killings? Was it not enough information or giving them everything they needed? Was time a factor? Maybe they just needed to get out of there before the authorities showed up? Maybe it was that they gave them the name of the next person in line.

She settled on a plan. Give him enough information, a mix of truth and believable lies, to keep him beating and burning her. Delay the tools and the final bullet as long as humanly possible. These were thoughts that passed through the mind of a young woman facing almost certain death at the hands of the man who had killed her father, brother, and niece in cold blood.

"Why were you in Europe, Ms. Pike?"

"You know the answer to that already."

"Please just answer my questions."

"I needed to get away. I was upset about my father and had paid for the whole trip already."

"Perhaps we need a few more minutes for the drugs to work."

She needed to be cleverer than that and immediately regretted making such an obviously false response. She could feel the heat of the burning cigar tip near the nape of her neck. His breath, charred and stale, was so close. If only she could flip her head back, she was certain she'd break his nose. But she couldn't.

"I don't know who you are, but I'm scared. I'll tell what you want to know if I know it, I swear. But my father was a mystery to all of us. He had a double life."

"I ask again, why were you in Europe?"

They already knew—or at least suspected—that it was about the money. There wasn't much point lying about it, but she also needed to drag it out and get something from him in return, fair trade in information.

"He left us some money that we never knew about. I went over there to find it."

"How much did he leave you?"

"I don't know exactly. It was held in different currencies and a bunch of different banks. You know how they are over there with security, so they are investigating our claim."

"That money belongs to someone else. It was stolen."

"I don't know anything about where it came from. No one will tell me."

They danced around the money for about ten minutes, Ana carefully feeding the information she guessed they already knew, avoiding as many details as she could. He never moved from behind her, but she sensed a second person in the room. He appeared from a dark corner of the basement, strode over to her, and stopped about five feet away. His face was completely covered in a balaclava, and he carried a pistol with a silencer on it.

From behind her, the man spoke close to her again. "The games are over now, Ms. Pike. We're going to pick up the pace a little." He reached over her shoulder and handed the cigar to his partner.

The first burn to the bottom of her feet was like no pain she had ever felt before. She screamed at the top of her lungs. He did the same thing to her other foot and in quick succession beat the wounds with the pistol butt. She felt the agony in every nerve in her body. Her eyes bulged, and the blood in her face burned.

Outside, Team Alpha pointed thermal cameras at the building. They had a pretty good idea what was going on.

"Four individuals on the ground floor of the building, one seated in a reclined position, one standing in front of that person, and one person seated behind on what looks like a stool. A fourth individual is guarding the front door, the only available entrance to the building. There are two loading bay doors on the far side, but they were locked from the inside when we checked them out."

"Get one of the those loading bays open now. No noise. Control center, do we have any active phone signals from inside the building? How many? Just one? Okay. Is the negotiator here yet? Okay. Send him over. What do you think, Agent Benoit? Go in hard now and neutralize them as quickly as possible or have the hostage negotiator see if he can talk them into coming out?"

Pascal, stunned to be suddenly asked a strategic question, rubbed his stubble. "Ukrainian mobsters don't come out with their hands up. It's part of their code, *Vorovskoy Zakon*. These guys will protect their boss, whoever that is, at all cost. They don't trust the authorities and may even have been arrested in their home country and treated poorly while under interrogation. They will get as much as they can from her, kill her, call their boss with the information, then come out shooting without regard for their lives."

Isherwood was pleasantly surprised that Benoit agreed with his own assessment of the situation. He'd expected the Frenchman to suggest talking and negotiating, an unconscious bias he held against European law enforcement and their resistance to the use of force.

A voice came through on the radio. "We've found two skylights on the roof that we can use to access the building. It drops us about thirty feet away, so it'll be an immediate gunfire situation. Opening the bay days, once we break the locks, will be noisy for sure. I think we go through the skylights, throw down some flash-bangs and smoke grenades then drop in and take them down quickly."

"Draw up the plan, gather the team, and walk me through it. I do not want this hostage killed, and I want at least one of these guys alive."

Balaclava man tried to revive Ana. He'd attached a hose to a small spigot on the outer wall and hosed her down. The urgent bruises on her face were purple and swelling already. She was missing a couple of teeth, and her nose was broken. Blood was running down her chin and soaking her blouse. The man seated behind her lit a fresh cigar, unmoved by her suffering.

The noise of the water spray gave Team Alpha the advantage. Neither of the captors heard the footsteps on the roof or the creaking sound of the rusty hinges on the skylights. Flash-bangs followed by smoke grenades and heavy boots splashed into the water puddles on the filthy concrete floor. Red laser sights scoured the gloom. There was shouting and gunfire. It was all over in a matter of seconds. Two men—the balaclava man and the front-door guard—lay dead, and the other writhed on the ground, trying to stop the flow of blood from an upper-chest or shoulder wound.

Isherwood and Pascal ran in through the front door, the Frenchman heading straight for Ana. She was alive but barely. The EMT crew dashed over to her, shoving Pascal aside, releasing her bonds and removing the remnants of the blood-soaked gag hanging around her neck.

Isherwood pulled out his camera and took a picture of the surviving man. "Sending it to you now," he said into his phone.

The wait for the answer was interminable, but when it came through, Isherwood was shocked.

"Anatol Palatnik. Son of Oleksandr Palatnik and nephew to Maksym Palatnik."

Pascal was not shocked. It was entirely possible that Oleksandr was behind all this and perhaps the boss of the Ukrainian Malina in Brighton Beach. It was certainly the simplest explanation, but Pascal's instinct was that it was Maksym.

What if he hadn't disappeared in a 1989 purge led by the KGB but was in fact living in the United States? He'd paid the Draftsman to do his dirty work for years, knew that photographic evidence of their crimes existed, and wanted to make sure that nothing ever saw the light of day. And he wanted his money back. How did he make his escape from Ukraine? And how was it possible not to surface at all in twenty years?

It was simple. He had a new identity. And someone had brought him here.

"*Agente* Isherwood, there is nothing to suggest that Brandon Pike ever met Oleksandr. Also, the way these criminal organizations work, the boss would never send his only son on a killing rampage. We know, however, that Pike worked for Maksym Palatnik for many years. It is my belief that Maksym Palatnik is alive and living in America under an assumed identity, and it is he that put the contract out and sent his nephew to the killing."

Chapter 47

P ascal's seemingly outlandish claim—circulated by Isherwood and the FBI liaisons throughout the intelligence community—eventually landed on the desk of Sam Sternwell. And he knew right then that his career was going tits up, right before his eyes.

It was really just a matter of how badly the agency's reputation would be damaged and how public his own fall would be. Would it happen in shadows and maybe leave him with a future in private sector consulting or lobbying? Or would it be an epic fall from grace as the scapegoat for the illicit activities of UNDERCUT, his name splattered all over the evening news? He had almost nothing to do with UNDERCUT aside from a one-day interaction with its two main players in Istanbul two decades earlier. And yet he would take the fall for operations conceived and executed by his predecessors. The outcome depended on what he did next.

To convince others to find truth in your lies, you have to first successfully deceive yourself. Sternwell's career was a mix of a thousand deceptions that had little or no impact on his life outside the walls of Langley. There were maybe a dozen secrets—the operations currently being investigated by Congress, for example—that he would be ashamed to share with his family. But this FBI investigation would be the final nail in his coffin.

He was one of only three or four people who knew for sure that Maksym Palatnik, now known as Mikel Borova, had been allowed to rebuild his criminal organization in Brighton Beach with agency protection. Now, without consulting anyone, Palatnik had initiated the ritual execution of his former CIA friends and colleagues for reasons that were not entirely clear—at least to the FBI and INTERPOL.

Sternwell knew very well the loose ends that Palatnik was tying off. But why had he put his own nephew in charge of the hit squad? With all the cold-blooded killers available for hire in the New York metro area and the loser shit bags trying to climb the ranks of the Malina, why had he chosen a member of his own family?

It felt personal. Resentment that Oleksandr escaped before the Nazis invaded and left him behind to die in camp at Bogdonovka with thousands of other Jews? Why had Anatol used the Draftsman's own weapon, a gift from his uncle's most loyal enforcer, to kill them all? It would inevitably lead back to the Malina and its leader, Mikel Borova, the silent hand of the Ukrainian Malina in America. It made no sense.

Regardless, this annoying fuck of a Frenchman from INTERPOL was half right. Maksym had been living in the United States under an assumed identity, but that was no longer the case. He was safely out of the country, beyond the reach of the FBI and probably INTERPOL too. His brother, Oleksandr, was also under CIA protection offshore, on a beach somewhere with a drink in his hand. The fear now, of course, was that the killing might not even be over. There were a lot of loose ends.

Ana Pike was a loose end. Still recovering from her injuries in hospital, she made it clear to the FBI that her mission now was to expose this organization and take it down. By all accounts, she was a good investigative journalist. For now, she had round-the-clock protection, but it wouldn't last forever.

Pascal Benoit was a loose end. Convinced that Maksym Palatnik was alive, he was going to build the rest of his INTERPOL career around closing the dozens of open and cold cases with links to the Ukrainian mafia.

And Anatol Palatnik was a loose end. So far, he wasn't talking and was safely locked up in the Metropolitan Correctional Center in Manhattan awaiting trial. The grand jury convened to bring charges against him would be underway within the week. Subpoenas for every known associate in the Malina would go out, and a lot of people would be nervous.

It was time to come clean with EXDIR Atwater. He pressed the intercom button on his desk that connected to his assistant.

"Marjorie?"

"Yessir?"

"Please see if you can find some time on Director Atwater's calendar for this afternoon. It's a top priority. Make sure his assistant knows it's important and to clear thirty minutes if she can, okay?"

"Yessir. I'll let you know when its scheduled."

Three days in a Mount Sinai hospital bed was more than Ana could handle. They ran tests, took X-rays, and made her walk up and down the hallway, but she wanted out. The security detail checked IDs for anyone coming into her room and followed her wherever she went.

Special Agent Isherwood stopped by each day to update her on the case. Today's news was that district attorney for the State of New York was convening a grand jury to gather information ahead of the indictments against Anatol Palatnik. The jury was already seated, and the proceeding would start the following Monday. It was likely that she would be the first witness called by the DA.

"You'll need to stay put here and recuperate for a couple more days. We have you well-protected here, and once the subpoenas start going out to Palatnik's associates…well, you know…things could get dicey."

"I'm going to need better food and steady supply of decent wine, or I'm going to lose it before I ever get to the courthouse."

After he left, she was still unsure whether or not he had agreed to her demand. Perhaps she wasn't clear enough. Hospital food was hospital food, even at the best medical institutions.

It was quiet, and she was alone. Isherwood was gone, and the early morning flurry of nurse checks and tests were over. In an hour, the staff would be back for her physical therapy. She grabbed her phone and called Mattinson's number again, her third attempt to reach him in the last day or two. So far, all voice mail and no return call.

"Hello, you've reached James Mattinson. I'm so very sorry to have missed your call. Please leave me a message at the beep, and I will return your call at my first opportunity."

"Hi, Mr. Mattinson. It's Ana again. I'm really starting to worry. I hope you are okay. Anyway, I'm still at Mount Sinai hospital, and they tell me I'm going to be here a few more days to recuperate and make sure someone doesn't kill me before the grand jury. I wanted to check to make sure that all the transfers were taken of and that you had control of my father's money. If you could give me a call back as soon as you get this and let me know. They have me in and out of tests and doing physical therapy, so just leave a message to let me know everything okay."

She opened up her laptop and looked up his web page for the address. His office building was managed by a company called Piccadilly Market Enterprises, headquartered in London. She called the number.

"Yes, hello. I'm trying to reach a tenant in your building on Piccadilly Square in Manchester, and I haven't been able to get through. Would it be possible for you to connect me with the front desk or the building manager?"

"Certainly, could you hold on a sec?" So cheerful and, at the same time, formal in the way that only an English customer service person could be.

Muzak.

A very official yet soothing voice chimed in. "Good afternoon and thank you for calling 25 Piccadilly Square. How can I help you today?"

"Hello. I'm trying to reach one of your tenants, James Mattinson, and I'm not able to get through."

"Oh, dear. I'm sorry, ma'am, but Mr. Mattinson is no longer in this building. He didn't inform you?"

"He's gone?"

"Yes. Lorries showed up a few days ago. I was a little upset that he didn't say goodbye, if I'm honest. He was always so polite and friendly."

"Have his other clients called looking for him?"

"I don't know what Mr. Mattinson did, ma'am, but I can't recall him having more than one or two visitors as long as he was here. Said he was in finance and his clients were all over the world."

He was talking, and she could hear the sounds he was making, but nothing was registering. She had transferred millions into an account under his control, and now he was gone. Without warning and with their money.

"Thank you. I'll try the head office for his forwarding address."

"Certainly, ma'am. Have a…" but she had already hung up.

Her next call was to Pascal.

"*Bonjour! C'est Pascal Benoit. Comment puis-je vous aider?*"

"Pascal, it's Ana. Listen, Mattinson has vanished. I called him three times and got voice mail. Then I called the building manager for his office, and apparently, he cleared out three days ago." She heard him swear in the background. "I wanted to check that all the money had been transferred into the account. I presume it was frozen?"

"It was not frozen. We were waiting for the final transfers to be made. I will call back to the office. It is late afternoon in Lyon now. We may not get an answer until the morning. In the meantime, I will see what I can do to find out if he left the country. I have some contacts in the Manchester Metropolitan Police. You focus on healing, and I will take care of this."

Mattinson was gone, and he had taken the money with him. She could feel it in her gut. Her worst fear was confirmed an hour later when Pascal called back to say that the account had been frozen yesterday but only contained 3.9 million euros. There was a record of a one-way flight to Istanbul under Mattinson's name but no record of him passing through Turkish passport control or connecting to another flight. It was entirely possible that he was still in the UK and INTERPOL and Scotland Yard were working together to track him down.

"I'm sorry, Ms. Pike. I feel responsible for this. However, the greater danger now, I believe, is that whoever killed your father and his colleagues will be even more ruthless. I must call Agent Isherwood to secure protection for the rest of your family. We may have captured one of these monsters, but there are more waiting to take his place."

She cried, hard. Not about the loss of the money but out of anger. Her father had trusted Mattinson for years and encouraged her to trust him too. And now he had betrayed them both.

Chapter 48

Sochi, Russia, 2009

It was a fifteen-hour flight from New York. Maksym had no idea where they were going. They made two stops to refuel, but he didn't know where. It was dark outside, no lights or landmarks to give any clues to the location. He wasn't sure whose plane it was, but it was definitely a step up from the military transport that brought him the United States all those years ago—leather seats and a TV screen in the back of the seat in front. He was getting the royal treatment.

In the seat next to him, the grim-looking fellow who brought him this far had little to say. He kept his Ray-Bans on throughout the flight, eyes forward, and his hand close to the firearm holster by his ribs. When you think about American government security types, he was the stereotype—cold, efficient, hyperaware of everything, and seemingly incapable of saying more than two words in a row.

Once in a while, a very attractive flight attendant stopped by to take his food and drink order. He loved the way she leaned into him to better understand what he wanted. Maybe it was that he kept his voice intentionally low. Convinced she gave him the eye, he brushed a stray shoulder against her backside as she passed by with the drinks trolley. It was firm, and he imagined that she had strong thighs from pushing the cart up and down the aisle. There was just something about the strength of her stride that attracted him. When she turned and shot him a look, he apologized for the indiscretion and passed it off as an incidental contact.

Nonetheless, he felt emboldened. He watched her make coffee and giggle with her associate at the front of the plane. Their blouses and skirts were so tight, their voices a melodic singsong of "whatevers" and "oh-my-gods." They touched each other in ways that suggested they were intimate, brushing imaginary things off each other's shoulders and touching each other's hair. The more he watched them together, the more he thought they were doing it for him.

His gaze lingered a little too long. and she caught his eye for a second but not in good way. At first, her look was harsh and disgusted. He didn't feel any embarrassment and shame. Maksym had none of that in him. He just smiled instead and looked down at his vodka tonic for a moment. Her face softened, changing from seeing him as a leering serial pervert to the way a pretty young girl looks at an old man and thinks of her grandfather. Her whole body relaxed. and it was clear that from that moment, she would care for him in a granddaughterly way. It pissed him off because what he wanted to do was fuck her in the bathroom.

Maksym forgot that he was in his eighties every day.

When they landed for the final time, there was a car waiting on the tarmac. The familiar smell of the Black Sea filled his nostrils, but it wasn't Odessa.

As he approached the top step, the lovely flight attendant said, "Welcome to Sochi, Mr. Borova, home of the 2014 winter Olympics!" *Very nice*, he thought, *not a bad place to retire at all.*

At sea level, it was still very warm, the sweaty breeze off the Black Sea surging north from Turkey. Sochi was the beach playground and summer holiday spot for influential and wealthy Muscovites and oligarchs. By October, however, the holidaymakers had closed up their dachas for the winter, and the resorts on the beach were running off-season rates to attract business. The ski resorts of Gornyy Kurort Roza Khutor and Gorki Gorod up in the Caucasus mountains wouldn't see much action until mid-January.

The airport sat to the south, so they drove up the coast before heading up a steep and winding road that went from fresh new tarmac to uneven gravel and eventually to unpaved dirt. They passed Stalin's summer dacha, "Green Grove," on the road up. The two-story building looked more like a motel than the home of the Soviet leader. Now a museum, it apparently showcased some of the unusual quirks of the diminutive and mercurial autocrat from the private pool on the second floor that was only five feet deep to the small army cot he slept on. The house was also devoid of carpets so he could hear every footstep, and the exterior was painted to pea green as camouflage. The local driver told him that the tourists made it as far as Green Grove and then turned around.

"You know? I met Stalin once, not long before he died."

The agency chaperone, actually a local embassy official, turned sharply and said, "Really?" He was young, and so, to him, this was like talking to someone from a bygone era, a relic from the past.

"*Da*. I was surprised by how short he was. I'm not tall, but he only came up to my shoulders! 1952, Poland. It was a big textile conference. We had your man there for security. Maybe he wasn't your man by then. He might have still been with Brits. Anyway, we had this big display with some kind of fancy weaving machine that the Americans were trying to sell to the Soviets, and Stalin stood admiring that giant thing for a long time. He turned to me, I was representing the Soviet side of the delegation, and said, 'Do we really need the fucking Americans to build this for us? We will do it ourselves. Fuck them!'"

The chaperone let the "your man" comment pass, but he was pretty sure this guy shouldn't be talking about Stalin and an agency field operative in the same breath. No doubt someone back in Langley was listening in. Let them handle it.

"I didn't even think Americans could do business with the Soviets back then."

"They couldn't. It was very complex, but both sides turned a blind eye if it made sense and could be kept quiet."

He really didn't care anymore. He was home again. They were recording it all, but he was safe again.

"Our company was a joint venture between America and the Soviet Union with the British in the middle. It was supported by the KGB, the CIA, and MI6. We passed information back and forth about each other, and it became like an unofficial channel of communication. We just made the money as a legitimate business, at least it started out that way."

They lapsed into silence. The embassy officer didn't know what to say.

"It's a shame that the intelligence services abandoned that form of cooperation. It kept everything stable. The rules were the rules, everyone understood them. There were spies, double agents, triples, all betrayers and deceivers but rarely killers."

But everything changed that night in East Berlin in 1978. The Draftsman killed a KGB officer and was arrested trying to escape. He was interrogated in the basement cells of Hohenschönhausen and then exchanged on the Glienicker Bridge. At great personal risk, Maksym had secured the release and exchange. After that, everything went to shit. No one followed the rules anymore, and no one felt safe.

Maksym was not the type to get nostalgic about the past, but this felt like his retirement—a house up the road from Stalin's summer dacha, his old *Prava Ruka*, Andrey Kutnetzov somewhere in the area also.

A mile later, they pulled into a driveway.

"We're here," the driver announced.

Maksym's new home—five thousand miles from Brighton Beach and one thousand from his birthplace in Odessa—was set back from the road and well-hidden behind tall pine trees. It was small in the front, a typical, unassuming A-frame ski house with a turnaround driveway.

The agency chaperone in the Ray-Bans handed him the keys and told him lay low for a few months. He got back in the car and drove away without another word, leaving Maksym standing in the driveway with a single suitcase at his feet.

When he opened the door and stepped inside, he was pleasantly surprised to find a lovely woman in her fifties with a big smile and an even bigger chest preparing a meal in the kitchen. She turned and smiled at him. "Mr. Borova! How lovely to meet you. My name is Irina. I'll be your housekeeper and chef." Things were definitely looking up!

A deck off the back of the house had a wonderful view of the ocean and pricey resorts in the distance. He spent his first afternoon there, with a blanket on his legs, and when it cooled off in the evening, Irina brought him glasses of warm Glühwein.

"This will keep you warm. It's a tradition on the Austrian side of my family to always have a pot of it ready in the winter."

Apparently, her mother was from Vienna and her father Russian. There had to be a story in there, but it was too early to probe, so he let his imagination take over.

Her parents would have been young during the war, likely in their late teens. Maybe there was some kind of sordid episode between a teenage girl living under the Nazis and a liberating Red Army soldier. Perhaps her family were Nazi loyalists and she wasn't, and when the Second Ukrainian Front of the Red Army launched the Bratislava–Brno Offensive to liberate Vienna, the young girl decided to get back at her parents by having an affair with a brave Ukrainian soldier.

He would find out in time.

They settled into a daily routine, but the days—and then the weeks—passed slowly. He leered at her. At first, it didn't seem to bother her, but eventually, she took every opportunity to clean another part of the house or spend time in her own quarters "writing letters to her mother in Vienna" or "taking care of the house accounts."

Meanwhile, Maksym climbed the walls. He was under house arrest. How he was going to make it through the coming months of solitude? This wasn't him. Even at eighty-three, he couldn't sit still. He needed to be doing, directing, deciding. He didn't drink wine often, but the house had an impressive wine cellar. It was dingy, smelled of dirt and old cedar, but it was packed with Bordeaux and Burgundy reds and whites from Loire and Alsace. He decided to learn about French wine. He found a shelf of books on wine, food, and table setting in the study, grabbed a few, and decided to become a sommelier. It took about five minutes for him fall asleep on the deck every time he opened one of the books.

The weeks dragged on. Hannukah came and went without much fanfare. Irina wasn't Jewish but pretended to be interested in the holiday, and in January, the temperatures dropped. The snows came early.

One day in midwinter, a taxi dropped its passenger at the end of the long driveway and drove away. This was a man who knew and had lived in the secret world, endured harsh conditions, but was older now and softer, more comfortable in the stuffy offices of Whitehall than out here in the wild.

It was snowing unusually hard for February. He had been led to believe this place was temperate even in the winter. He was grateful for his Crombie overcoat and Burberry woolen scarf, but his Gucci shoes were not a great choice, and the icy wetness bit into his toes. He turned up the collar on his overcoat and tightened the scarf around his neck. They told him there were wolves in the area, so he picked up his pace and marched at a full clip down the driveway toward the house. Instead of enjoying the crunch of the snow beneath his feet and the flakes falling on his shoulders, he worried about the damage it was doing to his expensive clothes.

He was not at all sure how this whole thing would go. Palatnik was not expecting him and would be shocked when he realized who his guest was. He knocked on the door. No one answered, so he knocked again.

The door opened, and a beautiful woman, in an apron and holding a large spoon, looked at him without saying a word.

"Pardon me for intruding. I was hoping to speak to Mr. Palatnik...excuse Mr. Borova."

"And who should I say—"

"My name is James Mattinson..."

An old man appeared behind her. He was wearing a bathrobe, smoking a cigarette. At first, the old man was confused then quizzical as his mind searched the cobwebs of his memory banks for recognition. It was awkward, and the woman looked at her boss for guidance. She looked from one man to the other, hoping for some kind of clarity about what was happening in front of her.

Finally, Maksym's eyes widened and he uttered, "Giles Bancroft."

"The very same," he said as cheerfully as he could manage. There was a long and awkward pause while everyone figured out what the next move should be. It fell to Irina, but she couldn't hide her confusion around the names.

"Mr. Mattinson…I mean Bancroft, you'd better come inside. You are not really dressed for a Russian winter."

"It's been a very long time, Mr. Bancroft."

"The name's Mattinson now, James Mattinson. If you don't mind, can we stick to that?"

"Operational security?"

"Sure, but I'm not here on official business actually."

The poor woman was horribly confused by what was going on.

"Madam, I'm an old friend of Mr. Borova. I do apologize for the unexpected intrusion." He stuck out a frozen hand, the veins raised in the pale skin of his thin hands. She took his hand gently.

"Pleased to meet you, sir. I am Irina, the housekeeper. Please come in. and I'll get you some Glühwein." She led him into the living room. A small fire burned in the fireplace, just enough to warm the living room, and she tossed another log on before disappearing into the kitchen and leaving the two old men to their conversation.

"She seems lovely. You are very…," he said cheerfully.

"What the fuck do you want, Gi— Mattinson? I haven't heard from you in thirty years, and now you show up in the middle of the night?"

Giles looked around before speaking, just in case someone was listening. They were listening, of course. "Perhaps we could go out on the deck. It's such a lovely evening."

Classical music played in the background. "Haydn's *The Seasons*? An interesting choice, Mr. Borova."

"Irina is Austrian, grew up in Vienna. Her taste in classical music is better than mine. I have no taste as a matter of fact. I let her choose, and Haydn is one of her favorites. They all sound the same to me."

The frivolous small talk got them to the door leading to the back deck. When they were safely out of earshot, Maksym asked, "Why are you here? After all this time?"

"Well, I owe you a great debt, as you no doubt remember. I am here to repay it. You saved my life and my career."

"And as a I also recall, Mr. Bancroft or Mattinson or whatever name you go by now, you betrayed me, like so many others. From that Romanian schmuck who identified my family to the Nazis to the fucking Draftsman who kept enough records to put me in the Supermax in Colorado where they are sending my nephew and everyone in between, I was betrayed. And now I can add you to the list. You chose the Draftsman over me. I gave you and your masters everything they asked for, the inside track on everything and everyone happening in the Soviet Union, for more than thirty years. I risked everything. I walked through the minefield for you people and asked nothing in return. In the end, you and the Americans chose him over me. And I gave him millions to do your work and the Americans work."

They both knew this was horse shit, that the money paid to Draftsman was CIA and MI6 money, and that they had extracted Maksym before the Soviet Union collapsed and the KGB purges reminiscent of the Stalin days started. The truth was that Maksym was a liability to everyone—ruthless, undisciplined, and self-serving. The chip on his shoulder was enormous, but Mattinson had no intention of paying the price of everyone else's sins.

"I'm not interested in playing games here, Palatnik. I'm here to pay a debt, buy your silence, and never have contact with you or anyone else involved in this mess again. I have control of the Draftsman's money, more than seventy-five million dollars, and I'm going to share it fifty-fifty with you. Your people have killed too many going after this money, and the noose is tightening. Your nephew is going to prison. Your brother has been accused of money laundering and fraud. The CIA got you out of America before the FBI figured out who you were, but they are washing their hands of you. They are not coming back, I'll guarantee you that. In fact, I suspect your next visitors will be Putin's FSB friends. There's a reason they put you back on home soil. No need to bother with that ridiculous Polonium-210 poisoning business. You remember Litvinenko, I presume? I think you know what they'll do once you are in their hands with your background."

From an inside pocket, Giles pulled out a small manila envelope. "This was one of my last final tasks before suddenly leaving MI6 to deal with a so-called health issue." He took out a new British EU passport, birth certificate, and driver's license. "These are in the name of Antoni Kaminski, the son of Polish immigrants who arrived in England in the early 1920s to escape the Jewish pogroms in Warsaw. He was born in Lancashire, where his father worked in one of the mills. They are untouchable. Here's a plane ticket to Malé in the Maldives, part of the Commonwealth, so no visa questions to deal with, and an account at the Bank of Ceylon with thirty-five million dollars. Unfortunately, Ms. Austrian Big Tits will not be going with you."

On cue, Irina appeared with two glasses of Glühwein. and they toasted each other. Poor Irina was none the wiser.

The next morning, a taxi pulled up in the driveway to take the new Antoni Kaminski to Krasnador International airport for the flight to Malé. The weather had turned ugly during the night, changing from light snow to freezing rain and wind. As he climbed into the car, the old man was grateful to know that his days of shit weather were almost over. For the third time in his life, his slate was being wiped clean, his past erased from the historical record, his crimes untraceable.

The taxi pulled forward, and as he took one last look through the blurred rear window, he could see Mattinson and Irina standing in the doorway. He thought he saw the Englishman reach into his overcoat pocket for something, a gun. She turned, her face a mixture of fake sadness and real relief, to go back into the house. Mattinson put his hand on her back, gently ushering her inside. She seemed to welcome the attention of the elderly but still dashing Englishman, but he had one last loose end to tie up. Such a shame.

Maksym turned back around and asked the driver, "How far is it to airport?"

"About five hours."

"What? I thought it was about thirty minutes."

"That's Sochi airport. It's being rebuilt for the Olympics. No international flights right now except for private jets, bigwigs from

Moscow and their oligarch friends. Place is crawling with FSB types too, checking everyone's papers. Krasnodar is much safer for a man in your situation, if you know what I mean."

Clearly, this man was not a regular taxi driver. He looked the part all right—a few days off beard growth, untidy hair, and a car that stank of cigarette smoke and body odor.

He stuck his arm back over his shoulder, a crumpled pack of Winston's in his hand. Maksym took one. "What the hell. I'm going to reek of cigarettes by the time we get there anyway."

An hour later, Mattinson climbed into his own taxi headed for the airport. He'd dragged body of poor Irina into the woods behind the house where the wolves and bears would take care of her remains as they stocked up for the rest of the winter. He wasn't a natural-born killer. At the last minute, he had almost decided to let her live.

By the time anyone made contact with her, he rationalized, both he and Maksym would be long gone and beyond reach. What was the harm in sparing her? In the end, even he decided not to take any chances and shot her in the back of the head when she wasn't looking.

It had taken him a good twenty minutes to drag her body to a back door, down the steps, and down into the line of trees on the hill-side. After cleaning up the blood, he showered, changed into some clothes left behind by Maksym, and combed in some fresh Brylcreem to darken his hair a little. From the front-hall closet, he took a thick woolen overcoat—much warmer than one he arrived in that he'd also used to slide Irina across the tile floors, leaving that one was in the woods with her body—and marched out the front door without looking back.

His driver was clearly FSB, silently monitoring his every move in the rearview mirror. His job was to get him to the airport and watch his back. Presumably, defectors got cold feet at the last minute all the time. It was no doubt dangerous to have your hands on a steering wheel with your back to a cornered animal.

His flight wasn't heading for the Maldives, or any place warm for that matter. Instead, he was planning to take a two-hour flight from Sochi to Moscow's Sheremetyevo Alexander S. Pushkin International

Airport where he would seek asylum and perhaps be granted permanent residency as an MI6 defector.

They were expecting him, of course.

For his plan to work, he needed to give them something worthwhile. He worried that too much of his intelligence was old news and not worth much. Operation UNDERCUT would have been worth something twenty years ago, but not today. The Draftsman and his work for the CIA, MI6, and the KGB as a double and triple agent? The Cold War intelligence gambits were long forgotten, and the Draftsman and his retinue were all dead anyway. Maksym Palatnik, a.k.a. Mikel Borova, a.k.a. Antoni Kaminiski? Possibly. The Russians had long memories when it came to the misdeeds of one of their own. Betraying Maksym might be enough, and the money trail would be easy to follow.

What they really wanted—and what he would hold back as long as possible—was intelligence on China and the intelligence operations it ran all over Asia and within Russia. Of particular interest was Her Majesty's new consul-general at the British Consulate in Hong Kong, Dame Victoria Slocum, who had vacated her role as minister counselor to Moscow months earlier to take on this new position. Rumors were circulating around Whitehall that she would become the next British ambassador to China. She and Giles were colleagues and friends from her days at MI6 where she served as a liaison with the Foreign Office in his final year running the Russian directorate in 1991. Together, they had moved to the next rung on the ladder by joining the China directorate. Dame Victoria left MI6 to join the Foreign Office when the Labour Party took office in 1997. She rose steadily through the ranks, serving in British embassies in Kiev and Warsaw before her posting to Moscow.

About a month before her posting to Hong Kong in mid-2009, Giles—who had more of an emeritus role at MI6 by then—welcomed her request for a meeting, and she had stopped by his office at Vauxhall Cross for a chat. They had reminisced about the old days and the bestowing of the Order of St. Michael and St. George for her Foreign Office work in Eastern Europe and Russia. He asked, perhaps a bit rudely, why she had never married. She had taken the question in stride and said, "I never met a man good enough to compete with my work for my energy nor one that was willing to live the life I wanted to lead."

As he sat in the taxi, it struck him how devastating his defection would be to the Service and how many people would worry about their safety. How many networks would they roll up out of the simple fear of exposure? How many years would it set them back? It had been a very long time since someone with his seniority and tenure had gone over. It was almost a relic of a bygone era. Why on earth was he doing it?

The answer was easy. Greed and proximity to power. Putin's inner circle of former KGB officers and newly minted oligarchs would welcome a kindred spirit like Giles.

The taxi driver stiffened, sensing a change in his passenger. "We're here."

The rear opened suddenly. He turned to see three men in dark glasses standing close to the door. "This way please, Mr. Bancroft. We will escort you through security and make sure you get on the plane safely."

Whatever second thoughts he might have had, it was too late now. These men would make sure he made it to Moscow, no matter what. He stepped out of the car, the chilly breeze blowing up the coast from the south. He felt like a fool. Maksym was heading off to the sunny Maldives, and he was going to plead for asylum in Moscow in mid-February.

When all was said and done, no one would understand his choice. Back at Vauxhall Cross, the repercussions would ripple through the organization. Why didn't anyone see it coming? What was he involved in that, after forty years of service, would lead to this betrayal of his country?

But Giles Bancroft—the careful operator and opportunist that he was—felt the noose tightening. It was time to cash in his chips.

Chapter 49

Vauxhall Cross, London

B y the time they got into the office, everyone at MI6 knew
that Giles Bancroft, the legendary former head of the Russia
division, had defected.

After dropping off the radar, he'd resurfaced overnight, all
smiles and handshakes for the cameras, on Russian television at the
Kuznetsky Most headquarters of the FSB in Moscow. The chaos that
followed was unlike anything the Service had experienced since the
hysterically paranoid days of the Cambridge Five, more than a half
century before.

In the hours before sunrise, senior officials sped through
Lambeth in their chauffeur-driven Range Rovers toward Vauxhall
Cross. At 8:00 a.m. on the dot, the secure mobiles of all 2,500 of the
staff buzzed simultaneously. As they trudged across Vauxhall Bridge,
a bitter cold wind roaring up the Thames, they reached into their
pockets and purses. What they heard was a broadcast message from
chief of the Secret Intelligence Service, Sir James Lovewell, better
known by the moniker "C." He alerted everyone to Bancroft's reap-
pearance, warned them not to discuss the matter with family, friends,
or the press, and reminded everyone of their commitments to secrecy.
More information would follow for those authorized to hear it, of
course. Many exchanged horrified looks with colleagues. Others just
shook their heads in disbelief. It was going to be a very long day.

It was rare, but defections still happened, just without all the
fanfare. Usually, the traitors were caught in the act or while trying to
escape after spying for the Russians, Iran, Chinese, or North Korea.
But sometimes, they made it out and got the chance to start a new

life in their sponsor country. Behind the scenes, governments nego-tiated for their return to face the consequences of their betrayal. If there was someone worthy of a swap, it happened in the shadows, and no one in the press or general public need be any the wiser.

But Bancroft was the first senior MI6 officer that anyone could remember to appear on Russian television, rubbing salt in the wound of his former colleagues. It was astonishing. What on earth could have prompted this earth-shattering move from the old man?

By 10:00 a.m., C was back in his office, staring out of the sixth-floor window, recovering from the tongue lashing he'd received from the PM and his chief of staff. His office faced south, down the Thames toward the abandoned Battersea power station. The same thoughts passed through his mind every time he stood there, Such a shame to let Battersea go to ruin and become a bloody eyesore. Time to move the office to the north side with a view of the Houses of Parliament instead. But he didn't want to be the kind of chief that created a lot of unnecessary bother for the building-management people. Nonetheless, he felt he deserved better.

His predecessor—a longtime MI6 officer who had served in some of the most godforsaken corners of the globe—had established this as the chief's office, leaving more desirable locations for his underlings. Appointed in 1997 when Labour took office, his tenure had been mercifully shortened when he ran afoul of UK/US politics by being a bit too vocal in ministerial circles with his skepticism about the evidence surrounding Saddam's weapons of mass destruc-tion. No one had a strong appetite to challenge the Americans so openly, and having the head of MI6 voicing his opinions was detri-mental to transatlantic relations.

But today, the view from his office was trivial given the situa-tion in front of him.

Around 5:00 a.m. Greenwich Mean Time, the phone next to his bed with a direct line to Ten Downing Street rang. Prime Minister, who was apparently "incandescent" according to his chief of staff, wanted an immediate briefing. C had dressed quickly, kissed his sleeping wife goodbye, and headed for the door. He picked up an official-looking envelope from the floor by his front door and climbed into the back seat of his Rolls headed for Whitehall.

"Bloody hell, Lovewell! You'd better have some good news for me on this. I've known Bancroft for thirty years, had the bugger over for dinner not six months ago in fact, and now...now, he shows up in Moscow wanking off the bloody KGB! What the hell is going on?"

"Well, Prime Minister, it obviously came as a shock to all of us, and we really don't have much information to go on yet. He informed us that he was going on holiday to the BVI, submitted all the right forms, got approval, and showed tickets and hotel reservations at a luxury resort in Tortola. He didn't take the flight or check in at the resort. We sent someone around to his house last night, and the place was sealed up tight. And then this was delivered to my house overnight."

It was the large manila envelope, postmarked February 17, that he had grabbed on his way out of the house that morning. Inside was a long typewritten note.

"Let me see that. What is it? Some kind of bloody manifesto?"

He seated himself behind his desk, papers in one hand, pipe in the other, and read.

"Good god," the prime minister exclaimed when he was finished. "Do you believe him?"

"Right now, we just don't know. We'll need people to dig back through the history and verify it. Obviously, he was involved in a lot more than the Draftsman operation, but that's the only one he specifically mentions. There was never a whisper of a stain on Bancroft's character from the day he joined until now. But showing up suddenly on Russian television after stealing millions from the Draftsman's family and sharing it with his killer doesn't give a great deal of confidence in the integrity of his word."

"He sounds almost delusional. I'm going to get crucified during Question Time on Wednesday! I'm going to need some answers. Langley must really have their knickers in a twist right now. I'm sure I'll get a call from the president at some point today. He'll be looking for us to share the blame."

"Quite so. The director of CIA Operations, Sam Sternwell, resigned overnight, but we don't think it was related to Bancroft's sudden popularity on Russian television. The pressure of the FBI/INTERPOL investigation has been building for a while, and the whole enhanced interrogation investigation was pointing toward him, so it may just be a coincidence. I'll keep you updated on any new developments, Prime Minister, and you can expect a complete report on the implications of all this within twenty-four hours."

"Good. You'd better get on it then." The prime minister looked down at the telephone on his desk. It was his awkward way of dismissing someone from his presence without having to say anything. Lovewell nodded and marched toward the door.

Back at Vauxhall Cross, Lovewell waited anxiously for the first reports reviewing Giles's operational history. Analysts were busy scouring through old files and records with a fine-tooth comb, looking for any sign of betrayal or malfeasance. The first briefing by the analysts was in thirty minutes and would last an hour. A second stream of analysis was focused on the intelligence he passed to the Soviets, what he described as "rubbish" in his letter. What exactly had he given them? That briefing was scheduled for noon. The third avenue of exploration was, of course, his relationships. Many people within the building had personal and professional relations with Giles, but he was equally well-connected in the halls of Whitehall, the Foreign Office, and with foreign intelligence services. All needed to be inspected, and a good many would be called in for interviews. Some would be polygraphed. That briefing would take place at 1:00 p.m.

He broke his own rule and pulled out his bottle of Nikka Yoichi ten-year-old single malt Japanese whiskey and a Waterford Crystal tumbler glass from his desk draw. He was going to need his steadiest nerves today. The Nikka would help.

Five minutes before the scheduled start time, the analyst team reviewing Giles's operational records came into the secure briefing room to set up. They connected their laptops to enormous LCD screen at the far end of the room and positioned themselves appropriately for the meeting. C strode in with his air of confidence and approachability, said hello to everyone individually, but avoided the usual pleasantries that generally consumed the first ten minutes of his meetings.

"Time is short today as you know, so let's get down to it. We have about an hour to get through this, and I want to make sure there's time for my questions as we go." He pressed his palms together and pursed his lips, his universal signal to everyone present that it was time to get going.

A young woman in a conservative gray wool skirt and blazer cleared her throat and launched the first part of the presentation.

"We'd like to start with the central operation that Mr. Bancroft referred to in his letter as it was clearly the most significant undertaking of the first twenty years of his MI6 career. Our review of the operation falls into two parts, the MI6 operation that ran from 1948 to 1965, officially, and then the CIA-led Operation UNDERCUT that ran from 1964 to 1990, ending, unofficially, with the collapse of the Soviet Union. However, it is the transition between the two was somewhat unconventional and gave us the most concern. Our assessment is that Mr. Bancroft approached the CIA, and not the other way around as the official records shows, and offered the services of the Draftsman, Bruce Lasher, and Maksym Palatnik to the Americans. We believe this because he invited a CIA officer, one Robert Schier, to participate in a classified debriefing of Draftsman at Dolphin Square safe house in 1964. The inclusion of Mr. Schier was not authorized by anyone in the chain of MI6 command. And we are quite confident that a full transcript and recording of that debriefing was given to the CIA. This was also not an authorized transfer of intelligence. The debriefing lasted about six hours and provided the CIA with the complete history on the Draftsman's operations in Eastern Europe."

The presentation lasted exactly thirty-five minutes, leaving ample time for questions and debate. Very little of it was surprising to Lovewell. The assessment of the team felt credible to him. Giles treated the Draftsman like some kind of lovechild, conceived, nurtured, and treasured in a way that his other more conventional operations were not. When MI6 got cold feet around the operation and instructed Bancroft to shut it down, it felt to him like his child was being taken away. He took steps, deceptive steps, to smuggle his lovechild over to the Americans without approval. He surreptitiously sought out and maintained a relationship with the Draftsman and Lasher, who as it turned out was also on the CIA payroll.

One surprising development was that it was Giles who engineered the prisoner exchange for the Draftsman in East Berlin with help from Maksym Palatnik on the Soviet side. The man going the other way was Robert Tompkins, a US Air Force clerk who confessed in 1965 to passing photos of secret documents to the Soviet Union while he was based at the Office of Special Investigation at Tempelhof Air Base in West Berlin. He'd been sentenced to thirty years and sent to Lewisburg Federal Penitentiary. Giles secured his release, put him on a plane to Berlin, got him to Glienicke Bridge, and sent the surprised and disheveled convict staggering across the bridge into the welcoming arms of the KGB.

"So we're certain that Bancroft secured the release of Tomkins and got him to Berlin and not the CIA? Why wouldn't they have a hand in that process?"

"He maintained very close ties to the CIA and shared intelligence with them throughout Operation UNDERCUT. He continued to run agents for us in Eastern Europe, notably Poland, Czechoslovakia, and Yugoslavia. Bruce Lasher was a CIA field agent who ran agents in the south, Romania, Ukraine, and Hungary, one of whom was, of course, Maksym Palatnik. It is our belief that Bancroft and Lasher maintained close contact and that Bancroft provided him with intelligence which was then passed back to Lasher's handler at Langley, Robert Schier. It does appear that it was a bit of a one-way street, however, and not properly authorized. Our assessment is that Bancroft traded intelligence for access, allowing him to stay involved in UNDERCUT all the way up to 1989 when the Autumn of Nations revolutions began to have a real impact on the governments under the thumb of Moscow in Eastern Europe, which was the goal of UNDERCUT since its launch in 1965."

"Okay, thank you. Excellent work on short notice. Please keep digging, and we need to know what he gave the Americans in exchange for his access. I'll need a draft report by the end of the day, please."

The noon meeting started five minutes late. The lead analyst, sweating profusely in response to the delay that left C sitting in the secure conference room by himself, apologized and explained that the picture of the counterintelligence that Bancroft gave the Soviets was still incomplete. There were unexplainable gaps in the records that required more time to investigate.

"It's fine. Tell me what you have now. Let's get on with it."

"Thank you, sir. I'll summarize our early assessment by saying that the intelligence we believe Mr. Bancroft gave to Soviets was not sourced from any UK intelligence service. He maintained separate files within the network that under normal circumstances would not draw much attention. He could have encrypted them, but he chose to password protect the files, and the password was his father's birth-date in reverse, so they were easy to access."

"So where did the intelligence come from?"

"We think it came from the Americans, most likely from Bruce Lasher and Robert Schier who were running UNDERCUT. It was very clever stuff, if I'm honest, material relating to the economic data from countries in Eastern Europe that was inaccurate but not so inaccurate as to be obvious, NATO military plans, armaments, troop counts and locations that were off in one way or another, lists of spies operating in the Soviet Union on behalf of the satellite countries which were inaccurate. It really seems like the information he passed was created to plant seeds of distrust between Moscow and the governments of the Warsaw Pact. And since, that was the goal of UNDERCUT from the get-go... Now, I think I know what you are going to say next. If Bancroft kept all this stuff separate, made it easy for us to access, and only included material that support the argument that he didn't hand over anything valuable, does that not raise the possibility that it was all just too easy for us to find and therefore not real that the real information is somewhere else and more incriminating? The answer to that question is yes, that is possible, but we need more time to find it."

After the meeting with the analysts focusing on the nature of Giles's relationships, the picture was clearer. Together, Schier, Lasher, Pike, Palatnik, and Bancroft masterminded the execution of UNDERCUT, sometimes with full knowledge of their superiors, but for the most part, they ran it like a covert operation with little oversight or accountability.

"We had two avenues of investigation, sir, the money trail and the catalog of photographs referenced in the letter. From the money trail side, almost 170 million euros was deposited in banks around Europe, but the funds were rarely touched, which means they weren't for operational costs and more likely payment for work completed. The sources varied, but they had one thing in common. The source of the deposit was always a legitimate or a shell company controlled by or in business with Maksym Palatnik. It will take months to track all the flows, especially if our friends at the CIA were providing operational funding. As noted by our colleagues earlier today, Director Bancroft maintained easily accessible records on our network and one such file included copies of the photograph catalog referenced in the letter to you. Without going into too much detail, it is safe to say that includes some nefarious characters and gangsters and also known enemy agents operating in Eastern Europe."

The next morning, at Ten Downing, C delivered the preliminary assessment to the prime minister. Bancroft hadn't appeared on Russian television again, and the British Press—unlike them to be so slow on the uptake, if we're being honest—hadn't picked up the story. Bancroft was not a public figure, and no statements of who he was and what he was doing in Russia had been made. It was unlikely but still possible that the firestorm would be contained inside Vauxhall Cross.

Perhaps he would get to keep his job after all unlike Sternwell at Langley.

Chapter 50

Romford, Essex

At home that night, a tumbler of his trusty Nikka on the ornate side table next to the reading chair in his library, Lovewell read the letter from Bancroft one last time before tossing it in the fire.

Dear C,

By the time you read this, I will be beyond reach. You may have seen me on Russian television, and, no doubt, all hell is breaking loose over there. I feel that I owe you an explanation.

The man you know as Giles Bancroft is in fact a German, born to a Russian mother who fled the anti-Jewish pogroms in Kiev after World War I and ended up in Berlin. There, she met my father, a German soldier from Leipzig, a Marxist and a Jew. They married in secret as neither family was in favor of the union and started a family together. We moved to England in 1931 after my father was beaten by the Nazi SA during a pro-Marxist rally. It was the last straw for him. I was two at the time. We changed our family name from Baumann to Bancroft.

By the time I finished primary school, my father had joined the Soviet OPGU and was working under-cover recruiting spies in London's universities. My father encouraged me to attend Cambridge, spend time with others with Communist leanings, and then undertake a life of espionage on behalf of the Soviets. While I did not share my father's political fervor, I wanted to please him. You can imagine how pleased he was when I joined the Service. He saw opportunity in it for himself but was blind when it came to me.

I assure you that, throughout all my years in MI6, I never betrayed the Service or my adopted country. I resisted the pressure from my father and his handlers, instead feeding them false information when pressed. Whatever I gave them, they took hook, line, and sinker, but it was all rubbish. When my father died in 1965, he went to his grave believing I served his cause. I did not. I regret deceiving my father, but I do not regret staying loyal to Britain.

As you know, the Draftsman was my brainchild. I used my relationships in the Jewish diaspora to establish the connection between two brothers separated by the horror of the Nazis. I handled the merger of Lawrence Textile and Saco-Lowell then recruited Bruce Lasher to connect with Maksym Palatnik in Odessa. I placed the Draftsman inside Palatnik's criminal organization and orchestrated those early operations. On the instructions of my superiors, I turned the operation and its network over to the CIA and their man in London, Robert Schier, in 1964. MI6 just didn't have the stomach for it anymore, with defections, mole-hunting, and other scandals to address. I was devastated and disillusioned. I had betrayed the dreams of my father for MI6, and in return, they betrayed me.

Schier and the CIA turned the Draftsman into a real killer, not me and not MI6. Yes, I did place him in some situations that warranted violence, but they were few and far between. The CIA had other plans for him, plans that would lead him down a path he wasn't prepared for. We stayed in contact. He trusted me. Together, we assembled a collection of photographs and documents to catalog his CIA activities. We set up bank accounts around Europe to deposit the money he was paid by a variety of unsavory sources. They used the Lawrence Textile connection to funnel money to Palatnik and companies controlled by his cronies.

Before he was extracted and moved to America, the Draftsman wrote a will, so I established solicitor credentials and created a new identity, James Mattinson, that could be activated at the right time. Several months before he was killed, he called to say that he had a terminal cancer diagnosis and would need me to talk to his daughter Ana, the executor, and protect his family.

In the end, I betrayed both him and his family. As efforts by Palatnik, the FBI and INTERPOL to track down the binder and the money intensified, I feared the road would eventually lead back to me. Maksym was untouchable, protected by the CIA and surrounded by his loyal Malina. He had the Draftsman, Schier, and Lasher killed, and it was only a matter of time before his hit squad showed up at the home of James Mattinson. I convinced Ana Pike to put all the money in a single account under my control, stole it, and then split it with Palatnik to keep him away from me and the rest of Pike's family.

You are probably asking why not just take my half of the money and disappear. Why go to Russia and cause so much chaos for my friends in the Service? I have no family left in England. The only family I have is from my mother's side. I made contact with them years ago and look forward to building the relationship with them all. The Russians will protect me, and my long-lost family will, I hope, embrace the return of their prodigal son. The Russians also believe that I have been feeding them valuable intelligence for more than thirty years and will use my relocation to celebrate that. I hope.

I am not the brave man I once was. I asked myself who would protect me when everything about the Draftsman, Palatnik, UNDERCUT, the countless assassinations, and the killing of Draftsman and his CIA handlers came out. The answer was no one. I chose the Russians. They will probably interrogate me, and I have to have something to give them. I'll give them the Draftsman and the CIA plot to destabilize the Soviet Union, UNDERCUT. It's ancient history now, and most of the players are dead. It may not be enough, but I assure you that I will give them nothing else.

I have no doubt that at some point you will hand this letter to the prime minister, and so here are my words for him. Prime Minister, I'm sorry. I pray that my actions don't cost any unnecessary lives. There is no need to order the roll up of networks across Europe or conduct mole-hunts into your intelligence services. The blame will eventually fall on the CIA and the Americans. This was their operation, not ours.

Maksym will probably spend what remains of his sordid life looking over his shoulder. I'm sure you could find him hiding in his British protectorate if you try, but I cannot live a lonely life and be on the run.

I have the utmost respect for you, C, and I hope you understand the terrifying choice I had to make.

Sincerely,
Gerhard Baumann
a.k.a. Giles Bancroft
a.k.a. James Mattinson

Chapter 51

Columbia University, New York, 2014

Coincidently, Ana Pike was awarded the Pulitzer Prize for Investigative Journalism on the fourth anniversary of the day that Anatol Palatnik was found dead in his cell at the Manhattan Metropolitan Correctional Center. He was being held on charges of first-degree aggravated kidnapping of Ana and second-degree murder in the killing Robert Schier in Connecticut. He died, and was disposed of, in the most appropriate manner for the man he was—strangled in his cell by the brother-in-law of one of Maksym's Pakhan who was an MCC prison guard. To make the attack look like a prisoner-on-prisoner assault, he was violated with a broomstick.

His autopsy had confirmed asphyxiation as the cause of death, indicated by petechial hemorrhages in his eyes, foam in his airways, and the fracture of his hyoid bone. Significant blood loss from rectal and colonic injuries were also noted. All the charges were dropped, including three counts of second-degree murder in Florida for the killing of Sean Pike and Bruce and Regina Lasher, denying all his victims their justice. The MCC guard who killed him vanished without a trace, last reported taking a flight to Venezuela where the trail went cold.

The body was claimed by an "unknown relative" and hastily cremated—except for his head, which washed up on the banks of the Hudson River several weeks later. It was discovered by a jogger in Riverside Park, mere steps from where Ana now sat in Pulitzer Hall at Columbia University for the award ceremony.

So four years and more than a hundred thousand miles of investigative travel later, Ana sat at the table in Pulitzer Hall with her editor at the *Times*, Robert Penfold. The paper had been a great supporter of her investigation into the Malina, putting her up for weeks at a time in Odessa and Tel Aviv. Her work, hand in hand with Pascal, led to the arrest of more than a dozen high-level members of the organization, including Maksym Palatnik who had been picked up in the Maldives less than a week earlier. It seemed likely that his extradition to the US would happen eventually. For now, he was in custody in a Malé prison cell, a frail old man, shriveled dark by the sun.

The lights dimmed, and the polite applause began as Maureen Harper, cochair of the Pulitzer Committee, stepped to the podium. Her introduction was both touching and inspirational, and Ana was bursting with pride when she stepped onto the biggest stage of her life.

"Thank you, Maureen and the entire Pulitzer board. Thank you so much for this tremendous honor. I'd also like to thank the *New York Times* and my editor, Robert Penfold, for taking a chance on my story and giving me the freedom to follow the truth into every corner of the world. And thank you, Pascal, wherever you are today, for being such a great investigative partner these last few years. There are so many others that I just don't have time to name here today. They'd yank me off the stage before I got through them all.

"Needless to say, this was almost five years of very painful work. My father and I were only close for the last six months of his life, and I thought that I finally knew him. I could not have been more wrong. I didn't know him at all. He wasn't just a killer. He was a hired killer. Is one any worse than the other? And yet between jobs, he returned home to his wife and children and resumed a normal middle-class life as if nothing had happened, deceiving us all for so many years. My father, as it turns out, was a letter writer, not prolific but a letter writer nonetheless. He wrote to my mother many times over the years from wherever he was in the world. I found his letters in a hatbox in her bedroom closet after her death.

"We worried that the murder of her husband, then her youngest son and granddaughter, followed by my own brush with death at the hands of Anatol Palatnik was too much for her. She felt betrayed by his secret life, that he had soiled the sanctity of their life together with his double life of crime and espionage. She worried he had other secrets, a second family perhaps, that no one knew about. But even she had us fooled. She knew all along, perhaps not the details but certainly the bigger picture. I remember her saying once, 'Ana dear, we are English, and if you don't have some relative who does odd work for the government, then you really aren't English at all.'

"She never told us about the letters. A few she never opened, and I haven't been able to bring myself to open them either. If she didn't want to open them, perhaps I should abide by her wishes and leave them that way, at least for now. But today, I want to read you an extract from two of his letters, ones that she did open. The first is dated 1988.

> *My dearest Addie,*
>
> *We got you know who out of the country today, but I spent the better part of two days locked in a shipping container filled with rats. I think we beat the Soviet authorities by hours. Not sure what happens next, but there are others working for us here who need to be extracted. The whole system is collapsing over here, and the security forces in every country are hunting down their enemies, perceived or real.*

"The second is dated August 17, 1981, and speaks to his life in the shadows after Eastern Europe. It reads:

> *I don't know, yet, why I am here. I rode eighteen hours in the back of a truck, hiding underneath crates of chickens, to get to this place. We were stopped by soldiers every ten miles to check the driver's papers. The constant gunfire rattled the chickens. They shat through their cages, so I had to keep my eyes and mouth very tightly closed whenever the truck stopped. I could see nothing of the landscape, the people, or anything, only smell and the sounds. It*

smelled of blood and death. Blood, especially when left to pool without being cleaned up, has a metallic odor like iron. There must have been a lot of it to be so prominent. And the sounds, yelling, gunshots, scared animals screeching, and then the crying in that order, all the time, over and over again.

But now, I have a balcony overlooking the Tonle Sap River, a steady supply of Sombai, and a mosquito net. I'm safe from my malaria-carrying attackers here under the net, but I'm also trapped. I can watch the everyday life of the traffic on the river, but I can't touch anything. When I leave this room for work, I'll disinfect it, and it will be like I was never even here. Is this any kind of life?

I woke up sweaty and confused this morning. I thought I was back in Malaya before we got married and had the children. Do you remember those days? I actually got up and dressed with a plan to go straight to the radio tent to start my listening shift. It took me a minute to remember that I'm a middle-aged man, a million miles from home, waiting for the order to do something evil in the name of freedom and democracy.

And I realized that, for all the love there is in the world, there is ten times more hate. For all the wealth and good health, there is a hundred times more poverty and suffering. And for every decent leader serving his people, there are dozens of cold-blooded slaughterers killing his own in the quest for power.

What they make me do only makes the situation worse. I want it to end. Wherever I go, I leave a trail of blood but with a pocket full of money.

I will be home soon,
Your loving husband,
Bran

"In the far corner of the auditorium, Sam Sternwell watched her speak. They caught each other's eye. For a second, she froze then gave him a conspiratorial smile and nod before continuing on with her speech."

Preview

Dig Two Graves
Second Novel in the Draftsman Series

Seoul, South Korea, 1979

T he Draftsman focused on his breathing—long, slow breaths in, slow, long breaths out—as the limousine turned onto Changuimun-ro, the tree-lined road that wound through the Buam-dong neighborhood to the security gate of the fabled Blue House presidential palace compound.

The palace was surrounded by mountains. To the north, the mighty *Bukhansan*, the "mountain north of the Han River," was flanked on the left by *Naksan*, "the Azure Dragon," and *Inwangsan*, "The White Tiger" on the right. To the east was Mount Namsan, the protective mountain of the capital, Seoul. On the south end flowed the Cheonggyecheon stream and the Han River.

These natural protections—and the one-road-in-one-road-out system—would make the Draftsman's escape difficult.

The Blue House had been the venue for many successful and failed assassinations in its nine-hundred-year history. The most recent—known as the January 21 Incident—was in 1968. North Korean infiltrators stormed the palace in a bid to kill South Korean President, Park Chung-hee. The President had survived—and was still in office—but twenty-eight North Koreans, twenty-six South Koreans, and four Americans were killed in the raid.

Today's "incident"—whether it succeeded or failed—would be one for the history books. The Draftsman's name would be attached to one of the most brazen assassination attempts in recent history—a CIA assassin and his target, a senior foreign affairs official, placed at his same dinner table inside a Korea Central Intelligence Agency (KCIA) safe house within a presidential palace for a dinner with the heads of covert operations from a dozen Asian countries.

"Brazen" was an understatement.

The planning for the operation was a master class in patient agency tradecraft that combined intelligence gathering by a dozen field agents and their informants, matched with carefully planned diplomatic maneuvering and scientific innovation. There was no room for error, and it had to be executed with such perfect precision that it never made it into the newspapers.

The CIA had initiated the plan in 1976 after DC lobbyist Kim Dong-seon was charged with successfully bribing members of the US Congress to keep US troops in South Korea. A year later, he was indicted on charges ranging from illegal campaign contributions to failing to register as an agent of the KCIA. He testified to it all in a grand jury hearing in exchange for immunity that almost brought down the Speaker of the House. And then he disappeared, was given a new identity, and retired to a three-thousand-square foot condo on a golf course in Arizona with his one-time secretary.

He was also the cousin of Kim Son-jae, a diplomat in Korean Ministry of Foreign Affairs, which meant, of course, that he was really KCIA. The CIA had it on good authority that he and Yee Xiu Ying, who ran counterintelligence operations on the peninsula at the Central Investigation Department of the People's Republic of China, were lovers, a fact confirmed by Dong.

Dong's real value to the CIA was the information he had about President Park Chung-hee's policy known as "Nordpolitik" to befriend North Korea's main allies, the Soviet Union, and China as a means to improving relations with the Kim Il-sung regime. The relationship between Kim Son-jae and Yee Xiu Ying was one of the many elements of that policy. It was in US interest to disrupt any flirtations between their key ally in the region and their biggest threat.

The CIA wanted Kim Son-jae gone, but it wasn't for the Draftsman to know why. His job was to take the shot—from the inside and somehow get out without leaving a trace.

As the plan started to come together in the spring of 1978, the best assassin they had, the Draftsman, was still shuttling back and forth between East and West Berlin. Six months later, he was arrested crossing the checkpoint, thrown in prison, interrogated, and exchanged for a Soviet spy—just in time to begin his training for this mission at the Farm in Williamsburg, Virginia. It would be, without a shadow of a doubt, the most dangerous mission of his career in the killing business.

The girl in the back seat of the limousine next to him was a beautiful local model who spoke no English and was hired to escort him to the dinner. That was her cover at least. Despite the limited amount of clothing she was wearing, she was well-armed—a Heckler & Koch P7 9mm tucked into a small purse that she would leave in the car for the getaway and a long red pin in her hair as sharp as a Korean fighting sword.

The Draftsman had his Makarov wedged between the seats, but he would enter the safe house carrying only a small air gun that looked more like a Montblanc pen to deliver the single shot of ricin sealed inside a tiny sphere made of a platinum-iridium alloy. Kim would feel the pellet shot and wonder what it was. A few hours later, he would develop a severe fever and, if everything went as expected, die in hospital within a day or two. The Bulgarian Secret Service had used a similar weapon the year earlier to kill the dissident journalist, Georgi Markov, although the delivery mechanism in his case was the tip of an umbrella converted into an air pistol.

There were three guards standing in line at the steel gate across the one road that led to the Blue House, a line of black limousines forming in front them, waiting for the gate to go up and grant access. The Draftsman's invitation to the dinner was based on his cover as a diplomatic attaché to South Korea for the US State Department.

Every attendee was in the intelligence business but had a similar sounding cover.

Eventually, the heavy gate rose, and the driver of the first limousine pulled forward, extended a paper through the open window, and received a curt nod from the guard to go ahead. The Draftsman and his dinner escort exchanged a final look and, at the same time, said, "*Vremya igry.*" Game time.

About the Author

Simon Yates, lives in Marblehead, Massachusetts, with his wife Shannon, their children Lily, Ben and Chloe and the family dog, Parker. Brought up in Blackburn, Lancashire, Simon and his parents moved to the United States quite suddenly and under a cloud of mystery when he was 15 and settled in Greenwich, Connecticut.

Printed in the USA
CPSIA information can be obtained
at www.ICGtesting.com
CBHW020031020824
12556CB00038B/360